PENGUI
THE W

Aruna Chakravarti is a well-known academic, writer and translator. Prominent among her many publications are her translations of Saratchandra Chatterjee's *Srikanta* and Sunil Gangopadhyay's *Sei Samai* (*Those Days*) and its sequel *Pratham Alo* (*First Light*), published by Penguin Books India in 1993, 1997 and 2001 respectively. She is the recipient of several awards, among them the Vaitalik Award (1986), the prestigious Sahitya Akademi Award (1996) and the Sarat Puraskar (2004). Her first novel, *The Inheritors*, was published by Penguin Books India to critical acclaim and was shortlisted for the Commonwealth Writers' Prize 2004.

The Way Home

Contemporary Bengali Short Fiction

EDITED BY
ARUNA CHAKRAVARTI

PENGUIN BOOKS

PENGUIN BOOKS
Published by the Penguin Group
Penguin Books India Pvt Ltd, 11 Community Centre, Panchsheel Park, New Delhi 110 017,
India
Penguin Group (USA) Inc., 375 Hudson Street, New York, New York 10014, USA
Penguin Group (Canada), 90 Eglinton Avenue East, Suite 700, Toronto, Ontario, M4P
2Y3, Canada (a division of Pearson Penguin Canada Inc.)
Penguin Books Ltd, 80 Strand, London WC2R 0RL, England
Penguin Ireland, 25 St Stephen's Green, Dublin 2, Ireland (a division of Penguin Books
Ltd)
Penguin Group (Australia), 250 Camberwell Road, Camberwell, Victoria 3124, Australia
(a division of Pearson Australia Group Pty Ltd)
Penguin Group (NZ), cnr Airborne and Rosedale Road, Albany, Auckland 1310, New
Zealand (a division of Pearson New Zealand Ltd)
Penguin Group (South Africa) (Pty) Ltd, 24 Sturdee Avenue, Rosebank, Johannesburg
2196, South Africa

Penguin Books Ltd, Registered Offices: 80 Strand, London WC2R 0RL, England

First published by Penguin Books India 2006

Anthology copyright© Penguin Books India 2006
Introduction copyright© Aruna Chakravarti 2006
The copyright for individual pieces rests with the authors or their estates
Page 281-82 is an extension of the copyright page

While every effort has been made to trace copyright holders and obtain permission, this
has not been possible in all cases; any omissions brought to our notice will be remedied
in future editions.

All rights reserved

10 9 8 7 6 5 4 3 2 1

ISBN-13: 9780144001064 ISBN-10: 0144001063

Typeset in Sabon by S.R. Enterprises, New Delhi
Printed at Pauls Press, New Delhi

For Milu...

CONTENTS

Introduction

A translation is an attempt at communication on behalf of a culture, a tradition and a literature. The choice of authors and, more precisely, the most significant areas of their work are the first steps towards this communication, for translation must be a valid exercise. The choice of a target language is equally important, for the wider its usage the larger the scope of transmission. The use of certain languages as filters also raises questions of power and hierarchy. For example, when a work from one of the regional languages of India is translated into English it becomes the representation of a small provincial culture for a powerful international culture. It is from judicious exercising of such choices that national, even regional themes and ideas become international ones.

The operation, however, is fraught with difficulty. The more divergent the two literary traditions and the wider the gap in space and time, the greater the skill required to bring them together in a meaningful way. A writer, revered in her own country, is tested through a translation by people who judge by an altogether different set of assumptions. If the translator fails to speak forcefully and meaningfully across the language barrier she is doing her writer a serious disservice.

Beauty and Fidelity. These are the twin ideals the translator is chasing; swinging sometimes this way, sometimes that. The golden mean, the exquisite harmony in which the strands are woven so lightly and easily that they raise no dust, is the committed translator's El Dorado—forever sought; forever elusive.

There is another dimension to the attempt. The very act of translation entails the filtering of image and idea from one sensibility to another, raising questions of race, sex, religion and personal history. Translation, with its deep racial, cultural and gender implications, serves as a measure of the growth of a language and the extent of domination of one language over another. At another level, the very process of transference reconstructs cultural identity and reframes the boundaries of language, idea and perception, thus changing the terms of affiliation. How much of oneself can the translator allow to seep into her work? How much shall she guard against? A translator of today working on a nineteenth-century Bengali classic, for example, may, quite unconsciously, orient it to the expectations of a present-day international readership. A woman, translating the work of a male author, may find herself giving it a gender slant. In both cases the shifts may proceed from natural human impulses and not from deliberate choice or premeditation. Should this be seen as a betrayal? Or as the expected consequence of the filtering of images and ideas from one sensibility to another?

Regarding the collection presented here, I would like to make a few observations. To begin with, the task assigned to me of selecting and translating fourteen of the best stories by contemporary Bengali authors was daunting from start to finish. For one, it was hard to determine what constituted 'Contemporary Bengali'. I was not sure of the time frame involved. It obviously carries on to the present day. But when did it start? Post Rabindranath? Post Saratchandra? Or even later? After Bibhuti Bhushan and Tarashankar? I decided to include the last two authors in my collection and begin my quest from there. Scholars of Bengali literature may have problems with my decision. I can only beg them to bear with me.

The second hurdle I encountered was the choice of stories. The wealth, both qualitative and quantitative, of short fiction written in Bengali is so vast and varied that selecting fourteen stories was almost impossible. I tried to pick the ones which not only combine economy of expression with storytelling ability and rhetorical skill but also offer some significant comment on the human condition. I admit, of course, that many good stories have been left out. I hope to make amends for the lapse in a second volume.

Some of the stories in the collection have shared themes and patterns. They may deal with the same subject matter or even employ the same devices. For example, there is a strongly stated gender theme in a large cluster of stories. Sushila of Bibhuti Bhushan Bandopadhyay's 'Aniseed Flower' is the young daughter-in-law of a harsh, conservative Brahmin family living in a remote village of Bengal. In her youth and innocence she doesn't realize that to survive in the society in which she lives she is required to mould herself in an acceptable stereotype. Her faith in her natural instincts and her spirit and independence are seen as a complete violation of the norms of rural middle-class living—not only by her family but the entire village. Two other stories take up the same theme: Ashapurna Debi's 'Cactus' and Suchitra Bhattacharya's 'Shikha's Address'. But the overall effect of each story is different. Whereas Sushila's resistance is naïve and unthinking, Bharati's and Shikha's are powerful and intellectually expounded. By seeking to redefine their role and image, and by demanding equality with men in economic and social spheres, they challenge the very basis of the world they occupy.

The impact of triple talaq on Muslim women is visible in Narendranath Mitra's 'Sap'. The romantic and lyrical exposition of the theme makes 'Sap' one of the most beautiful stories in this collection. The element of irony inherent in this story, however, does not distract the reader from the writer's main intention which is the examination of some significant human problems sparked off by archaic notions and warped interpretations of the shariat. A similar approach is visible in Bani Basu's 'In the Opinion of This House'—an ironic representation of notions of female emancipation. It also deals with the conflict between reality and illusion and demonstrates the way people spin flimsy webs about themselves as a protection against unpleasant realities. Rajshekhar Basu's 'Anandibai' is yet another comical exposé of relations between the sexes. Although the characters are flat for the most part and the story fairly stereotypical, the economy of language, the intensity of effect, and the benign bland humour make it one of the best stories in the comic tradition. Though the other characters remain static, the central character is shown as having altered his view of himself and his destiny. It is a consequence of the insight he has gained in the conflict through which he has passed.

Two stories, 'The Way Home' and 'The Crossing', explore and analyse innate human values. In the first, Sirshendu Mukhopadhyay employs the twin motifs of perilous journeys and surreal worlds, using fantasy to disguise universal truths but ultimately revealing them in the context of tribal folklore and ancient wisdom. A perilous journey is undertaken, too, in Samaresh Basu's 'The Crossing'—not magical and illusory as in Sirshendu's story but harrowingly real. 'The Crossing'—a brilliant compound of plot, characterization, point of view, language, tone, atmosphere, imagery and symbolism—is one of the most powerful stories in this collection.

Three stories have a weak, marginal man at the centre of the narrative. But the techniques of delineation are widely divergent. In 'The Brahmin', Tarashankar Bandopadhyay starts out with a character both comic and despicable— a stock type which he then develops far beyond its original dimensions. At the end of the story Purna Chakrabarty escapes the confines of his type and transcends it. He becomes an archetypal figure—a symbol of tragic human experience. Exactly the opposite happens in Premendra Mitra's 'The Story of a Coward'. The writer skilfully manipulates the elements of the plot to provide the reader with a heightened perception of a common human weakness—the inability to take a decision. Nothing is solved for the protagonist at the end of the story. His conflict goes unresolved and he gains no insight. The reader, with his greater awareness, knows that life for the protagonist will go on in the same way for he was given a second chance but lacked the guts to take it. Haran of Gajendrakumar Mitra's 'The Faithful Retainer' is also a stock figure—a timid, bumbling, middle-aged man shamelessly exploited and degraded by his own family. The technique employed here is somewhat unusual. Haran is seen not through the eyes of the omniscient narrator, but the narrow limited perspective of his neighbour—the narrator of the story. Suddenly, right at the end, the focus shifts and Haran is given voice. The implications of the story change dramatically and the reader's perception of Haran and the other members of the family undergoes considerable alteration.

Three other stories with separate themes make up the rest of the collection. Jyotirindranath Nandi's 'King of the Forest' celebrates the preservation of our natural habitat and makes an environmental statement through the depiction of an old man who, having given up the artificiality and boredom of his life in the 'sick' city of Kolkata, has retired to the country and made himself one with nature. Though alienated from his son and daughter-in-law, he succeeds in making a connection with his grandson. Perplexed and hesitant at first, ten-year-old Moti gradually becomes a willing participant in his grandfather's way of life.

The tragic travails of Partition have been delineated in a host of Bengali short stories. Prafulla Roy's 'The King Is Dead, Long Live the King' has been chosen out of many for its unusual sub-theme. It speaks, not of this side of the border, but the other. It deals not with the rigours of flight and rehabilitation of refugees, but with the strange reversal and counter-reversal that Partition brings in the destiny of a young Muslim peasant.

Sunil Gangopadhyay's 'The Fugitive and the Stalkers' is the only story of this collection that depicts the 'harrowing seventies'—when the Naxal movement let loose a trail of rampant lawlessness and wanton murder in Bengal. Three boys, trapped in a vicious cycle, are fugitives and stalkers by turns. They yearn for the simple joys of life— a hot meal, a warm bed, and the sight of a much-loved little sister—but know no way of escaping the deadly spiral which is whirling them towards annihilation.

The stories in this volume were chosen with the idea of offering a cross-section of the best of Bengali short fiction to the non-Bengali reader. I hope the collection will find favour with my Bengali readers as well. I hope they will be enabled to hear the voices of the authors— albeit in another language—and perceive each nuance of the subtexts. The translator has perforce to stand between an author and her readers but in her heart she cherishes a dream: of finding an ideal language—a common language that all mankind can share.

Aruna Chakravarti

Anandibai

Anandibai

Rajshekhar Basu (Parashuram)

Seth Trikramdas Karorhi, proprietor of a chain of business houses, was sitting in his Delhi office, signing cheques, when the orderly came in and left a card on the table. *M. Zulfikar Khan*, Sethji read, glancing out of the corner of his eye at the gilt letters. 'Ask him to wait,' he said. Then, gesturing to the orderly to leave the room, Trikramdas went back to his cheques. Minutes later, after the secretary had left with a sheaf of papers in his hand, Trikramdas rang the bell. 'Send the gentleman in,' he commanded, pointing to the card.

'Adaab Arz,' M. Zulfikar Khan greeted Trikramdas from the door. 'I'm coming from the Intelligence Bureau, Sethji.'

'Oh!' Sethji's face fell. 'Is it something to do with the income tax again?'

'I don't know about your income tax. A very serious charge has come to the department.'

'Against me?'

'Against you.'

'Why? What have I done?'

'You have married three women—'

'Is that all?' Trikramdas laughed in relief. 'That's no crime. I'm a Hindu. I can marry a hundred women if I choose. I don't have to restrict myself to four like you.'

'Hai! Hai!' Khan Saheb exclaimed, waving his hands in despair. 'You've learnt to make money. Lots of money. But that's all. You don't keep track of what's happening in the country. Hindus, Buddhists, Jains and Sikhs can have only one wife at a time. The law was passed recently and—'

'What are you saying, Khan Saheb?' Sethji cried out, thunderstruck. 'I had no idea there was such a law in the land! I do business, Khan Saheb. Big business. Ask me about licences and taxes—I have them all on my fingertips. But this . . . what you're saying is impossible! I simply don't believe it. My uncle, Seth Harchandji, is having a wonderful time with his two wives. There's no charge against him.'

'The case is quite different. He had married both women prior to the passing of the law. But you—you've married your three quite recently. Prepare yourself to face trial and conviction, Sethji. You'll have to pay a hefty fine. You may even be imprisoned for as long as ten years.'

'Siyaram! Siyaram!' The old man's jowls shook with fear. 'What am I to do now? Is there no way out, Khan Saheb?'

'You're an elderly man and respected in business circles. We wouldn't like to embarrass you. I give you one month's time to sort out the problem.'

'How much money do you think—?'

'You'll have to get rid of two wives by the end of the period and keep only one. How you tackle the job and how much money you spend on the transaction is your headache. I can't help out in any way. As for . . . ' Khan Saheb coughed delicately and cleared his throat, ' . . . the understanding between you and me . . . that is quite another matter. We'll take it up later. At leisure.'

'Ho Ramji! Ho Parmatma!' Trikramdas struck his forehead with the palm of his hand. 'I've married one

Rajshekhar Basu

according to traditional Hindu rites, one by the rites of the Arya Samaj and one through a civil ceremony. Which one can I set aside?'

'Don't worry, Sethji. All you need to do is shell out a few lakhs. Buy two of them off with hefty sums. Get them to sign declarations that they are not your legal wives—only partners in pleasure. The rest will be easy. We at the Bureau will hush up the matter. But there's no time to lose. Get yourself a lawyer as fast as you can.' Rising to his feet, Zulfikar Khan added, 'I'll take my leave now and return a week later. Adaab!'

Trikramdas Karorhi was a little over fifty with a marital career graph that was strange—to say the least. Like most other men he had had one wife till only two years ago. She had died, suddenly, leaving him inconsolable and encumbered, besides, with the responsibility of half a dozen children. Unable to bear the burden of her loss, he had married Anandibai three months after the tragic event and then two others in rapid succession. He had, however, kept the fact of his last two marital ventures carefully hidden from friends, relatives and Anandi.

Anandibai was the only child and heir of Harjivan Lal, dewan of the erstwhile ruler of Khajauli, and extremely wealthy in her own right. On her father's death, some months ago, a distant cousin of his had landed up, from who knows where, and tried to lay claim to the property. Seth Trikramdas had stepped in at this juncture, married Anandi with the help of her maternal uncles, and brought her vast estates under his control. Anandi was twenty-five years old, not good looking at all, and had a quick temper and a sharp tongue.

The registered offices of Sethji's chain of companies were located in Delhi. But there were branch offices in Kolkata and Mumbai which he visited three or four times a year. A couple of months after his marriage, Sethji went on a tour to Mumbai and was invited to dinner by the branch manager Kishen Ram Khobani. Kishen Ram was a Sindhi who had left Karachi after Partition and settled in Mumbai. He was a man of impeccable taste and his manners were elegant and refined. Sethji was highly impressed with the warmth and cordiality of his reception, his beautifully furnished flat but above all by his wife and sister-in-law.

Sethji was an old-fashioned man with a conservative attitude towards women. He had never had the privilege of meeting modern ladies and conversing with them. But he had never regretted it either, fervently believing that women from good families kept themselves decently in purdah. But now he found himself completely charmed by Kishen Ram's sister-in-law Rajhans Jhalkani. What a beauty she was! And how vivacious! Her powder-blue salwar and midnight-blue kameez set off, to perfection, her exceedingly fair neck and arms. Her pale-green veil, spangled all over with silver stars, rested, light as gossamer, on a dazzling white bosom. Her laughter rang like bells and her voice, as she coaxed Sethji to try 'a little more of this' and 'a little more of that', fell like a stream of honey in his ears.

The meal over, Sethji drew his subordinate aside and asked him a number of questions about his sister-in-law. Rajhans was an orphan, he was told, and lived with the Khobanis. Her only brother ran a business in Singapore and was earning good money but he didn't care to look after her. Rajhans was a good actress and singer and nurtured the ambition of joining films but her sister and brother-in-law would not allow it.

Sethji made up his mind that very evening. 'I would like to marry Rajhans,' he told Kishen Ram. 'Arrange it without delay. I'll keep her in great luxury. She'll have a flat of her own, here in Mumbai, and I'll spend the better part of the year with her. She will want for nothing.' Needless to say, Trikramdas did not disclose the fact of his earlier marriage. Kishen Ram, believing his boss to be a widower, agreed to the proposal. Rajhans, too, gave her consent. She could have objected to the groom's age but didn't. The marriage took place according to the rites of the Arya Samaj. A flat was bought for the bride, close to her sister's, and filled with comforts. Within a few days, Rajhans moved into her new home.

A couple of weeks later, Trikramdas visited his Kolkata branch. The manager, a Bengali gentleman by the name of Paritosh Horh Chowdhury, was an extremely efficient officer and very cultured and westernized in his style of living. That night at dinner in Horh Chowdhury's Alipur residence, Sethji made the acquaintance of his wife and sister.

Miss Balaka Horh Chowdhury was not as fair as Rajhans. But she had so much more style! Such sophistication! Her fine silk sari swirled and floated about a form as slim and supple as a reed. Huge dark eyes shone from out of a face as delicately oval as an egg. Her silky black hair was twisted into a careless knot at the nape of a long arched neck. She had very sophisticated manners and spoke English like a memsahib. She spoke Hindi too in a faltering voice and with a quaint accent. How sweetly the words fell on Sethji's ears! She was extremely well educated and accomplished too. Her brother told Sethji that Balaka had done her MA in Bengali literature and sang and danced so beautifully—no one in Kolkata could compete with her. Producers and directors of film companies were wearing out the soles of their shoes trying to get her to act in their films. But Paritosh wouldn't allow it.

Sethji was totally smitten. 'Miss Balaka,' he said humbly, 'I would like to marry you.'

'Very well,' she laughed—a delicate peal of silvery laughter. 'But the trouble is . . . I can't live in Delhi. It's much too hot. And I won't be able to eat your dal roti. I have a very sensitive digestion.'

'Arré! Arré!' Sethji made haste to soothe away her fears. 'I have no intention of taking you away from here. I'll buy a house, right here in Alipur, close to your brother's. You can live in great comfort. And I'll spend eight to nine months in the year with you. I have neglected the business in Kolkata sadly in the past few years. I must take it up in all seriousness from now on and make it boom. As for eating dal roti, who says you must do anything of the kind? Enjoy your rice and fish curry as you've always done. I have nothing, personally, against fish. Except . . . except that it smells terrible.'

'I'll cook it for you with essence of roses. You'll think you're eating kalakand.'

Balaka had heard from her brother that Sethji was a widower. She gave her consent to the marriage with alacrity. Her brother and sister-in-law were thrilled as well. The marriage took place, in the registrar's office, twenty days later.

Over the next couple of years, Sethji moved from city to city and wife to wife with the utmost ease. Life had never been sweeter. And then . . . like a clap of thunder M. Zulfikar Khan had walked into his office.

Mr Khajanchand BA LLB was a well-known solicitor and a close and trusted friend of Seth Trikramdas Karorhi. It was Khajanchand who helped him out with his tax problems and other legal matters that happened to vex him. Sethji sent for him that very evening and told him of M. Zulfikar Khan's visit.

'Tch! Tch! Tch!' Khajanchand clicked his tongue in annoyance. 'You've behaved very childishly, Sethji! You say you trust me. Yet you never dropped a hint about the Kalkatta-wali and the Mumbai-wali. You should have taken my counsel before offering them marriage. You've committed a big blunder and—'

'Forgive me,' Sethji folded his hands before the lawyer and said humbly. 'I was so ashamed of myself . . . you see. At my age . . . and with a wife living . . . I couldn't face up to what I had done. But surely there's a way out? Who else but you can show it to me?'

Khajanchand thought for a while and said, 'There's no need to tell Anandibai anything just yet. She'll feel very hurt and humiliated and might create a nasty scene. You'd better tell the other two though. They're modern girls and won't weep and beat their breasts like Anandibai. They'll be wild with fury and hate you for what you've done. They may even threaten to divorce you which will be a blessing in disguise. Pay them handsomely and your two managers as well. You may have to spend a couple of lakhs—a sum that, to you, is peanuts.'

Trikramdas hemmed and hawed. The advice Khajanchand gave him wasn't quite what he wanted. 'Khajan bhai,' he said plaintively, 'I need to expand my business and for that I must meet people from the highest rungs of society. I must throw parties for ministers and big government officers. Who will play hostess for me? Anandi?' He shook his head dismissively and added, 'Rajhans and Balaka are ideal for the job. If I have to divorce one of the three it must be Anandi. It will hurt me terribly. My heart will burst with grief. It will be a big financial loss as well. All her property . . . Tch! Tch! But I'm ready for it. The trouble is I can't make up my mind about the other two. Which one to keep and which to give up? However . . . '

Here, Sethji went into deep thought. 'All things considered I think I like Balaka the best. If, God forbid, she decides to leave me, I'll settle for Rajhans. Don't worry about money. I can easily spend up to fifteen lakhs.'

Khajanchand explained, at great length, that Anandibai was Sethji's true, legal wife and that her claim was superior to that of the others. Divorcing her would not be easy. Sethji might have to take the help of her wicked uncle. Besides, the loss to his assets was not to be scoffed at. But Trikramdas was not convinced. He was determined to drop Anandibai and keep one of the others.

'Very well then,' Khajanchand rose to his feet. 'Break the news to all three of them. See how they take it and let me know. I'll proceed with the matter after hearing from you.'

Trikramdas didn't waste any time. Catching the next flight he went to Mumbai and drove straight from the airport to Rajhans's house. Rajhans was sitting in the drawing room, deep in conversation with an elegantly dressed young man. 'Sethji!' she exclaimed on seeing her husband, 'I had no idea you were coming! Why didn't you write?' Then, turning to the young man, she introduced him. 'This is Mr Jhumkamal Matkani—a distant cousin from my father's side. He is a brilliant accountant. You must sack the old man in our Mumbai office and give Jhumkamal the post of accounts officer.'

'I'll think about it,' Sethji said. 'But I have something else to discuss with you first. It's very important.'

After Jhumkamal left, Sethji told Rajhans about his three marriages. His voice faltered and the muscles of his face were slack with anxiety. But her response was quite the opposite of what he had anticipated. 'Wah Sethji!' she exclaimed gaily, rolling over the sofa in mirth. 'You're a colourful man and very romantic! So what if

Rajshekhar Basu

you have two other wives? It doesn't bother me one bit. The only thing is—no one must know. By the way, you'd better get the flat registered in my name as soon as possible. The officers in the municipality are harassing me no end and—'

'I'll do that,' Sethji rose to his feet, 'but I can't spend time with you today, Rajhans. I have urgent work in Kolkata. I must leave immediately.'

Arriving at Kolkata airport, Sethji drove straight to Balaka's house in Alipur and walked into her beautifully furnished drawing room. An extremely handsome gentleman was at the piano, playing a merry ditty to which Balaka danced, her feet tapping out the rhythm in swift, neat strokes. 'Sethji!' Balaka exclaimed, frozen in mid-dance. 'Why this sudden visit?' Then, pointing to the gentleman, she asked Sethji, 'Have you met my cousin Mr Loton Kumar Bhorh? No, of course, you haven't! His father was a second cousin of my mother's. He's a wonderful dancer. I'm learning "pigeon dancing" from him. Would you like to see what I've learnt?'

'Not now,' Trikramdas shook his head. 'I'm in a hurry. I have something important to share with you, Balaka.'

Sethji waited, heart in mouth, as Loton left the room. The time had come to break the news to his beloved Balaka! How would she take it? What could he expect? Fury! Indignation! The humiliation of a woman scorned! But Balaka merely put a finger on her dimpled cheek and stared at him with huge, wondering eyes. 'Oh Sethji!' she said at last. 'You've been flitting from flower to flower like a humming bird, haven't you? What a libertine you are! Come, come. There's no need to look so ashamed. You're married to three women. Where's the harm in that? You don't have to worry about me. I'm not a jealous type. The only thing is . . . keep the news to yourself.

Don't go spreading it everywhere. Ah! Yes—I almost forgot. I need a new car desperately. The old Austin is giving me endless trouble. Just write out a cheque of twenty thousand. I'll do everything else.'

'That's no problem,' Sethji said. 'But I'll have to leave you now. I have urgent business in Delhi. My plane leaves in an hour.'

Arriving in Delhi, Sethji drove straight to Khajanchand's office and apprised him of all that had happened. Then the two went to Sethji's house. Khajanchand waited in the drawing room while Sethji went upstairs to break the news to Anandibai.

'What's wrong with you?' Anandi exclaimed, coming into the bedroom where her husband waited for her. 'You've been away for three days without even leaving a message!' Then, peering into his face suspiciously, she added, 'You don't look well at all. What's wrong? Trouble with the government?'

Trikramdas lowered his head in shame and told her the whole story. Anandi heard him in stunned silence for a while. Then, pulling herself together, she advanced upon him menacingly, arms akimbo, eyes rolling. 'What did you say you've done . . . you . . . you?' she screamed at the top of her voice.

'Shh! Softly, Anandi!' Sethji cried, alarmed. 'You'll frighten the children. Everything will be fine. Don't worry. Don't worry at all!'

But Sethji's assurances had no effect on her. Anandi danced a tandava all about the room, threshing her limbs in a fine frenzy. Bengali may be a fine language but it has its limitations. It is no match for Hindi in its vocabulary of abuses. The stream of adjectives describing Sethji and his fourteen generations of ancestors that issued from Anandi's lips, like water from a hosepipe, was fit to drown

Rajshekhar Basu

Sethji in a sea of self-loathing and despair. 'Forgive me, Anandi, forgive me,' Sethji cringed and begged with folded hands. But Anandi wanted none of his apologies or his promises. 'Don't dare open your mouth, you dirty mole of the gutter! You street cur!' Anandi screeched, gnashing her teeth. Flecks of angry froth starred the corners of her mouth as, springing upon her husband like a tigress, she clawed his cheeks with her nails. Then, stepping back a couple of paces, she pulled the solid gold bangle from her arm and flung it at his head. Jhan! Jhan! Jhan! The heavy circlet found its mark and fell to the ground. Sethji's forehead cracked open and the blood came running down his nose and cheeks. He screamed and fell to the ground in a faint. Anandi screamed, too, then running to her puja room collapsed on the floor. Tears ran down her cheeks and her body was racked with terrible sobs.

The whole house was in an uproar. Hearing the commotion, the members of the family came rushing to the scene. The women clamoured around Anandi, clicking their tongues in sympathy. Khajanchand ran to fetch a doctor, and the maids and servants scurried about, harassed, trying to keep up with conflicting orders.

Seven days later. Sethji lay in a comfortable armchair on the balcony upstairs, the long pipe of his hubble-bubble sputtering gently at his lips. There was a bandage on his forehead and bits of sticking plaster on his cheeks but otherwise he looked quite well and cheerful.

'Well, Sethji!' Khajanchand walked in and seated himself in a chair by his side. 'How do you feel today?'

'Better,' Sethji wagged his large head from side to side. Then, coming straight to the point, he said, 'Look here, Khajan bhai, I've made up my mind. I want to cut off all relations with Rajhans and Balaka. You'd better go to

Kolkata and Mumbai immediately and make the arrangements. Give them whatever they want and get rid of them. Those two care only for my money—not for me. But Anandibai loves me and wants me.' Raising his head he sniffed the air a couple of times. 'Can you smell the delicious aroma floating up from the kitchen? Anandi is cooking khichdi for me. And do you see this muffler? Anandi knitted it for me with her own hands.'

'Excellent decision, Sethji!' Khajanchand beamed at his client. 'I'm so glad the two of you have made up. Don't worry about the others. They'll be taken care of. You'd better arrange to take Anandibai on a pilgrimage to Mathura, Brindavan and Dwarka. It will make her very happy.'

Anandi nursed Trikramdas back to health in no time at all. Balaka and Rajhans were paid off and even M. Zulfikar Khan got a fat wad of notes. A few days later, Anandi dispatched a trusted servant to Kolkata; to the king of astrologers—Jyotishchandra Jyotisharnab. In return for a thousand rupees he sent her an amulet that guaranteed her husband's devotion to her for life. This she hung about Sethji's neck with loving hands.

The astrologer did his job well. For, in later years, Sethji was often heard commenting to his closest friends: 'All women are witches—all, except Anandi.'

Rajshekhar Basu

Aniseed Flower

Mouri Phool

Bibhuti Bhushan Bandopadhyay

Dusk was about to fall. In the bamboo grove, behind old
Ramtanu Mukherjee's house, clouds of glow-worms
flitted about ready to light their lamps for the night. The
taal palms growing around the pond were heavy with
hanging bats. Past the meadow and pond, beyond the
rice fields, streaks of rose and orange from the last rays
of the setting sun still clung to the rim of the earth. It was
a romantic hour and the scene alluring enough to inspire
a poet to write a few verses. Suddenly, the peace and
tranquility were shattered by sounds of violent quarrelling.
It came from within the Mukherjee household.

A pious Brahmin and a disciple of Shibkrishna
Paramahansa, Mukherjee Moshai made it a point to offer
oblations to the gods each evening. For this he needed
two hundred grams of pure ghee. Procuring so much ghee
every day was no easy task. But he managed it somehow
and kept it, jealously guarded, in a bowl on a high shelf,
away from the prying eyes of other members of the family.
That evening, on taking down the bowl, he discovered
that it was empty. The culprit was Sushila, his daughter-
in-law. She had stolen the ghee and used it all up to make
snacks for the evening meal.

Ramtanu Mukherjee had just returned from the subdivisional court where he had appeared as a witness on behalf of the Chowdhuris. The prosecuting lawyer had grilled and harassed him quite a bit.

'Weren't you the chief witness in the Panchu Rai versus his brother lawsuit in May?' he had asked him sternly. 'The boundary wall case?'

Mukherjee Moshai had nodded in affirmation.

'And in the Kanshona riot trials, were you not the chief witness for the plaintiff—the elder Chowdhuri?'

The old man had gulped nervously and admitted that it was true. He had appeared on behalf of the elder party.

'And isn't it also true,' the lawyer had rammed at him ruthlessly, 'that a few days later you appeared on behalf of the younger Chowdhuri in their property dispute case?'

Ramtanu Mukherjee couldn't recall this fact at first. When had he appeared on behalf of the younger Chowdhuri? But the prosecuting lawyer's fierce probing and Munsif Babu's stern glances had activated his memory. He had . . . yes, it was true . . . he had appeared as witness for the younger party. And it was in this very court only last month.

What transpired after that—how the prosecuting lawyer had exchanged scornful glances with the munsif and passed the most acerbic comments on Mukherjee Moshai's credibility; how the shamed and humbled Ramtanu Mukherjee hadn't known where to look in that courtroom filled to overflowing with lawyers and clerks—need not be mentioned here. Suffice it to say that Mukherjee Moshai had left the courtroom in considerable agitation, comforting himself, all the way home, with thoughts of the hour when he would light the lamp in his puja room and, surrendering his spirit burdened with worldly cares at the feet of his guru, enjoy the bliss of

Bibhuti Bhushan Bandopadhyay

holy communion. Reaching home he had performed his ablutions and taken down the bowl from the shelf when the shocking discovery was made. The ghee he had secreted away with so much faith and hope had been drained to the last drop.

For the next half hour the inner quarters of the Mukherjee household became the scene of a *kobir ladai*, a duel in which the opponents challenged each other, in verse, to come up with a fitting reply to their respective volleys. Sushila, initially embarrassed at being caught stealing, soon pulled herself together and, throwing herself into the slanging match, gave her father-in-law as good as she got. The words that fell from her lips were hardly befitting those of a good, dutiful daughter-in-law still in her teens. Ramtanu Mukherjee, maligned and abused in court and humiliated by his son's wife at home, couldn't contain his fury. Launching on a comparative analysis of the two lineages—his own and that of his daughter-in-law—he took pains to point out the merits of his own and the demerits of hers, using such difficult Sanskrit words and phrases in support of his argument that only those educated in Vidyasagar's *Kuladarsha Vidya*—knowledge of ideal lineage—could even pretend to understand them.

At this point, Mukherjee Moshai's son Kishori came home. He was about twenty-five years old. Not being well educated he worked as a scrivener in the zamindar's court on a salary of nine rupees a month.

Entering his room, Kishori was surprised to find that the lamp had not been lit. Changing his clothes in the dark he went out to the pond to wash his hands and feet. Returning half an hour later, he saw that the house was still pitch dark. Suddenly, out of the dark, Sushila's voice came ringing out. Addressing the wind perhaps (there being no one nearby with whom she could be conversing), Sushila said that it was impossible for her to live in her husband's home any longer and that the bullock cart should be sent for, first thing in the morning, so that she could go back to her father's house and give her bones a well-earned rest.

Kishori heard what she said but did not favour her with a reply. Entering his room, he lit the lamp, picked up the bamboo stick from behind the door, walked out of the house, and went to the small gymnasium set up by some idle youths of the village in the vestibule of the Chowdhuri mansion. The young men of the neighbourhood assembled there each evening, practised their wrestling and rehearsed the plays they performed, at intervals, for the entertainment of the villagers. Kishori was in the habit of attending these assemblies, often staying till late at night.

Ramtanu Mukherjee sat outside the house for a long time. Hari Rai, his neighbour, who dropped in for a smoke every now and then (it was more to save his own tobacco than out of love for the old man) was witness to his declaration that he had made up his mind to proceed to Kashi forthwith for, at his age, etc., etc. The reason for Ramtanu's decision to seek *vanaprastha* was his daughter-in-law. Sushila was a source of continuous trouble in the family. She was not only careless and inefficient in her household tasks but flew into a rage if anyone pointed out her defects. Not that she was able to get the better of her parents-in-law. But it wasn't for want of trying.

Kishori came home at midnight to find his meal laid out in a corner of the room, and his wife fast asleep on the bed. He ate in silence and was about to lie down when Sushila awoke.

'When did you come?' she asked, sitting up and rubbing her eyes. 'Why didn't you call me?'

Bibhuti Bhushan Bandopadhyay

'Why should I call you?' Kishori answered coldly. 'Don't I have hands? Can't I eat by myself?'

'Eat by yourself then!' Sushila cried, losing her temper. 'What is this—a house or an enemy stronghold? Why do all of you needle me all the time? I'd like to know what I have done!' Bursting into tears she pressed her face into her pillow.

Kishori was alarmed. His wife was always looking for an excuse to make a scene. And now—in the middle of the night! Really! This was too much! All he had done was refrain from disturbing her and eaten his meal. Was that a crime?

'Do what you like in the morning,' he said brusquely. 'Now move over and let me sleep. I didn't call you because you were sleeping. But if that's a crime I'll pull you out of bed by the hair of your head in future.' Sushila made no reply. Pressing her face deeper into her pillow, she tried to suppress her sobs.

Next morning, at dawn, the zamindar sent for Ramtanu Mukherjee. He was to come immediately as his services were required in tutoring some new witnesses for the trial. Just before leaving, Ramtanu said to his daughter-in-law, 'Start the cooking as early as you can, Bouma. I'll have a quick meal before going to court.' On returning home, he was surprised to find his wife in the kitchen and his daughter-in-law putting out clothes to dry in the sun. Hearing her husband come in, Mokshada poked her head out of the kitchen door and bellowed in a voice resembling a watchman's on night duty, 'I'll have to walk out of the house one of these days, if things go on like this. I've been begging and begging all morning, "Start the cooking, Bouma. Put the rice to boil." I've all but fallen at her feet. But does she care to obey? Now, at nine o'clock,

Her Royal Highness has had her bath and is ready to do the cooking.'

'I'm not a paid servant,' pat came the answer from the courtyard. 'Have I been sitting idle? Aren't there other chores? Sweeping, swabbing, washing the clothes, fetching water—I must do all that *and* finish the cooking by eight o'clock. Is it humanly possible? If I'm not quick enough why don't you do some of it yourself?'

At this, Mokshada rushed out of the kitchen, spud in hand, screaming and leaping about like Shiva dancing the tandava. Suddenly, a boy of ten or twelve appeared on the scene. He was very dark, thin and worn with malaria, and he carried a split bamboo cane in his hand. He was bare-bodied, despite the freezing cold, with only a torn filthy *gamchha* knotted around his loins. He was the son of Atar Ali, the thatcher from the next village. His father having died the year before, all he had in the world were a widowed mother and two little sisters. They were very poor and lived a hand-to-mouth existence. The boy went from door to door singing *hapu** for a few copper coins. He came to this village often enough but this was his first visit to Ramtanu Mukherjee's house. Ramtanu and his wife weren't exactly reputed in the village for their charity and benevolence.

A strange succession of sounds sprang from the boy's throat as he whirled round and round, drumming his armpits and lashing his bare back with the bamboo. Ramtanu Mukherjee had had a gruelling morning, drilling three ignorant villagers about what they were to say from the witness box. But the more he tried to put them through their paces the more confused they got. Taking out his frustration on the hapless boy, he snarled,

---

*A form of rural music now extinct.

'Stop! Stop this nonsense at once! Go home. Or find another house.' Startled at the vehemence in the old man's tone, the boy stopped and walked slowly out of the house. Sushila had been stretching out her husband's *dhuti* on the line and watching the boy, round-eyed, all this while. Seeing him leave, she hurried after him and beckoned him to come closer.

'Where do you live?' she asked.

'In Harishpur, Ma Thakrun,' the boy answered.

'Do you live with your parents?'

'My father died last year, Ma Thakrun. I live with my mother and two sisters. I'm the eldest.'

'Is that why you go around singing like this? Ha ré! Does it bring you enough to live on?'

Tears had risen to the boy's eyes on hearing Ramtanu's harsh rebuke. Now, Sushila's kind face and sympathetic words brought them tumbling down his cheeks.

'No, Ma Thakrun,' his voice broke as, wiping the tears away with a malaria-shrivelled hand, he said, 'people don't care to hear all this any more. If I could sing really well I would have joined a jatra troupe. We are very poor, Ma Thakrun. We don't get enough to eat. And in this terrible cold . . . '

'Wait here,' Sushila said. 'I'll come back in a minute.'

Restraining her tears with difficulty, Sushila ran into the house and pulled out a sheet from the clothes rack. Then she ran out again and thrust it into the boy's hand. 'Take this,' she whispered, 'it will keep you warm. It's very thick and almost new. Hide it under your arm. No one must see it. Go quickly.' The boy stood staring at her—sheet in hand. Seeing him hesitate, Sushila cried out in panic: 'Go! Go quickly before someone sees us.'

Coming into the kitchen a moment later, she saw that her father-in-law had started eating his morning meal.

The boy's misery had softened her feelings. 'Shall I serve you something more, Baba?' she asked in a gentle voice.

'You don't have to serve anything,' Mokshada snapped from the other end of the kitchen. 'Haven't you served him sweet words in plenty? Now, if you are in the mood to finish the cooking, kindly come over here. If not, just say so plainly and I'll do the rest—even if it kills me.'

Ramtanu didn't say a word. Finishing his meal in silence, he rose and went away. Had Ramtanu spoken to his daughter-in-law, had he asked her for something—even a pinch of salt or a wedge of lemon—her anger would have evaporated. What she couldn't stand was meanness and sarcasm. And if she thought someone was trying to get the better of her, was trying to corner and humiliate her, she lost all control. Hurling herself in the fray she gave as good as she got.

A couple of months later. It was the end of March and quite warm already. Kishori walked into his bedroom very late one night to see his wife sitting on the floor, writing a letter by the light of a lamp. The rest of the house was dark and the others were fast asleep.

'Whom are you writing to?' he asked.

Sushila covered the sheet of paper with the end of her sari and looked up. 'Why should I tell you?' she asked, smiling mischievously.

'Don't tell me if you don't want to,' Kishori said dryly and added, 'but give me my dinner as quick as you can. It's very late and the grind will start again from dawn.'

Sushila had thought that her husband would insist on seeing the letter and she would tease him by pretending to hide it from him. Actually, she was not writing a letter at all. It was a ploy, one she had used frequently in the past, to start a conversation. He spoke so rarely to her these days and even when he did . . . Her woman's heart thirsted for words of love, for the romance they had shared in the early months of marriage. It was with the hope of rekindling the old flame that she had forced herself to keep awake and had laid this simple snare. But Kishori hadn't walked into it. Sushila was extremely disheartened by her husband's response. She sighed and, putting away pen and paper, served his meal. Kishori ate in silence and prepared to go to sleep. Sushila went to the kitchen, did the last of her chores, had her own meal and returned to the bedroom to see her husband still awake—tossing and turning on the bed from the heat. Hope rose in her breast. Lying down beside him she laid her second snare. 'Tell me a story,' she begged in a little-girl voice. 'You haven't told me a story for s-o-o long! *O go*! Please tell me . . . '

In the early years of their marriage, Kishori used to regale his child bride with stories from the *Arabian Nights*. Sushila would listen to them, night after night, her eyes wide with fascination. Wonderful tales of jinns and fairies, of vast deserts where death lurked in wait for the unwary traveller, of palm groves with fountains in them throwing up jets of rubies and pearls. Of young handsome princes who fought against armies of demons single-handed and won beautiful captive princesses. Of storms at sea and . . . oh! so many wonderful things and people.

The stories were so thrilling and exciting! Sushila pretended that they were real. That the incidents were actually happening and that she and Kishori were at the centre of it all. Investing her young husband with all the virtues of the prince, she sent him out on perilous journeys over sea and land. She dressed him up in brocade and pearls (her knowledge of royal attire was derived from the few jatra performances she had seen) and agonized over his travails. When he walked through miles of arid desert without a drop of water to drink or was buffeted about in a ship on stormy seas, a lump rose in her throat and she stroked the storyteller's face and hair tenderly. It was in this way that she had first come to love her husband. Five or six years had passed but Sushila was still wrapped in the web of the old enchantment.

Kishori, however, had matured considerably since then. 'Hunh!' he grunted dismissively. 'Tell a story indeed! Work yourself to death all day and humour your wife all night. Do you have any idea of how hard a man's life is? For people like you who sit comfortably at home . . .'

Another girl would have shut up at this point. But Sushila had a stubborn, wilful streak in her. 'One story,' she insisted. 'It isn't all that late!'

'*It isn't all that late*!' Kishori repeated, mimicking her voice. 'Do you have any idea of time? Now lie down and be quiet. I need my sleep.'

Sushila felt her temper rising but she controlled it. 'What sort of husband are you?' she smiled up at him. 'Here I'm begging and begging and you aren't even . . . O go! Just one story. Even a small one will do.'

'Aah!' Kishori sat up with an exclamation of disgust. 'This is getting intolerable! You scream and quarrel all day. And now—even in the middle of the night! Can't I ever have some peace?'

Saying that she was responsible for all the quarrelling that went on in the house was the surest way of wounding Sushila. Stung to the quick, she cried out angrily, 'I'll scream and quarrel as much as I choose. If you don't like it, send me home to my parents. Is it my fault that it's so late? You spend half the night idling and gossiping with your friends and I have to stay awake to serve your meal. As if I don't work like a slave all day. Only I know what I go through. But does anyone care? All you think of is yourself and . . .'

Bibhuti Bhushan Bandopadhyay

Kishori tried to ignore her and go to sleep. But as her voice rose, turning sharper and shriller, he suddenly lost patience. Sitting up with a start, he picked up the palm-leaf fan and brought the stump viciously down her back several times. Then, dragging her off the bed by the hair, he pushed her out of the door. 'Get out!' he snarled. 'Out of my sight! Hateful creature! Day and night—it's the same! Won't give me a moment's peace.' This was not the first time. Though no such precedent had been set for him by the princes of Arabia, Kishori often punished his wife in this manner. Shutting the door, he examined his hands by the light of the lamp. They were bleeding from the long scratches inflicted by Sushila's nails.

It was Ekadasi. The night was on the wane but the sky still glimmered with moonlight as white and tender as jasmine petals. The air was filled with the scent of lemon flowers and the nightingale sang passionately from the branches of the mango tree. Sushila lay on the floor, outside her bedroom door, fast asleep.

Morning came. The members of the household rose and went about their tasks. 'Finish your work quickly, Bouma,' Mokshada said to her daughter-in-law. 'The Chowdhuris are going to offer puja at the Shiva shrine today. They've invited us to accompany them.' The Chowdhuris were the zamindars of the village and Ramtanu Mukherjee lived, virtually, under their protection. He made a living by helping them in their lawsuits, bearing false witness himself, and tutoring bogus witnesses.

Around ten o'clock, after all her work was done and the morning meal eaten, Sushila wore her best sari and followed her mother-in-law to the boat which was to take them down the river, to the shrine. It was a two-hour journey. A young woman, sitting with the zamindar's wife, looked up eagerly as Sushila stepped into the boat. She was a relative of the Chowdhuris and had come from Kolkata to participate in the rituals of Raas Purnima, a festival celebrated each year in March on the night of the full moon. Her father-in-law was a rich man of the city and her husband well educated. He was an MA and a deputy magistrate.

Though pleased at the prospect of spending the next two hours with a girl of her own age, she found it difficult to make the first move. The carelessness with which Sushila's midnight-blue sari was wrapped around her, and the old-fashioned way in which her hair was plaited and bound, proclaimed her to be an ignorant, unsophisticated village girl. It was also obvious that she came from a poor family.

The city girl sat quietly with her eyes on the water as the boat, cut adrift from its moorings, skimmed rapidly down the river. A little distance away, the zamindar's wife was regaling Mokshada with an account of all she meant to do, all the money she meant to spend on the successful conclusion of her Savitri *brata* pledge. Mokshada listened, round-eyed with awe and admiration. But the lady's guest started getting restless. She was educated and had some idea of how civilized people behaved. The unashamed boastfulness of her hostess's pronouncements left her feeling awkward and embarrassed.

After sitting silently for a while, the city girl looked up to find a pair of large, dark eyes looking at her, curiously, from behind a low veil. Turning to her companion she asked, 'What's your name?' Sushila answered, hesitating a little, 'Srimati Sushilasundari Debi.' Her voice sounded slightly suspicious.

The city girl was amused at Sushila's manner. 'Why is your face all covered up?' she asked, laughing. 'There's no one here but you and me. Throw back your veil and

Bibhuti Bhushan Bandopadhyay

come closer. Let's sit together and chat.' Putting out her hand, she lifted Sushila's veil and was charmed by what she saw. Though dark, the face was the loveliest she had seen in her life. Looking at it she was reminded of the *kalmi* creeper that covered the river bank with its lush, wild foliage. The face was young and supple, bursting with health and sap, and glowed with a cool green radiance. One look and the sophisticated city girl fell in love with her simple village counterpart.

'Who is the lady with you, sister?' she asked. 'Your mother-in-law?'

'Yes.'

'Come closer. Let's enjoy the view together. Where do your parents live?'

Sushila was much more relaxed by now. 'My parents?' she repeated. 'They live in Shimlé.'

'Shimlé!' the girl exclaimed. 'In Kolkata?'

Sushila was puzzled. 'Is there a Shimlé in Kolkata?' she asked wonderingly. 'My father's village is quite close to this one,' she confided. 'Ten or twelve miles away. One has to go in a bullock cart.'

The two girls sat together, looking out at the fields of millet and mustard that stretched along the bank. All these—miles of open sky, fields and river—were new to the stranger and she exclaimed with delight at everything she saw. Pointing to a bird with blue-green wings, she cried out, 'What a beautiful bird! What is it called?'

'Why! That's a kingfisher,' Sushila was surprised. 'Haven't you seen one before?'

'I've never been out of Kolkata, sister,' the other girl said ruefully. 'Only once, when I was very young, I went with my father to Chandannagar. This is my first visit to the country. What's growing in that field?'

Sushila's eyes followed the pointing finger. The boat was passing a field of aniseed, gay with tufts of green-white flowers waving in the breeze. Sushila's mouth lifted in a smile. She had stood in awe of the city girl at first. The latter's exceedingly fair complexion, elegant silk sari and blouse, and glittering necklace had heightened her sense of her own inadequacies. She had felt shabby and awkward. But now, seeing her companion's ignorance of the simplest things of life, she felt a gush of sympathy. Fancy not recognizing a field of aniseed! Or a kingfisher! Kolkata was a strange place indeed and its inhabitants deprived of even the most ordinary things.

'That's *mouri*,' she said, smiling tenderly at her companion. 'Can't you smell the flowers? Don't people eat mouri greens in Kolkata? Why, even here, there are so many . . .'

The city girl responded by saying that she didn't know about the past but present-day Kolkata had no aniseed fields or any fields for that matter. Of course, one could never tell what might happen in the future.

An hour later, by the time the boat came to a halt, the two had become good friends. Sushila's companion had confided in her a great deal. She had talked of how much her husband loved and admired her and all the sweet things he said to her. As she listened, Sushila felt a pain welling up in her heart. This pain was always with her. She bore it in silence, keeping it hidden from the eyes of others. But, every now and then, it reared its head. Her husband had also loved her at one time. He had petted and cajoled her and told her stories. He had held a cone of paan to her mouth, every night, and begged her to eat it and redden her lips. Thoughts of Kishori as he was once, and of the rough, harsh stranger he had become, brought the tears, sharp and stinging, to her eyes.

The two wandered, hand in hand, in the shadows of the great trees that lined the bank. How beautiful everything was! The bright blue sky hanging like an inverted dome above lush green fields! The flocks of cranes and egrets that rose from the water, their wings flashing like silver spars in the sun. 'Come sister,' the Kolkata girl said. 'Let's pledge a bond of friendship.'

'Let's,' Sushila cried out delightedly. 'What shall we be to one another?'

'*Mouri phool*,' her companion replied. 'The aniseed flowers we saw on the bank as we were coming . . . '

Sushila agreed happily. Moving towards the river, they lifted palmfuls of water and chanted a few words. And thus they pledged a bond of eternal friendship.

'Bouma!' Mokshada called at this point. 'Come this way.'

The two walked in the direction of the shrine—a small, dilapidated brick structure standing under the spreading branches of an ancient banyan tree. The place was packed with people. A little distance away, an old woman was selling herbs and potions. She had remedies for every problem, she claimed—from finding a lost cow to bearing a male child. She was surrounded by women buying her wares. Sushila's companion pulled her by the hand and led her to the shrine. 'Come, Mouri Phool,' she said, 'let's see what's going on there.'

Sushila went with her but, after a while, she slipped silently away and came and stood near the potion seller. Her customers had gone and she was alone. 'What do you want?' she asked.

Sushila tried to speak but could not. Her face flamed with embarrassment.

The potion seller smiled. 'You don't have to say anything. I understand. But why do you worry? You're very young. There's plenty of time. Many women bear late and—'

'It isn't that,' Sushila made haste to contradict her. 'It's—'

'I understand perfectly now,' the potion seller smiled her toothless smile. 'Your husband neglects you. He goes to other women. There's nothing new in that. I'll give you something—never fear. You'll get results in a month.' Picking up a small dark-green root she thrust it into the girl's hand. 'Here. Grind it to a paste and feed it to your husband. But be very careful. No one must know. The charm won't work otherwise. It will cost you eight annas.'

Sushila was horrified at what the old woman had said. Her husband went to other women! Was that possible? Her heart sank at the thought. Unfastening the knot at the end of her sari she took out an eight-anna bit and handed it over. She had brought the coin from home to spend on something if she fancied it. Her mother-in-law didn't know. Had Mokshada known she would have taken it away. Hiding the root in a fold of her sari, Sushila made her way back to the shrine.

The puja over, the members of the zamindar's party took their places in the boat.

'Will you be staying a while longer, Mouri Phool?' Sushila asked her friend as the boat glided over the water towards their village.

'No sister,' the city girl replied, 'I'll be leaving in a day or two. But I'll never forget your sweet face. You're the priceless gem I've picked up on my first visit to the country. I'll remember you all my life.'

Sushila's eyes glistened with tears. No one had treated her with so much kindness before. All she had heard about herself was that she was stubborn and quarrelsome and gave no one any peace. Pulling a gold ring off her finger, she took her companion's hand in hers and said, 'Wear this ring for my sake, Mouri Phool. It's my mother's. She gave it to me after the wedding. I wish I had something better to give you but . . . Every time you see this you'll be reminded of your poor Mouri Phool.'

'Are you mad?' the girl pulled her hand away with a laugh. 'How can you give away something that belonged to your mother? No, sister, I can't take this ring. I'll remember you without it. Believe me. And now, promise that *you* will never forget me.'

'Never,' Sushila's voice shook with emotion. 'Never. Never. Dear Mouri Phool! You must have been my sister in a previous birth.' Then, giggling self-consciously, she chanted, 'Mouri Phool! Mouri Phool! Mouri Phool! My aniseed flower of the field by the river!' Putting her arms round the city girl's neck she buried her face in her shoulder. Her companion held the lovely face in her hands and kissed the streaming cheeks over and over again. Her eyes misted with tears as she bid farewell to the strange, wild girl with her deep dark eyes and poignant smile.

A few days later . . .

Kishori was away from home on some work and wouldn't be back for a day or two. The zamindar's lady had sent for Mokshada that morning to help her prepare for the festivities that would mark the successful conclusion of her Savitri brata. Just before leaving, she said to her daughter-in-law, 'Finish the cooking as soon as you can, Bouma. I won't have time to do anything today. I'm going to the zamindar's house and might be very late in returning.' Mokshada need not have said what she did for the simple reason that all the work of the house was done by Sushila anyway. She rose at dawn, scrubbed the utensils, washed the clothes, fetched water and did all the cooking. There had been a maid in the house to do the more strenuous chores but she had been dismissed soon after Kishori got married. Sushila didn't mind the work, heavy though it was. She was strong and energetic and could work day and night if kept in good humour.

Sushila finished all her chores, bathed and started preparing to cook the morning meal when she discovered that there wasn't a stick of firewood in the shed. Ramtanu would send for a labourer, once a month, and get him to chop a pile of wood for the kitchen. But he hadn't done so for several months now though Sushila had reminded him many times. She had managed, so far, by scouring the jungle behind the house, picking up faggots and lengths of dried bamboo, then chopping them into the right size for the kitchen hearth. Seeing that his daughter-in-law was collecting the wood herself, Ramtanu thought, *Why send for the labourer and waste a rupee*? That she was grumbling about it was of no consequence. Complaining and grumbling were part of her nature.

But, today, at the sight of the empty shed, Sushila lost her temper. There was no one in the house on whom she could vent her anger and that infuriated her even more. 'How much longer can I go on like this?' she cried out indignantly to the sky and air. '*Finish the cooking early*! That's all I hear every day. That's all this family cares about. But how am I to cook without wood? Am I to stuff my arms and legs in the hearth and set them alight? There's no wood in the shed, I've said over and over again for the last two months. But does anyone care to hear? I won't do the cooking today—that's that. Do all the chores, collect wood *and* cook all the meals! Is this a joke? I'll keep everyone starving today. Only then will they learn to heed me.'

Walking out of the kitchen she came to the *dalan* and sat for a while, grumbling to herself. After half an hour or so, she had an idea. *I could grind the spices in the meantime*, she thought. Going back into the kitchen she set to work.

Around ten o'clock, a fair, pretty, young woman peeped in at the kitchen door. 'Didi,' she whispered fearfully.

'Who is it?' Sushila looked up from the grinding stone. 'Oh! It's you, Chhoto Bou. Come into the kitchen. Don't be afraid. Thakrun isn't home.'

The girl was dressed in a threadbare silk sari, dating from the time of her wedding and all the ornaments she wore was a pair of conch bangles. She held a brass bowl in her hands. One glance at the unlit hearth and she exclaimed, 'O Didi, you haven't started the cooking!'

'Start the cooking indeed!' Sushila made a face. 'This family's lucky I haven't smashed the pots and pans to pieces.'

The girl's eyes widened in horror. 'Don't even think of such things,' she pleaded. 'Begin at once. You know what these people are like. They'll—'

'I'll teach them a lesson today. What do they think I am? A bonded slave? Sweep, swab, fetch water, collect firewood, cook all the meals. Hunh!'

The girl understood in an instant. 'There's no wood in the house?' she asked, then added quickly: 'Give me the chopper. I'll get you some in a minute.'

'Why should you? Let the members of the family do their own work. For two months now, I've been telling them that there's no wood in the shed, but nobody cares to listen. Today, I'll teach them a lesson they'll remember all their lives. You sit quietly and watch the fun.' Sushila gave a short laugh.

'No Didi,' the girl's eyes darkened with anxiety. Sushila's wilfulness alarmed her. She knew what the older girl's parents-in-law were like. There might be fun coming this way but there was no doubt in her mind that it was Sushila who would be at the receiving end of it. 'No Didi,' she repeated, 'don't try any tricks. Start the cooking, I beg of you.'

The girl was Ramtanu's cousin Ramlochan's daughter-in-law and lived next door. Ramlochan was a widower and very poor. In the absence of a mother-in-law it was she who had to fend for the family. The poor girl had a tough time making ends meet. In consequence, she was often seen in Ramtanu's house, bowl in hand, asking for rice, salt or oil. She asked for them as loans but could rarely return what she took. She was mortally scared of Mokshada, who sent her away empty-handed most of the time, and if at all she gave anything it was always after a lengthy lecture. Moreover, she always remembered what she had given and insisted on its return. Sushila was careless and absent-minded and, more often than not, forgot what was owing to her. Even when she remembered she didn't care to take it back. 'It's only a measure of rice,' she would say to the girl. 'You don't have to return it. Slip away quietly before Thakrun catches you.'

That day, intent on teaching her husband and in-laws a lesson, Sushila didn't notice that the girl held an empty bowl in her hands. She grumbled away for a while, then looked up from the grinding stone. 'What about your own chores, Chhoto Bou?' she asked. 'Have you finished your cooking?'

The girl smiled sheepishly. 'I—I—I . . . ' she stammered, 'took some oil from you the other day. I haven't been able to return it. There isn't a drop in the house. My father-in-law will send for some in a day or two. Then I'll . . . that's why—' she finished lamely.

'Oh!' Sushila understood. 'Let me see how much is left in the jar. Even we are short—' Picking up the jar of oil she poured its entire contents into the bowl of her diffident, penurious, gentle sister-in-law. 'Please Didi,' the girl cast an imploring glance at her benefactress as she rose to depart, 'begin the cooking, I beg of you.'

But Sushila turned a deaf ear. 'Run away before anyone catches you,' she cautioned. 'I'll teach everyone in this house a lesson. I'm determined—'

Mokshada arrived at noon to find the kitchen hearth cold and empty and no sign of a meal. Flaring up (she really had every right to do so) she leaped about in rage and called the whole world to witness what she had to endure day after day. Ramtanu came in a while later. He was so shocked by what he saw that he didn't know how to react. Walking away from the scene he sat outside and began puffing at his hubble-bubble. In the meantime, mother-in-law and daughter-in-law went for each other hammer and tongs. Mokshada screamed abuses at all fourteen generations of Sushila's ancestors. Sushila had answers for everything Mokshada said. If the truth were to be told not even her worst enemy could accuse Sushila of being a quiet, docile daughter-in-law. The quarrel had reached fever pitch when Kishori arrived, suddenly, on the scene. He was to have returned a few days later but, having finished his work, he saw no reason for staying away.

At the sight of her son, Mokshada began screaming louder than ever. Kishori had travelled a long distance and was tired and hungry. What he saw infuriated him beyond endurance. Though unaware of what had actually happened, the full force of his anger fell on his wife. Picking up a length of bamboo from a corner of the courtyard, he leaped up on the dalan and entered the kitchen. Sushila, still grinding her spices, looked up to see her husband, bamboo in hand. For the first time that day she was truly frightened. Her face went white and she put up her arms to shield herself. Kishori dragged her up viciously by the hair and flung her onto the kitchen floor. Then, striking her several times with the bamboo, he grabbed her by the neck and pushed her, out of the door, to the dalan and from there to the courtyard below. Unable to keep her balance, Sushila fell in a heap with her face to the ground. Kishori would have beaten her some more if Ramtanu hadn't come in at that moment and stopped him.

In the house next door, Ramlochan's daughter-in-law had fed her husband and his father and was just sitting down to her own meal when she heard the clamour and came rushing out. Peeping from the back door she saw that the courtyard was full of people. The neighbours had heard the sounds of beating and come hurrying to see the fun. Now they huddled together in groups, nudging and whispering to one another. Sushila stood in the middle of the courtyard. Her face and arms were coated with dust and there were splotches of turmeric on her hands and sari. Her hair, unfastened from its knot, streamed down her back. A few unruly locks tumbled about her cheeks. Above the wall that separated the two properties, Ramlochan's face could be seen looking on curiously, his mouth twisted in a sly grin. The young woman's heart thudded painfully at the sight of Sushila in her turmeric-stained sari with her dust-covered hair, standing, so helpless and forlorn, in the middle of the yard. *Poor Didi!* she thought. *Poor innocent, unloved Didi!* Sharp, scalding tears stung her eyes and ran down her cheeks. She felt Sushila's humiliation keenly, but what could she do? She was too young and too shy. She dared not interfere. But when old Ganguly Moshai came hobbling in, hookah in hand, and called in a loud hectoring voice, 'Why Ramtanu! What's going on?' she couldn't bear it any longer. Stifling her sobs with difficulty, she ran to the dazed, bewildered girl and, taking her by the hand, led her out of the yard. Tears streaming down her face, she wiped the dust and sweat off Sushila's with the end of her sari and whispered,

'Darling Didi! Why didn't you listen to me? I told you not to . . .'

The next day at noon, Mokshada came into the kitchen where Sushila sat cooking. Kishori, seated on a plank in the dalan, was waiting for his meal. Sushila, her back to him, had ladled dal into a bowl and was mixing something in it. A smaller bowl with some greenish paste clinging to the rim stood by her side.

'What are you doing, Bouma?' Mokshada asked, her voice sharp with suspicion. 'What are you mixing in the dal?'

Sushila turned around, startled. Seeing her mother-in-law, her eyes grew large with fear. Guilt and embarrassment were stamped all over her face. Her reaction confirmed Mokshada's suspicions. Picking up the bowl of dal, she peered into it. There was a tinge of green mixed with the yellow. 'What is this?' she asked sternly. 'What have you mixed in the dal?'

Sushila tried to speak but could not. Her face turned from flame to ashen grey.

And now Mokshada set up a wail that could be heard all over the village. 'O go!' she cried, running out into the courtyard. 'My son would have been poisoned if I hadn't caught her at it. We are nurturing a serpent with milk and honey! A demon! O go! What have we done to deserve this?'

Kishori rose from his plank and joined his mother. Ramtanu came rushing in from the puja room. Neighbours flocked from all sides. Mokshada held the bowl out for all to see. 'Look for yourselves!' she howled. 'You think I'm to be blamed for all the quarrelling that goes on in the house! You think I'm harsh and cruel to my daughter-in-law! Baba Taraknath . . .' here, Mokshada brought her palms together and touched her forehead, 'has saved the day. If I hadn't come into the kitchen by chance . . . '

A courtyard full of people heard that Ramtanu's daughter-in-law had tried to poison her husband. Some expressed their astonishment. Others smiled snidely and said, 'It was to be expected. Women with loose morals won't stop at anything. We knew her character was flawed. Only, living in the same neighbourhood, we didn't . . . ' There was one lone voice which said, 'Has anyone checked the stuff? It might be something quite harmless.' But the suggestion was drowned in the shower of abuses that fell from Mokshada's lips. Old Ganguly Moshai turned to Ramtanu and said ponderously, 'Thank your guru your son has been saved this time. But no more risks. Get rid of her as soon as you can. The Shastras recommend banishment for evil wives. Not another day in the house.'

The rest of the day was spent in confabulation. By evening it was decided that Sushila would be sent away to her parents next day at dawn. Everyone concurred in the decision. The sooner the village was rid of her, the better. Who knew what she would do next? Besides, the presence of a girl like her in the neighbourhood would send out wrong signals to other daughters-in-law.

That night, Sushila was made to sleep in another room. This was Mokshada Thakrun's arrangement. Since the evil creature was to be sent away the very next day, the separation from her husband might as well start from now.

Sushila spent a sleepless night. The windows of the room in which she lay were wide open and squares of moonlight fell on her as she tossed and turned on the floor. She had never felt so wretched in her life. So full of misery! She was young and foolish and ignorant of the ways of the world. She thought she could get her own way if she protested forcefully enough. But the events of the last

Bibhuti Bhushan Bandopadhyay

two days had left her dazed and bewildered. She had been punished and beaten by her husband often before but not in public. Not with her parents-in-law and a courtyard full of people looking on. Consequently, she had never felt such pain! Such humiliation! Tears flowed down her cheeks at the thought of how her husband had beaten her. Her back throbbed from a deep cut with the split edge of the bamboo. One hand, put up to defend herself, was lacerated with shards from her broken bangles. Her dear husband! He had loved her so tenderly only five or six years ago. He had kept her awake all night, petting and caressing her, telling her stories. He had held a paan to her lips and begged and begged . . . For some reason, memories of the paan Kishori had made her eat came drifting into her mind over and over again. The moon rose higher in the sky, round and radiant, filling the room with silver light.

It was the end of March. Tender, coppery-green leaves had started sprouting on the branches of the trees. Above their heads, a veil of sunlight, flimsy, hazy with dancing motes, drifted gently to and fro all day. Long, lazy summer days filled with the perfume of new buds and blossoms floated away, over the river, and came to rest in the shadows of the silk cotton tree. The nights were filled with birdsong. Flitting from one bamboo frond to another in the grove behind the house, cuckoos and nightingales sang joyfully in the moonlight.

No one loves me, Sushila thought as she lay on the floor. *No one except Mouri Phool*. She had received a letter from her friend only a few days ago. Mouri Phool had written that she missed Sushila so much she cried for her each night. Mouri Phool and Chhoto Bou! They were the only ones. Poor Chhoto Bou! She had so many troubles. If she, Sushila, grew rich some day she would take care of Chhoto Bou. But how? Her husband had decided to send her away. *Un hunh*! That was nothing. He hadn't meant it. Not really. He was a good man and he loved her. He was tense and angry all the time because he didn't earn enough money. Mouri Phool's husband was rich and influential. He would find Kishori a good job. Then all would be well. She would write to Mouri Phool tomorrow. Once he earned well, she and Kishori would set up a little house of their own. She would keep it very clean and neat and fill it with comforts. She would cut down expenses by planting pumpkin seeds in the yard and trailing the vines over a machan. They wouldn't need to buy pumpkins any more. Everyone said she was careless and disorganized. Once in her own house she would show them what a good housewife she was. Suppose the house caught fire? What would she do then? But no! Who would set the house on fire? Chhoto Bou? Of course not. If anybody did anything so wicked, it would be her mother-in-law. The kind of person she was—she could do anything.

What was that floating in the moonlight outside the window? She couldn't see it properly. She strained her eyes but it was shadowy and blurred. *Perhaps it's a fairy*, she thought, *like the ones in Kishori's stories. The ones who flitted about in the moonlight over the river and above the clouds*. What was that melody drifting into her ears? It sounded like the strains of a flute. Someone had played the flute on her wedding day. She could remember the tune—sweet, poignant and filled with nostalgia. Why didn't people play the flute any more? There were so many lying on the bank of the river . . . The postman was bringing a letter from Mouri Phool. A big, square envelope, red as *alta*, and smelling of rose petals.

Next morning, seeing that her daughter-in-law hadn't risen, Mokshada peeped into the room. Sushila lay unconscious on the floor, her eyes red as hibiscus, her body burning with fever. No one came near her for a whole day and night. The day after, alarmed by her condition, Ramtanu sent for the doctor. As he stooped to feel her pulse, Sushila cried out in high delirium, 'Mouri Phool! O Mouri Phool! What they are saying is not true . . . I didn't . . . I only . . . '

She died shortly before dusk. Her husband's family breathed a sigh of relief. They could live in peace at last, free from quarrels and unpleasantness. And when, soon after Sushila's death, Kishori brought his new bride Meghlata home, everyone was charmed. Such a lovely girl! So intelligent and hardworking! So thrifty and careful. Some time later, when Kishori secured a well-paid job in the estate of the Pals, everyone in the village pronounced Meghlata to be the goddess Lakshmi incarnate.

The other wife, the stubborn, wilful, quarrelsome girl was forgotten in a few days. No one takes her name in the village any more.

The Brahmin

Agradaani

Tarashankar Bandopadhyay

If one took a wooden staff six to six-and-a-half-feet long and, wrenching it cruelly from the middle, bent it towards the ground it would look exactly like Purna Chakrabarty. Yet, thirty years ago he was quite a different proposition— an upright young man of thirty-two, tall and dark and straight. 'Look! Look!' people cried out to one another the moment they saw him approach, 'there comes the ladder!' If the men who laughed at him were adults, Purna would walk over calmly to where they stood and, holding their eyes with his own steely ones, enquire gravely, 'Hmph! What's so funny?'

'Nothing, Dada . . . just enjoying a joke.'

But someone in the group would give it all away. 'No, Dada,' he would announce, 'they were laughing at you. "The ladder's coming," was what they were saying.'

Purna Chakrabarty would grin, revealing all thirty-two of his perfect teeth. 'Right!' he would agree enthusiastically. 'If you climbed up on my shoulder I could send you straight to heaven. Treat me to a fine meal and I'll do it with pleasure.'

'But a fall from those heights would hurl us down to the pits of hell. What do you say, Dada?'

Purna Chakrabarty would search his mind, frantically, for a fitting reply. But, fortunately, he was rarely called upon to make one. Glancing out of the corner of his eye he would see a knot of children playing in the alley. They would beckon to him, for children loved Purna Chakrabarty. Excusing himself, Purna would stride away in their direction.

With the children in tow, Purna Chakrabarty would steal into his neighbours' orchards and strip the trees of their fruit. It might be the Roys' mangoes one day or the Mians' guavas the next—he marauded them without a prick of conscience. Clouds of wasps and bumblebees, attracted by the pungent smells of ripe, juicy fruit, buzzed and droned aggressively around him—even threatened attack. But he was unfazed. Comfortably ensconced in a fork among the highest branches, he would cram the fruit, in handfuls, into a greedy red mouth. 'But you're eating it all yourself,' the children would wail from below. Then he would give the branches a tremendous shake, sending showers of star-apples or roseapples to the ground. 'Eat children! Eat!' he would cry lustily—the words slurred and indistinct from a mouth too full.

'Purna Kaka!' one of them would call out. 'You're not supposed to eat now . . . why, you haven't even started your puja!'

'It's only fruit!' Purna Chakrabarty would reply, grinning from ear to ear. 'There's no harm in fruit. I'm not eating rice—'

The story needs to be told properly. It all started thirty years ago when Shyamadas Babu, a wealthy man of the village, held a great religious ceremony and invited a large number of Brahmins to the feast that followed. There was a reason for the occasion. Shyamadas Babu was childless—his wife Shibrani having had the misfortune of bearing five stillborn infants one after another. When all his efforts, that is intervention with gods and humans, came to naught, Shyamadas decided to remarry. Shibrani, pregnant once again, begged him to desist with tears in her eyes. 'Wait till the birth,' she pleaded. 'If I fail you this time I won't say another word. I'll arrange a suitable match for you myself.'

Though he had little faith left in her, Shyamadas could not bring himself to set aside her plea. He agreed to wait a little longer but he took some precautions first. He arranged a great Putreshthi yagna in his own house besides sending offerings to the temples of Kashi Vishwanath and Tarakeshwar. And at the vast assembly of Brahmins that feasted on his goodly fare, he went from one to the other, head lowered in humility over folded hands, and sought their blessings.

Purna Chakrabarty sat with his three sons in a corner but they had five leaves between them. This fifth portion was Purna's by right, for it was he who had gone on foot from village to village and invited all the Brahmins on Shyamadas Babu's behalf. This was how he was paid for his efforts at each celebration in Shyamadas Babu's household. And not Shyamadas Babu's alone. Purna Chakrabarty was a familiar figure at all ceremonies—big and small—where Brahmins were fed, not only in his own village but in the surrounding five as well. Clad in a dhuti so short it barely covered his knees, and an upper cloth with the hundred names of Kali stamped on it (it could well be called an heirloom—it was so ancient), he would come bustling into the courtyard in question, uninvited, calling out in a strident voice, '*Koi go*! Is anyone there? I've come to see the master.' Then, on the master's appearance, he would rattle off in a tone of mixed familiarity and unctuousness. "Here we are, *Karta*! Now, how many Brahmins would you like me to invite? We'd better settle the details. There isn't much time left.' Then his eyes, darting this way and that, would catch sight of the maids cutting up a couple of giant-sized carp in thick fat chunks. 'Mm . . .' Purna would lick his lips. 'The fish looks good. Plenty of oil in the innards. *Hoosh*!' A tremendous shout to ward off a kite floating lazily against the warm blue sky, and a muttered, 'Darned kite—would have swooped on the fish if I hadn't been looking.' This was Purna Chakrabarty.

Purna was always striving to prove his worth to the neighbours. He would walk from village to village on the darkest, coldest winter nights, shivering in his threadbare dhuti, collecting Brahmins for someone's feast. On the hottest afternoons, in the peak summer months, he could be seen on the same errand, striding on his long stork legs, a wet gamchha wrapped around his head, the scorching dust seeping into his feet through the holes in his torn slippers. And all this only for a leaf full of food.

To go back to our story. On the day of the Putreshthi yagna, Shyamadas Babu came up to him where he sat eating with his sons and said, 'Shall I send for some more fish, Chakrabarty?' Purna had eaten some twenty pieces already and was now sucking on a fishbone. 'No, Karta,' he said. 'I've kept some room for the sweets. Hari Moira has huge balls of *chhana bara* swimming in syrup in his wok. I've seen them.'

'Yes. Yes. Sweets of course,' Shyamadas nodded, smiling. 'But some fish before that. A head perhaps?'

'A small one.'

The sweets started arriving by the time Purna finished eating the fish head. 'Clear your leaves,' he commanded his sons. 'Make room for the sweets, otherwise they'll fall into the gravy and taste salty.' Then to one of them: 'Eh! You've eaten nothing! You haven't even finished your fish.' Reaching out with a long crab-like hand he plucked the half-eaten piece off his son's leaf and put it in his mouth. Then, craning his long neck above the other eaters, he called out to the man who was serving the sweets: 'Here! Here! This way.'

The other men in his row nudged one another and smiled snidely. 'Look at his eyes,' one whispered. 'He's gobbling the food with his eyes as well as his mouth.'

'The look in his eyes makes my flesh creep,' his neighbour whispered back. 'I make it a point to sit as far away from him as I can.'

The man serving sweets had reached Purna Chakrabarty's group by then and placed four pieces of chhana bara on each leaf. Purna Chakrabarty reared up for a fight.

'I should get eight for my take-home leaf,' he glared at the man. 'It is my right.'

'But you always get four, Moshai.'

'That's when you serve two on each leaf. You're serving four this time. So my take-home leaf should get eight.'

Drawn by the commotion, Shyamadas Babu hurried to the scene. 'Serve him sixteen sweets,' he commanded the man. 'He takes on so much of my responsibility for no wages at all. Come, put sixteen sweets—'

'But the leaf is full,' the man muttered.

'Here,' Purna Chakrabarty unfolded the cloth on the upper part of his body and held it out. 'Put them in this.'

'Be here first thing in the morning, Chakrabarty,' Shyamadas Babu said before moving away. 'Come for breakfast.'

'Certainly. I'll come as soon as I can.'

'Apply to the Babu for the post of a jester, Chakrabarty,' one of his neighbours called out with a grin. 'In the old days kings kept men like you as court jesters.'

'Hmph!' Purna Chakrabarty had finished eating and was tying his take-home leaf in a large red gamchha.

Tarashankar Bandopadhyay

'That would make you happy, wouldn't it? As for me—I'm a Brahmin. Nothing can shame me. I wouldn't mind being court jester if it brought me goodies like these.' He rose with a laugh.

Reaching home he handed the gamchha to his eldest son and said, 'Go, give this to your mother.' His second daughter had heard her father and brothers coming and had rushed out to greet them. 'The sweets!' she exclaimed, her eyes round. 'What about the sweets?'

'I'll give them to your mother myself.'

'No!' the girl screamed at her father. 'You'll hide them, I know it.'

'Off with you!' Purna tried to shoo her away.

'Ma!' the girl shrieked in a voice like a siren. 'Ma! Come here quick. Baba is keeping the sweets for himself. All sixteen of them.'

'Sixteen!' Purna exclaimed as though struck with horror. 'Who said there were sixteen? I got eight. That too after a big fight.'

Chakrabarty's wife had been a great beauty in her youth. Though battered by the unceasing assaults of poverty and want, some of it still endured. Her form was thin and shrivelled, her clothes soiled and frayed, and her hair rough and tangled from lack of oil. Yet Haimavati, even now, was the 'golden goddess' her name denoted. Gold that had lost its lustre but was still recognizable. Her eyes were wide and beautiful but the expression in them was harsh; even cruel. She was like a desert of sand—smooth and golden from without but arid and pitiless from within. No love flowed out from her—for her husband or her children.

Seeing Haimavati approach, Purna panicked. 'I—I only said,' he stammered, 'that she wouldn't be able to carry it. The wench screamed as though—' Haima stared at his eyes with her own glittering ones and put out a hand. 'Give it,' she said in a steely voice.

'Don't give Baba any of it, Ma!' one of the boys called out to his mother. 'He's eaten—my god! How he's eaten! And Babu has invited him to breakfast tomorrow.'

'Get out of my sight,' Haima snarled at the boy. 'Get out! Why don't you die—all of you? Die! Die! Give my bones some rest.'

Somewhat emboldened, Chakrabarty took a step towards his wife and said, 'Look. Just look at the way he talks about his father. Even a peasant has better manners.'

'If he has the manners of a peasant he's doing well enough,' Haima turned on her husband. 'What can you expect from the son of a *chamar*? Do you give your children food enough to keep them alive? Or clothes to hide their nakedness? Do they get an education? Or medicine when they are sick?' Fire rained from her eyes and sparks flew, scorching Purna's rhino skin till he squirmed. 'Yet they don't die. They live on and on to torture me. Sons of demons! Indestructible!'

Chakrabarty didn't dare open his mouth in the presence of his wife. When she left he breathed deeply and shifted his feet. 'See if you can find a piece of betel nut or myrobalan,' he whispered to his son. 'But don't trouble your mother for it—whatever you do.'

That evening, after her day's chores were done (there was no dinner to cook since Purna and the boys had eaten enough for two meals and what they had brought back had been sufficient for the rest of the family), Haimavati sat, legs spread out on the floor, patting her youngest child to sleep. Her husband squatted by her side, trying to win her over with exaggerated concern and compliments. But, so it seemed to Purna, his words were falling on deaf ears. Her face was as hard as ever and she didn't even care to

Tarashankar Bandopadhyay

glance at him as he spoke. Purna was desperate. The truth of the matter was that he knew Haima had saved the chhana bara for the next day's breakfast and they were, at the moment, stored in a pot in the reticulated bag hanging from the rafter in the kitchen. But Purna was dying, simply dying, to eat some of it. The food he had eaten had disappeared without a trace—like a sprinkle of water on the bare parched earth. His stomach craved chhana bara. Greed rose like tongues of flame from his abdomen, setting his chest, throat and palate afire.

Even as Purna continued to coax and cajole her, Haimavati lay down beside her son and fell fast asleep. She was pregnant again and got so exhausted by the end of the day that she couldn't keep her eyes open after dusk. Purna gazed on his sleeping wife's face for a few minutes, then, tiptoeing towards her, opened the knot at the end of her sari and drew out the household keys.

The children were awake at dawn, dancing about their mother and demanding their share of chhana bara. 'You must give me a whole one, Ma!' the eldest boy pleaded, pulling at her arm. 'Why only one?' the mother scolded, flinging off the offending hand. 'I'll give you leeches the whole lot to put into your stomachs—the bottomless pits!'

But, opening the door of the kitchen, she got the shock of her life. The strings of the bag had snapped—someone had pulled at it with force—and hung loose and tattered. The pot lay on the floor, broken in several pieces. Most of the chhana bara had disappeared. Only three or four lay rolling on the ground among the shards. Haimavati picked one up. It was as light and dry as a leaf. Something, human or animal, had sucked all the syrup out of it. Haimavati's lips curled in a cruel, mocking smile.

'Purna,' Shyamadas Babu said to the Brahmin, 'the mistress is very keen that you stand guard outside the birthing chamber this time.'

There was a belief in this part of Bengal that if a Brahmin kept vigil outside the birthing chamber on the night of a delivery, the child would be born safe and sound. Shibrani had specially asked for Purna because all the children his wife had borne were alive and healthy. Therefore, it was very probable that he had greater powers over the evil spirits that flock at a birth than the other Brahmins of the village.

'But . . . but,' Purna hesitated. 'If my wife—'

'No ifs or buts, Chakrabarty,' one of the toadies who hung around Shyamadas Babu cut him short. 'You'll get the most wonderful meals, a bed as soft as butter. What's your problem?'

At these words, happiness bubbled up in Purna's breast. 'If you command me, Karta,' he grinned ingratiatingly, 'how can I say no?'

'Wait for me, Purna,' Shyamadas put a hand on Purna's shoulder. 'I'm going in for my breakfast. I'll tell them in the kitchen to send some refreshments for you.'

In a few minutes a servant appeared with a wooden plank under his arm and a bell-metal platter full of sweets in his right hand. He held a glass of water in the other.

'Come, Chakrabarty,' another toady urged. 'Begin your meal.'

'A pitcher of water . . . ' Purna murmured to confirm his status as a Brahmin, 'I must wash—'

'Fall to it! Fall to it!' the toadies called out encouragingly. 'Just say *Ganga Ganga Om Vishnu*. The impure will be purified in an instant.'

Tipping a little water from the glass, Purna rinsed his mouth, sprinkled a few drops on his right hand, and sat down on the plank. A while later, Shyamadas Babu came into the room where Purna sat eating and asked, 'Have they served you enough, Purna? Have you had your fill?'

'Yes, yes, Karta,' Purna spluttered. He had a whole chhana bara in his mouth. 'I've eaten so much there isn't room for a sesame seed in my stomach.'

'Look Purna,' Shyamadas Babu said to him, 'if, through your efforts, my lifelong desire for a living son is fulfilled, I'll give you ten bighas of land. And for all the years you live you'll get a daily allowance of prasad from the temple of Singhabahini.'

Purna's eyes glittered and the saliva squirted in his mouth. Singhabahini's prasad! All his life! He knew that Shyamadas Babu's family deity, the lion-riding Durga, was served all the delicacies one could imagine.

'Do I take it then,' Shyamadas Babu continued, 'that you agree? That our deal is clinched?'

'Of course, of course, if huzoor—' Leaving his sentence unfinished, Purna called out to the khansama who was crossing the room with a plate on which the remains of Shyamadas Babu's breakfast lay. 'Ei! Ei!' Purna cried. 'Come here.' The moment the plate came within reach, the Brahmin, oblivious of his position, swooped like an eagle on some uneaten *sandesh* and *malpoa* and crammed them into his mouth.

'Arré! Arré!' Shyamadas Babu exclaimed, aghast. 'What are you doing, Purna? These are remains from my plate! They would have served you more had you asked for it!'

Purna had realized his folly but it was too late. 'A king's prasad,' he mumbled. 'Why do you call it remains?'

He saw the assembled company staring at him and hung his head in shame. Presently he rose and shuffled quietly out of the room.

Reaching home he found the house in turmoil. 'Some animal has torn the bag, broken the pot and eaten all the sweets,' his second daughter informed him tearfully. 'Dada got angry and hit Ma. Ma fell and hurt—' Sobs, rising from her small chest, swallowed the rest of her words. Rushing to Haima's side with a pitcher of water and a palm-leaf fan Purna gazed at her face with tears in his eyes. Haima lay in a dead faint, her face white as marble. But the moment she opened her eyes and saw her husband, she shrieked, 'What are you? A man or an animal! Shame on you! Shame! Shame!' Purna clasped her feet in his hands. His lips trembled. He tried to speak but couldn't. Haima pulled her feet away and cried, 'If you touch me once again I'll knock my head on the wall and dash my brains out!' Exhausted, she sank back on the bed and lay for the rest of the day in a death-like stupor.

Towards evening she opened her eyes. Purna, who had been sitting by her side all this while, now told her of Shyamadas Babu's offer, adding, 'You say you expect the child around the same time as the mistress. Who'll keep vigil for you? I'll go to Shyamadas Babu tomorrow and tell him I refuse.'

'No! No!' Haimavati cried out agitatedly. 'I want it dead this time! Dead! I tell you. I want to be free. And if you get the land, the others will eat.'

The births were expected towards the beginning of the monsoon. That evening a servant from Shyamadas Babu's house came to call Purna. 'The mistress is in labour,' he informed him. 'The master has asked you to come quickly.'

An agonized look came into Purna's eyes. Haima wasn't feeling too well either.

'Go,' Haima commanded.

'But—'

'Give my bones a rest. Go—I say.'

Tarashankar Bandopadhyay

Purna sighed and went out with the man. Reaching the zamindar's house, he found Shyamadas Babu sitting in state, surrounded by his friends and toadies. 'Ah! You're here, Purna,' he called heartily. 'Good! Go into the kitchen and get yourself a meal. I'm very busy—as you can see.'

Only too delighted to obey, Purna hastened to the kitchen and accosted the cook. 'What's cooking? O Thakur Moshai!' he exclaimed, peering into the wok on top of the hearth. 'What a wonderful smell! Is it fish or mutton?'

'Mutton,' the cook replied. 'A goat was sacrificed this morning and—'

'Hmph! Just the thing for a rainy evening! How much longer will it take? Can I have a little to taste?' Picking up a *sal* leaf from a pile in the corner, he twisted it into a cup and thrust it in the cook's direction.

'What a glutton you are, Chakrabarty!' the cook muttered none too pleased. 'It will take a while for the meat to soften.'

'Give me some as it is. I don't mind—as long as it isn't blood raw!'

With a sour face the cook ladled out a portion into the cup. Purna slurped appreciatively. 'Hmph!' he said. 'The gravy's perfect. Your cooking is truly marvellous.' The cook grunted, not caring to reply. Purna tried again. 'I haven't eaten better mutton curry in my life. No one in these parts can beat you for—'

'Please go away, Chakrabarty,' the presiding deity of the kitchen snapped at his admirer. 'Let me do my work in peace. I'll send for you when the meal is ready.'

Purna had just risen to obey when he saw his eldest son at the kitchen door.

'Baba!'

'Yes. What is it?'

'Ma's had a son. Come home quick.'

'How's she?'

'The midwife couldn't come. She's alone.'

Purna hurried home to see his wife lying pale and spent beside her newborn—the umbilical cord still unsevered.

'Go call the sudras' midwife,' Haima said to her husband. 'Our own midwife is attending the zamindar's lady. She can't come.'

The sudras' midwife arrived in a few minutes and did whatever was to be done. 'A beautiful boy!' she gushed. 'Only to be expected with both parents so handsome. The mother particularly—'

'Go back to the master's house,' Haima prodded her husband. Purna demurred a little but Haima pushed him out. 'Go this instant,' she commanded.

At midnight, the zamindar's house came alive with the sound of blowing conches and excited voices. 'A boy! A boy! The mistress has had a son.' The doctor, who had been sent for from the city, sterilized his instruments in boiling water and cut the cord with utmost care. Then, washing the tiny body with warm water, he wrapped it in clean muslin and handed it to the midwife.

Haima accosted Purna the moment he reached home the next morning. 'O go!' she cried, sounding worried. 'The baby seems to have caught a chill. He's burning with fever.' Purna seemed taken by surprise. He grunted, then, turning on her, he cried, 'I told you repeatedly that I would stay by your side! But would you listen? The spirits—'

'That's nonsense,' Haima waived the spirits away. 'He'll be all right in a while I suppose. Now kindly bestir yourself and get him some milk. He won't get a drop out of me. I'm as dry as a bone.'

Not having a single paisa on him, Purna picked up an empty pot and walked over to the zamindar's house. The inmates bustled about, busy with the new birth. No one

Tarashankar Bandopadhyay

deigned to cast a glance at him. Only the khansama called out in passing: 'Go home, Thakur. We can't give you breakfast this morning. We're busy.' Purna's face fell. Pot in hand, he came out and stood on the veranda where a servant crouched surreptitiously in a corner, taking a couple of quick pulls at a hookah.

'Ei Baba,' Purna whispered ingratiatingly. 'The cow must have been milked by now. Can you give me some—?'

'You want milk?' The man laughed insolently. 'What a glutton you are, Thakur!' Then, after puffing silently for a while, he added solemnly, 'No. The cow has not been milked. The baby's sick. Go home.'

It must have happened some time during the night but no one had noticed. Wearied by hours of hard labour, Shibrani was fast asleep. So was the midwife. Much later, when the sun had risen well over the horizon, Shibrani awoke and asked for the baby. But, taking him in her arms, she got a shock. The child's limbs twitched painfully. The face was the colour of wax and the lips were turning blue. Shibrani burst into tears. History was repeating itself. The same symptoms as in the others! This child would die too. Sending for her husband, she cried, 'O go! Fetch the doctor. Quick!'

The doctor arrived a few hours later. After examining the baby carefully, he turned to the father and sighed. 'Could I speak to you in private for a minute, Shyamadas Babu?' he asked.

'The boy?' the midwife frowned worriedly.

'I'll leave some medicines.'

Shyamadas Babu's maternal aunt stood in the doorway and ordered the midwife to bring the child to her. Seeing its condition she struck her forehead with her hand and, fixing her eyes on the weeping Shibrani, said in a doleful voice, 'It's your destiny, Ma. Who can change it? Tch!

Tch! It's the same story every time. The child has to be taken away. It breaks my heart to say it but how can I let a child die in the birthing chamber in a new mother's arms?'

In the privacy of the next room the doctor was talking to Shyamadas Babu. 'I would like to ask you a question if you don't mind.'

'What is it?'

'Do you suffer from a venereal disease?'

Shyamadas Babu's face turned pale.

'I guessed as much,' the doctor said. 'Ah! The follies of youth! You are suffering the consequences. No child of yours will ever live.'

'This one too?' Shyamadas Babu's eyes brimmed over with tears.

'This one too. I can't hold out any hope.' With these words the doctor walked out of the house, leaving the zamindar staring after him, his eyes glazed with shock.

In a while Shyamadas Babu's aunt sent for him. Sharing her doubts about the child's survival, she added, 'Letting a newborn die in its mother's arms is highly inauspicious. There are customs, beliefs. After all we are Hindus.'

Shyamadas Babu could not deny it. Custom and tradition were the twin pillars on which the entire fabric of Hinduism rested. And so the dying baby was taken from the weeping mother and laid in a corner of the veranda with the midwife in attendance and the Brahmin keeping vigil for the messenger of Death. In the birthing chamber, Jamuna, the maid, was given charge of the weeping mother.

The monsoon sky was dense with cloud. Purna sat by the dying child, smoking funnel after funnel of tobacco. His lips twisted in a bitter smile. The child at home was sick too. But he would live. *Destiny!* he thought sorrowfully.

Who can fight her? How much better it would be for Purna if his own son died and this one lived! Ten bighas of land. A platter full of Singhabahini's prasad every day. He would be saved. But no doctor in the world could save one from his fate.

The child moaned and twitched, distracting Purna from his thoughts. Turning to the midwife he said with a touch of impatience, 'Do something.'

'What can I do?'

'Give him some water for God's sake.'

The midwife obeyed but the water wouldn't go in. It spilled out all over the tiny chin. Curling up in a corner, the midwife said, 'Why don't you go to sleep, Thakur? What is to be gained by keeping awake?' But Purna sat on, staring at the starless sky. It was pitch dark—as dark as his future. If only the child would live! Lifting his sacred thread he touched it to the boy's forehead. Suddenly, a thought struck him, a thought so bizarre that he shuddered violently. 'No! No!' he muttered. 'Not that. Never that!' Sweat broke out on his forehead and streamed down his face. Packing a fresh funnel with trembling hands he took a deep pull.

An hour passed. Purna glanced at the snoring midwife curled up in her corner. He cocked a ear in the direction of the birthing chamber. The mistress's weeping had ceased. Worn out with pain and anxiety she had, presumably, fallen into a fitful slumber. Purna's eyes burned as fiercely as the embers in his hookah. In his head was a jumble of thoughts. *If only . . . ten bighas of land . . .* his agony would be over . . . *this child would die before dawn . . .* he was sure of it . . . *then?* His own son was a bonny babe just like his mother . . . he wouldn't look out of place in a zamindar's house!

Another thought struck him. It flashed like a bolt of blue lightning through the meshes of his brain, numbing it with shock. His son would be the zamindar's only child! He would inherit all the property. Purna stood up in his agitation. Sin, unheard, unseen, beckoned to him from out of the dark. He tiptoed towards the baby. A sudden gush of fear ran through his veins, chilling his blood. He stepped back. But it was only for a second. The very next saw him creeping towards the door, the half-dead baby in his arms.

Purna was assailed by the strangest sensations as he walked rapidly through the forest towards his own house. There were snakes and scorpions in the dense undergrowth, moths and insects above his head. But he strode on, undaunted. They couldn't harm him. He knew that. They wouldn't dare. For, he had done that which no man could dream of.

There was no door to the birthing shed where Haima lay, sleeping the sleep of the dead. Only a broken fence rattling in the breeze.

Purna walked back on feet as light as the wind. It was almost dawn but the zamindar's house was still plunged in sleep. Purna laid the bundle he carried in the tiny crib and stretched himself out at its head.

The child stirred in his sleep and whimpered softly. No one heard him except Purna, but Purna lay still, holding his breath. Another whimper—fretful, uneasy. In the birthing chamber adjoining the veranda, Shibrani heard the sound and started weeping again. And now the child let out a wail. It was the wail of a healthy newborn proclaiming its presence in the world, demanding sustenance.

Jamuna opened the door and stepped into the veranda. Shaking the midwife awake she scolded, 'Is this how you do your duty?' Then, turning to the Brahmin, she cried,

'Thakur, O Thakur! Don't you hear the child cry? Keeping vigil indeed!' Muttering beneath her breath she added, 'Both sleeping like corpses.'

The midwife sat up with a jerk. Jamuna went on grumbling at her, 'Don't you hear the child fretting and whimpering? Give it some water—quick.' The midwife rose hastily and, fetching a spoonful of water, tipped a couple of drops on the baby's lips. A little pink tongue came out and lapped it up. Then the tiny rosebud mouth opened for more. 'O go!' the woman called out excitedly. 'The child's drinking the water! Come and see!' People came rushing from all parts of the house to witness the scene. From within the birthing chamber Shibrani heard the commotion and rose to her feet. Her legs shook with exhaustion as she tottered to the door. 'Bring him to me,' she commanded imperiously. 'He's my son and he'll stay with me.'

A few hours later . . .

The house was buzzing with gossip. The child had been miraculously restored. He was God's gift to the mistress. God's and the Brahmin's! Purna Chakrabarty had sacrificed his own son's life for that of the master's. For the baby sleeping in Haima's arms was discovered dead at dawn.

Purna got his ten bighas of land. And every afternoon an immense platter heaped high with Singhabahini's prasad arrived at his house. Haima was calmer now, less embittered. But Purna hadn't changed. He went sniffing around wherever there was food to be had just as he had done all his life. His sons went to school now. They came back and grumbled to their mother. 'We feel so embarrassed at the way Baba behaves! The boys in school tease us and call us sons of a clown. Tell Baba he must consider our feelings.' But if Haima even attempted to remonstrate with him, Purna shouted her down. This was so out of character that Haima stared at him not knowing what to make of it.

Suddenly one night, ten years after the birth of her son, Shibrani passed away. Everyone envied her her good fortune. It was the height of a woman's glory to die in the prime of her life, leaving behind her husband and a son who would perform the rites to perfection. That morning, as Shyamadas Babu sat with his friends planning the *shraddha*, Purna Chakrabarty hobbled in and sat down with the others. 'The arrangements are lavish indeed,' he remarked, 'but what about the Brahmins? Will they be given take-home pots?'

'Of course,' one of the men sitting with the zamindar replied.

'Containing what?'

'A *luchi* as big as a sieve and a *ledikeni* the size of a bolster.'

A roar of laughter followed. Shyamadas Babu, who was frowning abstractedly all this while, snapped at the man who had made the joke. 'Can't you ever be serious in your life?' Then, turning his eyes on the man who had just come in, he asked, 'What news? Were you able to find anybody?'

'No, master. The line has vanished without a trace.'

'Try somewhere else then. A shraddha is not complete without an Agradaani.'*

*An important ritual of a Hindu funeral is the feeding of the newly departed spirit. Rice, milk and ghee are mixed together, formed into a lump called *pinda* and offered to a Brahmin who eats it on behalf of the spirit. The Brahmin who agrees to play this part is called an Agradaani and his generations are condemned to carry on playing it till the line lapses.

'Yes. But the trouble is that there are so few of them. There isn't another within forty miles.'

'What about our Chakrabarty?' someone suggested. 'Why don't you take the Agradaan, Purna? What do you care about the stigma?'

Shyamadas Babu stirred in his seat. 'Quite true, Purna,' he said, looking up hopefully. 'Think of the advantages. I've set aside twenty-five bighas of land for the purpose. And if you agree I'll arrange for a special fifty rupees to be paid to you each year from the accounts. *O ré!* Who's there? Bring some breakfast for Chakrabarty Moshai. Fill the plate with the sweets that came from Kolkata last evening. Heap it high.'

The vast gathering that assembled on the day of the shraddha was witness to the scene in which the zamindar's son and heir performed his mother's last rites with Purna Chakrabarty sitting facing him—his hand outstretched.

The eating of the pinda in the cowshed should have been the last scene in this drama. But life is rarely what it ought to be. The selfish, greedy, gluttonous Purna Chakrabarty hadn't eaten to satiety even after swallowing the pinda offered to him by his own flesh and blood. Fourteen years after this shraddha came another. This time Purna flung himself at the master's feet and, clinging to them wildly, howled like a child. 'I can't, Karta! I can't. Don't make me. I'm a poor wretch, and mockery and humiliation have been my just deserts. But not this. Never this. Flesh and blood couldn't endure it.'

Shyamadas Babu sighed and drew his feet away. 'I know how you feel, Purna,' he said gently. 'You've seen him and loved him from the day he was born. But if I can bear it, why can't you? I, his father, and the tender young girl, his widow, are to perform the shraddha. Is it easy for us? Besides, where can I find another Agradaani? You'll get ten bighas of land and . . . '

The heir to the zamindar's estate, his only son, had died a few days ago, leaving behind a young widow and a two-year-old boy.

In the cowshed, on the day of the shraddha, Purna Chakrabarty put out his hand and received the food offering on behalf of the departed soul from the newly bereaved widow.

The priest performing the ritual called out encouragingly, 'Come Chakrabarty. Eat. Eat your fill.'

Tarashankar Bandopadhyay

The Story of a Coward

Janaika Kapurusher Kahini

Premendra Mitra

Karuna brought me the morning tea herself. At the sight of the many eats that went with it I could not resist a smile. 'The climate here must be good for the appetite,' I said. 'But remember—I came only two days ago. My appetite, unfortunately, is still what it was in my native Bengal.'

Karuna only smiled and pushed the dishes towards me.

'Why are you being formal with me?' I asked as she turned to leave the room. 'I would have understood if Bimal Babu—but . . . '

Karuna cut me short. 'Perhaps what I'm doing is only on behalf of Bimal Babu! You don't mind, do you?'

Then she smiled and left the room.

I sat mulling over the cup of tea. I had to admit, even to myself, that Karuna's behaviour was very, very odd.

It's not that I expected Karuna to do anything dramatic. In fact, that was a prospect I had dreaded. That is why, at the outset, I was so pleasantly reassured by her calm serenity. But somewhere, in some quiet corner of the self, there was a sense of hurt vanity that gradually started surfacing. There was no need really, I thought, for such a drastic change of attitude. It was true that the sun had set on our relationship but some faint touches of colour could still have clung to the clouds in the west. If Karuna had been cold and silent I would have been happiest. I would have understood that her detachment was only a mask behind which she was hiding her real feelings.

But Karuna was neither overtly emotional nor entirely devoid of emotion. She was completely natural.

Of course I could have told myself that I did not care. In fact that is what I should have done. After all, we had lost ourselves among the many people in this vast world and I had neither hoped nor feared that I would ever see her again. Yet, when we met once more, I found that though I believed I had forgotten Karuna completely I wanted her to have remembered me. This little bit of presumption was not unnatural when one considers the past.

It had been a day of such incessant rain that I was forced to spend it in my mess room—unable to get out. Towards evening the servant boy came up and said that a girl was waiting to see me. When Karuna walked in, I was shocked and embarrassed.

'You are surprised, aren't you?' she said.

'Yes, I confess I am—' Then, in an effort to soften the blow, I added hastily, 'But you are completely wet!'

Karuna lowered herself into a chair. 'If one goes out in the rain one has to get wet,' she laughed, 'but don't worry about me. Even if you do, you won't find dry clothes for a woman in your room.'

'There is a married couple in number 10,' I ventured.

Karuna laughed again and said, 'You mean you will borrow a sari and blouse for me?' Then she became serious. 'Come and sit down. Wet clothes won't hurt me. You must be wondering why I came.'

I did not answer. Karuna sat in silence for a while. Then she rose abruptly and, throwing herself against my chest, burst into tears. 'They are taking me away to Patna. Uncle wrote a letter—' she said between sobs.

It was not that I did not understand. I only pretended not to when I said, 'Have your college vacations started?'

'No, no, you don't understand,' Karuna cried out agitatedly. 'They won't keep me here. If I go I'll never come back.'

I took her cold limp hand in mine and sat in silence. Yes, I too was suffering but not like Karuna. My love lacked the wild passion that hurls itself rebelliously against impediments.

Karuna lifted a tearful face and said, 'I'm not going. I won't go. Why should I?'

I did not reply. I could not bring myself to agree with her. I knew her rebellion would be futile. I tried to make light of the situation. 'Perhaps what you think is not true,' I said.

'It's not a question of thinking. I *know* they will take me away and keep me under lock and key. They believe it's the best medicine for girls like me.' Smiling bitterly, she added, 'I told them I was going to college and came away to you. I did not want to come to the mess. But what else could I do? You do not visit Aunty's house any more. Besides I could not have spoken so freely there.' Karuna was quiet for a moment. Suddenly she became insistent. 'Can't we do anything? Will you let them take me away?'

With what sweet words and promises I soothed Karuna and left her at her aunt's house that evening need not be mentioned here. Suffice it to say that despite my suffering I could do nothing. Karuna was taken to her uncle's house in Patna and subsequently married off. It was not that the news gave me no pain. But now, on mature reflection, I realize that the misery of the days that followed stemmed only from an awareness of Karuna's sufferings. What it

is to have loved and lost, I sensed through Karuna's fate—
not my own. I completely failed to recognize the measure
of egotism that was mixed with such sentiments. Even
when Karuna's image grew dim in my mind, somewhere
deep down within me there was a belief that *she* would
never forget me. When that belief was dealt a severe blow
I was aware of a strange sensation—one hitherto unknown
to me.

When Karuna came to my room again she would have,
had she cared to, noticed a subtle change in my manner.
She picked up the plates and said, 'You haven't eaten
anything.'

Putting the last touches to my toilette, I turned to her.
'Formality breeds its own kind, Karuna. Had I cleaned
out the plates you would have thought I was starving.'

'You are harping on what I said!' Karuna sounded
offended.

'I have an incurable weakness for harping on the past,' I
made my voice deep and emotional.

Karuna had turned away. I could not see her face. But
when she spoke, her tone was light. 'You mean you have
cured your other weaknesses?' Then, as she saw me rise
from the chair, 'Surely you are not going out so early!'

'Yes, I must enquire after the car.'

'My husband will inform you when it is ready. He
wants you to wait till he returns.'

'I must sit and chat with you till then?' I tried to smile.

'Why not?' Karuna smiled too.

My voice changed. 'You say this so easily, Karuna.'

'Is it supposed to be difficult?' Karuna's face was both
smiling and bewildered.

'Are you being true to your heart? Are you not afraid
of yourself? I am.'

'I think you're crazy.' Karuna left the room with a smile, leaving me quite embarrassed. She didn't come back for a long time. Bitterness welled up in my breast as I paced to and fro. I don't know if it was against Karuna or against my own self. What a mockery of fate this was! Why did I have to meet her again?

I had been in the middle of a motoring holiday when my car broke down suddenly last night. I was grateful that it had happened in a town and not in the jungles through which I had passed. Yet, to be stranded at night in a strange place is not a happy experience. After wandering for hours in a tonga in vain search of a hotel or dak bungalow I came back to the mechanic's shop where I had left my car. It was there that I met Bimal Babu. Seeing a fellow Bengali in distress he insisted on taking me home. I may have protested a little but to no avail.

Bimal Babu's house was situated at the far end of the town. When we reached there we found the house dark and silent. 'The servants must be asleep,' Bimal Babu explained as he knocked on the door. 'I was not supposed to have returned tonight.'

After a while a lady came, lantern in hand, and, opening the door, said in a muffled voice, 'I was asleep. You said you weren't coming tonight.'

Bimal Babu smiled and said, 'I was fated to do a good deed. But for me this gentleman would have been shelterless in a strange town.' The lady stopped abruptly in the act of moving away and stood scrutinizing me. Bimal Babu was still talking. 'Wake up the servants and ask them to make up a bed in the outer room,' he instructed his wife. 'The gentleman might find it a little uncomfortable but—'

'So what if he is a little uncomfortable? After all he is among strangers,' Karuna laughed.

Bimal Babu shot a sharp glance at me and asked his wife: 'Do you know him?'

'A little.'

'How extraordinary!'

'Why? I have been married to you for three years. The twenty before that were not passed in solitary confinement.'

Bimal Babu laughed and said, 'Give the gentleman a sample of our matrimonial felicity by all means but don't keep him out in the cold.'

I felt it was time I said something. 'I am a businessman, Bimal Babu,' I said, 'I don't trust samples.'

Karuna's manner had given me a jolt.

Karuna came back to the room after a long time. She had changed her clothes. Anticipating my question, she said, 'I have to go out. Would you like to come with me?'

I picked up my shawl. 'Command me,' I said smiling. 'Where do we go?'

'Shopping.'

'Shopping?' I was surprised.

'I do a lot of the shopping myself. When my husband is away I have to.'

'But Bimal Babu is here.'

'Oh! I forgot to tell you. He has sent word that he can't come home today. He has been held up.'

Karuna said this quite calmly. But I stopped short. 'Then—'

'Then what?' Karuna interrupted. 'Are you afraid that with Bimal Babu away you won't be looked after?'

'It isn't that, Karuna,' I said, my voice deep and quiet. 'I'm thinking—'

'If you start thinking in the middle of the road, I'll have to go on by myself.'

I walked along with her. The area seemed quite deserted. A few houses were scattered here and there but most of them were empty. After walking for some time I couldn't help asking her, 'Will Bimal Babu be returning tonight?'

'Probably not. He may have to stay away for three or four days.'

We walked on in silence. Karuna glanced at my face several times. 'What are you contemplating so seriously?' she asked at last.

'Perhaps I ought to go back tonight.'

'But your car will not be repaired by then.'

'The garage can send it straight to Kolkata. I'll go by train.'

'Why are you in such a hurry? What are you afraid of?'

I stopped in the middle of the road. 'I'm afraid of myself,' I said.

Karuna laughed quite loudly. 'So what?' she said. 'That won't harm anyone!'

I could not bear that laugh. On an impulse I took her hand in mine and asked in a trembling voice, 'What if something happens that harms *you*, Karuna?'

Karuna did not draw her hand away. But she shattered my emotions with a mocking laugh. 'How is that possible?' she said. '*I* am not afraid of myself.'

I let go of her hand and said, 'Your confidence may be misplaced. Such a wave may come into your life that will shatter your anchor and toss you in mid-ocean.'

The same mocking smile appeared on Karuna's face. 'You're right,' she said. 'I have not been put to the test.'

I do not know what I would have replied to this. Fortunately for me there was no need to, for we had reached the heart of the town.

In the morning, when she was dressed for going out, I had seen one aspect of Karuna. At midday, when she sat fanning me while I ate an elaborate meal, I saw another. The wide red border of her sari was partially drawn over her head, covering the thick wet hair streaming down her back. I had never seen her looking so beautiful. Waving the fan, she held my eyes with her own deep ones. 'What is it?' she said. 'Have you not seen me before?'

'I really feel I haven't.'

'That's possible.' She smiled a strange smile. 'Tell me, what did you think of my going out shopping alone?'

'I felt that I had discovered you afresh.'

'Really? But don't forget to give poor Columbus his due.'

'Someone may have a claim prior to Columbus.'

'Someone may, but he has no document to prove it.' She laughed uproariously at her own joke.

I ate for some time in silence, then remarked, 'Not everyone values a document. It is only a piece of paper that can be burned to ashes.'

This time Karuna did not smile. She searched my face for a long time, then rose to her feet with an abrupt movement. 'I'll fetch the dessert,' she said.

However, it was the cook, not Karuna, who brought the dessert. But she came to my room after a while and, handing me a cone of betel leaf, said suddenly, 'So you are leaving tonight?'

I stared at her. Did I see or was I only imagining a restless flicker in her eyes?

'So be it,' I said, 'I'll go.'

'What do you mean? You sound as though I am sending you away. I asked you to stay but you insisted on going.' There was an edge to her voice that could not be mistaken.

I smiled. 'I'm not blaming you. I really have to go, Karuna.'

Karuna tried to smile. 'I knew you could not go on staying in a hole like this. There's a train this evening at six-thirty—the only one today. Don't forget.'

There was no need for me to try to remember. Long before the due time, Karuna had had my things packed, sent word to the garage, and ordered a tonga to take me to the station. The journey to the station would take only fifteen minutes but Karuna made me leave an hour earlier. Just as I was getting into the tonga, she came close to me and said, 'I don't know what you are thinking of me. Perhaps that I'm trying to get rid of you.'

'That thought is my sole consolation.'

Karuna laughed. 'When so little can console you, you don't deserve anything better.' The tonga started moving and the creaking of its wheels drowned her laughter.

The story should have ended here but it did not. I reached the station with plenty of time to spare. Keeping my things in the waiting room I wandered aimlessly about. Finally I came and stood near a bookstall, wondering what to buy. Suddenly my eyes fell on a form standing next to me.

'Karuna! You?' I cried, startled.

She smiled wanly. 'I—just came.'

In the faint light of the station lamp, Karuna's face looked pale and drawn. Moving away from the stall, I said, 'I don't quite understand. What is it?'

Karuna smiled again and said in a sombre voice, 'I've burned the document.'

For some time I stood dazed and uncomprehending. Then I burst out, 'What are you saying, Karuna?'

'Am I saying something extraordinary? Cannot a wave powerful enough to shatter the anchor come into my life?' Karuna's voice was heavy with unshed tears. She came close and whispered against my chest: 'Can't you take me away? Can't you? Why don't you speak?'

Utterly bewildered, I stuttered, 'I . . . you . . . take you away?'

'Don't worry about where. Anywhere. Only take me with you.'

I was struck dumb. A terrible panic seized me.

'You will suffer pain and humiliation, I know. But I too have abandoned all pride, all shame, only to share that suffering with you.' Karuna was looking at me with pleading eyes. What could I do? What could I say? It was I who was responsible for what had happened. Like a fool I had opened the floodgates of her dammed-up emotions. How was I to turn back the torrent that threatened to sweep me off my feet?

'There is something that you have not considered,' I said in a voice that did not even fool me. 'Do you have the power to fight the storm that will inevitably follow? Will not years of struggling against it render us hateful to one another?'

Karuna was looking at me with a strange expression in her eyes. Gradually, her face changed. Her mouth twisted in a smile. She said in a voice that was completely transformed, 'Thank you for your advice. It came in the nick of time. I was on the point of unhooking my anchor.' She laughed out loud. I stared at her. Was all this a pretence? Was her intention only to seek out my vulnerable spot and make a mockery of it?

'Go,' Karuna said in an amicable voice. 'Your train is about to leave. And mine is due any moment—'

'Your train?'

'Aunty and Uncle are coming from Kolkata. They don't know the house, so I thought I would come to meet them. Are you disappointed to hear that?'

Not another word was said. I started climbing the over-bridge to the next platform where my train stood. I looked back once and saw Karuna bending over the books in the stall. Had she really come to take her aunt home? I will never know.

The Family Retainer

Ekti Galpa

Gajendrakumar Mitra

The big double-storeyed house next to ours had been lying vacant for so long that I was sure it would continue to do so for all time to come. There were several reasons for my conviction. The house was huge, inconveniently so, and dark and gloomy. Practically no sun and air penetrated its interiors. It was obvious that the man who had designed it had only concerned himself with the number of rooms he could build without a thought for their ventilation.

Consequently, when, one morning, I caught sight of a party of workmen repairing the house, I was filled with curiosity. Approaching the scene I found our neighbourhood doctor Bhupati Babu standing by, issuing instructions.

'Good morning, Daktar Babu!' I called out heartily. 'What's going on? Have you bought this house?'

In asking this question I was guilty of hitting below the belt. For though he has been around for a good many years, Bhupati Babu's practice is still far from roaring.

'No brother,' Bhupati Babu gave a pained smile. 'I've rented it.'

'Rented it! Such a big house?'

'It's for my father-in-law who has just come from Burma. He's lucky to have escaped before the bombs came raining down. Had he waited—who knows what would have happened? Astute man that he is he could foresee the future and—'

'Then he must have come some months ago,' I cut in. 'Where is he staying now?'

'Well! He stayed in a hotel for the first seven months—squandering a heap of money. Then, after his luggage arrived, he moved to a house in Sahebpara. But now, with the sirens screeching all over the city, he wants to move away from the centre and live in the suburbs. You understand?'

I understood. Bhupati Babu's father-in-law was an immensely wealthy man and had been distinguished by the title of Rai Bahadur. He had been medical adviser to three or four large firms in Burma, drawing a salary of two thousand five hundred rupees a month. He was also part owner in a timber business and ran a dispensary which brought him additional tidy sums. We had all this information straight from the horse's mouth—his son-in-law. What we hadn't heard from Bhupati Babu, only gleaned from the gossip women indulged in, was that the Rai Bahadur had two wives. One was the Bengali woman he had wedded in his childhood, the other a Burmese lady of considerable wealth and influence without whose help his meteoric rise in an alien country would never have been possible. It was out of deference for the latter's wishes that he hadn't returned to India though he had longed to do so for many years. Now, by an amazing stroke of luck, she had died and set him free even as the threat of war loomed over the horizon. The Rai Bahadur was not a man to miss opportunities. He had wound up his business with alacrity, sold his properties and returned to India with several lakhs of rupees. But even here, in Kolkata, he hadn't sat idle for long. On the strength of his Rangoon background he had found suitable employment for himself in several top British firms.

'Will he need such a big house?' I asked Bhupati Babu after a while.

'Not for himself . . . er . . . I'm moving in too, you see. The Rai Bahadur is very keen to . . . My mother-in-law won't hear a word. She insists on having her daughter's family with her.'

'So you'll be a resident son-in-law?' I asked with a smirk.

'By no means,' Bhupati Babu answered indignantly. 'I shall maintain a separate establishment. This is a large house with many rooms. Of course I won't have to pay rent—'

'You won't have to pay for a good many things,' I muttered to myself. Then, raising my voice, I added, 'What about your father? Is he moving in with you?'

'N-n-no,' Bhupati Babu sounded a trifle embarrassed. 'He'll be staying with my younger brother. In Sodepur.'

So much for the first day. Bhupati Babu shifted to the new house a week later, followed by his father-in-law who arrived, amidst a lot of hustle and bustle, some time after that with his family. Eight truckloads of furniture and household goods accompanied them. The Rai Bahadur and his wife were tall, stout and dark—the former a few shades lighter than his wife whose skin was the colour of unpolished ebony. No wonder she had agreed to put up with a co-wife, many of us thought. With a complexion like that no woman has the right to make a fuss. It was also clear to the neighbours where the doctor's wife had got her looks from. We had heard that the Rai Bahadur had paid Bhupati Babu's father a dowry of ten thousand rupees as compensation for the colour of his daughter's skin.

Be that as it may, there was no doubt that the new arrivals contributed substantially to the entertainment of their neighbours by supplying them with abundant material for gossip and speculation. Whoever passed the house stopped short in his tracks and looked up to see what was going on. Then, in the evenings, at the congregation in our outer veranda, each one contributed his findings. With all the information pooled together we learnt that the Rai Bahadur had another daughter, also ebony-hued like her mother. The girl obviously had a husband (she was always dressed to the gills) but there was no sign of him. He must have thrown her out, the neighbours conjectured, or he may be living abroad. The two daughters were the Rai Bahadur's only progeny and would eventually inherit all his property. For that reason they were treated with extraordinary care and affection. But the younger daughter, Bhupati Babu's wife Priyobala, having lived away from her parents for many years, had received less than her fair share of pampering. Her sister Rajbala had appropriated it all and was, consequently, disliked and resented by her. Indeed, it was quite true that Rajbala's saris and jewels were far grander than her sister's and her children were better clothed than their cousins. The latter had looked on enviously in the first few days of their coming together under the same roof. However, the Rai Bahadur's wife had been quick to make amends. Clothes and toys started arriving for Priyobala's children in large quantities.

Poor Bhupati Babu! He must have heaved a sigh of relief. His struggle to make ends meet was over. Needless to add, no signs of a separate establishment was to be seen.

We, of the suburban middle class, have little notion of how the rich live. Seeing it for the first time was an experience indeed. For lack of a garage the Rai Bahadur hadn't bought a car. But he travelled everywhere by taxi. Property dealers and agents were wearing out their soles running after him with offers of plots and houses. But he wouldn't commit to anything before the war was over.

The best fish and vegetables were sent to his house by the vendors, and the women of the family didn't lift a finger. They didn't need to. The Rai Bahadur employed a whole staff of domestic servants—a cook, an ayah, a maid and a serving boy. In addition, there was an old family retainer and it was he who, out of all the Rai Bahadur's possessions, drew our greatest envy.

Haran, for that was his name, was a small, slight midget of a man. He must have been quite fair once but, exposed to the harsh light of many Burmese suns, his complexion had turned a coppery brown. No one could fathom his age. His hair, though black enough, had thinned down to a few wisps which he combed carefully over his balding pate just before going out. His skin wasn't loose but it had lost all lustre and was dry and wrinkled like old parchment. At home he wore a semi-soiled dhuti which climbed high above his knees, and a vest with as many holes in it as a sieve. When he went out, as he often did, to the post office or the laundry or with Bhupati Babu's lunch to his chamber in Ballygunge, he simply lowered the dhuti six inches and drew a green printed shirt over the torn vest. His feet were always bare. No one had ever seen him wearing shoes. He must have been with the family for many years, the neighbours speculated, for only the master and mistress called him by his name. He was Haran da to everyone else—servants, children, Bhupati Babu et al.

How hard the man worked! And with what loyalty and devotion!

A large portion of the house was visible from my window and so I was, whether I wanted to or not, witness to a great deal of what went on there. Haran rose at the crack of dawn, when the rest of the household was cocooned in slumber, and set the kitchen fires alight. This duty was really the servant boy's but he had to be called a dozen times before he condescended to rise. Time was precious and Haran couldn't afford to lose any. Once the boy was up, Haran packed him off to the milkman's and came and stood outside the cook's room. It was several knocks and quite a while later that the great man could be seen opening his door. By the time he made his appearance in the kitchen, after performing his ablutions, Haran had fanned the fires till they were roaring, boiled the kettle, made the tea and served it to the master, mistress, their daughters and son-in-law. Now, the cook took over. While he set the milk to boil, Haran got the children's breakfast ready. Toast, milk, biscuits, sandesh and fruits were fed to the young ones every morning, and only Haran, not even their mothers, could conduct this operation with smoothness and efficiency. Coaxing and threatening by turns, luring the really fractious ones with bribes of toffees and toys, he managed to make each one eat his portion.

After the children were fed it was time to think of the adults. Breakfast at the Rai Bahadur's was a lavish affair. Luchi, fried potatoes, fritters, halwa, singhara, sandesh and rosogolla were on the daily menu. The cook prepared these delicacies in his kitchen, the nitty-gritty of peeling, washing, mixing and grinding being left to the maid. But she absented herself without notice quite often and then Haran could be seen carrying out her duties. After everyone had eaten, Haran found a few minutes for a gulp of tea. That is if he wasn't rushing off to the market on a pressing errand. When he did find the time, however, a cup of tea didn't suffice. He had a mug—a huge enamel one, which he encouraged the cook to fill to the brim and from which he sipped the hot, sweet brew with oohs and aahs of satisfaction. On his way to the market he indulged in one small luxury. Sitting for a few minutes in Chhontu's shop

Gajendrakumar Mitra

he smoked a bidi. This bidi was a gift from Chhontu to the servant of his most affluent customer. Haran loved an occasional smoke but bidis were banned in the Rai Bahadur's household. The fumes gave the mistress a headache.

Haran had to make a trip to the fish and vegetable market every morning—sometimes two or even three trips as the situation demanded. I often saw him come in, staggering under the weight of two huge bags, then leaving them inside, rush out again. After the daily market errand came a succession of duties.

'Have you paid the telephone bill, Haran? Tomorrow's the last day.'

'Go find out what happened to the clothes. The washerwoman took them a good ten days ago.'

'Have you brought my suit from the drycleaners, Haran da? No? I reminded you yesterday.'

'What did the tailor say, Haran da? You didn't go? Really. You're so forgetful!'

Demands and complaints like these came from the adults. There were others from the children.

'My pencil, Haran da?'

'Have you seen my geography book, Haran da?'

'Haran da! I can't find my shoes.'

At ten o'clock, after the children had been bathed, fed and sent to school, Haran went to the post office to collect the master's mail for the day. The rest of the morning was taken up in attending to the household's essential needs. Coal, wood, rations, grocery—it was Haran's responsibility to keep the larder and storeroom stocked at all times.

At noon I could hear the cook call out patronizingly to a red and perspiring Haran who had just returned from his various errands. 'O Haran da! Are you on a fast today?' Haran's thin face would light up as he asked eagerly, 'Have you kept some breakfast for me?' Some days the cook handed him a plate with some cold, leftover luchis. And on others he shook a negligent shoulder and said, 'Sorry, Haran da, there's nothing left.' But Haran's enthusiasm wasn't dampened in the least. 'Give me a bowl of *muri*,' he said, 'and some of your fried potatoes.' Squatting on his haunches on the kitchen floor, Haran would eat his muri with relish.

After lunch had been served and eaten and the members of the family retired to their rooms for siesta, Haran had a bath followed by a meagre meal which he ate alone sitting in a corner of the kitchen. He got an hour's respite after this which he spent in Chhontu's shop, smoking a bidi and dozing off at intervals.

The children came clamouring home from school soon afterwards, to be washed, fed and taken to the park by Haran. Then, after an infinite number of other duties, Haran sat down to his dinner with the other servants. This was the best hour of Haran's day. He chatted of this and that and a smile broke out on his thin, tired face.

Who wouldn't envy another the possession of such a servant? Our neighbour Phatik Babu, who had recently been promoted to head clerk, would ask from time to time, 'How much does he get? If I offered some more—'

'Impossible!' The rest of us made haste to disillusion him. 'Haran won't leave the family. Don't you see how attached he is to all of them? Why would he work so hard otherwise?'

Five weeks after their arrival, the Rai Bahadur's wife came to our house with her younger daughter. This was in the nature of a social call aimed at getting to know the neighbours. My sister-in-law, flustered at the sight of such a great personage, busied herself in making her visitors comfortable. On being asked if she would like to have a cup of tea, the lady answered, 'Well! To tell you the truth I drink a lot of tea. But only of the best. I can't bear to put my lips to an inferior brew.' Then, turning her eyes this way and that, she said, 'Looking at your household I get a feeling that you eat and drink well. Don't you agree, Priyo? It takes me just a glance to know how a family lives.'

Boudi stared at her in wonder. But only for a moment. Then she bustled off to organize tea and snacks for her guests.

An hour or so of small talk followed tea. It was dominated entirely by the lady's reminiscences of the past. She rattled off, non-stop, an animated description of the princely life she had lived in Burma; of the prestige and dignity of her position; of how everyone, including the governor, had respected her and deferred to her opinions; of the luxuries her grandchildren had taken for granted. In the middle of her account, just as she paused to take a breath, Boudi blurted out the question. 'Where's your elder son-in-law? Is he still in Burma?'

This seemingly innocent question had the strangest effect on our guests. Priyobala darted a glance at her mother, then picking up a magazine buried her face in it. The Rai Bahadur's wife fixed her gaze on a pumello tree growing outside the window and sighed. Boudi's face turned red with embarrassment. From my vantage point in the next room I observed all three faces: one lowered with shame, one shocked into silence, and one stamped with guilt. Boudi was, obviously, ashamed of her intrusion into their lives and so was I. There was a history of pain and humiliation in connection with the Rai Bahadur's elder son-in-law. I was convinced of it. He might be dead or he may have deserted his wife and children. It was difficult to tell from a distance if Rajbala wore sindoor or not.

'You would never have guessed the truth,' the lady turned her eyes from the tree, 'if I chose to keep it hidden. The trouble is—I can't tell a lie. I'm always blurting out the truth. My husband scolds me for it ever so often. The fact is—' She gulped and hesitated. 'It's . . . it's my bad luck . . . I'm ashamed to say—'

'You don't have to say anything,' Boudi cut in quickly.

'No, child,' the lady shook her head, 'the truth will come out some day. How long can I hide it? The fact is— we had no son; only two daughters who were much loved and pampered. When the time came to wed the elder one, the thought of parting with her was so hard to bear that I begged my husband to look for a son-in-law who would live with us. As you know there aren't many Bengalis in Burma and so it was difficult to find a suitable boy from our own caste and clan. After a lot of searching, we found one, a nice-looking, fair boy, studying in school. Our Raji was very young at the time, only ten, so it seemed a good match. The father demanded ten thousand rupees which we paid and brought the boy home. We took him out of his old school and put him in a better one. We kept tutors for him. The Rai Bahadur wanted him to become a doctor and take over his practice when the time came. But destiny willed otherwise. All our efforts went down the drain. The boy hated his books and resisted learning with all his might. He made no friends among boys of his own age and class. He preferred hanging about the kitchen and chatting with the servants. Then, after failing in the matriculation examination for the sixth time, he declared he wouldn't go to school any more. We were mortified but there was nothing we could do.'

The Rai Bahadur's wife paused a moment to catch her breath before continuing. 'We tried to get him interested in his father-in-law's affairs. Even if he couldn't take up

Gajendrakumar Mitra

the practice he could look after the property and business. He would be our manager. But even that drew a blank. All he wanted to do was odd jobs about the house. And so it went on. Three children were born. And then, of course, we left . . . He isn't really as old as he looks. It's just that—'

Boudi couldn't catch the drift. 'Is your son-in-law here?' she asked, staring at her guest.

'O Ma! Don't you understand? It's Haran. The man who does the errands and . . . '

Haran! Haran da was their son-in-law! I was shocked and so was Boudi.

'It's not our fault,' the lady said defensively, looking at the stunned expression on her hostess's face. 'He has neither self-respect nor the will to do anything else. "So be it," my husband said. "I'll tell myself I've kept a steward to look after the household." That is why, this time, he was determined to get a qualified doctor. Our Priyo was married only the other day, so to speak.'

Boudi couldn't contain herself any longer. 'But his clothes!' she cried aghast. 'Surely something could be done about them.'

'That's the way he likes to live. No one can do anything. It's our bad luck.' The lady sighed.

Silence descended on the room. Boudi broke it with a question. 'What do his children call him? Haran da?'

'Y-y-yes,' the lady answered. She sounded a trifle embarrassed. 'They hear everyone call him that. So, naturally . . . Besides, it's better for them not to know he is their father.'

Many months have passed since that day. Haran da and I are now good friends. I keep a stock of bidis with me and offer him one whenever I see him. His brow, frowning at all times, clears at the sight, and the wrinkled parchment on his face stretches out smooth and bright. A rare smile lifts the corners of his mouth and eyes. He chats of this and that—mostly about his life in Burma. He had parents and siblings whom he misses to this day— his little sister in particular. A girl as fair and pretty as a lotus. Who knows what happened to her, he muses. Did the bombs kill her? Or did she fall into the hands of Japanese soldiers? There was a Burmese girl he'd been very fond of. A beautiful girl. She had been so hurt on hearing of his impending marriage that she had stopped talking to him altogether. Who knew where she was now? He had lost touch. He had been forced by his wife's family to break with his past. Haran da's anecdotes are confused and out of sync and his memories fleeting and fragmented. He doesn't seem to be able to focus on any one subject and keeps flitting from this to that. I suspect that his brain, under continuous assault by the unnatural life he leads, has turned vague and fuddled.

'How did all this happen, Haran da?' I asked him directly one day.

'All what?' He looked up at me, his light, somewhat myopic eyes as innocent as a child's.

'How did you manage to descend to the level of an unpaid servant?' It was a cruel, insulting question but I dared to ask it. I knew Haran da didn't have the guts to hit back however great the provocation.

Haran da sat silent for a while, his head sunk into his neck like that of a weary old tortoise. 'How it all happened I can't say,' he mumbled at last. 'They treated me very well for the first few years. I had a lavish life and was smothered with care and affection. Nothing was too good for me. That, perhaps, was part of the problem. I wasn't bred for that kind of life, you see. Besides, to tell you the truth, I wasn't happy. I felt hurt and bewildered at how life had changed for me. I came to look on my father-in-law as an evil man who had the power to buy me and mould me in his own image. I decided to resist that power, to frustrate him in his efforts. I could have done much better in school had I wished. I wasn't really a dull student. He and his wife knew that well enough. They had made all the enquiries. They wouldn't have bought me otherwise.'

'Then?'

'Then—?' Haran da shrugged. 'When they realized that they couldn't make me toe the line, that I had actually willed myself to become a lowly, subhuman creature, they started treating me like one. I was spurned and neglected and kicked around. And, strange to say, the more cruelly they treated me the more I shrank within my shell. Instead of hitting back I submitted meekly to their will. Somewhat like a dog—you know. An abused dog. All I could do was cringe and obey.' He paused for a moment to puff at his bidi. 'The trouble was that I had nowhere to go. And, by that time, it had become too late to start a new life. I had neither education nor skill in any trade. So, like a caged bird, I clung to my perch. I had forgotten how to fly. And now when I'm being ground in a millstone, I suffer the pain in silence. I've lost my voice. I've lost even the will to flap my wings.' Throwing away the charred butt of the bidi, Haran da rose to his feet. 'I must go now,' he said. 'Some of the master's friends are to dine here tonight. I've been ordered to do the shopping.' Haran da smiled and hurried away.

Haran da's smile was placid, his countenance serene. But I was agitated beyond endurance. I couldn't bear his humiliation. As the days went by my desire to get him out of the house and give him a new lease of life grew in intensity till it became an obsession. 'Why are you huffing and puffing like that?' Boudi would ask me, laughing. 'It's not your problem.' Then, getting serious, she would add, 'What they've done is very wrong of course. Uprooting a boy from his natural habitat, draining the sap out of him, then blaming him for growing up warped! I wonder at the wife. What sort of woman is she? Preening like a peacock in rich saris and jewels with not a care for her husband. Doesn't she realize she owes it all to him? If he were to die, she would have to cover her neck and arms—not with gold—but a soiled *thaan*.'

I kept on thinking and finally came up with a plan. 'Haran da,' I accosted him one day, 'would you like to go away from here?'

'Go away?' Haran da was flummoxed. 'Why? Where?'

'Anywhere.'

'What would I eat?'

'You could work.'

'What work? I'm not fit for anything.'

'That's what you think! What if I were to get you a job?'

'How is that possible? I'm not educated enough and—'

'It's the post of a bearer in a government office. The salary isn't princely of course. About fifty-five rupees, including allowances. I'll find a place for you to stay, too. You can live on your own with dignity.'

Haran da was silent for a while. 'This is my father-in-law's house after all,' he said at last. 'I'm under his protection. Would it be wise to give it up for a bearer's job? What would people say?'

'Protection! Father-in-law's house!' I exploded like a bomb. 'You call this a life, Haran da? As for the job—don't scoff at it. Hundreds of matriculates are wearing their soles out for a bearer's post. As for what people will say—you'll work in a different part of the city and live there. How many people know you here in Kolkata?'

'That's true enough,' Haran da agreed slowly, hesitantly. 'The trouble is—it's been a long time . . . I've become used to . . . let me see. Give me a few days to think it over.'

Following this exchange I didn't lose a single opportunity to press my point. Wearing him down became an obsession with me. I felt I had to, simply had to, fan the cold damp ashes of his soul and set it aflame. I got a strange kick out of it, a thrill of conspiracy. But Haran da wouldn't respond. He was frail and enfeebled, both in mind and body, and afraid of taking a decision. When pushed too far, beads of sweat appeared on his brow and he looked this way and that in an effort to escape.

'To leave one's children . . . ' he mumbled defensively one day. 'It isn't easy.'

'Children!' I cried indignantly. 'Do they know you're their father? What good can possibly come from staying with them? On the contrary if you go away now, if you show them you have a spark of manhood left in you, they'll come to respect you in time. They may even want to take you back. You can return, then, with your head held high.'

'Let me see,' Haran da murmured. 'I'll think about it.'

Then one day, after being severely reprimanded by the Rai Bahadur for some minor error in the accounts, he came to me and burst out, 'To hell with everything! You're right. This life is intolerable. I've made up my mind. I'll do the bearer's job. You make the arrangements, brother. Only . . . only I can't tell them I'm leaving. They'll create such a rumpus—I'll start wavering again. I'll slip out in secret and—'

'Are you sure?' I peered sharply into his face. 'If you change your mind it will be horribly embarrassing for me.'

'No, no! I won't change my mind. I promise.'

'Very well then.'

Getting a job wasn't very difficult those days. I had no problems in making good my boast that I would rehabilitate Haran da. The very next day I wrote out an application and within a week I got Haran da the job of a bearer in the building adjacent to my office. I also found a tiny room quite close by, paying a month's advance rent from my own pocket. I managed to furnish it, too, with some bare essentials—a reed mat, a pillow, a palm-leaf fan, a bucket and a few other such items smuggled from my own house. It was decided that Haran da would slip out one morning, at the crack of dawn, with only a dhuti and a shirt wrapped in a newspaper. I would be waiting for him in the street outside from where I would take him to his new home. I was in a fever of excitement. It seemed to me that this was my battle and I was determined to fight it and win.

I rose from my bed at four o'clock on the appointed day (I hadn't slept a wink the whole night) and came and stood outside my door. But where was Haran da? I kept glancing at my watch. Four-thirty . . . five . . . five-thirty . . . six. At six o'clock I went up to the terrace and peered over the wall into my neighbour's house. Haran da wasn't in the kitchen either. The cook was lighting the fire. Coming back to the street where I had been waiting all this time I accosted the servant boy just as he was leaving for the milkman's.

'Where's Haran da?' I asked roughly.

'Haran da's sick. He's burning with fever.'

'Fever! Since when?'

'Since last night. And why not—may I ask? With it pouring cats and dogs these ten days, the house is as damp and cold as a tomb. But Haran da insists on sleeping on the floor. That too in the veranda.'

There was no sign of Haran da for the next three days. Then, on the fourth, he appeared, thin and frail, shivering under a threadbare cotton shawl. 'Haran da!' I cried out. 'You've messed it all up, haven't you? What kind of fever was it? Influenza?'

Haran da raised his eyes to mine. I saw that they had sunk in their sockets and that his face was pale and worn. 'The fact is,' he said slowly, 'that the worry was killing me.'

'What worry?'

'About leaving the family and going off to do a bearer's job.'

'My god! Does that mean you're giving up the plan?'

'Yes, brother. Forgive me. I know you went to a great deal of trouble but the truth is . . . the truth is . . . I can't live without them. The bonds are too strong for me to break.'

'Bonds with whom? Your children?'

'Why only the children?' Haran da averted his eyes, fixing them on the grey wall opposite. 'The wife too. She doesn't seem to notice me as a rule. But that night when the fever came she forced me to leave the veranda and come into her bedroom. She made up a bed for me with her own hands. I've been . . . er . . . sleeping in her room for the last three nights. She loves me . . . perhaps . . . just a little. You see, don't you,' he said, lifting his eyes, soft and pleading like a dog's, to mine, 'why I can't leave my wife and children and go off to live among strangers?' There was a sheepish smile on his face. A weak, foolish face but I saw contentment in his eyes. 'I must go now,' he rose to his feet, 'to the municipal market.' Taking a last pull at his bidi he flung the butt away. 'Priyobala has been yearning to eat a *chachhari* made with *bhetki* bones for the last three days. Bhetki bones!' He gave a short laugh.

'Pregnant women and their whims and fancies! Who can understand them?'

Haran da bustled away in search of bhetki bones—a small, worn midget of a man in a soiled dhuti and printed shirt. Today, of course, he has a shawl wrapped around his shoulders. An old, frayed, threadbare cotton shawl.

Cactus

Cactus

Ashapurna Debi

Sometimes, perhaps once in a lifetime, what you need desperately falls into your lap when you are least expecting it. That's exactly what happened to Bharati. It came to her when she had given up all hope; when she and Sisir had hit the rock bottom of despair. The offer left her stunned. She didn't know how to react. She went through the rest of the day in a daze. Going from class to class she took her lectures in a state of suspended animation, waiting only for the moment when she would reach home and break the news to Sisir. From time to time she pulled herself together and rehearsed the scene. How would she do it? What would she say? With what hand-and-eye gestures?

At a time when their lives were swamped with the anxiety of finding a suitable house, when taunts and abuses were part of their everyday life, when every weekend was dedicated to roaming the streets of the city for a *To Let* sign, and when reading the newspaper meant keeping one's eyes glued to the 'Houses and Properties' column—at such a time the offer had come like a gift from heaven.

Was Bharati homeless then? Far from it. The first-floor flat that Sisir had rented for quite a few years before he married her was convenient in many ways. And for a long time after she had come to it as a bride she had been treated like a favoured daughter-in-law by the landlady who occupied the ground floor. Sisir's mother had been the landlady's best friend, and after her death the landlady had taken her place with the son. 'Bouma! Bouma!' she had called out to Bharati a dozen times a day with bowls of cooked vegetables, kind words and motherly advice. But of late things had altered. Reports of rising rents, of landlords making a fortune by raking in tidy sums, had set the good lady's temper afire. And now, from a loving mother and mother-in-law, she had turned into an archetypical landlady who wanted her tenants out at any cost and didn't mind resorting to the lowliest of tricks to achieve her end.

She took to lighting two coal ovens just beneath Bharati's window so that the smoke rising from it would make its way into their bedroom and subsequently assail their lungs and nostrils. She made it a point to lock the gates at nine, virtually making them prisoners for the night. If she saw wet clothes draped over their balcony wall she complained loudly that they were impeding her movements. And if the little boy's rubber ball fell into her courtyard by mistake, she thought nothing of flinging it out on the street with an exclamation of disgust. 'Whatever you do,' she advised everyone who visited her, in a voice so clear and penetrating that Bharati was forced to hear it, 'never, *never* let your house out on rent. Tenants are a vicious lot. They enter your house as meek as lambs, then sit on your chest for life. And not one life, mind you. For generations to come!'

In short, the lady was employing all the tricks of the trade she knew. But Bharati and Sisir, though dying of mortification, didn't know what to do. They just couldn't afford to move. Rents were rising every day. If this week's paper carried an offer of 'two rooms, a kitchen and a bathroom' for two-hundred-and-fifty rupees, the rent for the same accommodation jumped another seventy-five the next. And by the week following . . . But the worst, the unkindest cut, was the fact of a one-time beloved friend turning into one's bitterest enemy.

This very morning . . . Ghontu was playing in the balcony, running around a little more spiritedly, perhaps, than usual when the mistress's voice came floating up, honey sweet, from the ground floor. 'Bouma, O Bouma! Do mind the boy a little. I'm a poor woman and my house is old! It is about to crumble to pieces under your son's feet. There is no question of repairing it since I'm not likely to get it back in my lifetime.' Bharati, who was about to leave for college, didn't care to enter into an argument just then. She turned, instead to the eight-year-old boy and begged him to play quietly while she was away. But Ghontu, who for some reason had a holiday, wasn't likely to obey. What eight-year-old would miss the opportunity of doing exactly what he felt like while his parents were away?

'Who knows what is waiting for me when I get back home,' Bharati thought with a little flutter in her heart. Yet, not so long ago, the family downstairs had cared for Ghontu exactly as if he was their own. They had kept him with them all day—bathed him, fed him and put him to sleep. Without their help, Bharati had to admit, it might not have been possible to keep her job. Mashima, the landlady, had held her in such high esteem those days. 'You girls of today are truly wonderful, Bouma!' she had gushed. 'Look at you. You are cooking and cleaning, caring for a husband and child and bringing home a fat salary as well. And women like us. Worthless parasites!'

But the wheel of time had turned and their relationship had entered another phase. A phase in which barbed comments came hurtling from below, tearing at the eardrums. 'There! See! See with your own eyes! The mother's leaving for the whole day, silk sari fluttering, handbag swinging! And the neighbours are left at the mercy of the little monster. This is really the limit. Flesh and blood can't endure it any more.' And all this from a woman who had fed Bharati pickles and tasty titbits when she was pregnant and had never failed to add the words 'my golden moon' while referring to the baby after he was born.

One of the reasons for this drastic change could be Bharati's gradual metamorphosis from a semi-literate girl-bride to a woman with a doctorate and a high-paid job right before her eyes. Anyhow—that was not Bharati's concern. Her concern was to find a way out of the situation in which she and Sisir were trapped. And, suddenly this morning, the opportunity had come. The managing committee of the college had offered her the wardenship of the girls' hostel on the acceptance of which she would be given fully furnished quarters on the campus. The college building was old but the hostel was brand new and the warden's cottage had all the modern amenities that Bharati had, hitherto, only dreamed of. No wonder Bharati went about all day like one in a dream. She hadn't accepted the offer right away, of course. She had said she would think it over and let them know. But, in her heart, she knew there was nothing to think over. She could easily take on the added responsibility. She liked the girls and they liked her. That solved half the problem. As for the administrative work involved, she had confidence in her own ability. She wouldn't fail. Before her acceptance, before sharing the news with Sisir, before even reaching home, she had started making plans for the future.

Stepping into the house that evening she saw that Ghontu had gone out to play. The maid had just lit the fire and set the milk to boil. Glancing at the coal oven she suddenly remembered that the kitchen in the warden's bungalow had a gas range. That's why it was so neat and clean. Bharati, who had inherited her mother-in-law's possessions and her pattern of living, hadn't had a chance till date to live the way she wanted to live. She had yearned for a different lifestyle—neat, light and modern. Her chance had come at last. Her heart lifted at the thought.

'Sharada,' she called out to the maid, 'why did you let Ghontu leave the house without drinking his milk?'

'Really, Boudi!' the maid snapped at her, caring not a whit for her status as lecturer of a college. 'The things you say! Don't you know your own son? Is he so meek and obedient that he'll stay home if he's asked to?'

'Well! You ought to try and keep him in the house till he has had his milk at least. Has he been very naughty all day?'

'Naughty! He's driven everyone mad. The landlady came up a while ago and lambasted—'

Reports of this nature were neither new nor unexpected. They usually left Bharati feeling small; annoyed with her son. But today she thought: 'What rubbish! A child is a child. He can't be expected to behave like an adult! How dare the landlady barge into my flat and scold my son? It's because she thinks we are at her mercy; because we don't have the money to rent another house!'

Waiting for Sisir in a fever of impatience, she rehearsed the scene one last time. How would she break the news? Hesitating a little . . . laughing a little?

Yes, that is exactly what she did.

'Something happened in college today,' she said. A tinkle of laughter followed.

'Something or the other happens in your college every day,' Sisir smiled. 'What is it?'

'Nothing much . . . only . . . the college authorities made me an offer.'

'Arré Baba! Is this a suspense story? That you're telling it bit by bit? What *is* the offer? Are they sending you to England?'

'Stop teasing me. Listen, Moshai. They've offered to make me warden of the girls' hostel.'

'Really!' Sisir exclaimed in astonishment. 'What made them pick you as worthy of the honour?'

'They must have seen something in me,' Bharati tossed her head and blushed like a young girl. 'I have lots of good qualities. Only you don't see them.'

'Hmph! I hope you didn't jump with joy and accept—'

Bharati stared at her husband. She hadn't accepted, yet, of course. But something in her husband's manner annoyed her. She had expected him to be delighted and he wasn't. Why? Was it because she hadn't told him about the house? It was obvious, wasn't it? But perhaps it hadn't entered his head.

'Why shouldn't I jump with joy and accept?' she demanded testily.

'It isn't an easy job,' Sisir's voice was guarded.

'I take delight in tackling the difficult.'

'Maybe you do. But this isn't a difficult mathematical problem. It's a complicated business and—'

'Complications can be ironed out if one is honest and sincere.'

'Don't depend on it. Girls today are a discontented, rebellious lot. Handling them is not easy.'

'It's become fashionable nowadays to blame the young; expect perfection from them. But what example are we, their elders, setting them? Are we models of patience, humility and good behaviour? One can see where the problem lies if one is objective. In any case, my students are not like that. They love me and—'

'It doesn't take much time for love to change to hate,' Sisir laughed. 'Mashima loved you at one time.'

'You have something there,' Bharati laughed with him. 'But whatever you say I'm not rejecting the offer. If for no other reason—because it will enable me to walk out of Mashima's house with my head held high. One of the perks that go with the job is a rent-free, fully furnished, modern dwelling filled with all sorts of comforts.'

Yes, this was how Bharati had rehearsed the scene. Now, having acted out her part to perfection, she sat back to enjoy the applause, to see the light flame into her husband's eyes. But where was the applause? Where the light?

There was a moment's silence. Then Sisir said, 'So you're taking this rent-free, fully furnished, modern dwelling?' His eyes were sombre. His voice held a touch of derision.

'Arré! What is the man saying?' A peal of laughter came floating on the air and entered Sisir's unwilling ears. 'Of course I'm taking it. I'm so thrilled—I've been waiting to tell you about it all day. But you—you worry too much. If I work hard and do my job well, why should the girls not be satisfied? As for the house—it's beautiful. I'll turn it into the most comfortable home you can imagine. And if we give up this house,' here Bharati broke into another laugh, 'Mashima may start loving me all over again. "You're going away, Bouma!" she might say with tears in her eyes. "I'll be so lonely without you." You're right. Nothing's impossible in this world.'

It was true. In this world nothing was impossible. Sisir, instead of sharing Bharati's happiness, turned on her suddenly and said, 'Where's the question of giving up this house? You're getting the quarter. Not I.'

'The things you say!' Bharati threw up her hands in despair. 'Do you think only I'll be allowed to stay there? That my husband and son won't?'

'I can't say anything about your son. The problem, as I see it, lies with your husband. Your employers may, very kindly, allow me to take shelter under your roof. But whether or not I would like to is a different matter.'

'Could you kindly tell me what you mean? In plain Bengali?'

'It's plain enough in my opinion. I'm not exactly looking forward to being the only male in a world of females.'

So this was what it was all about. Bharati heaved a sigh of relief. 'The warden's bungalow isn't attached to the hostel,' she explained. 'It's in a different part of the campus. Even the entrance gate is separate. Besides, don't forget that though the hostel is for girls, the college is co-educational. The wife of the warden of the boys' hostel lives quite happily in her husband's quarter.'

Sisir burst into a laugh. 'Is it the same thing? Women follow their husbands and make homes for them wherever they go. Forests, mountain peaks, caves.'

Bharati's blood froze at these words. For the first time she felt frightened, truly frightened. She felt as though a vicious, gigantic bat had cast its venomous shadow on the bright, beautiful dream she had nurtured all day. Her voice, when she spoke, was quiet. 'Wives follow their husbands but not willingly—at all times. They go because they are compelled to.'

She understood, quite clearly now, where the problem lay. Her husband wouldn't live in a house which was hers by right. The old, age-old male ego! Men still found it impossible to think of their wives as equals. They had the same mindset as when they had taken girls of ten and twelve from their birth homes and locked them up in their own for life. When they treated them like slaves. When husbands embellished their own images with titles like *Lord* and *Master* and a wife was simply *Woman*. Why were men so blind? Couldn't they see that times had changed? That women were educated? Financially independent? That they had earned the right to be treated as equals?

These thoughts flashed through Bharati's mind but she took care not to express them. 'My goodness!' she exclaimed instead. 'Here I am sitting and chatting while the snacks are getting cold. Have a quick wash and have your tea. Worrying, arguing, discussing and speculating! We can leave all that for later.' Thus she built a dam in the sea. But what are a few sandbags against a tidal wave?

Three hours later . . . Ghontu was asleep and Bharati and Sisir were about to settle down to their dinner when the wave came hurtling from below, hitting them with such force that they almost lost balance. It came in the form of Mashima whom both were snidely referring to as *the landlady* these days. Mashima's name was Charulata. Though Bharati and Sisir knew her name they hadn't troubled their heads about it all these years. But they were doing so now. Particularly Sisir. 'Rightly named,' he muttered now and then. 'Like the heroine of Rabindranath's *Ruined Nest*. Ours was such a happy nest. And look how she is ruining it!'

Well, her entry certainly ruined the moment Bharati had been looking forward to and planning for the last three hours. She had rehearsed the scene all this while and was just ready to play it. She would smile sweetly, pout fretfully, entreat her husband with tears in her eyes. She would try all her wiles, use all her charms and convince him that what she was proposing was good for them both. She had to bring him over to her way of thinking before he barked out a command and forbade her to take on the job. But Mashima's entry and the scene that followed nipped the tender bud and forced the flower rudely open. 'Baba Sisir,' she called as she came up the stairs, 'the time has come, I think, to speak out openly. You must get yourself another place. I'm finding it difficult, in many ways, to keep you. The boy particularly—he's so unmanageable, I live in constant terror of the house tumbling to pieces about my ears. Consider this a notice and look for another flat.'

Sisir who had always treated her with respect, called her Mashima, and deferred to her opinions, mumbled humbly, 'I am looking. I've been looking for a long time . . . ' when Bharati's voice, cold and clear, cut into his. 'There's no such thing as notice in this day and age Mashima,' she said. 'Not when tenants pay the rent each month.'

The landlady was startled. She hadn't expected such words or such a tone of voice. It had been *her* privilege, hitherto, to shoot the darts. She hadn't imagined that one would come springing back and hit her. Her face darkened with humiliation.

'I belong to another age and another time, Bouma,' she said with whatever dignity she could muster. 'I neither know nor care to know what goes on now. The simple fact is—my Anil is to be married and I need the extra space. You'll have to vacate—' Turning around, she walked away in high dudgeon, not giving either of them a chance to answer her.

'You heard that?' Bharati lifted her head and looked piercingly into Sisir's eyes.

'Yes. I heard that,' Sisir replied. 'I'm hearing things like that all the time. But you shouldn't have spoken as you did.'

'What shouldn't I have said?'

'That part about the law and the rights of tenants. It wasn't fair.'

'It wasn't *fair*?' Bharati echoed.

'That's what I think.'

'Yet you're the one who is always saying that protest is necessary. That submitting to a wrong is as good as supporting it.'

'I don't deny it. But you—you have always argued otherwise.'

Bharati stared at her husband in exasperation. She didn't know what to make of his contradictions. If the truth were to be told it was entirely through Bharati's efforts that their relationship with Mashima had retained a semblance of decency so far. Sisir lost his temper every now and then and was prone to snap back but Bharati stopped him each time. She knew that once the mask of civility was ripped off, there was no knowing to what depths both sides would sink. 'Don't start a slanging match for God's sake,' she had begged often. 'It's most undignified. Let's keep our cool and try to get out as fast as we can.' And Sisir would reply, 'It's getting worse and worse. Our silence is only encouraging her. One needs to protest sometimes.'

Yet, today, he had changed his stance completely.

'She came into the flat this afternoon,' Bharati informed her husband, 'when we were away. She scolded Ghontu, wrung his ear.'

'Wrung his ear!' A shocked exclamation from Sisir.

'That's exactly what she did. Ask Ghontu if you don't believe me. "Both your parents are working," she told him. "Tell them to build a mansion for you to jump about in. Why do you go on staying in this old, ugly house?"'

'Hunh!' A grunt from Sisir.

'What do you mean by "Hunh!"?'

'It's our double income that's at the root of it all. It's irking her.'

Bharati fixed her eyes on her husband's face. It was dark and brooding, mysterious. She wondered what he meant by that last remark. Was he hinting that bringing in a double income was an aberration of some sort? That if the neighbours found it irksome one couldn't blame them?

'Well!' Bharati's voice was sombre, 'since it is not possible to revert to a single income and thereby remove Mashima's annoyance, we can do the next best thing. Vacate. I hope you'll overcome your scruples now and go tell Mashima that we're moving out next month.'

Sisir's voice was sombre too. 'I'm not mad,' he said quietly.

'What!' Bharati's face flamed and her hands trembled in agitation. 'Are you telling me,' she said with a catch in her voice, 'that you've made up your mind to stay away from the quarter simply because it is mine?'

'Not for all time to come,' Sisir chewed out the words sardonically. 'Who can look into the future? It's possible that I'll land up there some years from now, bedridden, an invalid.'

'You're trying my patience so that I lose my temper. But I won't. And I won't let you behave so foolishly. I'm taking the job and we're all getting out of here. All—you understand. If I can live in your house why can't you live in mine?'

'All questions don't have to be answered.'

'There is no answer to this one. Tell me the truth. Why can't you come with me? Where's the obstacle?'

Now Sisir's mouth twisted in a smile. Touching his chest he said, 'Here.'

'I guessed as much. But you'll have to give up your silly scruples.' In an effort to lighten his mood, Bharati giggled like a schoolgirl. 'I have rights too—you know. Come, be a good boy. Let's walk out of Mashima's house as soon as we can. Honestly—everything apart—the thought of leaving all this unpleasantness is such a relief.'

'It's not so bad. Besides, we *are* looking for another place,' Sisir reminded her solemnly.

'We've been looking for ages. And we may go on looking for all eternity. But will anything come of it?'

Words, words, words! Arguments and counter-arguments. Sisir's cool disregard of her feelings, his indifference, his obstinacy stiffened Bharati's ego, strengthened her resolve.

'Very well!' she said at last. 'You stay with your venerated Mashima. Work hard for her son's wedding and overeat at the feast. I've made my decision. My future is mine alone.' Her last words startled her. Had she really meant what she said? She felt a twinge of guilt. She had been harsh, too harsh. But what could she do? Was she not human? Was she not made of flesh and blood? Sisir insisted on ignoring the positive aspects of the case. The peace and privacy that would be theirs, the enhanced resources, the joy of living in beautiful surroundings. He clung, perversely, to the one negative point he saw—the diminishing of his status and prestige as male and head of the family.

Anger and resentment rose in Bharati's breast. 'Oh!' she thought bitterly. 'You think you'll win each time simply because you are male? You think your word is law? Why? Why? Am I not human? Do I not have the right to take some decisions? If I can improve my financial situation, the quality of my life, my prospects—why shouldn't I? Because it makes a dent in your ego? I realize now that I should have been tougher, more demanding. All these years you've taken advantage of my civility, my unassuming nature, my gentleness. I've worked like a slave from dawn to dusk. I've served you hand and foot. But you—have you ever even passed me a glass of water?'

The unhappy past, unhappy now at any rate, washed over Bharati in waves. She saw how she had rushed back from college, day after day, changed into a shabby sari and fallen to work, getting the house ready for Sisir's return. She had swept and dusted, put away books and toys, bathed and fed her son and sent him out to play with strict instructions to return before dusk for Sisir liked to see his son when he came home. And in the midst of all this she hadn't forgotten to make a special snack to go with Sisir's tea. And after all her work was done she had made herself fresh for the evening for he hated to see her looking tired and unkempt. There was a gap of about two hours between the times she and Sisir returned. That's what made all this possible. But was it always easy? Didn't she often feel an overwhelming urge to fling her bag on the floor and collapse on the bed? But she controlled the urge. 'Poor Sisir,' she thought. 'He'll be worried if he sees me lying down. It's my duty to keep him relaxed and happy.' She had done her duty. But had he? Had he ever considered her happiness? Could he not say to himself now, 'Poor girl! She's never asked for anything. If my living in her quarter makes her happy . . . '

No. Sisir was made of different mettle. 'All these years,' the more Bharati thought the clearer the images became, 'we've lived a one-sided life. We've followed one goal— taking care of your joys and sorrows, your needs and aspirations, your whims and moods. Why? Why? Because I'm courteous, diffident, eager to please? Yet . . . '—and this thought came to Bharati for the first time in her life— 'if I weren't so gentle and considerate, so sensitive to your feelings, I would have reminded you that my position as senior lecturer of a reputed college is much higher than yours—an ordinary clerk in a private firm. What you earn in a month, I earn in twelve days. Leaving all other considerations aside, the enhanced salary that I'll be getting if I take on the wardenship is not so small that a petty clerk like you can scoff at it.'

Tears of self-pity gushed into Bharati's eyes and rolled silently down her cheeks. 'Where was the question of reminding him,' she thought sadly, 'when I never thought of it myself.' Today, only today, battered against Sisir's cruel, implacable will, the floodgates had opened.

Yet, the next morning, when the principal asked her if she had taken a decision, she said, 'I've thought it over. I don't think I'm fit for the job.'

'Why don't you leave that to us?' the principal smiled. 'We know what we are doing. Just put down your signature—'

Still Bharati hesitated. The principal reasoned with her. So did the other members of the faculty. 'You're a fool,' her best friend, Lila Ghosh, scolded. 'It's your husband, isn't it, who is at the bottom of this? He should have been born two hundred years ago. It's at his command that you're sacrificing this wonderful chance. If the offer came to me I would turn a somersault with joy.'

'Am I not? Turning a somersault—I mean?'

'Stop speaking in riddles. The age when husbands commanded and wives obeyed meekly is gone. Look at the world around you.'

'You're right,' Bharati said suddenly. 'I'll take it.'

Right. But what was right? Bharati's life went dreadfully wrong. Totally out of gear.

'Very well,' Sisir said quietly after she told him that she had signed the agreement. 'Go if you're determined to and take Ghontu with you. I'm staying on.'

Bharati was frightened. She felt the earth slipping beneath her feet. 'Believe me,' she told her husband that night, laying her head tenderly on his chest. 'I told the principal that I wasn't fit for the job . . . that I was refusing. But he insisted. So did everyone else. The problem, you see, is that I don't have a valid reason—'

Sisir's chest moved just the slightest bit away from the head that had laid itself so humbly, so lovingly on it. 'Your husband doesn't wish to live on the campus,' he said coldly. 'That, I suppose, isn't a valid reason?'

'O go!' Bharati humbled herself, brought herself down to the dregs of her soul. 'People make mistakes sometimes. Treat it as a mistake I've committed inadvertently. You're my husband. Support me. Save me from the humiliation that will surely follow if—'

'I?' Sisir laughed. 'I save you? You've just signed a bond taking on the responsibility of a hundred and fifty young women. And you can't save one woman—yourself? These are hardly the words I expected to hear from a highly educated, financially independent, liberated female like you.'

He wouldn't relent. No—he would never relent. He would put the entire weight of his personality solidly against the prospect of a smooth harmonious life, a life light and easy, in comfortable, aesthetically pleasing surroundings. He wouldn't let Bharati live the life she had craved for years; had craved but never demanded because she didn't know that she had a right to demand. Men were cruel, selfish. They didn't know that no matter how well educated a woman might be, how high profile her job, what she yearned for in the secret recesses of her heart was a neat, pretty home—a nest in which she could love, cherish and nurture her family.

Didn't know or didn't care to know? Or that, taking advantage of this weakness in a woman, they enjoyed all the comforts of a well-run home while pretending that

Ashapurna Debi

they didn't need any of it, perpetuating the belief that a home for a man was wrought neither out of his love nor his dreams. It was only a lodging where he got his meals and a bed for the night. That a man provided all the paraphernalia required for setting it up only out of consideration for a woman's needs. He himself was austere by nature, undemanding—a helpless creature yoked to a partner whose demands were unceasing. In consequence they didn't suffer a twinge of guilt when they cruelly repudiated and ignored the small, humble aspirations of their womenfolk.

Bharati lay awake for a long time after Sisir fell asleep. So many thoughts flitted through her head. She remembered the time they went to attend her sister's wedding in Barasat. Her mother had begged them to stay the night. 'You can go to the office tomorrow morning from here, Baba,' she had told her son-in-law. 'I'll give you an early meal.' But Sisir had ignored her mother's entreaty. He had insisted on returning. And Bharati? Fearing that he would be uncomfortable without her, she had come away with him.

Another time . . . Memories of Sisir's heartlessness and indifference to her wishes rose, one by one, like witnesses in the dock. Memories that had lain buried in her heart all these years, which would never have reared their heads, perhaps, had her life not moved towards this crisis. Bharati forgot that she was a highly educated woman with a PhD degree; that she was a senior lecturer in a reputed college, respected and revered by so many. Like a helpless, thwarted girl-bride, spurned by her husband, she wept—the silent tears coursing down her cheeks and falling on her pillow. Her only consolation was that there was no witness. No one had seen her bitter battle and her utter defeat and humiliation.

But was Sisir completely unaffected? Was he not fighting a battle too? Was he not suffering? Feeling thwarted, humiliated? He had his own perspective. Everyone does. And from that perspective Bharati appeared arrogant and high-handed, self-centred, bent on seeing only her own point of view.

The trouble was that they had been so happy together all these years, so self-sufficient, that they had no friends, no one before whom they could unburden themselves and seek advice. Consequently, the two confused young people, unable to resolve their dilemma, had perforce to follow their own inclinations and, in doing so, prove to the world how far they could go, how much they could change.

At the opening of the next scene, we see Bharati living with Ghontu in a neat, charming little house decorated to perfection with plants and pictures, books and goldfish, bright cushions and covers. She has kept a boy servant who spends the whole day dusting and sweeping, scrubbing and polishing with his small hands till the house sparkles like a jewel. She also has a maid who comes in twice a day to do the rest of the work. She cooks on the gas stove set on the kitchen table and washes the clothes in a mound of lather in the washbasin. Bharati looks at her, from time to time, with something like envy in her eyes. She remembers the dark, sooty kitchen where she had had to cook for years on a smoky coal fire; the bathroom with its cracked cement floor where she had washed clothes out of a tin bucket and dreamed of a spotless bathroom with a gleaming white washbasin. Yet now that she has realized all her dreams, she doesn't feel enthused enough to even wash a handkerchief or fry a couple of potatoes for her son.

Who knows why?

Is it because Bharati is rich now? Because Bharati's free time is spent in chatting with the friends who drop in every evening? Who sit in her charming circular veranda, drink her tea, and keep her company. The chief of these ladies is Lila Ghosh. 'Really!' she exclaims every now and then, 'your husband is the limit! It isn't his male ego that's the problem as you believe. It's jealousy! He's jealous of you. That's what. Jealous! There's a lot of that between husbands and wives. They keep it under wraps out of consideration for the joint business they run.'

'How do you know so much?' Bharati smiles faintly.

'Observation, child!' Lila laughs. 'Simply by observing the world around me.'

'Is that why you never married?'

'No,' Lila giggles self-consciously. 'The truth is that no one wanted me. But I don't mind admitting that even today, at my age and with my looks, if someone asks "Will you?" I won't say "No".'

Peals of laughter ring in the glazed veranda. Teacups tinkle. Bone china teacups with a pattern of roses. The aroma of the finest Darjeeling tea scents the air. Curtains rustle in the breeze. The cactus growing in pots on the window sill keep vigil. Some are straight and steady, looking up at the sky. Others spread their thorny arms, all bent and crooked, towards undefined boundaries, creating the illusion of warped, misshapen humans silhouetted against the glass. Bharati looks at them and thinks, 'It's not so bad really. I'm quite all right . . . '

At this moment the maid appears. 'Shall I give Khoka his dinner, Didimoni?' she asks.

'Why?' Bharati flies off the handle. 'So that you can wrap up and run off home? He's not to eat before nine o'clock. He must study till then.'

'It's not I who am in a hurry,' the woman retorts indignantly. 'The child is half-asleep. He's been nodding over his books for the past half an hour.'

She sweeps out of the room.

There's a moment's silence. Then one of the ladies murmurs, 'It's hard on the child. He gets a bit lonely . . . perhaps.'

'Yes,' Bharati looks at the slanting shadows on the glass and mutters, 'I should send him to a boarding school. There'll be other boys of his age—'

And Sisir?

Well, to tell the truth, Sisir hasn't done too badly for himself either. In scene three we see that Sisir has moved out of his upstairs flat and found shelter in Charulata Mashima's household. Mashima is looking after him like a son. No ordinary son either—but as one who has been dealt a cruel blow by the world and needs all her motherly care and affection. She bemoans his fate constantly and scolds her daughters if she finds a broken button on Sisir's shirt. Those who think that all this concern is only an act are quite wrong. The fount of love in her heart for Sisir was real. Time and circumstance had dammed the flow for a while. They had embittered her, made her shameless and cruel. But now the stream is flowing again, clear and bright and strong.

A few coats of lime wash to the walls of the flat upstairs have yielded excellent results. She has a tenant now who is paying her full market rent. And Sisir is her paying guest. He forks out a substantial amount each month for a creaking bed in the drawing room and two humdrum meals a day. Has Sisir rented the drawing room then? No. He lives in half of it. The landlady's eldest son, Anil, who has always slept in the drawing room, continues to do so. Shameless disregard of the proprieties has brought

Ashapurna Debi

the good lady a pile of benefits. 'What harm then,' she thinks, 'in going a *little* further? In stooping a *little* lower?' She is helped in the matter by Sisir himself. 'Why not?' he tells Charulata Mashima when she makes the suggestion. 'Let Anil sleep in his usual place. What difference does it make to me? It's a big room.'

Is Sisir so insensitive, then, that he doesn't realize the lowliness of his situation? If he does, he is certainly giving a wonderful performance. He has managed to persuade not only the people around him but himself that he doesn't mind in the least. 'Anil has always been like a younger brother to me,' he tells himself. 'What a terror he was as a child! And how my mother pampered him! Besides, I am getting all I need. Why should I complain?'

There is something to be said about a life free of responsibilities, of bonds, of people's expectations. There's a rhythm to it, a certain cadence. Sisir has acquired it in exchange for a handful of rupees paid out on the first of every month. After that—nothing. No more worries. No more running after salt or coal or oil. Bharati's voice doesn't come ringing into his ears, as it used to, with a hundred commands and complaints. 'Is it true that one can't buy bread without a coupon any more? What a nuisance!' Or 'Has the substance called oil disappeared from the market? I've been telling you to pick up a tin for the last three days! But you never have the time to do anything for me.' Or 'Bring a packet of tea leaves on your way back from your walk. The tin is empty.' Or 'You're free today. Why don't you take Ghontu to South Tailoring? He needs some shorts and shirts.'

No. All the sounds that had jarred on Sisir's nerves are things of the past. No one requires anything of him any more. He has found refuge in a 'silent' world, a world of total freedom from care. The faint tinkles that enter his ears come from outside that infinite silence. They have no weight. They drift past on delicate wings, leaving no echoes. Anil holds forth enthusiastically on the triumphs and defeats of his football team. Mashima's daughters scold him tenderly. 'You're so-o-o absent-minded, Sisir da! Why didn't you tell us your water jug is empty?' Sisir smiles, enjoying their concern. And when Mashima sits by him, while he eats his meal, waving a palm-leaf fan and lamenting, 'You'll ruin your health this way, Baba. You're eating less and less each day,' tears spring into Sisir's eyes. His heart quivers with an unknown emotion. Is it joy or pain? Mashima makes it a point to remind Sisir of his mother and the deep love and friendship the two women had shared. 'Ah!' she says, 'it makes my heart bleed to think of the past. Didi was such a loving mother! She used to spend the whole afternoon making a stack of ghee-soaked *rutis* for you to eat after coming home from college. Those days are gone—never to return.' Mashima's voice becomes heavy as if with unshed tears and she sighs often. She brings up Bharati's name, too, from time to time. 'I don't understand Bouma's attitude, Baba,' she says. 'To break up a lovely family! And for what? Her own self-advancement. Women like us can't even dream of doing such a thing.' To give her her due, these laments may be genuine. It is possible that she really doesn't understand.

Women have always been susceptible to males in distress. Males abandoned by their partners, left to fend for themselves in a comfortless world. 'The poor helpless boy!' Mashima thinks and her heart swells with indignation against the egoistic, self-centred wife. She quite forgets that Bharati's selfish egotism has earned her a heap of benefits.

Does this mean that Bharati and Sisir have lost contact altogether? That husband and wife, father and son don't see each other any more? By no means. They do see each other. Every Sunday. And why not? After all, the separation isn't legal. Sisir doesn't go to Bharati's house, of course. Bharati comes with her son. She has to sit in Mashima's drawing room while Sisir is getting ready and, sometimes, even has to have a cup of tea. Ghontu gobbles up the snacks served to him, then whispers to his mother, 'Can I go up to the roof?' The roof used to be his play area and he still has his kites and thread roll there, tucked away under the water tank. Bharati doesn't like the idea. She shakes her head and looks severe. But Mashima ignores her and calls out encouragingly. 'Of course, child! Go up if you like. The new tenants are good people. They won't mind.'

In a while, Sisir enters the room all shaved and bathed and ready, and the three go out together. They spend the day wandering around the city. Sometimes they see a film. Sometimes they visit the zoo or the circus. They always eat out on Sundays. And when they come back, their arms are laden with presents for Ghontu. Toys and sweets, clothes and comics. Sisir pays for everything. In accordance with an unwritten agreement, the Sunday expenses are all his. Even the most detached observer can see that Bharati and Sisir plan the day as Ghontu's day. A day of the week they have put aside for Ghontu's sake. Only to give him pleasure.

Does that mean husband and wife don't talk to each other? Of course they do. They laugh and talk and exchange pleasantries that hang lightly on the air before drifting away. They cause no tremors in the blood, no flutters in the heart.

And at dusk, just before parting, they hold each other's eyes and murmur softly, 'See you, then.' Sisir taps Ghontu on the head playfully and says, 'Ghontu babu is growing into such a big boy. Soon he'll be taking *us* out. What do you say, Ghontu babu?' Ghontu turns his head aside so that his parents can't see his eyes. It is during moments like these that Bharati and Sisir realize that Ghontu is truly growing up.

And, sometimes, when the 'fast-growing' Ghontu's attention is elsewhere, Bharati turns to her husband. Like Ghontu she doesn't let him see her eyes. 'So you won't come to my house—ever,' she murmurs. She doesn't look up even when he answers with a laugh, 'Have I said that?'

'No you haven't,' Bharati sighs and falls silent.

'I could go some day—' Sisir says casually. 'Any day.'

'Strange!' Bharati muses. 'Why don't I ever fall ill? If I were to fall ill . . . ' She imagines the scene. Bharati is ill, dangerously ill. The college authorities have sent for Sisir.

But the scene remains in the imagination. The very next Sunday, Bharati is seen in Mashima's drawing room, healthy and beautiful and radiantly alive. She has deliberately come a little late, hoping that she won't have to wait; that Sisir will be ready and waiting for them. But that doesn't happen. Sisir likes a lazy Sunday morning. He doesn't feel enthused enough to get ready for the day till he actually sees them. Bharati has no option but to walk slowly into the house and stand outside Mashima's kitchen. Ghontu shifts his feet restlessly. He would like to go up to the roof but he doesn't badger his mother any more. He is a big boy now—very quiet, very well behaved. There's no doubt that he's being brought up well.

Bharati, Sisir and Ghontu's lives have fallen into a pattern. Week after week it remains the same. They get together every Sunday morning, bright and cheerful and looking forward to the day. They part in the evening—the glow gone from their hearts. Yet, the surprising thing is, they no longer look on this arrangement as strange or abnormal. They have accommodated each other. Their lives fit.

Ashapurna Debi

Bharati spends her Sunday nights staring up at the ceiling. But she wakes with the dawn, as usual, and goes about her duties. She gives the goldfish their food. She turns the cactus towards the sun and thinks, 'I must buy a few more.'

At the end of the day, Sisir returns to the room he shares with Anil and flings himself on the bed. He starts planning the next week's jaunt. Where would he take Ghontu next Sunday? What would he buy for him?

Human beings are wonderfully resilient, wonderfully strong! That's because they've learnt the art of adjustment. A series of adjustments—that's what the cycle of life is all about. They've understood that. Yet they never cease to concern themselves about themselves. Never cease to worry and agonize! One wonders why!

King of the Forest

Boner Raja

Jyotirindranath Nandi

'Trees talk to me.'

'Branches? Or leaves?'

'Leaves, branches, buds, flowers and fruit. They whisper in my ears.'

'Will they talk to me too?'

'Of course they will,' Sharada pulls his grandson closer. Then, taking his small head in his hands, he touches it to the trunk of an old almond tree. 'Press your ear against the bark,' he laughs softly. 'You'll hear it speak.'

Moti does as he is told. He presses his ear against the bark, black and gnarled with age, and stands absolutely still. Summer is at its peak and hot winds are blowing the branches wildly about. The dark-green leaves, strong with sap, make rustling sounds as they race against the wind. Moti's hair blows gently in the breeze. Sharada has no hair on his head—only an expanse of shining pate. But there are tremors in his whiskers and on his lips. These, of course, are not caused by the wind. Ten-year-old Moti realizes that. He knows that his grandfather is holding a bubble of laughter in his throat. A bubble of silent laughter. Dadu is naughty like a little boy. Moti wonders if there are other old men or women who are naughty like him.

'Do you hear the tree speak?'

'No,' Moti makes a face and shakes his head. He moves his ear away and says, 'I can't hear *anything*.'

'Thoo! Thoo!' Sharada turns his head and spits vigorously into a patch of yams growing in the jungle. He isn't holding any laughter in his throat now. The full lips under his whiskers are pressed together. The almond tree is waving so wildly in the wind that the Haldibon bird sitting on a branch flies away in panic. Sharada looks at the fluttering wings and sighs. Then he turns to his grandson. 'You've lost your hearing, child,' he says solemnly. 'It's the result of living in the city.'

'Is that so?' Moti looks into the dust-brown irises of his grandfather's eyes for a while. Then, baring his milk-white teeth in a smile, he laughs and shakes his head. 'Why!' he exclaims. 'There's a guava tree in our house on Beadon Street! And a huge gulmohar just outside the gate. Those two don't speak.'

'The Beadon Street trees!' Sharada makes an ugly sound in his throat. 'They've turned deaf and dumb with the noise they hear all day. Traffic rumbling, horns blaring, radios shrieking! It's a wonder they still live and breathe.' Sharada clears his throat and spits another blob of phlegm into the yam leaves. 'But it won't be for long. They're close to death.'

Moti is silent. He stares into his grandfather's eyes. 'Here the trees see and hear nothing but themselves,' the old man explains, 'and the grass and shrubs and creepers at their feet. See how lovingly the *aparajito* and *jhumko* are twining themselves about that hoary old trunk!' Sharada points a finger. 'And do you see those birds among the leaves? Flocks of them—rainbow-hued. They rub their beaks against the stalks and peck at the fruit, trilling all the while.' He looks expectantly at the boy.

'Yes,' Moti murmurs.

'And the trees in Beadon Street!' the old man exclaims. 'What do they have around them?' Two small flames flicker in the dust-coloured eyes. 'Stone, mortar and burning tar at their feet! Brick roofs, four storeys high, above their heads! And entangled in their branches? Not vines and creepers but electric wires, biting into them, sapping their strength.' The grandfather looks at the boy and the latter nods in affirmation. His toenail fiddles with the grass at his feet. 'Consequently,' the old man goes on, 'the trees in the city have lost their tongues. And their ears.' He spits ferociously, once again, into the patch of yams.

'Do trees have ears, Dadu?'

'Of course they do. Ears, tongues, eyes, noses—they have all the senses we have.' The grandfather nods solemnly at the boy. Moti's big black eyes, shining with excitement at the thought, dart here and there. Sharada walks ahead. Moti follows. Leaving the yams behind them they come to a slope of grass, below which is a pool of water. It isn't really a pool. It is last night's rain caught in a hollow. Some of it has seeped away but what stands is still knee deep. Moti clambers down the slope and puts a tentative toe in the green water. In a flash, hundreds of frogs, speckled black and emerald, appear from who knows where and leap into the water, causing a tremendous splash. Moti is startled at first. Then he laughs and claps his hands.

'Why don't you catch some and put them in your pocket?' the grandfather suggests. 'See how fat and oily they are—and how smooth and yellow their underbellies.'

'*Dhat*!' Moti wrinkles his nose. 'What would I do with frogs?'

'Eat them. Fry them nice and crisp and—'

Moti nearly pukes with disgust. 'The Chinese eat frogs. We don't.'

'Hmm!' The old man looks solemn. 'You eat stale fish packed in ice for days. That's why you're as thin as a rake. Look at your chest. I can count the ribs, each one of them.' What he says is quite true. Moti is thin and frail. That is why his parents have sent him over to his grandfather's for the summer holidays. He is already looking better with all the fresh fish and pure milk he has had over the past six days.

The two wade across the water and stand in a little grove where seven or eight roseapple trees stand in a knot. They're so close to each other that their branches intertwine and there are deep pools of shadows at their feet. The grove is cool and dark. Moti looks up and sees the roseapples, hundreds and thousands of them—dark, glossy fruit in tight bunches, so closely packed they almost block off the sky. They are like monsoon clouds, Moti thinks, blobs of ink massed together. But all the fruit isn't purple black. Some bunches are rose flushed, some leaf green. *They look*, Moti sighs wistfully, *like innumerable clusters of gems—garnets, rubies and vibrant emeralds.*

'What are you staring at with your mouth open?' The grandfather gives him a tiny push.

'I'm looking at the roseapples. They're so pretty.'

'Hunh!' Sharada bursts into a laugh. 'They may be pretty but they won't jump into your mouth. You'll have to make some effort to eat them, you know.'

'Of course I know they won't jump into my mouth,' Moti replies, sulking a little.

Sharada ties his gamchha around his middle. He, like Moti, is only wearing a pair of shorts. His upper body and feet are bare. Moti looks askance at the old man. The muscles of his neck and abdomen seem carved out of stone. *Dadu is so healthy*, Moti thinks, *because he lives in the country. Baba is Dadu's son but he looks much older. His body is soft and slack and he tires easily*. Moti's father works in an office in Dalhousie Square. It's a big, red building. Moti has been taken to see it once. *If only Baba didn't have to go to office*, Moti thinks wistfully. *If only he could come and live here, he would grow big and strong like Dadu*. Moti makes up his mind that, once back in Kolkata, he would persuade his father to come here for some months at least. But, and now Moti's heart sinks a little, he knows his mother won't let him come. Ma is terrified of the country. 'What is there,' she argues, 'but jungles infested with snakes and jackals?' She had worried about Moti, too, when Dadu's letter came. 'With whom will he play?' she had asked her husband. 'Peasants and cowherds' sons? He'll say goodbye to his books and run wild all day! He'll learn rough manners and probably help the cowherds drive their cattle home.'

Moti's father hadn't paid heed to her fears. He had sent Moti to his grandfather with a trusted servant. But the boy loved it here. There were snakes and insects of course but there were so many other things too. Moti wished his parents would come and then they could all stay here forever.

Sharada has completed his fifty-ninth year and is going on sixty. Moti watches in astonishment as his grandfather scampers up a trunk, as lightly as a squirrel, and settles himself in a fork of the tree. Stripping the fruits off the branches he drops them into a fold of his gamchha. From time to time he pops one or two in his mouth. Some of the roseapples slip from his hand and fall on the grass at Moti's feet. Moti stoops and picks them up—great purple eggs bursting with juice. He looks up at his grandfather with a merry smile. Sharada's mouth is full of sweet and tart juice and pulp. His lips are stained a deep aubergine. And the irises of his eyes are no longer the dull opaque of desert sand. They are bright magenta, the colour of a roseapple seed, and they gleam with excitement like the eyes of a wilful child.

'Pretty! Pretty!' Sharada mutters as, leaping nimbly from branch to branch, he reaches the top of the tree. 'What's pretty to look at is also good to eat. But city folks have lost their appetites.' From his perch on the topmost branch Sharada converses with his grandson. 'Your house in Beadon Street is full of pretty things. Sofa sets and dressing tables, curtains and flower pots. There are neon lights on the walls and fine crockery in the kitchen. Your playroom is full of plastic toys. Your mother wears pretty saris and blouses in the morning and changes into better ones in the evening. Her mind is occupied all day with what to wear. What will look pretty? What prettier? As for your father—he leaves home every morning, wearing a smart suit and tie, a uniformed peon carrying his briefcase to the car. He works all day in a glass cage with a fan whirring overhead. He doesn't go hungry. No, I can't say that he does. For lunch, he has two boiled potatoes sprinkled with black pepper, a slice of bread spread with tinned butter, some vegetables stewed dry and a sweet made with powdered milk. That is what the doctor ordered—a balanced meal. And who is to contradict him? He's the most eminent doctor of the city and he has prescribed the perfect meal! Carbohydrates, fats, proteins and minerals in just the right proportions. And your mother! Her lunch is a mound of rice, a mess of stale vegetables and a curry made with yesterday's fish. It is sprinkled with powdered turmeric and chillies. She belches at the end of the meal, a sour belch, and wonders what to do next. See a matinee? She scans the newspaper to find out if a new film has come to town. Films!' Sharada makes a sound of disgust and stuffs an enormous roseapple into his mouth. 'You city people have the longevity of a firework! All flash and sparkle outside. And nothing inside. Only a moment's life! Polluted air and adulterated food have taken their toll and—'

'Don't climb so high, Dadu!' Moti cries out in alarm. 'The branch will break and you'll fall.'

Sharada laughs. His face looks like a mischievous monkey's peering down from between the leaves. 'Branches warn you before they break,' he shouts. 'They make a crackling sound. The problem in Beadon Street is that nothing can be heard above the noise of traffic.'

Moti looks on as a flock of birds surge upwards and disappear like a scattering of bright-green sparks against the hot blue sky. Others take their place. They perch on twigs and branches and peck at the fruit, chattering to one another. *Birds eat all the time*, Moti thinks, *just like Dadu. Dadu had a big bowl of kheer and muri and four enormous mangoes for breakfast. That was just a couple of hours ago. But from the way he's wolfing down the roseapples—it seems he's hungry again. He must have put away about a hundred already.* As if guessing his thoughts, Sharada cries out, 'Your stomach has shrunk to a wisp of rubber from eating too little. Now mine . . .'

Dadu was obviously referring to the kheer Moti had not been able to finish this morning. Kheer made from the purest, creamiest milk and cooked to a delicious consistency by his grandmother. The old man had grumbled about it in the morning. And now again . . . Moti lifts his hand to his nose and sniffs it. The wonderful aroma still clings to his fingers—the fragrance of kheer, of pure milk and ghee . . . Coming to his defence, Moti's grandmother had said to her husband, 'Leave the boy alone. Eating is a matter of habit. His appetite will grow as yours did. How much could you eat when we lived in

Kolkata? To see you now—frankly, I get surprised sometimes.'

'Surprised or frightened?' The old man had smiled. 'Why don't you come out with the truth?' Moti's grandmother had looked embarrassed and his grandfather amused. Stroking his smooth, hard belly he had said, 'I can't blame you. Stretching the ribbon of life too taut is dangerous. It might snap in two. Eating too much may result in a stroke and then—'

'What rubbish you talk!' the grandmother had cried out indignantly. 'Why should you get a stroke? You're not so old that death should be stalking you!' Dadu hadn't replied. He had turned, instead, to his kheer and mangoes and devoured it with cries of pleasure. Thakurma had ladled some more kheer into his bowl. She expressed her fears, now and then, about the amount he ate but there was no doubt that feeding her husband was the source of her purest happiness.

The ribbon of life. The phrase was intriguing. Moti thought of his father who was a poor eater. A handful of rice, a couple of luchis. 'No more! No more!' Baba always put up his hand to ward off extra servings. As if his belly would burst with another luchi or another spoonful of halwa! *Not a good sign*, the boy shakes his head worriedly. *Dadu is so much older than Baba and he— what if Baba . . . ? The ribbon of life! How long would it stretch . . . ?*

'Here! Catch!' Moti looks up startled. His grandfather has sprinted down the tree and stands in front of him. The gamchha tied to his waist is swollen with fruit and he dangles a plump bunch above the boy's head.

'I can't eat any more, Dadu. I'm full.' Moti steps back a pace.

The old man coaxes, 'On just a few windfalls? Come, eat some plucked from the tree. Try one.' He thrusts the bunch into Moti's hands. 'And now,' he says, walking jauntily ahead, 'I must show you my guava orchard and my star-apple trees.'

'Did you plant all the trees yourself, Dadu?'

'Not the roseapples,' Sharada spits into a bush. His spit is deep purple with roseapple juice. 'I bought the land because the trees were there.'

'And the mangoes? The ones we saw yesterday?'

'Those I planted myself. I spent a thousand rupees on the saplings and built up this enormous orchard.'

'They're good mangoes,' Moti says, trying to please the old man.

'Hunh! Himsagar and Mohanphuli. I don't care for any of the other varieties.' The grandfather looks up at the sky, then down at his grandson. The boy's face is red and hot and pouring with sweat. Two pairs of eyes meet. One old, one young. One light, one dark. Moti gives a nervous snigger. 'Ei! What's so funny, boy?' The old man's brows come together. Scanty brows with one or two white hairs sticking out of them. The ridges of his forehead are filled with sweat which glitters in the strong sunlight. 'Last year I planted five hundred rupees worth of Singapore bananas and pineapples,' the old man goes on. 'I'll show them to you.'

'I've seen the bananas—'

'I'll show you everything. One by one. Guavas and pineapples, sorrel and star-apples. Chikoos too—'

'I love chikoos,' Moti sucks the juices from his palate. The irises sparkle like black jewels from the whites of his eyes. Sharada walks on. Moti follows. Skirting the edge of a lake they come to a field planted with star-apple trees. Three rows with four to a row. Twelve trees in all.

Moti counts swiftly even as he stares agape at the clusters of translucent fruit that blink and glimmer like moonstones from out of a canopy of dark-green leaves. There are lots more birds here, more activity among the leaves. Parrots, mynahs, bulbuls and koels, preferring the crisp, sweet, milky flesh of the star-apples to the tart and tangy pulp of the roseapples, flit faster here, chirp louder. They chase the squirrels whose swollen tails bob up and down, up and down, as they slide and slither from branch to branch in search of sweeter fruit.

'What do you see, Moti?'

'Stars! Thousands of stars hanging out of a sky as green and velvety as moss.'

'Hmph! Very poetic!' the old man bares his teeth in a grimace and spits. Then, putting up a hand, he plucks a cluster of star-apples from a hanging branch and hands it to his grandson. Moti bites into one and cries ecstatically, 'Delicious!' Sharada plucks another bunch and crams a large star-shaped fruit into his mouth. Clear, sweet, transparent juice runs down his chin. Moti laughs and claps his hands. His sixty-year-old Dadu is a little boy at heart, a mischievous little boy. Moti has realized it only after coming here. *Goodness*! *Dadu is biting into his fifth star-apple. He's certainly stretching the ribbon of life*. Moti laughs again. 'What are we sampling next, Dadu?' he asks his grandfather. 'The pineapples?'

'No. Pineapples aren't fit to be eaten till the leaves change colour. We need some more rain for them to turn yellow and the fruit to ripen.' He looks down at the boy and is surprised to see a mischievous glint lurking in his eyes.

'Why do you smile, boy?'

'I have a name for you, Dadu.'

'What name?' Sharada beams with his secret happiness and crinkles his eyes at the boy.

'King of fruits.' A gurgle of laughter rises from Moti's small chest and trembles in his mouth.

'Hunh! I can think of a better name.'

'What is that?'

'King of trees.' Sharada crunches the last star-apple between his strong teeth. 'Do you know why? Because the tree comes first.'

Moti stares at his grandfather. He doesn't understand.

'Last year I didn't eat a single mango.'

'Why Dadu?'

'Because not one mango in my garden grew to maturity. Just when the trees were loaded with blossom a terrible storm came one night and stripped the branches bare. The trees were ravished and turned barren. But did I blame them for it? No. I worked harder on my mango trees than on any of the others. I spent all my time with them. The trunks of the roseapple trees were knee deep in purple fruit. The grass in the star-apple grove was carpeted with fallen apples white as hoar frost. I didn't even care to look at them.'

'Then you love the trees more than you love their fruit.'

'Exactly!' Sharada snorts. 'How much do I eat? How much can one man eat? Yet I spend thousands of rupees on my orchards. Birds and squirrels feast on the fruit all day. Wasps and bees get drunk on sweet juices. And at night the bats and owls have the fling of their lives . . . '

Moti thinks of the catapult he has left behind in Beadon Street, a tiny one made from a bent twig and a wisp of rubber. For want of birds and squirrels he used to aim at the electric poles and telephone wires and set them jingling and jangling. The sounds echo in his ears as he watches the plump squirrels dart up and down the rough trunks. He smiles at his grandfather, a sweet, sudden smile that shows all his pearly teeth.

'You used to have a car in Beadon Street,' he says inconsequentially. 'A yellow car.'

'Who told you that?'

'Ma. She was sad that you sold it.'

'Naturally I sold it. What was the sense of bringing it here?'

Moti hesitates. He looks around at the fields and ponds, woods and thickets, and agrees. There are no roads here.

'Wasn't I right in selling it?' the grandfather persists. He is very serious, as though he is really depending on Moti's opinion. Moti nods. Sharada grunts. It is a grunt of relief. 'I'm glad you approve,' he says. 'For a moment I feared you'd advise me to drive the car from tree to tree.'

'*Dhat*!' Moti considers the prospect and finds it funny. Not only funny but, on second thoughts, disastrous. 'The fruit lying on the grass would be crushed under the tyres,' he declares solemnly. 'And the noise of the engine would scare away the birds, bees and butterflies. They would fly off in panic.'

'Well said,' the old man pats the child on the head. 'Cars are worthless things. That's why I sold mine.' He starts to walk away.

'Except that—'

'Except what?' Sharada turns around and looks sternly at the boy. He doesn't like second thoughts. Moti's head is bent and his eyes are on the earth at his feet. He is scuffling the grass with his big toe. The old man understands. 'Our feet need to feel the sting of hot dust,' he explains gravely, 'and the caress of soft grass. Life isn't worth living without—'

So that's why Dadu doesn't wear shoes, Moti thinks. *Never ever. The king of trees goes barefoot all day.*

They've come out of the cool, green shadows of the

star-apples and are walking under a hard, brassy sky. The sun, at the zenith, is a ball of white-hot flame.

'It's very hot,' Moti mutters.

'This is the month of Jaistha,' the old man smiles, 'the best month of the best season of the year. The sun has to shine hard for the juices of fruits to sweeten.'

'That's true,' Moti murmurs in support of his grandfather's logic. He wipes the perspiration off his forehead with the back of his hand. The grandfather stops in his tracks. The boy stops too. Two pairs of eyes scrutinize each other. Moti sees that the irises of the old man's eyes are losing their dun colour and turning crimson with the heat.

'Where does it feel hottest?' Sharada asks. 'On the head?'

'Y-y-yes.'

'Naturally. The sun is shining right above it.'

Sharada spits—a big, fat, white blob. Moti watches in amazement as the hot dust shrivels it up in an instant and makes it disappear. 'Why don't you take that off,' Sharada points a finger at Moti's shorts, 'and wrap it around your head? You'll feel cooler and more comfortable.'

'*Dhat*!' Moti giggles at the old man's foolishness. 'What nonsense you talk, Dadu! How can I walk naked through the—'

'*I'm a bird/ I'm a cow/ I'm a fox/ I'm an owl/ I can see you*,' the old man sings in a quavering voice. Then, more seriously, he adds, 'Do you see any humans here? Who cares if you're as naked as the day you were born? Besides, the sun up there isn't the one you see in Beadon Street— weak and weary with shining on bricks and mortar, tar and asphalt; sick to near death of the fumes of factory chimneys and engines of trams and buses. Here he shines so bright and fierce that the land cracks into a thousand shards and the water bodies are sucked dry. He'll suck

Jyotirindranath Nandi

your brains dry too if you're not careful. Heed my advice. Take off your shorts and cover your head or else—'

Moti does as he is told. He is very embarrassed at first. His ears flame and his eyes are glued to the ground. Then he thinks, *What the heck! No one is looking at me. Only Dadu. And even he isn't looking. He's walking ahead. There's nothing wrong with*—

'I'm not prudish about shedding my clothes,' Sharada says conversationally. 'It's the best way to keep cool. One of my greatest pleasures on hot, humid afternoons is lying stark naked on the cool grass under the star-apple trees.'

'Does that feel good?'

'Wonderfully good!' Sharada laughs. He sounds like a child. 'A carpet of soft grass whispering against your skin. A canopy of dark-green leaves above you. Shadows flickering over your body—'

'Clothes are silly things,' Moti tries to please his grandfather. 'Years ago when men lived in caves and jungles they didn't know what clothes were.'

'Right,' Sharada agrees enthusiastically. 'People were sensible then. They knew that covering the body makes it hot and sticky and impedes movement.'

'Ma says,' and now Moti blurts out something he had been wanting to say for a long time, '"your Dadu was a big officer, a brilliant engineer. And look at him now. He lives in the country like a peasant."' Moti looks askance at his grandfather and waits, nervously, for a reaction.

'She can say whatever she likes,' Dadu is cool and unfazed. 'It doesn't bother me.'

'Ma was disappointed when you sold your house on Elgin Road.'

'I know that. The problem is that we are two different people—with different tastes and aspirations. She dreams of big houses, cars, clothes and expensive furniture and I of green, swelling meadows, stretches of cool water, trees and shadows . . . '

'Birds, bees, squirrels and insects,' Moti completes the sentence.

'Consequently,' Sharada goes on, 'your parents haven't a clue as to why I stay here. What I receive—' The rest of his speech comes out in a rush. As though the subject is so distasteful he wants it over and done with. 'Let them live on in a sick city, under a rotting sky, and dream of thrones and palaces. Let them fill their lungs with the poisoned fumes of mines and factories. They'll only be ravelling in the ribbon of life inch by inch.' Sharada's features are twisted in a grimace as he turns to his grandson.

'Will they die before you, Dadu?' Moti can't help but ask. 'My father and mother—will they . . . ?'

'The whole city will die,' Sharada sniggers maliciously.

Moti thinks for a moment, then asks worriedly, 'What will happen to the houses? The great big houses with hanging balconies?'

'They'll crumble to pieces and fall on the earth. Not a trace of them will be left.'

'What will happen after that? I mean when all the buildings have disappeared?'

'Grass will grow where they once stood. Flowers will bloom and fruit ripen on trees.'

'That will be wonderful, Dadu!' Moti's eyes shine at the prospect. 'Birds will flit among the leaves. There'll be clouds of butterflies.'

'Yes. That is what will happen. The world changes from time to time. It has to.'

Walking and talking at the same time, old man and boy come to a very pretty spot, a round pool with a sheet of water rippling and sparkling like green glass. Lotus leaves, large and round as *thala*s, are floating lazily on the surface. At one end is a thatch of water lilies. The leaves are shaped differently from the lotus. *They are like betel leaves*, Moti decides. Two bright crimson flowers have pushed their heads from out of a nest of leaves. Some more will bloom tomorrow and a whole host the next day for there are many buds and half-formed blooms standing on strong, taut stems. Grasshoppers flit from leaf to leaf, the green on their gauze wings glittering like emerald dust.

'Why is the lotus not blooming, Dadu?' Moti asks.

'It's the wrong season,' the grandfather replies. 'The monsoon rains nurture the buds and then, with the first clear days of autumn, they burst into bloom. Hundreds and thousands of them.'

Moti's heart lifts at the thought of seeing so many lotus flowers all together.

'Look under the leaves,' the old man pokes the boy in the ribs. 'You'll see fishes bigger than you.'

'Bigger than me!' Moti is startled. 'Then they must be very old! Is old fish good to eat, Dadu?'

Sharada is pleased at his grandson's interest in food. A warm, benign light shines in his eyes. 'Fresh fish is good to eat,' he replies. 'Old or young—it doesn't matter.'

Moti knows his grandfather is very fond of fish and eats tremendous amounts of it. Not one or two pieces like the people of Beadon Street. He sits twice each day in front of a thala full of rice surrounded by bowls and bowls of fish. Fried fish, stewed fish, fish cooked with vegetables and simmered in rich hot gravies! His grandmother hovers around while he eats and ladles some more into the bowls as soon as they are emptied. Sharada had informed Moti only yesterday that he had two ponds and a lake brimming over with fish. 'There's no food superior to fish,' he says now. 'Even the doctor in Beadon Street will tell you that.

Fish oils keep colds and fevers away. Why do you think doctors prescribe cod liver oil for weak, run-down people?'

'Hmm . . . '

'I've never needed cod liver oil,' the old man announces proudly. 'I eat chunks of fish, fried crackling crisp. Masses of them! Enough to frighten away the most intrepid cold.' Lights flare in the dun-coloured eyes at the thought and he swallows the juices that trickle into his mouth. 'I'm frightfully hungry,' he cries out, startling Moti. 'My stomach's making noises. It's calling for food.'

Moti pretends to be surprised. 'You can't be hungry!' he exclaims. 'You've eaten a big bowl of kheer and muri for breakfast. Then all this fruit . . . '

'I *am* hungry,' the old man growls. 'My stomach isn't the size of an allopathic capsule like yours. It's a barrel.'

Moti bursts out laughing. Sharada glances at the sky and says, 'It's nearing lunchtime. The fish must have been netted and sent home an hour ago. I told the fishermen I wanted chital today—huge, fierce, silvery chital from the pond in the north of the estate. Your Thakurma must have started cooking the *kalia*.'

'It is possible.'

'What do you mean by that? I know for a certainty that the old woman is cooking a kalia and—'

'I suppose you can smell it from here.'

'Of course I can. I can see it too. Fat wedges of chital simmering in red-hot gravy.'

Moti crinkles his eyes at his grandfather. The roles appear to have reversed. Moti has become the adult, his grandfather the child—a naughty, wilful, greedy child. The ribbon of life! Moti nods his head solemnly with his newly acquired wisdom.

'Are we going home then?'

'Yes. I have to go home the moment my stomach calls out for rice. Nothing else, nowhere else, for me then.'

'I thought we would see the pineapples,' Moti is teasing his grandfather now. 'And maybe the guava orchard after that.'

'The guavas are like stone nuggets. Even the bats don't go near them during this season. Wait for some more rain and then—'

Moti nods as though satisfied with this reasoning. Sharada unties the gamchha from his waist and hands it to the boy. It is heavy with fruit. 'These are for your grandmother,' he explains. 'The old woman won't sink her teeth into a single fruit I haven't picked for her myself. She turns sullen if . . . You may eat one or two, of course, if you like. Go sit in the shade of the myrobalan, child! It's cool and dark there.' Moti is glad to obey. He sinks on his haunches under the spreading branches of an ancient myrobalan tree. He wonders how long the tree has been standing there, looking down into the green water of the pool. But what is his grandfather doing? He has taken off his belt and is fumbling with the buttons of his shorts.

'Dadu . . . are you . . . ?' Moti cries out in panic.

'I'm taking a couple of dips.' The old man drops his shorts on the grass and stands, naked, ready to dive into the pond. 'I can sit down to my fish and rice as soon as I reach home without wasting time on a bath.' Sharada's voice is muffled, for he's already in the water. Moti's heart beats in a strange kind of way. Is it fear he feels or fascination? 'If this had happened in Maniktala or Sealdah,' he mutters to himself, 'where there are lots of people, shops, cars, trams, policemen . . . I would have thought he was a lunatic!' Moti had seen a lunatic once. Sitting in a tram on his way to his aunt's house he had seen, from the window, a completely unclothed man walking along the tramline. 'Lunatic! Lunatic!' People had jeered and laughed. Moti had laughed too. But now . . .

Moti averts his head and swallows nervously. Then, picking up courage, he turns his eyes on the pool. The old man's long, lean body is cleaving the water with neat, easy strokes. Sharada sees the expression in the boy's face and laughs. Then he ducks his head and disappears. One, two, three . . . Moti counts. There's no sign of his grandfather. But there's a rustling in the lotus leaves and a quivering among the lily pads that tell him he's down there. Moti stares into the water and wonders how long the old man's breath will hold. Suddenly a wild, sweet wind blows from who knows where and sets the leaves of the myrobalan dancing. A white cloud darts across the sun and hangs clinging to the edge of the sky. From somewhere in the jungle of reeds beyond the pool an egret calls. *Crik*! A kingfisher dives into the water with a shriek of triumph and comes up in an instant with a silver disc in his beak. Then, spreading his blue-green wings, he flies into the white-hot sky.

Moti feels terribly terribly happy. Taking a roseapple from the gamchha he pops it in his mouth. *Dadu has picked all this fruit for Thakurma*, he thinks. *It's his present for her. Baba brings presents for Ma from time to time. Boxes of snow and cream, tins of powder. Not star-apples and pineapples, mangoes or roseapples. No . . . never*. Moti sighs. He stands up and realizes, for the first time, that he, too, is naked. He's been naked ever since Dadu told him to take off his shorts and wrap it around his head to ward off the sun. Well, he is in the shade now and should be wearing his shorts. But he doesn't wish to. No—not in the least. He had loved the dark-blue shorts when Baba had bought it for him from College Street. But now he eyes it with distaste. *Clothes are useless things*, he says to himself. *They only make clutter and* . . . He longs to dive into the pool and float lazily over the cool water, his limbs brushing against the feathery fronds of the reeds and the papery edges of lotus leaves. But he dare not. He doesn't know how to swim.

A bird comes screeching across the pool and settles in a branch of the myrobalan. Its agitated cries fill Moti's ears but his eyes are on the water, on his grandfather's head to be precise. It bobs up and down, up and down, in an effort to, Moti is convinced, catch a glimpse of the large fish that lurk under the lily thatch. Who knows but he might grab one by the gills and bring it, threshing and struggling, to the surface, then fling it on the bank. One who loves fish as much as his grandfather does might well be tempted to do so.

Moti bends down to take another roseapple from the gamchha when he hears a laugh that startles him out of his skin. It seems to come from behind the myrobalan tree. Wheeling round he sees a girl standing by a thicket of cane. Her mouth is full of cane berries and she holds a spray of them in her hand. Her eyes sparkle like black jewels. *Her body*, Moti thinks, *is like a basak stem*. Dark and slender, taut and full of sap. It sways this way and that as she laughs, just as a black basak sways and shivers with every gust of wind.

Moti's ears flame with embarrassment. He knows why she's laughing. Quick as lightning he pulls on his shorts. 'Ei!' he turns on the girl and asks roughly. 'What are you staring at? What do you want?'

'Nothing. I'm only eating a cane berry.'

'*A* cane berry! You're eating a whole bunch!' Moti hisses at the girl. He is very angry and is perspiring furiously. The girl's sari is torn and as black with dirt as her body. But her teeth are surprisingly white. As white as the belly feathers of a crane. Looking at the shining, smiling teeth he feels a bit better. Suddenly his eyes fall on his grandfather's shorts, lying innocently on the grass, and his heart sinks. He knows the old man is swimming naked in the pool. What if he decides his bath is over and comes wading up to the bank?

'Ei!' he shouts in panic. The girl has dragged a bulging gunny sack to the trunk of the myrobalan and is making her way to the pool. 'Where are you going?'

'To get a drink of water.'

'What's in your sack?'

'Dead leaves.'

Moti stoops and examines the contents of the sack. There are two pineapples lurking among the leaves. Large pineapples newly cut, with sap dripping fresh from the severed stems.

'Where did you find them?'

The girl is scared at first. Bright black irises shift this way and that, revealing the whites of her eyes. Then she laughs. 'From Rajababu's orchard,' she waves a hand in the direction of the pool.

Rajababu! Moti is flummoxed. But the very next minute he knows whom she means. 'Rajababu will whip the skin off your back,' he tells her severely. 'Stealing pineapples! And they aren't even ripe!'

But the girl is unfazed. 'He won't,' she says with another flash of those crane-feather teeth. 'I eat fruit from his orchards all the time. He doesn't say a word.' Her head sways from the nape of her neck like a flower from a stalk and her nostrils quiver like its calyx. 'And now I'll drink my fill of sweet water from Rajababu's pool.' Swinging her slim hips she walks across the grass and stands by the water's edge. Moti looks on in horror. His teeth are clenched and his face is ashen. 'Dadu!' he wants to shout, to warn his grandfather. He opens his mouth but no sound comes. Terror, anger, hate, sorrow and bewilderment wash over his little heart in waves. His grandfather was neither a child nor a madman. He was a responsible adult. Sharada Ray, one-time eminent engineer and class-one officer with a huge, beautiful house in Elgin Road, had changed; had become an animal, a loathsome, frightening animal with no sense of right and wrong.

A trill of laughter breaks the silence of the woods. Moti raises his eyes. Sharada is standing in waist-deep water and the girl is laughing and pointing at something. Moti looks carefully. No, nothing is visible below the waist. Not even the navel. Moti swallows. A dry nervous swallow. Suddenly a gust of wind whips the leaves of the myrobalan and sets them quivering. There's a rustle among the reeds and the egret calls again. The white cloud clinging to the horizon is spreading over the sky in little wisps of silvery fluff. But Moti can't see or hear any of it. His eyes, ears, heart, mind and soul are fixed on the figure that stands smiling in the water.

Dadu is talking to the girl. He's moving his head, moving his lips and laughing with her. The girl sits down on the bank and dangles her feet in the water. She looks as though she is ready to sit there for a long time.

Arré Arré. Is Dadu making his way to the bank? Moti's heart misses a beat. If he comes just a little closer . . . didn't he just see a flash of Dadu's belly, the white hair around the navel glistening with tiny clinging drops? A shiver runs down Moti's spine. He can't breathe. He can't even swallow. Then, suddenly, he is calm again. Dadu has slipped back into the water. Only his head is visible. It is making its way to the lily pads. Relief washes over Moti's spirit in waves. He knows what his grandfather is doing. He's picking the crimson lilies for the girl.

Flowers in his hand Sharada dives into the water and disappears. He comes up in a few minutes. His head bobs up and down quite close to the bank. Moti shivers in apprehension. But no—the water is still up to his neck and his chin is resting on the waves. Lifting a muscular arm, Sharada flings the flowers on the grass. The girl picks them up. Then, wrenching them off the thick sappy stems, she tucks the lilies in her hair. The red petals quiver with ecstasy and dust their pollen on her blue-black hair. Bending her lithe body with a swift movement she drinks the water in palmfuls. Then, walking over to the myrobalan tree, she heaves the sack on to her hip and vanishes into the cane thicket.

Moti stares at the girl's departing back and heaves a sigh of relief. 'Good riddance,' he mutters. Turning to his grandfather he cries out, is able to cry out, 'Isn't it time you came out of the water, Dadu?'

'Yes,' the old man nods. 'Yes. It is time.' From the jungle of reeds beyond the pool the egret calls. Insistent. Passionate. The wisps of cloud are no longer floating like feathers in the sky. They have come together in the form of a lotus. A cloud lotus! Silver white, wondrous in its dazzling beauty. Moti's heart is filled with rapture. He beams at his grandfather as he climbs up the bank. Sharada's naked body is glistening wet. Water is dripping from his ears, fingers and the tip of his nose. *Dadu is like a tree*! Moti thinks. A tree that has lain embedded in the green, subterranean depths of the pool for ages and just been released into the light and air. The damp hair on his chest and belly is like moss, white-brown velvety moss clinging to a rugged trunk. Water dribbles from the moss in gleaming droplets and falls on the grass. The leaves of the myrobalan nudge one another, hiss and whisper.

Sharada pulls on his shorts and ties the belt firmly at his waist. Moti picks up the bundle of fruit. 'The water of this pool is wonderfully cold,' the old man says to the boy as they walk. 'Once in, you don't feel like coming out.'

'I have a feeling,' the boy says, 'Thakurma has finished cooking the kalia and is waiting for us.'

Sharada doesn't respond. He walks on, silent, as though in deep contemplation. His eyes are fixed on an insect with bright, red wings whirring close to his brow.

'Dadu . . .'

'Yes, child.'

'The girl stole two pineapples. They were in her sack.'

'Hunh!' Sharada laughs, a gentle mellow sound. 'She'll eat them, tart as they are, with salt and chillies no doubt.' His eyes are fixed on the red wings. 'Let her eat all she wants,' he murmurs. 'There are more than a thousand pineapples in my orchard this year.'

Moti sighs.

'Bats and caterpillars,' the old man goes on, softly, as though speaking to himself. 'Birds and squirrels eat all they want. Why shouldn't she? I have a lot so that all may have their fill.' He places a hand on Moti's shoulder.

Moti listens quietly. His legs are weary with all the walking but his mind is alive, wonderfully alive. He senses something within himself that wasn't there before. A soaring excitement, a restlessness, a strange tension akin to ecstasy. His grandfather's warm, wet hand is on his shoulder. He can smell the skin. Does it smell of fish? Of kheer? Of mangoes, roseapples, star-apples? No . . . no. Of water? Moss? No . . . not even any of those. Of what then? His mind threshes about, seeking an answer. Suddenly he has it, and happiness surges through his heart. The old man's skin smells cool and sweet. Of water lilies. Tender, moist, fragrant water lilies.

Moti understands. But only in part. He needs to know something else. Only then will his understanding be complete. In order to stretch the ribbon of life is it necessary to carry the perfume of lilies on one's person? He shakes his head perplexedly. His mind searches, eager and restless, as his feet walk on.

Jyotirindranath Nandi

Sap

Ras

Narendranath Mitra

Towards the beginning of November, Motalef began work on the grove of date palms that was the property of the Chowdhuris. This was the seasonal draining of the trunks of their clear sweet sap. Then, within a fortnight, he married and brought home Majukhatoon, the widow of his neighbour Razek Mirdha. The people of the village were astounded! Of course, this wasn't Motalef's first marriage—his previous wife had died two years ago. Yet, for a fine sturdy young man of twenty-five or twenty-six to choose as a bride a woman who was nearly thirty was strange, to say the least. It was true that Majukhatoon had no responsibilities to bother Motalef. She had an only daughter, whom she had wedded early into the family of the Sheikhs at Kathikhali. But, if she had no liabilities, she had no assets either. It wasn't as if her husband had left her boxes spilling over with silver and gold, or fields groaning with paddy. All she had were a few yards of bare earth on which stood a tottering little hut. And in looks she was no houri either. Except for the strong, healthy body that generally accompanies the clacking tongue of an arrogant female, Majukhatoon, it seemed to the village, possessed nothing that could lure a male and captivate him.

The women of the Sikdar and Kazi families were loud in their comments. 'She has put a spell on him,' they laughed. 'She has thrown dust in his eyes,' they said. Which meant that they believed a person's vision could be changed by means of secret incantations. 'Serves him right,' said Sakina, the youngest of the Munshi daughters-in-law. 'When Allah made his eyes, he must have forgotten to put the lids in. Have you not seen the way he squints at all the women? If she has thrown dust in his eyes he deserves it, the shameless one!'

She was not wrong. Motalef's glance went naturally askew when it came to women. His eyes seemed always on the lookout for a pretty face. To bring home a young beautiful bride had been his ardent desire, but he had never been able to afford the expense, for the price of a pretty girl ranged anything between a hundred and a hundred-and-fifty rupees. Of all the girls he had seen so far, he had been most attracted to Phoolbanu, the eighteen-year-old daughter of Elem Sheikh of Charkanda. She had been married the year before to Gafur Sikdar of the village of Koidubi, but had taken a divorce on grounds of cruelty. The truth was that Phoolbanu, whose head brimmed over with romantic dreams and whose body was voluptuous with the sap of youth, disliked her plain, elderly husband and picked up quarrels with him on the slightest pretext. However, not being a virgin did not lessen her charms. If anything, it heightened the lustre of her skin and brightened the sparkle of her eyes.

One evening, Motalef met Phoolbanu accidentally by the river bank of Charkanda, and Motalef saw in one glance that she was attracted to him as well. After all, he was quite handsome too, his body fair and slim in his blue lungi. And he had a wonderful head of wavy black hair, the likes of which was not to be found in a dozen

Narendranath Mitra

villages. Seeking out Phoolbanu's father, Motalef placed a proposal of marriage before him. But Elem turned a deaf ear. He had, he said, learnt from his experience, and never again would he give his daughter in marriage to a stranger, especially one without money. As Motalef rightly guessed, Elem wanted to make good the loss incurred in the divorce. And it was no small sum he wanted either. Not twenty, not forty, but a full hundred rupees.

Where was Motalef to find such a large amount? Morose and depressed, he was returning to his own village when he saw Phoolbanu making her way to the river bank, her water pot balanced provocatively on one hip. Glancing furtively around her, Phoolbanu gave a little giggle. 'Why Mian, surely you aren't going away?'

'What else can I do? Have you not heard of your father's absurd demand?'

'Of course I have,' was Phoolbanu's calm reply, 'but, if you must have something you like, mustn't you pay for it?'

'Oh! So the greed is not the father's, but the daughter's. If you are so expensive, why don't you go to the market in a basket, and set yourself up for sale?'

Motalef's anger amused Phoolbanu. 'Why in a basket?' she laughed. 'I shall sit on the scales and you shall weigh me against handfuls of gold and jewels. How else can I judge the size of your fist? How else can you prove your worth as a man?'

Motalef turned and walked away rapidly. 'Wait, wait, O handsome Mian. Listen to me,' Phoolbanu called after him. Motalef turned his head, sulky and petulant. Looking this way and that, Phoolbanu came closer. 'Listen to my heart,' she said, 'my father's daughter cares neither for money nor jewels. She only wants her lover to recognize her true worth, pay it and claim her with his head held high. Do you understand?' Motalef nodded as if he understood at last. 'But don't do anything rash,' cautioned Phoolbanu. 'Don't go selling your lands and fields.'

As a matter of fact, Motalef had no lands or fields to sell, but he was not going to disclose the truth. He said instead, 'Let the winter pass and I'll show you the size of my fist. I will prove to you my worth as a man. But will my beautiful Bibijan have the patience to wait and see?'

'She will,' was Phoolbanu's reply.

Returning to the village, Motalef tried to raise the money, but drew a blank everywhere—at the Sikdars, the Mallicks, the Mukherjees and the Munshis. The truth was that, having borrowed money, Motalef seldom bothered to return it voluntarily. It was always a nuisance getting it back from him. But though he got no money, he got a contract for draining about a hundred date palms as soon as winter set in. Half the sap would be his, half the owner's. Draining a tree was no easy job. The dead branches must be lopped off and cleared away, one by one. The special knife must be sharpened till it gleamed. Then, with its razor-sharp edge, the tip of the palm must be gently sliced away, a thin bamboo tube inserted, and a large earthen pot securely fastened so that the sap would trickle into it, drop by clear amber drop, through the long winter night. The drawing of sap is not like the drawing of mother's milk, which needs but a mouth to suckle. It is hard labour. And labour is not enough. It is an art that not many can master. The same blade that draws a jet of fiery blood when touched to the limb of a man coaxes a sweet liquid out of a gnarled old palm. But the tapper must be careful not to hurt the tree. He must caress while he cuts. A little carelessness and within a year the trunk will be fit only for sawing into logs. Never again will sweet juice trickle from it in melting drops. Never again will it fill a pot to overflowing.

Motalef had learnt the art from the master tapper, Razek Mirdha, renowned for his skill in three villages. Palms that were no more than deadwood came to life at the touch of Razek's hand. Ones that yielded only half a measure of juice when handled by others of the trade filled the pot when cut by Razek. Motalef had been his apprentice for a number of years. Not that he was the only one. There was Maqbool, of the Sikdars, and Ishmail, of the Kazis, eager to learn the art. But Motalef had been Razek's prized pupil. It was to him that Razek had taught all the nuances and given of his best, and on Razek's death a year ago, it was Motalef who had taken his place. He had become the acknowledged successor and to him fell the contracts that were once his master's.

However, draining trunks by the score and carrying home pots heavy with juice is not enough. The tapper needs a woman who can boil the juice till it thickens into firm cakes of fragrant molasses. This too is an art requiring long hours of labour, of crouching by roaring fires from dawn till dusk. Sap, after all, is worthless till it is transformed first into molasses, and then into money. Unfortunately, just such a woman was what Motalef lacked. His mother had died early in his youth—his wife two years ago.

A little after twilight, Motalef came and stood outside Majukhatoon's dilapidated hut.

'Are you awake, Majubibi?'

'Yes . . . who is it?'

'I am Motalef. Will you take the trouble to open the door? I have something to say.'

Majukhatoon appeared in the doorway. 'I can guess what you have to say. The sap season is here, and you need me to make the molasses. But this time you must pay me a quarter to a rupee. Not a pie less, Mian. I am sick in my limbs this winter.'

'Why blame the limbs, Bibi?' Motalef said sweetly. 'They do what the heart tells them. If the heart is happy, the limbs are healthy.'

'Well, whatever you say—not a pie less than a quarter.'

Motalef's smile became wider. 'Why only a quarter? If I offer you the whole, will you take it, Bibi?'

Something in his manner made Majukhatoon's heart beat fast, but she answered indifferently. 'Don't talk in riddles, Mian. If you really have something to say, do so, else let me go and sleep.'

'The night is meant for sleeping,' Motalef continued in the same vein, 'but when the heart is heavy the eyes will not shut, and the winter night is long.'

Now Motalef stopped beating about the bush and told Majukhatoon what he had actually come for. He would not, he said, compromise her in any way. He would send for the mullah, and they would go through a formal nikah after which she would be mistress of his home and heart. Majukhatoon was first astonished, then annoyed.

'I don't like your silly jokes, Mian,' she said. 'Is there a dearth of young women in the village that you should come to me?'

'Why should there be a dearth, Bibi? There are many, but all said and done, a young woman is no better than a pot of raw sap.'

Majukhatoon was amused at his comparison. 'Really?' she laughed, 'and what about me?'

'You!' replied Motalef, 'you are the molasses that satisfies a man's hunger. You are the toddy that intoxicates him.'

After Motalef had gone, Majukhatoon lay awake on her bed, her eyes staring in the dark. Her heart beat heavy and fast. Motalef was no stranger. They had known each

Narendranath Mitra

other from the time that he had been her husband's apprentice but, apart from a few pleasantries, nothing had passed between them. Nothing had been possible either, for Motalef had a wife and Majukhatoon a husband—a harsh, domineering, elderly man who filled her yard each winter with scores of pots brimming with date sap that had to be cooked into cakes of golden molasses. There was magic in Majukhatoon's touch. Her molasses sold at a rate two pice to a rupee higher than anyone else's in the market. Then Razek died, and all the date palms of the village passed to Motalef. Last winter she had been boiling the sap for him at two annas to a rupee but within a month he started suspecting her of stealing his goods and selling them secretly. There was a quarrel and the deal was off. This winter, Motalef had come up with a new proposal. It was not to bring his pots of juice to her yard, but to take her as his bride to his own.

A few evenings later, Majukhatoon, wearing a blue spangled sari and glass bangles on her arms, followed Motalef meekly to her new home. Dirt and confusion met her everywhere but she was undaunted. Tucking the edge of her sari at the waist, Majukhatoon picked up a broom and began sweeping out the piles of rubbish that had collected in the yard. She swept and swabbed the floors till they were smooth and clean. But Motalef had no time either for wife or home. Like a bird he flitted from tree to tree, slicing the tips, fixing the tubes, dividing the juice and bringing in his share of brimming pots. He had built a shed of jute stalks in the western corner of his yard in which a row of clay ovens burned. At these Majukhatoon worked from early dawn till late afternoon, tending the fires and stirring the boiling juice. Then she roamed the jungles for dried branches and fronds. At dusk, she sat chopping them into faggots. Her limbs were unwearied, her heart was light. After an age, it seemed to her, she had been given the work she loved, and a husband after her own heart.

Motalef took the molasses she made each day to the market and sold it at the highest price, for his were the prized goods of the season. At dusk, he went back to his trees. After the tapper removes his pot of juice in the morning, he fixes a bamboo funnel in its place. And into the funnel drips a thick opaque liquid that is the tree's yield through the day. In the evening the funnel is removed, the tree sliced afresh, and the pot fixed once again. The darkish substance obtained during the day is not wasted either. It is boiled into a sticky treacle, which is used to sweeten tobacco and is sold in the market at five or six annas a seer. Climbing over a hundred trees twice a day made Motalef's breath come in heavy gasps and his body stream with sweat, even in the bitter cold of January. The early dawn saw Motalef out among his palms, beads of sweat gleaming on his hairy chest like the dewdrops on the grass at his feet. Looking at him the villagers murmured in amazement to one another. It was true that Motalef was not an idle man, and draining a palm was his natural vocation. Yet, had anyone seen him work so feverishly before? Could it be that at last he had the wife of his choice under his roof? A wife he wanted to care for and give everything that money could buy?

One day, Motalef took three cakes of molasses and two pots of his best sap to Elem Sheikh of Charkanda. Placing them at his feet, he took out five crackling ten-rupee notes from a pouch at his waist. 'I give you half in advance, Mian Saheb,' he said.

'Advance for what?' Elem asked, surprised.

'Your daughter,' murmured Motalef.

Narendranath Mitra

'What is the use of bringing the money now?' Elem stroked the notes with a loving hand. 'I hear you are married to Razek Mirdha's widow. Why should my daughter live with a co-wife? Only to quarrel and scream at each other day and night?'

Motalef gave a sheepish smile. 'Don't worry on that account, Mian Saheb. While winter lasts and the sap is still running in the palms—only till then will Majukhatoon remain under my roof. With the first breeze of spring, everything old and ugly will be swept away.'

Elem Sheikh pushed a stool towards Motalef and put the hookah into his hands. 'You have brains, Mian,' he complimented. 'It is a pleasure to talk to you.'

Motalef met Phoolbanu for a brief moment on his way back. She had heard everything and understood the implications, but that didn't prevent her from pouting her full red lips at him. 'Who has turned out to be the impatient one, Mian?' she grumbled. 'Here I have been, waiting and waiting.'

'What could I do?' asked Motalef.

And indeed—what could he have done? A man needs a woman to give him the food and drink that sustains life, to boil the sap and make the molasses that can be converted into money to save his honour.

'Well, you have saved both your life and your honour,' taunted Phoolbanu, 'but what about her smell that is going to stick to your body after she has gone.'

Motalef was about to tell her that smells are not permanent. If so her body would also be reeking of Gafur Sikdar. He said instead, 'Don't let that worry you, Phooljan. We will sit on the river bank side by side, and you can scrub my body with soap and soda till all the foul odours vanish.'

Phoolbanu pressed the edge of her sari to her mouth and giggled. 'Really!' she said.

'Why not?' answered Motalef. 'Smell me after that and see if a new woman's new fragrance doesn't come wafting from my limbs. The south wind will be sweet with the scent of flowers, with the scent of your hair. Only be patient with me. Give me another two months.'

Phoolbanu assured him that she would wait.

Motalef was as good as his word. Phoolbanu did not have to wait long. The day he was able to put together another fifty rupees from the sale of his molasses, Motalef divorced Majukhatoon. He even told the neighbours why, loudly and clearly. Majubibi was a woman of loose morals. He did not like her relationship with her brother-in-law, Wahed Mirdha. Majukhatoon bit her tongue in shame and horror. 'Au! Au!' she cried, 'your face is beautiful, Moti Mian, but not your heart. So much evil is in you! Such treachery and deception! During the sap season you stuck to me like an ant, and now that it is over you drive me away like a dog.'

But Motalef had neither the time nor the patience to listen to her. The first warm breezes were turning the mango trees into globes of blossom. The branches of the *gab* were velvety with copper-coloured leaves. After winter came spring. After Majukhatoon came Phoolbanu—her face like a flower, her breath laden with the scent of petals. The neighbours all agreed that at last Motalef had brought home a suitable bride. 'What a beautiful pair!' they exclaimed. 'How she brightens up his home!'

Motalef had never been happier in his life. All day he worked hard as a farmhand on other people's land. In the evenings, he came home and made love to Phoolbanu. 'Let your cooking and housework be,' he would coax, tugging at her sari. 'Come and sit with me for a while.'

'Wait, wait,' Phoolbanu would laugh. 'How did you pass the winter months, Mian?'

'With the date trees,' was Motalef's unfailing reply. Breathless in his powerful embrace, Phoolbanu would gasp, 'Go back to your trees, Mian. A tapper's love is too much for me.'

'Sap runs in the trees only in the winter months, Bibi. But, the juice from your lips trickles sweet and fragrant through all the seasons, months and years.'

Majukhatoon was back in her little hut, trying to live out her days as of old. But it wasn't easy. The nights in particular were long and bitter. The neighbours were forever dropping in with accounts of Motalef's new wife and his passion for her. 'He is going crazy, the poor fellow,' they said. 'Crazy with love for his wife.' Majukhatoon's breast burned with impotent fury. She thought she would go raving mad with jealousy, that her heart would burst out of her lungs and kill her.

Moved with pity for her state, her brother-in-law, Wahed Mirdha, brought a proposal of marriage with Nadir Sheikh, a friend of his who lived across the river at Talkanda. Nadir was a boatman whose wife had died a month ago. He needed a woman who could look after his home and many children. A young girl would be of no use to him. She would be forever thinking of her youth and beauty, and would neglect the children. A middle-aged, sensible, hardworking woman was what he needed. A woman he could depend upon.

'How old is he?' Majukhatoon asked.

'About my age,' Wahed answered, 'fifty or fifty-one.'

Majukhatoon nodded. Yes, that was about the right age. She had no faith left in youth. Then Majukhatoon put another question. 'He is not a tapper, is he?'

'No, he is a boatman,' Wahed said in a surprised tone. 'He knows nothing about sap or trees. But why, Bou? Have you decided not to marry anyone who is not a tapper?'

'On the contrary,' answered Maju, 'I will marry a man only if he has nothing to do with draining trees and selling molasses. I am sick of the whole business.'

'Shall I talk to Nadir, then? He does not wish to wait long.'

'Where is the need for waiting?' Majukhatoon said.

A few days later, Majukhatoon sat with Nadir Sheikh in his boat and crossed the river to Talkanda.

'Thank Allah she's gone!' exclaimed Motalef. 'Weeping and sighing and cursing like a witch next to our doorstep. A good riddance! What do you say, Phooljan?'

Phoolbanu's laughter tinkled like silver bells. 'You are afraid of her, aren't you?'

'No. I am not afraid any more,' answered Motalef. 'Not now that the witch has vanished. Now, to open the eyes is to see a fairy. I am afraid of the fairy.'

'Why should you be afraid?' Phoolbanu asked, surprised.

'Because she may spread her wings and fly away any moment.'

'No, Mian,' Phoolbanu said seriously. 'The fairy has no need to fly, now that she has everything she wants. She is content. As long as her husband does not change.'

'While I have eyes to see, I cannot change,' answered Motalef.

Never were love and affection showered on a woman as Motalef showered on Phoolbanu. He would buy her favourite fish at the weekly *haat*, even if he had to borrow the money to do so. Eggs, vegetables, betel leaf and nuts he bought in abundance. 'Why do you buy so much betel when you don't eat any?' Phoolbanu grumbled at times.

'You keep puffing at your hookah, bhuruk, bhuruk, all day long.'

'The betel is for you,' Motalef would reply, 'to chew day and night and redden your lips.'

'Are my lips not red enough?' Phoolbanu would pout. 'Your lips have gone black with tobacco. You should take to eating betel.'

'A man's lips are not reddened with betel, Phooljan, but with the juice of a woman's betel-stained mouth,' was Motalef's answer.

Motalef had no land of his own. He worked as a sharecropper in the fields of the Mukherjees and the Mallicks. But Motalef was not a good hand at farming. The plots he tilled were small in comparison with those of others and the yield low. To eke out a living, he worked as a farmhand in the jute fields of the Sikdars and the Munshis. Weeding the fields, cutting the jute, soaking the plants, then putting them out to dry was all very hard work, and turned his fair skin to a dark tan in the burning sun. Not much of the jute he grew came home to his own yard. The Sikdars and Munshis paid him in cash. Only the Mallicks and the Mukherjees gave him a share of the jute that he grew in about four bighas of their land. Phoolbanu loved combing out the jute, but Motalef would not let her touch it. 'It is hard work,' he would say. 'Your hands will stink.'

'Let them stink,' Phoolbanu would answer with spirit. 'You work so hard in the hot sun. Why can't I do some work too? You talk a lot of nonsense, Mian.'

Towards the middle of October, when the paddy ripened, Motalef helped in the harvesting. Rowing out in a boat, he would wade waist deep in the water, cutting the paddy and binding and lifting the sheaves. But his shears would not move half as fast as those of Momin,

Karim, Hamid and Aziz. Motalef's hands were slow, his body heavy and clumsy in the water. Some days his back and underarms would be pitted with leeches.

Plucking them out with tender fingers, Phoolbanu would cover the spots with lime. 'Where were your hands, Mian?' she would scold. 'Why didn't you pull them out yourself?'

'The hands that were cutting the corn were with me, but the hands that had to pull out the leeches were left at home,' Motalef would reply.

Threshing the paddy he had cut, he would bring home his share to Phoolbanu, who would put it out to dry, then winnow it in flat bamboo trays.

'It is very hard work,' Motalef would murmur. 'You are straining yourself, Phoolbanu.'

'Who do you think you are talking to, Mian?' Phoolbanu would ask. 'Am I not a farmer's daughter? Or do you really believe I have come flying from the sky?'

After spring, came summer, and after the rains, autumn. And now winter was here once again—the season of sap, the season of Motalef's love. The cold was somewhat delayed this year, but Motalef decided to make good the loss by increasing the number of contracts. A good thirty date trees were added to his last year's quota, and he fell to work with feverish energy. Gone was the time for rest and relaxation, for teasing and making love to Phoolbanu. All day he worked like a demon, and no sooner did his head touch the pillow at night than he slept the sleep of the dead. Phoolbanu shook him with all her might, embracing his body with all the force of her warm young arms, but it wasn't a man she held, but the trunk of one of Motalef's own trees, stiff and unyielding to her touch. Under the thick cotton *kantha*, Phoolbanu shivered, yearning for the warmth of her husband's body against her own in the bitter winter night.

Along with dozens of sap-filled pots, Motalef filled his yard each morning with large branches of dry wood and piles of leaves and straw. 'Boil the sap,' he told Phoolbanu. 'Make the molasses as sweet and fragrant as yourself—the best and most sought after in the market.' But looking at the size and number of pots, Phoolbanu's face turned pale. Her heart beat rapidly. It was not that she had never made molasses. She had on one or two occasions, but never before had she even seen sap in such large quantities, let alone been told to cook it. Motalef laughed at her panic-stricken look. 'Don't be afraid,' he said, 'it is very easy. Only remember that the fire must burn as brightly and the juice bubble and froth as continuously as the passion in your breast.'

But sitting by the row of ovens from dawn till dusk, Phoolbanu's life force burned dimmer and dimmer—as low as the fires she tended. The sap simmered dully in the pots. The molasses was sometimes soft and sticky, sometimes burnt and bitter.

'What sort of a woman are you?' Motalef scolded her in harsh tones. 'I take so much trouble to teach you, but you learn nothing. What sort of stuff is this? Who do you think will buy it?'

Phoolbanu tried to smile. 'If you know how to sell, people will surely buy.'

But Motalef was not charmed by her smile. 'Then you go to the market and sell it yourself,' he said. 'If you get any customers, it will be for the sake of your pretty face—not for the quality of your wares.'

Now Phoolbanu was neither unintelligent nor lazy. Within a few days she learnt to make molasses after a fashion, but it was not of the quality that Motalef had sold the previous year. His old customers looked askance at his basket and said, 'What has happened to you this year, Mian? Last winter your molasses were the best in the market. The taste of it clings to the tongue to this day, but what you sold at last week's haat was very disappointing. Chhadan Sheikh's and Madan Sikdar's molasses are better than yours this time.'

Motalef's breast heaved with shame and indignation. Why? Why were his goods not selling as they always did? Why were his customers not happy? Why did he have to be flooded with so many taunts and criticisms? Was he not working as hard as he always did? Once again, at night, he tried to explain the process to Phoolbanu. 'When the molasses is ready for pouring, it should fall in a stream from the spoon,' he began, but Phoolbanu cut him short, saying irritably, 'Yes, yes I know. Now stop jabbering and let me sleep.' Suddenly, Motalef thought of Majukhatoon. They had spent so many nights last winter discussing ways to improve the quality of their wares. She had never lost patience, never complained of fatigue or lack of sleep. She had listened eagerly to all his suggestions and agreed with him.

Next day at noon, Motalef came home bearing a heavy load of firewood. Putting it down at the door of the shed he called, 'How is the molasses cooking today, Phoolbanu?' But no answer came from within. Astonished, Motalef looked into the shed. There were five pots of sap boiling in a row, but no sign of Phoolbanu. A queer smell was coming from the southernmost corner. Yes! It was just as he had thought. The molasses was burning in the pot. A wave of pain and fury convulsed Motalef. He called out in a choking scream, 'Where, where are you hiding, you bitch?'

Phoolbanu came running out of the house. She had been so delayed at her work for the last two days that she had had no time for a bath. Feeling sticky and

Narendranath Mitra

uncomfortable, she had left early this morning for the river bank and, rubbing her limbs with a little soap and soda, had taken a quick bath. Back home she had wrapped a blue sari around her and was just combing out her long black hair when she heard Motalef's scream and ran out, comb in hand. Motalef looked at her with burning eyes, then, rushing forward, he grasped her by the thick, wet hair that streamed down her back. 'Disgusting whore!' he screamed. 'Idling all day and preening before the mirror while the molasses burns in the pot. It is because of you that I am shamed before everybody. Insulted by everyone. The whole village is laughing at me.'

Phoolbanu tried to resist. 'Let go of my hair!' she screamed. 'Don't you dare touch me!'

Motalef picked up a strip of bamboo from the yard and, falling upon Phoolbanu, struck her again and again like a madman—on the face, arms, back and chest. A very temperamental man was Motalef. As importunate and unbalanced was his ardour, so overpowering and uncontrolled his rage!

Elem Sheikh came over from Charkanda and settled the quarrel. He scolded and threatened his son-in-law, but was not uncritical of his daughter's conduct. 'Take me home with you, Ba-jan,' Phoolbanu wept. 'I won't stay with this brute any longer.' But Elem was not prepared to do that. A little pampering and Phoolbanu would ask for another divorce. He calmed down his daughter, wiped away her tears, and persuaded her to remain with her husband. A marital quarrel, after all, was nothing to worry about. A couple quarrelled during the day and made up at night.

Elem was not wrong. After a while, Motalef himself made it up to Phoolbanu. And the next morning saw Phoolbanu among her ovens once again, boiling sap. In the late afternoon, Motalef took his basket of molasses to the market, remarking as he left, 'Another two months and you will be free from this heavy labour.'

'It is not all that heavy,' said Phoolbanu.

But these were only words, courteous words that sprang from the lips but did not touch the heart. After all, the language of the heart was not unknown to them. They knew each nuance, recognized all the cadences, the one who spoke as well as the one who listened.

One haat day followed another in weary succession. The season of sap was almost over. Motalef did not recover his lost prestige. His molasses sold at a price lower than others. But he no longer had it in him to quarrel with Phoolbanu. Back home from work he sat listlessly in a corner, puffing at his hookah. Every morning saw him among his trees, taking down his pots of sap—sweet date sap that his skilled fingers had seduced out of gnarled old palms, drop by drop through the dewy winter nights. But there was no thrill in it, none of the joy that had been his only twelve months ago. His body still streamed with sweat, but his heart was as dry as a jute stalk, as stark and empty as the noonday glare. It seemed to him that all the sweetness had gone out of his life, even though scores of pots, brimming over with juice, still filled his yard. Even though a woman's voluptuous form, bursting with sweetness and sap, filled his rooms with a heady fragrance.

One day towards the end of the season, Motalef met Nadir Sheikh of Talkanda at the haat.

'Salaam, Mian Saheb,' he called.

'Walaikum Salaam.'

'Are you well? Are the children well?' Motalef repressed the urge to enquire after Majukhatoon.

Nadir Sheikh gave a wry smile. 'Yes Mian, all are well by Allah's grace.'

Motalef hesitated a little before he said, 'I have good molasses. Why not take some home for the children?'

'Of course, of course,' Nadir smiled politely. 'Your molasses have always been excellent.'

Suddenly, Motalef made a confession. 'No, Mian,' he said, 'those days are gone.'

Nadir was surprised. What sort of trader was this who criticized his own wares? He asked cautiously, 'What is your price?'

Motalef cut him short. 'Don't worry about the price,' he said. 'I am giving you three seers for the children. Tell them their uncle sent it.'

'No, no,' Nadir Sheikh cried out alarmed. 'Why should you give it free and why should I take it?'

But Motalef persisted. 'Take it home this time, Mian. If you insist, pay me next time.'

Even while he said it, he was conscious of acute guilt. Like every year, this year, too, he was using all his trader's guile, praising his wares and pressing them on reluctant customers. The difference was that this time he knew he was lying. He knew his goods were mediocre and that those who bought today would come nowhere near him again.

After a lot of persuasion, Nadir agreed to take one seer of molasses free, but pressed the money for the other two into Motalef's hand.

Majukhatoon was furious when she heard what had happened. 'Give the molasses, if you like, to the children,' she stormed, 'but if I am my father's true daughter, I won't touch them with my foot.'

Several weeks passed by, but Nadir Sheikh avoided Motalef. Majukhatoon had threatened to leave him if he had anything to do with 'that man' as she now called him. Nadir feared Majukhatoon in his heart of hearts. A good worker and a very dependable woman was his wife, but totally uncontrollable when angry.

One morning a few days later, Motalef took two pots of his best sap and crossed by boat over to Talkanda. Walking past a spreading berry tree, he entered Nadir's yard. 'Are you home, Mian?' he called.

Nadir came out, hookah in hand. 'Who is it? Ah! Come in, Mian Saheb. But why these pots of sap?' Nadir's invitation was courteous though he was inwardly apprehensive. He whom Nadir's wife loathed with a venomous hate was here in person. Allah only knew what would happen now.

His fears were not ill founded. Through the curtain of split bamboo that separated the rooms from the yard, Majukhatoon had seen Motalef enter, and now she called her husband in and said in a voice loud enough for her guest to hear: 'Tell him to leave at once. Has he no shame left? How dare he come to my house?'

'Softly, softly!' Nadir whispered urgently. 'Speak a little lower, Bibi. He is a guest in our house. Even a dog or a cat is not driven out like this.'

'You don't understand, Mian,' Majukhatoon cried. 'There are some men who are lower than dogs and cats, more evil than Satan. Ask him why he has brought his date sap to my door. For me to drink? Does he have no fear left in his heart? Does he have no shame?'

Majukhatoon was not speaking softly. Motalef heard every word she uttered. Yet, surprisingly, her harsh words did not hurt or anger him. It was as if somewhere behind all this cruel abuse lay a touch of sweetness. As if her sharp grating voice and passionate words were releasing something that lay deep down in her heart. A strange sensation overwhelmed Motalef. He felt as if he had, with the tip of his tapper's knife, touched a vulnerable spot in the rough trunk of a tree through which was oozing now, drop by sweet clear drop, the sap of a woman's love.

Placing his pots on the threshold, Motalef called, 'Will you come out for a moment, Mian Saheb?'

Nadir came out, looking abashed. 'Sit down, Mian,' he said. 'Take a puff.'

Motalef took the hookah from Nadir's hand, but did not put it to his lips. He said instead, 'Will you put in a word for me to your wife?'

'Why don't you talk to her yourself, Mian? There's no harm in it.'

'I can't. I have some shame left in me still. You tell her that Motalef Mian did not bring the sap as a gift. He is not that much of a cad.'

Before Nadir could speak, Majukhatoon burst out angrily: 'Then why have you brought it?'

But Motalef continued to use Nadir as his medium. 'Tell her,' he said, 'that I have come to beg her to make some molasses with it which I can sell to some unknown customer at the next haat. I have not sold an anna's worth of real molasses this season. All I have done is climb from tree to tree. All my labour has been in vain.' Motalef's voice choked on the last sentence. He was about to say something more when suddenly, through the slits of the curtain, his eyes fell upon a pair of eyes, large and black and swimming with tears. Motalef looked on in silence. Nothing more was said. Suddenly, Nadir recalled his duties as host.

'Why, Mian,' he said, 'you are not smoking. Is the fire out?'

'No Mian bhai,' answered Motalef, 'it still burns.'

The Crossing

Parhi

Samaresh Basu

The two were without work. They sat idle, staring into space, the man leaning against the short stubby trunk of a leafy banyan tree, the woman curled up at his feet when, suddenly, a herd of animals came tumbling down the high bank, massed close together like a cloud. Grunting, hissing, snorting, snarling, they came—raising whirls of black dust, crushing dead grass and thorny scrub with their sharp hooves . . .

Forests of *ash-sheoda* and *kalkasunda* stretched as far as the eye could see. These were the natives, the aborigines of the land. Here and there, evading the eyes of the former, *peepul* and *pituli* trees and wild drumstick had crept up furtively. But, though trespassers themselves, they kept a stern eye on the shrubs and bushes growing at their feet. The land rose upwards to the north, not straight and steadfast but wavering, erratic, as though hobbling on painful feet. On the highest point above, there stood a factory shack. The rest of the bank was swallowed up in trees. From the west the earth sloped gently down till it merged into the waters of the Ganga.

It was the month of Ashadh—soon after Ambubachi when Mother Earth menstruates for four days, rendering her own body unclean. Only the waters of the Ganga are saved from the pollution of her touch. The Ganga becomes fuller and purer after each Ambubachi. Her waters swell and foam, ripple and dance. She becomes warm and voluptuous, gay and amorous. But though amorous, she isn't abandoned. She resists the mighty pull of the tide till, exhausted with straining against the weight of her own water, she crashes wearily on her banks.

The two sat staring at the river. With the steadily rising tide the water was moving swiftly, coiling and twining upon itself like a gigantic snake. Whirlpools were forming in the water. Small whirlpools—not dangerous to animals or humans. Only stalks, leaves and insects were sucked in, spun crazily around and swallowed without a trace. The river was playing a game. Weary with racing towards the sea it stopped now and then, danced a jig, then went on. Huge black clouds were winging their way across the sky, floating lazily, brushing against the waving tips of ash-sheoda and kalkasunda with quivering delight. From time to time they swooped on the water and, stealing a kiss from the crest of a wave, skimmed gracefully away. Strong winds were massing the ink-blue clouds in vast banks, then, upon a whim, tearing them asunder and sending the fragments flying to the horizon. The two had nothing to do. They sat passively watching river and sky when, suddenly, the sound of rushing hooves made them look up, startled . . .

This side of the Ganga was quiet and secluded. No humans or animals could be seen scurrying past, intent on their own business. Everyone, it seemed, was enjoying a siesta within the four walls of their own dwellings, safe from the brooding, threatening sky. On the other bank, the row of kilns stood idle. The brick-firing season was over. Some fishing boats could be seen drifting lazily over the water but they were few and far between. The two sat alone, facing the turbulent, swirling, orange river. To see them one would think that they had sat there for aeons. Caveman and cavewoman. Dark, shadowy, virgin forests behind them. Above their heads a primeval monsoon sky.

The man was as black as ebony with a harsh unpleasant face. His whiskers, though luxuriant, had a downward droop to them. There was something rough and ruthless about him, in the way he sprawled against the tree, his legs stretched out before him, his feet on the woman's thighs. The girl was dark too. A blurred mass of earth-coloured sindoor filled the parting of her tangled hair. The rag she wore barely covered her breasts and buttocks—the luxurious breasts and buttocks of a full blown woman. Bursting with the sap of youth like the waving tips of the kalkasunda. Naked. Vulnerable. The holes in her nose and ears were naked too. Crying out in deprivation. She pressed her breasts against the man's legs from time to time, scratched the wild tangle of her hair and, picking out the lice, squashed them between her thumbnails.

They had been sitting together under the tree since dawn. They had no work and, consequently, no food. The last time they had eaten was at sunset the day before yesterday. They had worked till last week, then the doors of the 'micipality' had shut in their faces. No work. No food. The strength was ebbing from their limbs. Shadows were darkening under their eyes. Marks of starvation were lining their faces.

The man had worked as a swineherd for Babu Nagin Prasad in the village. He was given no wages. Only food for two. A couple of months ago, his friend Nonku had come to the village. Nonku was head sweeper of the municipality, here, in the city. 'Come with me,' he had said. 'There are jobs in the city and good wages. If both of you work you can earn sixty rupees a month.' Nonku's

Samaresh Basu

chest was puffed up with the importance of his position as he twisted his moustache with an arrogant gesture. Sixty rupees! Baap ré! The man had hastened to agree. He had married only six months ago and was filled with lust for love and life. No fears assailed him. Not a twinge of doubt. 'There's no work a Nuth cannot do,' the villagers said often enough. It was true. Men and women of the Nuth community were known for their skill and intelligence. Besides, he and his wife were young and strong. What had they to fear? Without a word to Nagin Prasad they had slipped out of the village one night, and come to the city . . .

Sixty rupees? No, they hadn't earned that much. Only thirty-two rupees between them. That, too, for only two months. Then, thrown out of work, they were left with nothing except a shack in the sweepers' bustee.

No work. No food. 'Why are they dismissing us?' they cried out to Nonku. 'What have we done?'

'*Ot** is over,' Nonku explained patiently. 'They needed extra hands during *ot*. So they employed you. Now they don't.' He shrugged one shoulder.

'What shall we do?' they asked anxiously. 'What shall we eat?'

'Why do you ask me?' Nonku burst out angrily. Then, all of a sudden, the fire went out of him. His face started working. 'Hai Ram! Hai Ram!' he moaned. 'I've committed a grievous sin.' Striking his forehead with the palm of his hand he cried, 'I'm a son of a pig! A jackal's spawn! A sinner!' The men and women of the bustee came rushing to his side. 'Do not weep, Sardar,' they tried to comfort him. 'You're a good man. You meant well. Don't worry. Something will turn up.'

---

*Rustic mispronunciation of 'vote' or elections.

The two looked on in amazement as Nonku dried his eyes with alacrity and asked his consolers, 'You're sure?'

'Perfectly sure. Rest assured—all will be well.'

The neighbours fed them for seven days. But after that . . .

They had sat here all day yesterday and the whole of today because it was easier to bear hunger here than in the bustee where one looked on, tongue hanging out like a dog's, while others ate. Easier. But not easy. Two days of starvation and they felt the strength ebbing away from their limbs. Thud! Thud! Thud! What was that dull heavy sound? Their hearts or their bellies? They sat close to one another—their bodies touching. In the hope of shared warmth. In the hope of keeping the lifeblood flowing. Touching, smelling, squeezing, licking—they were keeping a terrible fear at bay. Fear that rose from the soles of their feet, turning their thighs and groins, chests and bellies, now to fire and now to ice. Exacerbating this creeping fear, the sky above their heads grew dark and terrible. At their feet the waters of the Ganga were changing colour. Looking like swirls of blood.

The south wind was pulling eastwards, making the river cackle with mirth, as though demented. Pushing their heads through the moist earth, streams of earthworms wriggled their way all around the pair. From the roots of the old banyan tree fiery red ants came rushing towards them in aggressive hordes. The tide had come and gone with a slow ebbing of the waters. Another tide was on its way when the creatures came rushing from the east. Rolling down the hill, like a cloud torn from the inky mass in the sky, they came—dark, obscene beasts with flinty eyes, pointed snouts and sharp thrusting teeth. Reaching level ground they dropped on their haunches and sat, male

Samaresh Basu

and female squashed together, skins touching, tails wiggling, snouts snuffling and snorting.

Frightened by the suddenness of their descent the pair sprang up from where they sat. Behind the swine were two men. One looked plump and well fed. He wore gold rings in his ears and had two gold teeth gleaming in the front of his mouth. The herd of swine was his. He had bought them in twos and threes from the scavengers of the bustees on this side of the Ganga. The man and woman had never seen him before but they recognized his companion. He was employed by the municipality to drive carts full of filth down to the river and he lived in the sweepers' colony in which Nonku had got them a shack. Throwing a sharp glance in their direction the cart driver turned to the man with the gold rings. 'I know these two, Mahashay,' he said. 'They could do the job.' Dropping his voice he added, 'They are out of work.' Gold Rings was staring at the woman who stood cowering behind her husband, clutching the rag at her breasts, trying, in vain, to hide their burgeoning beauty. The man looked at Gold Rings, curiosity and doubt mingled in his eyes. 'Mahashay,' the cart driver repeated, 'the two are out of work. They might be willing to . . . ' Now Gold Rings turned his attention to what the cart driver was saying. 'You think so?' he asked, then turning to the man, he said gruffly, 'You want work?'

Work! Work meant food. The man and woman looked up eagerly. The lassitude dropped from their limbs. Their chests and shoulders lifted.

'What work?' the man asked.

'You'll have to drive the swine, across the water, to the other bank.'

Baap ré! The tide was coming in fast. The river was foaming and swelling, lifting its waters in a weird dance.

Soon it would be flowing in full spate with deadly currents lurking underneath, catching man and beast unawares. The girl and her husband exchanged glances. Flames of hope laced with fear leaped up in their hungry eyes.

'We'll need a safety boat,' the man muttered.

He was justified. It was the rule. Whenever animals were driven across the river, a boat followed to help out in an emergency. But Gold Rings shook his head. He wouldn't waste money in hiring a boat. The hope flickered and died out of the starving eyes. The man and woman looked at each other again—this time in despair. It was only for a moment though. Then their eyes turned to the creatures sitting massed together like clots of black cloud. Sows mostly—with squinting eyes. One wasn't sure where they were looking. But that quick glance decided the issue. The adventurous blood of generations of Nuths leaped up in their veins. Their starved organs cried out for food. Sitting here endlessly was akin to death. They rose to their feet, as if in common accord, and tightened the rags that hung about their loins. But the woman was, after all, a woman. 'Can we do it,' she muttered, 'without a boat?'

'We'll have to,' the man replied.

Gold Rings was satisfied. 'Th-e-e-re!' he pointed a finger. 'Do you see the Shiv Mandir on the other bank? That's where you'll have to take them. There are twenty-nine in the herd. You'll get an anna for each. That makes twenty-nine annas between the two of you. Plus some mustard oil to rub on your limbs once you get there. Lose one animal and languish in jail for six months.' With these words he handed the oiled bamboo lathi he carried to the man. The woman broke off a long stem of kalkasunda and, stripping off the leaves, converted it into a switch. Now Gold Rings and the cart driver glanced at each other in surprise and dismay. They hadn't thought it would be so easy. That the pair would agree so readily. What if they lost the animals and their own lives in the process? They stared, half in fascination half in fear, as the man and woman took their positions on either side of the herd.

Ur-r-r-r-ah! The girl gave a long-drawn-out cry in a high, sweet voice.

A-a-a-hu! *A-a-a-hu!* The man repeated several times in a cracked tremolo. *A-a-a-hu!* *A-a-a-hu!* In rhythm. As though he was giving the beat to the girl's song. The sounds, rising from their starved bellies, were deep and sonorous and tinged with melancholy. Suddenly the woods were filled with the girl's song. The waters of the Ganga took up the strains and sent the echoes spinning with the wind to the breasts of the clouds. Wild, exotic, magical! Like webs of illusion. The creatures trembled in amorous response. Shuffling to their feet they lifted their pointed snouts and sniffed the air. Hams rubbing and scraping, tails rippling and curling, eyes gleaming and gloating, they massed together.

Ur-r-a-a-a-ah!
A-a-a-hu! *A-a-a-hu!*

The gold teeth glittered in the man's mouth. The cart driver looked on in appreciation. The gleam in his eyes matched those of the swine. And the two? The pain in their starved bellies dissolved, merged and mingled in the ecstasy of their song.

Dissolved but not disappeared. Another hunger—a controlled, disciplined hunger took its place, loosening the hard knot in their bellies as the summer sun softens the hard fruit and fills it with sweet juices. They would eat. Yes—surely they would eat. But there was work to be done before that. Hard, demanding work that had to be given all they had. The animals were no strangers. The man and woman knew them. They had raised their kind from the time they were children. But the river was unknown. This red river that cackled and snarled by turns with such malevolent intent! That sucked and pulled with the strength of a thousand elephants.

The girl shot a swift glance at the river, then squinted up at Gold Rings and the cart driver. 'No boat—nothing!' she muttered. 'Such a big river!' This was not an expression of dissent. She was a woman and a woman is in the habit of taking stock, of weighing her strengths and weaknesses against realistic odds. The man was a man. Puffing out his chest he gave a fierce tweak to his limp whiskers and said, 'Yes, a big river!' The last half of the sentence—'but we'll have to cross it'—was left unsaid. Yet it hung in the air with all the force and gravity of the spoken word.

'How much is twenty-nine annas?' the girl asked, knitting her eyebrows. 'Is it two rupees? Or less?'

'Three annas less than two rupees,' the man answered. The girl was pleased. A warm, sweet hunger rose from the pit of her stomach and spread to the rest of her limbs. Hunger for food. Hunger for work. They would meet the tide. Control it. Master it. They would take the herd safely across this vast stretch of water to the other bank.

But the woman was, still, a woman. 'The tide is high,' she remarked to her husband. 'Why don't they wait for the ebb?'

'They're business folk,' her husband answered, 'out to make money. They care little for the sufferings of their animals.'

In between their love calls to the herd, the pair counted heads. Two males. The rest were sows. One of the sows was pregnant. Sows carried gold in their wombs, giving birth to five or six, sometimes even seven, in a single litter. The girl looked at the expectant mother. Love and pity shone out of her eyes. Would the sow be able to make it to the other side? The thought worried her a little but she dismissed it with a shake of her tangled locks. Of course she would. She was young and sturdy and not too heavily pregnant.

The calls changed in tone and intensity. They were urgent now. Imperative. Suddenly, the man was stricken with a doubt. 'Huzoor!' he turned to Gold Rings anxiously. 'Have the swine been fed? It's a big river. And turbulent. They'll need all their strength to fight it.'

'Yes. Yes. They've eaten well.'

Good. The man nodded his satisfaction. They themselves were starving, of course. He and his wife. But the thought of the food they would eat after their work was done would keep them going.

The pair swung into action. The man raised his stick and swirled it above his head with a piercing shriek that rose straight from his navel. *Hanh-i-i-i*. The girl met the sound with one of her own. *Ur-r-r-a-a-a!* The cry, rising from deep within her lungs, filled the air with a poignant, bitter-sweet resonance. The animals were shocked into response. These were battle cries. Cries that goaded them into action. A wary look came into their flinty eyes as they pushed and jostled for space. On one side of them was a swirling lathi. On the other was a fiercely waving switch. Behind them a steep upward slope of thorny scrub. There was no option for them except to press on ahead. On and on towards the sheet of water that lay below.

The man flicked his lathi lightly about the backs of the animals, making them leap forward in alarm. *Khu-u-sh!* *Khu-u-sh!* Bristles rose and hides scraped against each other. The caked dirt on their bodies crumbled and flew up in clouds of black dust. Twenty-nine animals, huge and hefty, trapped in a circle of fear. Fear of a waving switch, a swinging lathi, a wall of thorns and a stretch of turbulent water under a terrifying ink-blue sky. The river was before them. It was high already and would rise higher. Swine loved water but only shallow enough to wallow in. They dreaded the river especially when the tide was high. Prickles ran down their backs, puckering the skin, setting it aquiver. In their eyes was the crimson horror of the turbid waters. Sounds of fear came bleating out of fat oily throats. What was happening? Where were they to go? A wave of terror passed over the herd.

And now the man was sending out mixed signals. Barks of sharp command *hanh-i-i-i-i* interspersed with gentle admonitions of *oi-ha-ha-ha-ha-ha*! *Oi-ha-ha-ha-ha*! which said, 'Come, come! It's not so bad. I'll see you across—never fear.' *Ur-r-r-r-a-a-a-a*, the girl kept calling in her sweet soprano but her eyes were fearful. Fixed on the rising water. The closer they came the higher it seemed. Swelling and foaming, snaking and twining with dangerous currents. The man was staring at the river too. His face was hard, his jaws clenched. They were nearly there. Soon they would be standing on the bank with the water curling about their feet. The swine were moving slowly, unwillingly. Pulling back. Pushing each other forward.

Suddenly, one of the sows sprang apart with a piercing shriek that seemed to shatter earth and sky. *No-o-o-o!* her voice cried out in mute desperation, making land, sky and river reverberate to the sound. *I won't go forward. No. Never.* The man's whiskers twitched with a lascivious grin. *It's not for herself the whore's running away*, he thought indulgently. *It's for the babies in her belly.* The girl ran after the sow with despair in her eyes. In her haste she stumbled and fell on the slippery mud of the bank. Rising, she prepared to run again when the man stopped her. 'Don't run,' he commanded sharply. The girl stood looking like a statue of black clay. Her full breasts

Samaresh Basu

like hard fruit, with taut stems at their tips, were caked with black mud. There was mud in her hair. She didn't look very different now from the swine she was tending. 'Keep calling!' the man said. 'She'll come back.'

They drove the swine along the bank with soft encouraging sounds. *Ur-r-r-r-r-ah*! and *A-a-a-hu*! *A-a-a-hu*! The pregnant sow had run a long way off. Suddenly, she stopped in her tracks and looked at the group with puzzled eyes. Lowering her head she sniffed at something on the bank and ate it, then lifted her snout in the air and screamed. The pair took no notice of her. She squinted her eyes at them, lowered her head, ate and screamed again. Then, with a yelp of surrender, she ran back and took her place in the herd. But she made her resentment obvious. Twisting her head like a stubborn ox she let the hate rain out of her eyes. *Devils*! she shrieked at her minders. *You're leading me to my death. You know you are. Cruel, cruel devils*! The man glanced at his wife. A signal passed. The time had come to take the plunge. To dash into the river with the herd. The waters were lapping about their feet already. Pushing forward. Curling back. The man called softly to the still screaming sow. *Hunh*! *Hunh*! *A-a-hu*! *A-a-hu*! as if to say, 'Don't be afraid. We'll take good care of you.'

Looking at the Ganga he folded his hands and murmured in deep devotion, 'Ganga! Ganga Mai!' The goddess river, taking no heed of his prayer, rushed past mumbling and giggling to herself. From time to time she seemed to stop and look at them. To say something. Only they didn't know what it was. Was she laughing at their foolishness? Was she saying, 'You little humans! You little starving humans! Don't you see how big I've grown? Yet you dare come near me. Nearer and nearer . . . ' Yes. That must be what she was saying. Laughing like a drunken slut. Her eyes veiled in mystery. Her waters turning crimson with unholy joy.

The man and woman looked at the river, their eyes sharp with enquiry. As though they wanted to scan her waters. To see what fears and mysteries lurked within her depths. What death traps lay in wait for them and their herd.

The two were like children—simple, innocent children with a courage that had never been put to the test. The girl was knotting the rags around her hips in readiness for battle. The rest of her was bare. Her strong, naked breasts rose proudly to the sky, like twin mountain peaks, defying storms and tempests. The man twirled his whiskers. Etched against river and sky he looked like a mountain crag, rough and unformed, but terrible. Invincible.

Yet their eyes pleaded with the goddess river. *Yes we are starving*, their eyes said, *and for that reason help us across. Gold Rings is a businessman. He's making his herd swim a river in full tide under an Ashadh sky. No boat. Nothing. Twenty-nine creatures. Arré Baap! And only two humans to guide them. Hai Baap! Hai Maiya! The creatures are innocent. We are innocent too. You know. You've been seeing us for the last two days.*

The river heard them and responded. *Kal kal jham jham*, her anklets rang like a dancing girl's. She moved towards them sinuously, luring them onwards, like a coquette, then danced back, leaving them staring in wonder. Higher and higher her waters rose. The man and woman retraced their steps a few yards, then moved forward. They were getting ready for the plunge. The animals looked at their minders with anxious eyes. Their ears quivered as though they were listening hard, trying to understand what the wind and water were saying. Their snouts snuffed and snorted. The pregnant sow continued to screech her protest though no one cared to hear her.

Now! The moment had come. The man barked a series of sharp commands at the girl. 'Climb upwards. Good! Now move forward. Stop. Stand where you are!' The girl obeyed. The swine were facing the river now. It was time to push them into the water. One shove. After that they would be sucked in by the tide. Husband and wife exchanged glances for the last time. Then a shriek rose in the air. A single shriek but it sprang from two throats. The man spun his lathi violently in the air. The girl brought her switch down heavily on the animals' backs. In a flash the herd was in the water. The two sprang in after them. The swine were well in by now. But where were they going? Pulled by the tide, the animals were flowing north. They had to be turned in the right direction. But how? A boat would have solved the problem but without it . . .

'Back to the bank, quick!' the man yelled. The water was up to their chests by now. Scrambling out of it they made a dash for the bank. Seeing them the herd prepared to follow suit. The water heaved and trembled as the beasts pushed and prodded and, touching snout to snout, whispered obscenities to one another. The sounds reached the ears of their minders, low and mysterious. The pregnant sow continued to protest but her voice was hushed and stricken.

The man and woman clambered up the bank and ran along it as fast as they could. By their side, twenty-nine enormous creatures floated on a red river. The man jumped into the water in front of the herd and proceeded to lash it with ferocious strokes, forcing the swine to change direction. And now the woman leaped in and brought her switch down on their backs. Up and down, up and down, the switch waved like a branch in a storm. The swine were trapped. The tide was coming in from the south. Only the west was open—a great sheet of water and that was the direction in which they were being driven. '*H-a-ih*! *H-a-ih*!' the man shouted in a commanding voice. '*Hum*! *Hum*!' the girl scolded gently. 'Keep going. Don't turn your heads.' The animals were pushing each other, hitting out with snouts and tails, snorting in fury. Floating with the tide was so much easier. Why were these two pushing them against the tide into a sea of turbulent water? What did they want from them? Their lives?

The man, now at the side of the herd, was finding it difficult to keep going. The water was pulling him backwards with tremendous force. And it wasn't a simple one-directional pull. It swerved from time to time, knocking him off balance. The girl was having a hard time keeping her position at the back. 'Push against the current,' the man shouted a warning. 'Keep pushing.' The girl was pushing with all her might. But the pull of the tide was too strong. She felt her chest crash against it, felt her arms and legs being ripped away . . .

There were no humans in the water now. Only a herd of swine. *Three males instead of two and twenty-eight sows . . .*

The bank had moved a good distance away. A strong south wind, leaping in and out of the river, made it quiver with exultation. In the absence of the tide this same wind would have turned killer. It would have raised walls of water, swamping the animals, drowning them.

And now a sharp wind came straining from the east. This was a danger signal. It cracked the cloud cover with strange lines of light. Blown asunder, the fragments massed together in knots. Some came sweeping down on

Samaresh Basu

the water. Others flew away to an unknown destination. An air of mystery hung in the sky. As though . . . as though something unholy was about to be revealed. The clouds were coming together again. Dense black clouds were massing together like a pack of bears. It didn't augur well.

The two were threshing their limbs with all their might, making the water seethe and foam around them. From time to time they swung lathi and switch. Their eyes, bleak with anxiety, were turned to the sky. The animals were flailing and threshing too. Suddenly one of them screeched—a long-drawn-out screech of agony. The two looked up startled. What was the matter with the sow? Had her leg been bitten off by a crocodile? Fear passed from the water into their bodies like electric currents, shattering their nerves, chilling their already icy spines. But no—they were quick to console themselves—nothing like that could have happened. The sow was perfectly safe. And so were they. '*Ha-i-ih*! *Ha-i-ih*! the man called softly. 'Don't be afraid. Keep going. Just keep going.'

And now the girl uttered a piercing cry. The man leaped from the water like a porpoise and looked in the direction of her pointing finger. Three of the sows had turned tail and were floating away in the opposite direction. Their intention was clear. They wouldn't go any further in this mad venture. The water was rising every minute. Swelling and foaming. The two humans were bent on killing them. But they wouldn't be led to the slaughter. The man gazed after the sows—shocked into silence. But it was only for a moment. Gathering his numbed senses together, in a flash, he swam after them with long powerful strokes. Face to face with the escaping creatures he brought his lathi forcefully down on the water, right under the rubbery nostrils, making them turn back startled. It was the pregnant sow and her friends. They were about her age. Not mothers yet but ready for mating.

Lifting his lathi the man swung it above their heads as, grunting and squealing, yellow teeth bared in a shamed grimace, they wobbled back towards the herd. 'Swine!' the man muttered in disgust. 'Spawn of a pig.' But there was amusement, too, in his voice. Amusement tinged with pity.

By now the girl had floated quite a distance away with the rest of the herd. 'Ei Haramzadi!' the man called after her. 'Do you want to leave me behind?' Abuses fell from his lips in a stream. Filthy, obscene abuses full of love and lust. Coming closer he met her eyes. His own were as red as *koonch* berries—no different from those of the swine he tended. The girl's eyes, in constant contact with the water, were the soft oozy pink of *karamcha* fruit. There was fear in them. Fear and suspicion. Both realized the danger they were in. The river was churning out deadly currents. In places, the water was being pushed up from below till it boiled over like a geyser, foaming and frothing before skimming away like a bird, white feathers flying.

The pigs had come together in a tight knot. Their mouths drooled. Their snouts emitted strange noises. They seemed to be whispering to one another, sharing secrets, making plans. They realized that here, in this high and turbulent river, death was very near. One slip and they would go under. Caution was necessary. Caution and unity. Only by staying together could they ward off the lurking presence of death. For the first time that day the swine started moving in a systematic, responsible manner. Taking care to follow the direction in which they were driven.

Two pairs of eyes were fixed on the river. The greatest of rivers! The holiest and the deepest! A river so vast, it seemed to have sucked the seabed dry. And they hadn't even reached the middle. Continuously assaulted by walls of crashing water, the nerves in their heads were strained to breaking point, like tightly stretched wires threatening to snap any moment. The water was cold but heat rose from the soles of their feet—a fierce consuming heat that burst out in beads on lips and foreheads, groins and armpits. Around them the water lurched and lashed about, like a drunken woman. It beckoned and called. *Come*, her voice rang in their ears, mocking, cruel. *Come closer*.

They had to go. '*Hé Mayi! Hé Ganga Mayi!*' they prayed. 'There's no choice for us except to press forward. Forgive us for lashing your breast with lathi and switch. In your great patience and endurance forgive us this sin. You know it is only to keep the animals going. We're humble swineherds who have undertaken this perilous crossing only to fill our starving bellies. We mean no offence Great Mother Ganga. People have crossed your waters from time immemorial.'

The girl felt her strength ebb slowly away. The hand clutching the switch was numb and listless. In her eyes lurked the fear of death. She was still pushing but her efforts were flagging. She kept slipping back. The man wanted to ask what ailed her but didn't dare. What if she answered, 'I have no strength left. You go on. Leave me to my fate.' No. Such words were best left unsaid. Suddenly, quite inconsequently, he thought, *Babu Nagin Prasad gave us forty seers of rice and two pigs for the wedding feast. And four barrels of toddy.*

The sky was coming closer, getting ready to touch the river. Suddenly, a flash of blue lightning came snaking from the west, rippled over their heads, and vanished. *Goom! Goom! Goodoom!* A clap of thunder burst into their eardrums. The animals were frightened. Abandoning the lines they had formed with so much self-discipline they ran helter-skelter. Within seconds the red water was starred with black dots. *A-a-i-n-n-h*! *A-a-i-n-n-h*! Squeals rose from frightened throats. Gasping at the gills like a katla fish, the girl rose to the surface and glided out over the water. Up and down, her switch went. The hand that held it was slow and heavy. Up and down. '*Hum Hum*,' her voice hummed, warm and comforting. 'Keep going. Just keep going. Let's get out of here as soon as we can.' And thus she got the herd together once again.

The tide had changed into a killer. It was gnawing viciously at the western bank. The moist earth yielded easily, willingly, to its rapacious teeth. Where was the Shiv Mandir? Why couldn't they see it? Ah! There it was, at the bend, where the river curved to the south. There, where the water was foaming at the mouth like a lunatic. The animals were back together and moving steadily ahead. But the humans couldn't keep pace. Battered by wind and water they floated about like flotsam and jetsam. The swine were looking at them with curious eyes. With eyes that said, *Why do you slip away? Stay close by us. Unity is strength.* The man and woman knew that too. And so they clung on desperately fighting a bitter battle.

All of a sudden, the two were thrown close together. The girl raised her face to her husband's. A wave-washed face with eyes as red as ripe fruit. 'How will we return?' she asked. 'Will they give us the fare for a boat?' The woman was a woman—worried about returning to her nest even before they had reached their destination. The man shook his head. 'I don't know,' he said simply. And then they were thrown apart again. The water here was as even as a sheet of metal. Not a ripple marred its smoothness. But terrible currents lurked underneath—currents that flung one a hundred yards away.

'Where are you?' the man called.

'Here.' Her voice reached his ears, muffled and indistinct. She was safe. She hadn't drowned. 'Is anything wrong?' He tried to smile as he asked this but, beneath the wet whiskers, the smile turned into a grimace. He felt worried about his wife. Yes. It was only now that he had begun to worry.

Wrong? The girl sighed. What a question!

'Nothing's wrong,' she answered.

Dusk was setting in. The sky was getting darker. Lightning flickered like tongues of flame. Like flicks of a whip it slithered over the backs of the swine. On wet, shining backs and heads. Thunder roared and rumbled and when it ceased, momentarily, the river took up the refrain. The beasts squealed in bursts of terror.

The two had forgotten their hunger. The only thought that devoured their brains and bellies was the thought of the crossing. They had to reach the other side. Dead or alive, themselves, they had to get the animals safely across.

The herd was moving more swiftly now. The pull of the water was stronger. The river was changing, reaching up to touch the sky. Rearing forcefully from beneath, hitting out at legs and arms, chests and stomachs. They were close together now. And close to the animals.

And now the girl seemed to be clawing at something with hands that had puffed up like the steamed cakes women made with newly harvested rice. Her head bobbed up and down. Up and down. *What is she doing?* the man thought. And then he saw. The pitiful rag she wore had slipped from her waist and she was fighting with the water for its possession. The man turned away. He couldn't meet her eyes. Eyes as dull and opaque as the red, turbid water. *Ramua played the flute on our wedding day*, he thought whimsically. *And now—this calamitous river.*

Chik! *Chik*! *Doom*! *Doom*! Lightning and thunder. Huge black beasts with yellow teeth bared in a frightened grimace. The man swallowed some mouthfuls of water. 'Are you there?' he called softly. 'I am,' the girl answered. Puffing and panting she posed a question. 'Twenty-nine annas is not fair payment. We've been tricked. Haven't we?'

'Yes.'

The Ganga heard them and her belly rumbled with laughter.

'We won't reach before nightfall. Where will we stay?'

Silence. The man's eyes were fixed on a point ahead. The current had changed direction. It was flowing south now instead of north. Had the tide turned? *Hé Ganga Mayi*! Would they be swept back with the ebb from where they came? No boat. Twenty-nine creatures. And only two . . . And then he understood. 'Whirlpool!' he shrieked. 'Beware! Beware!' The startled beasts, not knowing what to do, started moving towards him.

The western bank had been eaten away in a gigantic wedge, forcing the south-flowing water to move north. Causing the whirlpool that spelled death to animals and humans. *Arré Baap*! *Hé Mayi*! A sudden spurt of strength came, from who knows where, into the famished, half-dead bodies. The chilled blood started coursing, warm and strong, in their veins. The man lifted his lathi with a forceful arm and spun it violently in the air. 'Watch out,' he shouted. 'Beware! Beware!' He swam towards the whirlpool to prevent the beasts from approaching it. His wife, appalled at the dangerous course he was taking, tried to move towards him. But she couldn't. She felt something, a weight, slip away from her body, leaving her light and free. It was the rag she wore. *Hee*! *Hee*! *Hee*! the river bared her teeth and cackled, snatching it away from the girl's clutching hands.

Samaresh Basu

The man was trying to keep his position to the south of the herd and shouting, at the same time, till his lungs were fit to burst. This was to frighten the herd and keep it away from the whirlpool. To make the animals swim northwards in panic. *Arré Arré*. One of them was drifting south, away from the herd. She would be sucked into the inexorable maw of the whirlpool any moment. It was the pregnant sow. 'Stop her!' the man cried in a hoarse, cracked scream. 'Stop the stubborn, wilful bitch!'

'Come back,' the girl called out to the sow in an agonized voice. 'Do you want to kill yourself? To kill your unborn children?'

The sow was only a few feet away from the whirlpool. She had sensed her danger now and was screeching in terror. Threshing and flailing. But the water was too strong. All she could do was keep her position. The man wanted to swim out to her. To help her. But it was too dangerous. 'Come away,' the girl shouted to her husband. 'Leave her to die.'

Leave her to die? A young sturdy sow with a whole litter in her womb!

And now the rain came pattering down on the river in large ungainly drops. Rain! The man raised an arm to the sky and shook his fist at it. 'Whoreson!' he cursed, 'could you not spare us this? Have you no mercy?' His features were twisted with hate. It was an evil face now, a swinish, bestial face with yellow fangs and cruel red eyes. A predator's eyes, eyes that measured and took stock, gauged the distance between self and victim.

Spreading his lathi across the water he inched his body carefully forward. 'Push as hard as you can,' he called softly to the sow. 'Grab the lathi with your teeth.'

But the sow, though struggling desperately, was gradually drifting away. The man pushed himself a few more inches. He knew that this was the farthest he could go. And if she . . . A sudden violent threshing of the waters and, springing forward, the sow took the lathi in her mouth.

Relief washed over the man in waves. She was saved. The tip of the lathi was clenched firmly between her teeth. 'Keep pushing,' he shouted. 'I'm pulling as hard I can. I'll have to let go if my strength fails me.' The sow seemed to understand. She pushed with all her might. Her snout trembled violently with the effort. Red eyes and nostrils were distended. A few yellow teeth glittered in the gathering dusk. The bristles on her neck stood on end, hard and spiky.

Suddenly, without any warning, the lathi slipped into the water and man and sow, thrown together, began floating north. The lathi skimmed gaily over the breast of the river, then, meeting resistance at the bend, spun southwards and disappeared. The sow started screaming at the top of her lungs. *I knew it*, she cried angrily. *I knew you devils were leading me to my death.*

'Quiet!' the man roared at her. 'Ungrateful bitch! If you were mine I would flay you alive once we reached the bank.'

The girl was some distance away with the rest of the herd. She heard the sow's screams but the water was pulling her with an inexorable pull and she couldn't stop.

'What happened?' her voice reached her husband, muffled and indistinct.

'Saved,' the man called back.

They were close to the bank now. The girl and her herd had almost reached the spot where the Shiv Mandir stood. Where Gold Rings was squatting and gesticulating wildly, 'This way! This way!' This way!' But why wasn't she climbing out of the water? The man stared in horror as he saw her floating away. What had happened? Had she exhausted the last remnants of her strength and couldn't make it to the bank? He saw her head bob up and down. Up and down. She was drowning. Abandoning the pregnant sow he swam out to his wife and clasped her in his arms. As he did so he felt solid ground under his feet and was startled. Why then . . . ? He stared at the girl's face. A wet, weary face, pale and anguished, lips blue with cold. He saw pain stamped on it. Pain and shame. And he knew. Even before she whispered, 'I'm naked. The water is my only covering,' he knew.

'Wait for me,' he whispered back.

Leading the animals safely out of the water, all twenty-nine of them, he untied the gamchha he had knotted around his waist. Then, covering his loins with it, he flung his own small scrap of a dhoti into the water. Gold Rings and the two men with him laughed heartily.

'Making love in the river, eh!' they teased.

The sky was getting darker every minute. And now the rain came pelting down. Gold Rings led his animals to the bustee he owned this side of the river. The man and woman went with him.

Night had fallen. They had found shelter in a shack next to the pigsty which housed the swine they had driven across the water. They had received their twenty-nine annas and bought flour and vegetables. The girl had lit a fire and cooked a meal. They were eating now by the light of a burning faggot. Outside the shack, torrential rain was pelting down into a vicious, raging river. A wild east wind howled and lamented. The swine snorted and grunted in satisfaction.

The man and woman had been saved from a terrible death. They were eating a meal after forty-eight hours. But there was no light in the girl's eyes. Her face looked pale and haunted. She was putting up a hand, every now and then, and wiping the tears away from her cheeks. The man glanced sideways at her. He knew why. The scrap of cloth he had thrown out to her was so small it had left her breasts completely bare.

'Don't cry,' he murmured softly. 'Don't cry.'

After eating their meal the two lay down together. The girl was still weeping—the man fondling the shamed breasts. Suddenly, the tide was on them. Making the blood gush and gurgle, like a mad joyous river, through their veins. The girl put out a hand and extinguished the flame. And in the impenetrable darkness of a wild stormy night the two bloods pulsed and pounded, leaped and danced in an ecstasy of living. Caveman and cavewoman, they lay together with the elements raging and howling around them. Only a few electric bulbs flickering in the distance marred the timeless primeval quality of the scene.

His pleasure taken, the man began humming a song. *Yug yug paar ayil bani*, he sang softly, *pawan sut mahavir, Hoi Rama.*

His Rama slept a blessed, dreamless sleep even as rain and wind lashed sky, river and earth far into the deep dark night.

Samaresh Basu

The King Is Dead,
Long Live the King

Raja Jai Raja Aashe

Prafulla Roy

At the crack of dawn Razek could be seen sitting on the high veranda, outside the room facing east, dangling his feet over the edge. He wore a green lungi, gay with yellow stripes, and a vest of cotton mesh over it. Though the day had just dawned, his hair was carefully combed with a tall plume rising neatly from the middle. Waves of happiness welled up within him. And it wasn't only today. For some months now he had felt the tide of joy swelling, brimming over the banks of his heart.

The east room apart, there were two large rooms in the house—one facing north, one south. They were roofed with sheets of strong, sturdy tin, rippling artistically, charming the eyes of the beholder. The whitewashed walls were propped up with arches of sal wood and the floors were smooth with bright-red cement.

The courtyard beyond the veranda where Razek sat had a row of paddy bins at one end. At the other was a *shiuli* tree. Across the yard was a stretch of land covered with *pithkhira* and *sonal* bushes with a pond behind it. The monsoon had come and gone, swelling the water of the pond, sending it spilling over the edges, flooding the rice fields beyond till they looked like a single sheet of green glass stretching all the way to the horizon.

This enormous courtyard, three large rooms, pond, and ninety *kanis* of fertile soil yielding two rich crops a year were his—all, all his. A king's ransom! And eight months ago? But we'll come to that later.

It was the middle of October. The sky, washed by the monsoon rains to a pristine blue, was as clean and bright as it had been at the end of August. Soft clouds drifted over it like clusters of white flowers. The shiuli tree was loaded with blossom, the air drenched with its sweet dewy scent. And now the sun rose in the sky, round and full, its beams pouring into the courtyard like molten gold. Two tiny birds with tall red plumes flew in from who knows where and settled on the roof, billing and cooing, making love. The earth, as far as the eye could see, was touched by autumn's magic wand.

For many months now, Razek had sat thus, proud monarch of all he surveyed. It was a delicious pastime, a luxury he had never known before. This morning, as he looked out on his rice fields, he saw or thought he saw a boat cleaving its way through the water. In a few minutes he was sure of it. The humped straw roof was clearly visible above the tall green shoots and his eyes caught flashing glimpses of an ebony-black boatman plying the oars. There was nothing new in this. Boats could be seen floating across the fields every morning, going off to unknown destinations. He had no idea of where this one was headed and no curiosity either. He sat humming, and twirling his toes, enjoying the soft warm light and the sweet chirping of the birds and thinking about the past.

Alas! What a miserable life he had led for the past thirty years. From the time he was born! This green lungi and vest, this plume of well-oiled hair—where were they only eight months ago? Had the country not been divided, had Baikuntha Saha not been forced to flee Chhipatipur . . .

The rest of the thought was swallowed up. With a shock he saw that the boat had crossed the pond and come to a halt by his own bank.

Razek stared at the scene in consternation. Who had come for him? And why? He didn't have long to wait for an answer. Within minutes a man stepped out of the boat. It was Tohrab Ali—the wealthiest man of the village. The two hundred kanis of agricultural land he owned yielded three harvests per year. In addition, he had a herd of fifty or sixty cows and bullocks, a fleet of forty boats, several flocks of ducks and hens, and innumerable farm implements. Thirty field hands slaved for him all day, raising crops of paddy and jute, millet and lentils. He was headman of Chhipatipur village and the most respected landlord of these parts.

Tohrab Ali wasn't only rich and important. His tastes were refined and delicate and he took great pains with his appearance. Even this early in the day he was dressed in an expensive silk lungi and ruffled shirt. The tips of his leather sandals tilted elegantly upwards, and his hair and beard were dyed a bright henna red. Razek knew that the moment he drew near, a rich, heady scent of rose petals would come wafting from the dabs of cotton wool, soaked in *itr*, behind his ears. But why should Tohrab Ali step into his yard in the first place? Razek sat in stunned silence for a few moments, staring at the boat. Then, collecting himself, he rose with a spring and ran towards the pond.

'Bara Mian!' Razek exclaimed, his voice squeaky with awe and admiration. His hands rubbed against one another ingratiatingly.

'Yes,' Tohrab Ali smiled broadly and stroked his beard. 'I've come to you—'

'To me!' Razek couldn't believe his ears.

'Yes, yes—to you.'

Razek stared at his visitor, not knowing how to react. But Tohrab Ali was in full command of the situation. 'How long will you keep me standing by the pond?' he asked, smiling, crinkling a pair of small eyes darkened with kohl. There was a ripple of amusement in his voice. 'Won't you take me home?' Tohrab had never used such an intimate tone with Razek before and the latter didn't know what to make of it. Blushing deeply he stammered a welcome. 'Come, Bara Mian. Please come into the house.'

Leading his distinguished guest across the yard, Razek ran from room to room, nervous and flustered. Where was he to seat such an important personage? What was he to offer him? Unrolling a mat, he invited his guest to sit down, then, changing his mind, put it away hastily and set out a wooden stool instead. Tohrab Ali looked on amused. Razek's frantic endeavours at hospitality pleased him. 'Ease up, Razek,' he smiled kindly at the young man, 'I'll sit and rest presently. But first things first—I want to see your house and how you live.'

Razek shot a startled glance at his guest. Why was Tohrab Ali asking to see his house? Surely he hadn't come all the way, across fields and water so early in the morning, to pay a courtesy call! Was he plotting something? Tohrab Ali saw the flame of suspicion leap into Razek's eyes and made haste to quench it. 'There's nothing to fear, Razek,' he said gently, placing a friendly hand on the young man's shoulder. 'Your house and possessions will remain yours. I have no intention of taking them away from you.' Though his fears remained, Razek had no option but to do as he was told. The most important man of the village had expressed a desire to see his house and how he lived. Denying him was out of the question. Leading him from room to room, Razek showed him all his possessions, answering his questions painstakingly, satisfying him on every point.

The tour over, Tohrab Ali seated himself comfortably on the stool and asked, 'Do you have some tobacco in the house, Razek? I could do with a smoke.' Razek's face turned red with embarrassment. He should have made the offer himself. He would have if the niggling suspicion hadn't clouded his mind. Running into the kitchen he reappeared a few minutes later with a lighted hookah in his hand. Tohrab Ali took a deep pull, inhaling the rich fragrant smoke and said, 'Baikuntha Saha left you in charge of his house. You're the caretaker, aren't you?'

'Yes,' Razek murmured uneasily. He was still wondering what Tohrab Ali was getting at.

'What about the land across the pond?'

'That too. It's all his—'

'How much land?'

'Ninety kanis.'

'It's all been left in your charge?'

'Yes.' Razek's voice sounded stifled.

There was a few minutes' silence. Tohrab Ali puffed at the hookah, exhaling clouds of scented smoke. Then he said, 'It's nearly eight months since the Sahas left the village, isn't it?'

The man knows a great deal, Razek thought. 'Yes,' he answered in the same stifled voice.

'Do you know where they've gone?'

'They were to go to Kolkata. So I've heard.'

'Do you have news of them?'

'No.'

'Have you received any letters?'

'No.'

Silence once again. Tohrab Ali's brow was furrowed in thought. 'What do you think?' he asked at last.

'About what?' Razek didn't understand.

'Will Baikuntha Saha come back to the village?'

'How can I say?'

Tohrab Ali took another puff and muttered almost as though Razek hadn't spoken. 'He won't return. I feel it in my bones.'

Razek was silent.

'If he doesn't, all this property will become yours. The house and fields, the pond—why do I say "will become"? It *has* become yours.' And now Tohrab Ali asked Razek some more questions. It was clear he wanted to assess the exact value and extent of the property. Finally, rising to his feet, he said, 'Ah! I nearly forgot. The reason I've come—'

'What reason?' The question burst out of Razek before he could stop himself.

'I came to invite you to my house for a meal. Come tomorrow at noon. Nothing formal—just a little rice and dal.'

Razek wouldn't have been more startled if a bolt of lightning had fallen on his head. His body went limp with shock. The wealthiest man of the village, the most respected—for whom Razek had worked for years as a wage labourer—had come to his house and invited him for a meal. He opened his mouth to speak but no words came.

'Tomorrow, then,' Tohrab Ali rose to his feet. 'Don't forget.'

Razek bent his head obediently. The gesture was mechanical—like a clockwork doll's.

'We'll be waiting for you.' With these words, Tohrab Ali crossed the yard and strode purposefully through the bushes of pithkhira and sonal towards the pond. Razek stared after him. He knew he should have gone with his guest, should have escorted him right up to his boat. But his legs felt wobbly and he sat down on the floor with a thud. How could such a thing have happened to him? Even as he stared with vacant eyes, the boat began gliding over the green fields back from where it had come. It went bobbing and swaying till it became a speck in the distance and finally disappeared.

Razek kept sitting on the veranda for a long time after Tohrab Ali had left. Images of the past flashed before his eyes. In his head was a jumble of thoughts. He had been an orphan ever since he could remember. His first memories were of sniffing about, like a stray puppy, in the backyards of the Khans, the Mridhas and the Sardars. He even hung about the Hindu neighbourhood. Sometimes he was given something to eat. Most often he went hungry. Hunger pangs assailed him all the time. All day and all night. It was the only sensation he knew.

When he grew a little older he realized that living on people's charity was no life at all. For one thing, one could barely sustain oneself by it. For another, it was extremely demeaning. He decided to fend for himself. But how was he to find the means? He thought and thought and then an idea came to him. Determined that this would be his last stint at begging he went from door to door and acquired from one family a couple of lengths of bamboo and from another a coil of tough strong thread. His first fishing equipment was a rod which he fashioned from a length of supple young bamboo and a net which he wove himself. Next, he slit some reeds in fine strips and plaited them into a *dharmajaal* and a *polo*. The dharmajaal was a lattice screen planted in the river with a net behind it. When the tide rose, scores of large fish came tumbling over the waves and, leaping over the screen, fell into the net. The polo was a wicker pail with a handle. It was held in front of shoals of rapidly swimming fish and lifted up immediately afterwards to reveal dozens of tiny wriggling creatures trapped in the meshes.

Razek began his career as a fisherman in the ponds and pools, streams and waterholes of his own village. This was a land with more water than earth, and aquatic life teemed in their depths. If by chance, in an unusually dry summer, the water of the village was sucked dry, he would trudge the two miles across the fields to the big river. He would work feverishly all day and, at sundown, walk all the way to the haat at Sunamganj to exchange the day's catch for a few coins. Returning to his own village, he would seek out the homes of the poorest Muslims for shelter. Cooking his supper—a few handfuls of rice—over the dying embers of their kitchen fires he would eat his meal. Then, stretching out in a corner of the family's courtyard, he would sink into a heavy dreamless sleep.

For eight months in the year Razek fished for a living. In between he would work for a daily wage. He would cut the paddy for the Khans one season and comb out the jute for the Mridhas the next. But most often he worked for Tohrab Ali. There were other ways in which he supplemented his resources. After the harvests were reaped and taken away, a lot of paddy seed could be found fallen to the ground. Razek combed the stubble, even rummaging in the rat holes, and collected the grain painstakingly. What he gathered was enough to last him a month or two.

Life was an unending battle—against hunger and thirst, against the elements, and against mental and physical suffering. Razek's skin was burned black from exposure to sun and wind. His hair and beard were wild and matted from want of oil. His eyes were red and rheumy and his fingers covered with sores from constant contact with water. There was only one colour in his life—

the colour of sorrow. Deep, impenetrable, unending sorrow. He was dogged by it day after day, month after month, season after season. Spring, summer, autumn and winter. Cycle followed cycle in weary succession, inexorable, relentless—for thirty years.

One morning, as he walked waist deep through the water, carrying his dharmajaal, a strange sight met his eyes. The huge common outside the school building was packed with a motley crowd. An English band was playing. Several men were making speeches. They must have been impassioned ones, for Razek could see beards trembling, veins bulging thick in the speakers' necks. Presently, a green silk flag was hoisted high up in the air, whereupon the crowds cheered and clapped.

There were fireworks at dusk. Razek, who had looked on with vague, vacant eyes at the events of the morning, now felt a mild curiosity. Pushing his way through the crowd he asked a fellow villager, 'What is all the excitement about? Why these fireworks? Has anything happened?'

'Arré!' Arré!' The man turned around in surprise. 'Where has this idiot dropped from? Let me have a look at you.' Narrowing his eyes he peered into Razek's face, then exclaimed laughing, 'Of course! Who but Razek Mian could ask such a question? You've soaked your brain in water along with your limbs for so long that it has turned as turbid and addled as the rest of you. You know nothing and care less—'

'Stop talking in riddles,' Razek snapped back, 'and answer my question—if you have it yourself, of course.'

After this the man had explained the matter to Razek. People were rejoicing because it was a historic day—the day of the country's independence. Not only from the firangis—from the Hindus as well. What they had dreamed about for years, struggled for, sacrificed lives for, had come to pass. They had got their own land—a Muslim land. They had won their Pakistan. 'A day such as this,' the man had said, 'comes rarely. Once in many generations.' The celebrations had gone on all night. Razek had enjoyed the crowds, the lights, the colour and excitement. But next morning he was back again in the water, lugging his polo, setting out his dharmajaal.

A year passed. And, slowly, the village began to change. The Hindus started leaving Chhipatipur one by one. On a cold November morning, while spreading out his nets in the green, scummy waters of the pond, he heard that the Gosains had sold their house and lands for a song and left for Kolkata. A few months later the Bhuinmalis followed and then the Baruis, the Kumors and the Jugis in rapid succession. Chhipatipur took on an abandoned look.

The change that had come over the village had hardly any effect on Razek. He had to work so hard to keep body and soul together that he neither had the time nor the inclination to keep track of who went and who remained. In his life he had but one thought, one obsession. To reap the living harvests! To lure the fish from the bottom of ponds, pools and river, and ensnare them in his nets. But Razek's indifference was not destined to last. One cold, clear afternoon in January, as he gathered the fallen ears of paddy from a newly harvested field, old Baikuntha Saha came and stood by him.

'Do you wish to speak with me, Saha Moshai?'

'Yes.'

'What is it?' Razek asked curiously.

'I'm leaving the village and so—'

'Where are you going?'

'To Kolkata.'

'When will you return?'

'That is uncertain—'

Prafulla Roy

Razek hadn't asked any more questions but the old man had continued speaking. 'I have a request to make to you, Razek. You must look after my house and property while I'm away. Not without compensation of course. The rice and jute growing in the fields, the fish in the pond will be yours to enjoy. If and when I return you must give everything back to me. If I don't, all that I own—house, land and fields—will be yours forever.'

Baikuntha Saha and his family left Chhipatipur the next day, changing Razek's life and destiny. No need now for him to stand in waist-high water, till flesh and bones froze, to eke out a bare subsistence. No need now to sniff around for a night's shelter. He had never known such bliss, such peace and contentment. His limbs were filling out with hearty meals of fish curry and rice and his skin glistened with oil and good living. Gone were the rags he had knotted about his loins. Now he wore brightly coloured checked and striped lungis and vests of fine cotton. He combed his hair in a tall shining plume. Only eight months and he couldn't imagine life without these.

Thank Allah, the country was divided and Baikuntha Saha had to leave. Otherwise—

A chill passed through Razek's spine at the thought. But what was the meaning of Tohrab Ali's visit? Why did he have to seek him, Razek, out of all people to invite to his house for a meal? Was he plotting something? Fear gnawed in his mind like a mole and wouldn't let him rest.

Next morning, Razek sat on the veranda, the muscles of his face slack with anxiety. Ignoring Tohrab Ali's invitation was out of the question. But accepting it was not easy either. What was in the man's mind? Razek had spent the whole night trying to figure it out but he still had no clue.

At some point in his musings he rose, bathed and dressed. Almost unconsciously he donned a bright checked lungi and a freshly laundered shirt and, slipping his feet into a pair of raw leather mules, he walked past the pithkhira and sonal bushes to his boat.

Tohrab Ali's house stood on a sort of island at the extreme end of Chhipatipur village. It was a huge house with innumerable rooms built of bricks and mortar. It was packed with people. Tohrab Ali came hurrying out at the sight of Razek's boat. 'Ah, Mian!' he welcomed his guest with exaggerated courtesy. 'Why the delay? Had you forgotten?' Razek was so shocked—he stared at his host not knowing how to respond. Tohrab Ali had addressed him as Mian! Only the other day, he had snapped his fingers at him and called out commandingly: 'Razekya!'—a contemptuous sobriquet of his real name. Why even yesterday . . .

'Come, Mian,' Tohrab Ali took his arm. 'I've been waiting for you all morning.' Razek tried to say something but his tongue seemed to have tied itself up in knots and he couldn't speak. 'I would have waited a little longer then sent a servant for you.' Giving his arm a gentle pull, Tohrab Ali drew Razek into the house. Razek swallowed painfully and managed a few words. 'You came to my house, in person, Bara Mian, and invited me to a meal,' he said at last. 'Dare I stay away? How many heads do I carry on my shoulder?'

Tohrab Ali smiled and led his guest to a large room where a thick carpet, covered with a snowy sheet, was spread against one wall. On it were several cushions and bolsters. As soon as the men were seated, tall silver glasses of sherbet arrived. 'Have some sherbet, Mian,' Tohrab Ali offered his guest a glass. 'The meal isn't quite ready yet. One or two dishes are left—' Other members of the family took up the refrain: 'Yes. Yes. You've had a long ride in the boat and it's a hot day.'

After the drinks, tobacco and betel were served. Tohrab Ali took a few puffs and handed the hookah to Razek.

'No, Mian. No.' Razek shook his head. His ears flamed with embarrassment.

'Why not?' Tohrab Ali demanded. 'Are you a woman that you hang your head in shame?'

'It . . . it isn't fitting,' Razek stammered. 'I . . . I shouldn't be smoking. You are present and—'

'So what if I'm present? Come, take a pull.'

Razek took the hookah and, turning his back to Tohrab Ali, took a few surreptitious puffs. Then, handing it back with relief, he turned around to face his host once again.

After quite a while—the sun had crossed the zenith by then and was fast sinking west—a call came from within. The meal was ready and served. Escorted by Tohrab Ali and the other menfolk, Razek came and took his place on a large plank laid out on the dalan. Glory be to Allah! What a feast! Five or six varieties of fish! Mutton curry, payesh, a bowl of yellow milk thick with clotted cream, bananas the length of the Hindu God Krishna's flutes, thick sticky slabs of cream cheese . . .

Sitting next to Razek, Tohrab Ali kept coaxing him to try a little more of this and a little more of that. 'Eat, Mian, eat,' he urged. 'You're young. This is the age for a healthy appetite.' But the conversation, Razek noticed, was peppered with references to Baikuntha Saha. What was he doing in Kolkata? Was he likely to return to the village? What did Razek think? Razek had no answers. He ate diligently and in silence, his eyes fixed on the bell-metal plate in front of him, when a question from Tohrab Ali's old uncle made him raise his head and glance to his left. And then he saw her. Tohrab Ali's daughter Kamrun stood by a window. Her skin was a soft gleaming yellow—the colour of turmeric. In a face shaped like a betel leaf her features were etched with an artist's long steady strokes. Her carefully scalloped hair was set in shining waves around her forehead. Her pink lips were as thin and fluttery as butterflies' wings. She was as beautiful, Razek thought, as Princess Gul-e-bakawali of the fairy stories he had heard as a child.

The girl had probably been gazing at him for quite some time. Meeting his eyes, now, she blushed and, smiling sweetly, moved away from the window. It wasn't the first time of course. He had seen her often enough in the past when he had worked as a daily wager in her father's house. She had been so proud then! Proud of her beauty and her father's wealth. The world was at her feet and she knew it. If at all she deigned to cast a glance at Razek it was with scornful, contemptuous eyes.

The sun was about to set by the time the meal was over. Tohrab Ali did not press Razek to stay on longer. 'Go carefully,' he said as Razek took his leave, 'and come again soon. Come as often as you can.'

Tohrab Ali walked with his guest as far as the ghat and helped him step into his boat.

It was a beautiful evening. Sweet, wild breezes swept the boat along the waterways, setting the paddy stalks rippling and quivering. Clouds of glow-worms winked and glimmered in the dusk like globes of swinging lamps. But the old anxiety nibbled at Razek with tiny probing teeth. What was the meaning of all this? What was Tohrab Ali's game? Was all this warmth and kindness a trap to get Razek into his clutches? To grasp Baikuntha Saha's property?

From that day onwards, invitations to Tohrab Ali's house started coming thick and fast. Every two or three days, Razek was summoned to a meal on some pretext or the other. Tohrab Ali's hospitality, lavish and unflagging at all times, left Razek overwhelmed. He noticed one thing though and was surprised by it. Except for that first time, when she had looked at him from the window, Kamrun didn't come into his presence. She had displayed no such reticence when he had worked in the house. She had swept past him, time and again, flashing her beauty and her jewels in proud contempt of his manhood. There had been no question of observing purdah from him then. Why was Kamrun avoiding him now? Razek could come up with no answer.

Towards the middle of November, Tohrab Ali took Razek aside and said, 'I have something important to discuss with you, Mian.' Razek's heart sank. He knew Tohrab Ali was coming to the point. The mystery, which had stuck to his side like a thorn, giving him sleepless nights and days of anxiety, was about to be solved. Razek waited with baited breath but, whatever he had expected, it wasn't this. Tohrab Ali held Razek's eyes with his own ash-grey ones and asked, 'You've seen my daughter Kamrun, haven't you?'

'Yes.'

'I want you to marry her.'

Razek looked up with a start. His heart leaped wildly in his breast and his mouth went dry. 'What are you saying, Bara Mian?' he exclaimed.

'Why?' Tohrab Ali's voice was bland. 'What am I saying?'

'Marry your daughter? How is that possible? You're such a big man! So wealthy and respectable! And I . . . I've worked on a daily wage for you—for years. No, no . . . '

'That part of your life is over, Mian,' Tohrab Ali interrupted solemnly. 'You must learn to forget it. As for me being a big man—are you any less? Baikuntha Saha's lands are yours. His house and household goods, his ploughs and oxen, his pond teeming with fish—they are all yours. You are as wealthy and respectable today as I am. You've risen to my level.'

'But—'

'But what?'

'What will people say?'

'No son of a pig will say anything. They wouldn't dare. Besides—'

'Besides?'

'I have to see to my daughter's happiness. Who else in the village has ninety kanis of land? Such an elegant house and furniture? People! I don't give a crow's foot for people's opinions.'

Razek's heart was thumping so wildly he thought it would burst out of his chest. Kamrun! The proud beautiful princess would be his bride. This went beyond his wildest hopes and aspirations. Was he awake? Or was all this a dream? Now he understood Tohrab Ali's motive in seeking him out. His warmth and hospitality. He wanted him, Razek, as his son-in-law.

'What can I say then?' Razek mumbled, his face flaming with embarrassment. 'Please do as you think best. I'll obey you in all things.'

'After the harvest,' Tohrab Ali went on as though Razek hadn't spoken, 'will be the best time. You agree?' Razek nodded. His eyes were on the ground. 'That's settled then.' Tohrab Ali rose to his feet. 'I'll take my leave.'

Razek sat motionless, staring ahead of him, for long after Tohrab Ali had left. A sigh rose from deep within his breast. *Thank Allah, the country was divided!* he thought, his soul uplifted in gratitude. *Would such a fate have been mine if Baikuntha Saha hadn't left the village?*

The reaping of the harvest commenced a few days later. The cutting of the corn, binding it in sheaves, drying, winnowing and stacking in paddy bins took two whole months.

Towards the end of January, Tohrab Ali took up the subject once again. 'The reaping is over,' he said to Razek one day. 'It's time I sent for the mullahs and elders of the village.'

'Whatever you say, Bara Mian,' Razek mumbled. His eyes were downcast and his big toe circled the earth at his feet.

Tohrab Ali's eyes crinkled in thought. 'What's today?' he asked after a while.

'Wednesday.'

'I'll send the boat for you on Saturday afternoon. I'll inform the mullahs and elders too. We'll draw up the contract and finalize the details of the nikah and bridal dower on that day.'

'You don't have to send a boat. I'll come on my own.'

'No, no.' Tohrab Ali shook his head from side to side. 'I owe you that honour. After all, it's an auspicious occasion.'

After Tohrab Ali left that Wednesday, time just refused to budge for Razek. The blood pulsed and pounded in his head and danced in his veins, giving him no rest. He was in a fever of excitement. The hours went so slowly he felt he was traversing aeons. But, maddeningly protracted though it was, Thursday passed and Friday after it. On Saturday morning even the sun seemed to have come to a halt. It rose much later, Razek was convinced, than on other days and was crawling across the sky like a dying snail. It had taken ten hours, instead of one, to reach the top of the paddy field. There was no water in this season—only dry stubble. But a canal flowed by its side and Tohrab Ali's boat would come gliding along it. Razek paced restlessly up and down the yard, his eyes glued to the distant water. Why was the boat taking so long? Had Tohrab Ali changed his mind?

However agonizing the wait, it ended at last. As the sun crossed the zenith and started moving west, a boat could be seen inching its way along the canal, its hump bobbing up and down, up and down. Suddenly a great clamour rose in Razek's chest. A volley of sounds like the wild scraping of a host of fiddles filled his ears. His eyes misted over. The boat that was coming for him was no ordinary boat. His beautiful princess had sent a peacock barge. The peacock's tail was encrusted with gold and gems.

It had reached the bank now and someone was stepping out of it. Tohrab Ali? Should he walk towards the boat and . . . ? And then he saw who it was. It was someone he hadn't thought about in months, someone who hadn't appeared even in his most fearsome nightmares. His wildly thumping heart slowed down. It beat dull and heavy, like a lump of lead, in his chest. Sweat, cold as ice water, ran down his brow and along his spine. There was someone else with Baikuntha Saha. A man of about sixty. His looks and attire were those of a Muslim.

Razek looked with glazed eyes as the two men crossed the pithkhira patch and stepped into the yard. 'Why, Razek!' Baikuntha Saha exclaimed, smiling broadly. 'What luck to have found you at home! I was afraid you might be out. How are you? Is everything going well for you?' Razek stood rooted to the ground. He looked like the stump of a tree charred by lightning. He tried to speak but no sound came. The veins trembled in his neck, stood out like ropes. Slowly, very slowly, he managed a whisper, 'Saha Moshai! You?'

'Yes. It's me,' Baikuntha Saha replied, beaming. 'I wasn't able to inform you of my coming. It all happened so fast . . . I've just arrived.'

'Where were you all these months?'

'In a number of places—Kolkata, Bongaon, Dattapukur . . . I've settled down, finally, in Murshidabad.' Turning to his companion, he said, 'Sit and rest yourself, Amin Saheb. Fetch a stool, Razek, and prepare a hookah.'

The stool and hookah arrived. Baikuntha Saha seated himself on the floor and the two men talked of this and that. From time to time they flung questions at Razek. How many Hindus had left the village? Who were the ones that had stayed? What was the state of the country after partition? Had things improved? Razek made all the right responses but his voice sounded as though it had traversed a vast distance. Baikuntha Saha didn't seem to notice. 'So, Razek,' his big voice boomed heartily, 'how is life treating you? Well, I hope. Are you looking after the house and property?'

Razek's mouth twisted in a caricature of a smile. 'Why don't you see for yourself?' he said.

Baikuntha Saha rose to his feet on this invitation. 'Come, Amin Saheb,' he urged his companion. 'You've seen my fields and pond on the way. Let me show you the house.' Razek looked on, his heart hammering, his senses swimming. He felt the strength ebbing from his limbs. In his head was a jumble of thoughts. What was Baikuntha Saha doing in Chhipatipur? Did he mean to settle down, once again, in the village? If so, why hadn't he brought his wife and children? Who was the Muslim gentleman? He couldn't be from these parts because, if he was, Razek would have recognized him. What was the connection between the two? Why had Baikuntha Saha shown him his lands and was, even now, taking him on a tour of the house? The whole thing was a mystery. Razek racked his brain trying to answer some of the questions but could come up with none.

The two men returned in a while and took their places. 'Well!' Baikuntha Saha prodded his companion, 'what do you think?'

'Good! Good!' Amin Saheb nodded.

'Did you like the house?'

'Yes.'

Now Baikuntha Saha turned his attention on Razek. 'Ah! Razek,' he said. 'I must introduce you to Amin Saheb. He's a friend of mine—from Murshidabad. And Amin Saheb, this is Razek Mian. He is a gem of a person. Most trustworthy. I left him in charge of my property in my absence. You've seen with your own eyes how well he has looked after everything.'

Amin Saheb nodded.

'Razek,' Baikuntha Saha came to the point at last, 'I've decided to stay on in India. And that is why I've brought Amin Saheb along. Do you understand what I mean?'

Razek shook his head. He did not understand.

Baikuntha Saha looked around furtively and lowered his voice. 'I'll be making over all my property in the village to Amin Saheb.' Seeing the incomprehension on Razek's face he smiled. 'Let me explain,' he said. 'Amin Saheb wishes to migrate to Pakistan. In return for the house and land in Chhipatipur he will give me everything he owns in Murshidabad. This kind of transaction is called *exchange*. We'll send for the lawyer tomorrow and draw up the deed.'

Just as Razek opened his mouth to ask a question, the two men Tohrab Ali had sent as escorts stepped into the yard.

'We're a little late, Mian,' they said. 'You must come quickly or everything will get delayed.'

Razek stared at them with unseeing eyes. Baikuntha Saha was taking the house and fields away from him and giving them to Amin Saheb. The old equation had changed completely. Was there any sense, now, in accompanying these men? He remembered Tohrab Ali's kindness and warmth. His lavish hospitality. But that was because the old man was hoping that Razek would marry his daughter. Would he still want him as a son-in-law? Razek thought for a while. He might, he reasoned. Having come thus far he may not wish to go back.

Razek made up his mind. 'Please sit and make yourselves comfortable, Saha Moshai,' he said. 'I'll be back in a while.' Rising to his feet he followed the two men and took his place on the boat.

As Razek approached the house it became evident that a great celebration was on. The mullahs and elders had arrived and were seated in places of honour. The rooms were crammed with guests. Starting with the Khans, Mridhas and Sardars, all the respectable families of Chhipatipur had been invited. Rosewater was being sprinkled liberally. Betel and scented tobacco were being served. Bell-metal plates full of sweets and tall glasses of sherbet were making the rounds. Everyone cried out excitedly at Razek's entrance. He was, after all, the bridegroom. Jokes were exchanged. The place was abuzz with laughter and gossip. Razek's head was in a whirl. He could see what was going on but his mind wasn't registering. It felt blank and benumbed. Tohrab Ali noticed his absent-minded air and couldn't resist a dig. 'Why such a long face, Mian?' he nudged Razek slyly with his elbow. 'On a happy day like this?'

'Baikuntha Saha arrived this morning.' The words burst out of Razek before he could stop himself.

'Baikuntha Saha,' Tohrab Ali echoed. His voice sounded as if it was floating on air.

'Yes,' Razek continued hastily. It seemed as though he wanted to unburden himself. To rid himself of a demon that was straddling his chest. 'He has brought someone with him from India. A man called Amin Saheb. Baikuntha

Saha is going to gift him his house and fields in exchange for everything he owns in Murshidabad.'

There was a stunned silence. The mullah, elders and guests stared at Razek, their faces dark with anxiety. What was going to happen now? He could see the question in everyone's eyes.

'Then,' Tohrab Ali spoke at last, 'why are we sitting here? There's no question of a wedding.' He stood up and walked away, muttering as he went. 'What Allah wills is for the best! Why else would Baikuntha Saha arrive today of all days?'

Now the mullah and elders rose, one by one, and took their leave. The eminent men of the village followed suit. Razek was left alone, sitting by himself, in the room. He sat for a long time, then, rising to his feet, walked out of the house.

And now . . .

Day follows night in weary succession. Razek stands in the waters of pond, lake and river with his polo and dharmajaal. He scours the stubble in the fields for ears of fallen grain. His skin is turning black, once again, and his uncombed, unoiled hair and beard stand out from his face like clumps of straw. His feet have started to crack and his fingers and toes are festering from constant contact with water. He has taken to muttering to himself. If one listens carefully one can catch the drift of his words. 'Countries get divided,' he mumbles, shaking his head solemnly, 'and the Sahas and Jugis and Bhuinmalis leave the village. But what is that to you, you fool? What is that to you? Others come in their place. The king is dead. Long live the king!'

The Fugitive
and the Stalkers

Palatak o Anusharankari

Sunil Gangopadhyay

'You?'

Robi touched a finger to his lips. 'Shh!' he hissed. 'Is Pishemoshai home? Ashok da?'

Jayanti shook her head. 'No,' she murmured, surprised. 'Pishima should be home.'

'She is.'

Jayanti's eyes raked Robi's form from head to toe. 'Your feet are caked with mud,' she said presently. 'Go wash them at the tap in the corner of the courtyard.' Leading the way she looked back at her guest. 'Where have you been all these days?'

'I'm starving, Boudi. Please give me something to eat quickly. A bowl of muri will do.'

'Of course . . . come with me.'

Ascending the stairs they found Pishima on the landing. 'Who is it, Bouma?' Pishima peered out of rheumy, short-sighted, old eyes.

'It's Robi.'

'Robi! Come up, son. What are you waiting for?'

'I'm very hungry, Sejo Pishi.'

The old lady's feet shifted into position, expecting a *pronam*. But the famished young man had no eyes for them. 'Something to eat,' he turned his eyes on Jayanti. 'Make it quick.'

'Why are you in such a hurry?' the old lady cried. 'Won't you stay with us tonight?'

'I'll stay till Ashok da returns. I have something to say to him.'

'How's your father?'

'Same as usual.'

'And your mother? I haven't heard from her in a long time.'

'Don't you understand I'm hungry?' Robi snapped. 'Very, very hungry. Will you give me something to eat? Or only keep asking questions?'

'*Ma go*! What a temper! As though you haven't eaten for days!'

At this point, Jayanti walked in, holding a bowl full of muri in her hands. Robi saw, at a glance, that she had tried to make it appetizing with a scattering of spiced gram and finely sliced onions and green chillies. 'Have this to begin with,' she said. 'I'll bring you some luchis in a minute.'

'There's no need to fry luchis. This is good enough.'

'Some tea?'

'Tea would be fine.'

'You've lost a lot of weight in the last month,' Jayanti said conversationally. 'Why don't you look after yourself?'

'Ashok da is swelling like a balloon day by day. Why don't you look after your husband?'

'And your eyes are sunk in their sockets. How many sleepless nights . . . ?'

'Go. Put the kettle on. Quick.'

Robi flung a handful of muri in his mouth and, walking over to the window, peered with narrowed eyes into the

Sunil Gangopadhyay

gathering dusk. A few seconds later he saw them—three young men walking side by side, chatting in a leisurely manner as they went along. Approaching the house they looked up. Then, standing still for a while, they heaved a collective sigh and started walking towards it.

Robi set the half-eaten bowl of muri on the floor with a thud. Then, with swift steps, he walked out of the room, down the stairs and out of the house. Once outside he broke into a run.

The three had reached the house by now. Their eyes caught a flash of the escaping youth but they didn't hasten their steps or betray any emotion.

'He's escaped again,' Stalker No. 1 mumbled.

'Yes,' Stalker No. 2 nodded in agreement.

Stalker No. 3 took out a piece of paper from his pocket and peered at it. 'Where do we go from here? Dumdum or Srirampur?'

'Dumdum,' Stalker No.1 said.

'Then let's finish the job here,' Stalker No. 2 suggested.

Stalker No. 3 shivered slightly and thrust his hands deep into his pockets. 'It's turned cold,' he said. 'There's a shop at the crossroads, selling sizzling hot cutlets. Shall we—?'

Stalker No. 1 fished a bomb out of his satchel and hurled it at the door.

'Ah!' Stalker No. 2 exclaimed in a tone of satisfaction. 'Fine sound!'

'No need to rush,' Stalker No. 3 said comfortably. 'Let's have some cutlets.'

'Chandan! Chandan!' Robi stood outside a house, calling softly. No one answered. It was nine-thirty at night and the place a lane in a small mofussil town. The silence was broken by the occasional rattle of a rickshaw and the snarling of pi dogs.

'Chandan!' Robi called louder this time.

And now a young girl's form appeared in the balcony. 'Who is that?' she asked, leaning over the rail.

'Is Chandan home?'

'Dada has fever. He's asleep.'

'Open the door.'

'What's your name?'

Even as she spoke, some instinct made Robi wheel around. Two rickshaws had stopped on the main road at the end of the lane. Without another word Robi vanished into the night.

The three walked slowly towards the house.

'He didn't go in,' Stalker No. 1 said. 'I was watching him.' He moved towards the door, but before he could knock, it opened with a creaking sound. A girl of fourteen or fifteen, her sari wrapped carelessly around her, stood before him.

'Is Chandan really ill?' Stalker No. 2 asked.

'His temperature went up to a hundred and four today,' the girl said. 'Where are you coming from?'

'From Robi Babu. We've come to see your brother.'

'He's asleep.'

'Oh! All right then.'

'Any message?'

'Tell him three persons came looking for Robi Babu. He'll know what that means.'

'Do we need to do—you know what—now?' No. 2 moved away from the door towards the others.

'In my opinion—' No.1 hesitated.

'My younger brother is down with fever too,' No. 3 said ruefully. 'It's going to hit me next.'

No. 2 placed a hand on No. 3's forehead. It was cool. 'There's no temperature,' he said in a puzzled voice.

'I feel it rattling in my bones. Ah! What I wouldn't give to be able to creep into bed with a snug warm quilt over me.'

Sunil Gangopadhyay

'Let's finish the job here. No use wasting time,' No. 1, intent on his duty, reminded the other two.

'I haven't slept a wink for days,' No. 3 sighed. 'And the cold is killing me. Even God has turned against us. He's cruel, pitiless—'

'He's a bastard,' No. 2 said forcefully. 'Out to get our guts.'

No. 1 took a bomb out of his satchel and hurled it at the door. The sound of the explosion shattered the silence of the night. A volley of barks rose from the startled pi dogs.

Robi spent the night in the cremation ground on the bank of the Ganga. He tried to keep himself awake by pacing up and down and standing, from time to time, beside one or other of the four funeral pyres that were burning through the night. Knots of people stood around him but no one seemed to question his presence. His eyes smarted from the acrid smoke and tears ran down his cheeks. It was years now since he had wept at a death. Death meant nothing to him any more.

Suddenly a gush of love ran through him. But it was for himself. Placing a hand on his bare chest he stroked it gently. As though it was someone else's chest. As though it was someone else he loved.

At dawn, mingling with the crowd of bathers at the Ganga, he walked to Howrah Station from where he boarded a train for Srirampur. He caught Sushanta just as he was setting off for the market. 'I have to stay here for the day,' he said.

Sushanta didn't seem too pleased at this intrusion. 'My father is coming from Delhi,' he muttered.

'Just today. I must—'

'Shall I send word to Khokon? At Gosainpara?'

'No. No need for that.'

Robi slept the whole day, making up for nights and nights of lost sleep. He rose only once for a bath and a meal and slept again. His pants and shirt were so dirty that he couldn't bear to touch them to his clean, washed body. Wearing one of Sushanta's dhuti and kurta sets he glanced at himself in the mirror. He looked so different from his normal self that he gasped with surprise. *If with the change in my looks I could become another person*! he thought wistfully. Then he promptly went off to sleep and dreamed of a ship.

Dusk had fallen by the time Robi awoke. It was quite dark in the little room at the top of the house where he had found shelter. Coming out on to the roof he glanced furtively around the house. There was no one. A little later, Sushanta's wife Rupa came up with a cup of tea.

'Do you have an aspirin?' he asked, sipping at the tea.

'No. Shall I send out for some?'

'N-no. I get a headache every day around this time. It passes after a while. Has Sushanta returned from the office?'

'Not yet. He will—in a while.'

'Go down now. Send Sushanta up when he returns.'

'Would you like something to eat?'

'I'm not used to these courtesies. I ask for food when I'm hungry. Do you have moog dal in the house? Can you cook some for tonight's dinner? I haven't eaten moog dal in years—'

'In your house—'

'Please go down now. I wish to be left alone.'

After Rupa had left, Robi sat for a while in grim silence, his face turned to the wall. Then, putting his head in his hands, he squeezed his throbbing temples.

'It's dark in here,' Sushanta said, walking into the room. 'Why haven't you switched on the light?'

'There's a dog barking in the street,' Robi said, turning around. 'I've been hearing it for a long time now. I used to have a dog who barked just like that.'

Sunil Gangopadhyay

'Where is the dog now?'

'We used to live in Shibsagar those days. The dog was my constant companion. He was a good dog—gentle and docile. Then, all of a sudden, he changed. He became aggressive, hostile. People started getting scared of him. My parents said the dog had turned mad and had to be sent away. I resisted for a while, and then was forced to give in. One day he was taken out in a boat and left on a distant bank of the river. That bank, I was told later, got flooded during the monsoon and was inundated for months afterwards. That's why whenever I hear a dog barking in a lonely place, I . . . '

'Where are you going from here?'

'I don't know.'

'You may stay here for a day or two. We hardly use this room.'

Robi fixed his eyes on his friend's face. Moments passed. Suddenly he flung his head up and said haughtily, 'I don't need a roof over my head. I wasn't thinking of comfort when I chose my vocation.'

Sushanta's face hardened. 'You'll have to think again,' he said grimly. 'It isn't a street you're walking on. It's a blind lane.'

'You must have a gramophone at home. Do you, Sushanta?'

'A gramophone?' Sushanta was startled.

'*A happy home needs a gramophone*,' Robi sang. 'Haven't you heard the ad? A gramophone is a must for a set-up like yours!'

'This is what is generally referred to as the *arrogance of fools*,' Sushanta exclaimed indignantly.

At this point, Rupa came up and said to Sushanta, 'Three young men are here looking for you.' Robi jumped up and went to the edge of the roof. He looked around the house surreptitiously. Then, coming back into the room, he asked Sushanta, 'Is there a way out? From the back of the house?'

Sushanta gripped Robi's arm. 'You don't have to go,' he said.

'There's no time . . . ' Robi cried, trying to pull away.

'I'll speak to them. Why should we allow them to frighten us?'

'It's not fear I feel. It's disgust. There's no time!'

'Don't panic,' Rupa cried. 'Our neighbour has a telephone. I'll call the police.'

Robi ran out of the room without deigning to cast a glance at her. Vaulting over the edge of the roof he went shinning down a drainpipe. The noise of a train rushing by filled his ears . . .

'The numbering of the houses in this locality is peculiar!' Stalker No. 1 exclaimed. 'We have fifty-two here after thirty-six. What does it mean?'

'Some of them don't have numbers on the nameplates,' said Stalker No. 2.

'*Sala*!' Stalker No. 3 muttered. 'My legs feel like lead from walking the streets! When is it going to end?'

'Around this time last year I was the fugitive. It is more thrilling to be on the run.' No. 1 smiled at the other two.

'The day Bardhan was killed—' No. 2 began.

'There's a guava tree in my uncle's house,' No. 3 cut in. 'The fruit is green and has a red centre. I fell from it as a child and broke my leg. It hasn't felt the same since.'

'A guava with a red centre?' No. 2 sounded doubtful.

'You get that kind in Deoghar,' No. 1 said. 'I went to Deoghar many years ago with my brother and sister-in-law.'

'Let's finish our job here,' No. 2 prompted.

'Then we'll go home,' No. 3's face lit up. 'Have a hot dinner of rice, musur dal and mashed potatoes! Then a good night's sleep.' His voice trailed away.

No. 1 moved towards the door to speak to Sushanta. The other two took up their positions on the walls on either side . . .

'In which direction is the station?' Robi asked the man in front of him.

'Why are you trying to cross the field in the dark?' The man stared at him. 'The road's just there behind you.'

'Is there no way across?'

'There is. But it is long and circuitous. You won't be able to find it.'

'Leave that to me,' Robi snarled in desperation. 'Just tell me where it is.'

The man looked him in the eye for a moment. 'If you insist on walking cross-country in the dark,' he said calmly, 'you must find the way yourself.'

Robi threw him a burning glance before starting to run again. His eyes darted furtively this way and that. 'The thing to do,' he told himself, 'is to keep calm. Not tire oneself out.' He tried to regulate his breathing as he ran. In. Out. In. Out. He was alone in the field and the air was all his. But many before him had breathed the same air. Even people who had died years and years ago. Sweat broke out on his forehead on this cold winter night. Suddenly he bumped against a wall and stood still . . .

But it wasn't a wall. It was three men massed close together. They pinioned his arms and legs with the skill born of long practice. Robi didn't resist. He sank to his knees and covered his face with his hands. Stalker No. 1 tried to pull them away. 'Do you recognize me, Robi?' he asked casually.

'The three of you . . . Bardhan—' Stalker No. 2 gnashed his teeth at Robi.

'Bastard!' No. 3 shouted. 'You've given us quite a grind!'

Suddenly Robi remembered something. His little sister had asked him to buy her a box of coloured pencils. She had written several letters . . .

The knife did its work neatly and efficiently. But though the boy's chest and abdomen were cut to ribbons the three leaned over the prostrate form to make sure it wasn't breathing.

A sudden commotion made them turn around sharply. A group of nine or ten men were running towards them, shouting and flailing their arms. Were they cries of congratulation or slogans of revenge? They sounded the same. They always did. The three couldn't take a risk. They started running—each in a different direction.

The crowd reached the spot where the dead body lay. A collective cry rose in the air. It sounded like a pledge. Then, in the twinkling of an eye, the nine formed groups of three and, fanning out in different directions, dashed off in cold-blooded pursuit.

Stalker No.1 had become Fugitive No.1. The first of the three who were chasing him called over his shoulder to the third, 'How far can the bastard run? We'll have his guts in the end. Take the paper out of your pocket. Take a good look.'

Sunil Gangopadhyay

The Way Home

Gharer Path

Sirshendu Mukhopadhyay

My father went to a foreign land to seek his fortune; my mother to the mountains to pick faggots. Neither of them returned.

We lived in an earthen hut which had a crack in one wall. When the wind blew through the crack it made a whistling sound. From within the hut it sounded as though someone was standing outside and calling out to me. I was frightened and I clung to my mother for protection.

Every now and then, *ashwatha* saplings snaked their way through nooks and crannies of the walls. 'Cut it down,' Ma cried out to me whenever she saw one rearing its head. I had my axe ready, bright and shining, at all times. My eyes were always on the alert. A speck of green on the wall and I would rush to destroy it.

The roof hadn't been thatched in many years. It had large holes through which the rain came pelting down during the monsoons. To prevent ourselves from getting wet, we moved from one part of the room to another, Ma trying to shield me with a fold of her torn, damp sari. The floor became a swirl of mud. I've spent many nights like this locked tightly in my mother's embrace. Bitterly cold winter nights and nights of lashing rain made fearsome by the roar of thunder and the crackle of blue lightning.

My father had a horse, an old tired horse which couldn't do any work. But Baba loved it and so did I. I went with my sickle to the foothills where the grass grew tall and thick. I went each morning and came back with an armful of sweet rich grass and fed it to the horse sheaf by sheaf. I don't remember Baba at all. I was an infant, crawling on the floor, when he crossed the mountains and went to a foreign land, never to return. But he left the horse for me. When the horse munched the grass I gave him with his yellow broken teeth, I would throw my arms around him and rub my face against the dappled neck. I would pretend he was my father.

When Baba didn't return, Ma went out to the mountains to gather twigs and faggots. That was how the poor people of our village made a living. They left before sunrise every day and returned at dusk. 'Look after the house,' Ma would say to me as she was leaving with the others. 'Give the horse his grass and water. And, at sunset, be sure to collect an armful of leaves and light a fire just outside the hut. If I'm late in coming home I'll see the fire from a distance and know you're safe.'

And that's exactly what I used to do. Look after the house, feed the horse and light a fire at dusk. Sitting by it I would let my eyes wander far, far away, to the mountains which stood like a row of blue demons keeping vigil over our earth. Sometimes they looked dark and mysterious, their heads wrapped in cloud and mist. Sometimes they were aflame with the rose and orange hues of sunset.

The fire burned brightly for a while then dimmed and flickered and turned to ashes. Darkness descended. I was afraid of the mountain because it took my father. I feared for my mother too. I dozed, fitfully, beside the heap of burning leaves and waited for her footfall.

Sirshendu Mukhopadhyay

Ma used to tell me about Baba. How he climbed over the mountains, crossing lakes and streams and rivers till he reached the other side. She had no idea of how far the other side was. All she knew was that he would come back one day with a bag full of gold. I would get new clothes then. And new shoes. A horse would be bought for me, a playful little horse. I would sit on its back and gallop away, far away, to where the mountains meet the sky.

Ma would curse the mountain for obstructing the rest of the world. She would shake her fist at it. Her tangled hair would fly around her face. Yet she sought the mountain too. For it was there that she found the leaves and faggots, the nuts and wild figs that sustained life.

One evening she didn't return. The fire sank lower and lower, before dying out. The mountains disappeared in swirls of mist and darkness. But Ma didn't come back. At dawn I went looking for her. All the others had returned. 'Your mother has gone across the mountain,' they said, laughing, 'to look for happiness. You were the hurdle in her path. So she left you behind.' I didn't believe a word of what they said. I searched everywhere, in every nook and corner of every house in the village. But she wasn't to be found. 'Don't worry,' one of them clapped me on the back. 'You'll be a grown man soon. You'll be able to look after yourself. Start coming out to the mountain with us.'

I went out with them for a few days but my eyes and mind were not on the earth. They picked leaves and twigs. I stood and stared at the sky. I wondered why they said I was a hurdle in my mother's path and that she had abandoned me and gone to look for happiness. I had thought I was my mother's happiness. I had thought happiness was the power with which one fights sorrow and that my mother had that power because of me. Many years later I realized my folly. I realized that I was Ma's sorrow, Ma's suffering. She couldn't think of her own happiness because I was in the way.

My father crossed the mountain and went away. My mother didn't return. The only living thing I had left was the horse. But he was old and dispirited. He couldn't do any work. All he did was sit on his belly and doze the hours away. When I gave him grass, sheaf by sheaf, he chewed desultorily. When I gave him water, he drank. I looked after him the way a strong, sturdy son looks after an ageing father. Sometimes he dropped his huge grey head on my shoulder. I could feel his breath—hot, moist and laboured—against my neck. His head, a rough, hoary, rugged trunk, trembled gustily with every breath, and I could feel the veins throbbing beneath the dappled grey skin. Throwing my arms around him I would stroke his face and neck and feel comforted. I would feel as though I had found shelter under a spreading banyan tree. 'Your father rode this horse when he went out to marry,' the village elder said to me one day. 'Look after him well.'

I looked after him for the best part of the day. The rest I spent sitting outside the hut, staring at the mountain. The wind ran whistling past our empty house, carrying swirls of leaves on its wings. Sparrows danced in and out of the patch of *kurmi* greens. The air was heavy with the scent of wild coriander. In a little hollow beside the well, which the rain had filled to overflowing, a thrush jumped up and down, scattering beads of water from his flapping wings. Beads of bright water and two soft, grey-brown feathers lay on the grass. I sat idly by, watching. The blade of my axe turned rusty with disuse. Ashwatha saplings crept all over the walls like tiny green snakes.

The days passed. I gathered an armful of leaves at dusk every day and set them alight. I lay in the fading warmth of the dying fire and pretended that I was in my mother's embrace, that the soft heat that caressed my limbs rose from my mother's body. The lids slipped over my eyes, heavy as stones, and I drifted away on the wings of slumber.

The midwife who had assisted at my birth came to see me one day. 'You'll die of starvation at this rate,' she said. 'Come and live with me. I have no son. Only a daughter. The two of you can live happily together.'

'N-n-no,' I shook my head. 'I can't leave the hut. At night I dream that my father is coming back.'

The old woman snorted in disbelief. 'Just as that foolish wench—your mother—came back! What do you eat?'

'Whatever I get . . . berries, greens . . . '

The midwife went away muttering and scolding. From the next day, her daughter Chandra started coming at midday with a platter of rice in her hand. Setting it down on the ground she crouched on her haunches like a cat. Waiting, watching.

'What are you staring at?' I asked her one day.

'You,' she answered solemnly. 'Why do you stay at home all day with only an old animal for company?'

'I love him like a father.'

Chandra laughed. It sounded like a tinkle of silver bells. Then, looking into my eyes, she lowered her own and asked, 'Can't you find someone better to love? What can that old horse do for you? How far can it take you?'

Very far, I thought to myself. *One day I'll sit on its back and ride away, far, far away. To the east from where the sun rises. I'll be king of some realm one day.* Aloud I said, 'I don't know.'

Chandra rose to her feet. Pointing a finger at the hut, she said, 'Look, ashwatha saplings are creeping all over your house. Their roots, like sharp teeth, are digging deeper and deeper. Soon the walls will start to crumble and the roof will fall on your head. Scotch the vipers! Kill them!'

'They are like my mother,' I said, smiling at Chandra. 'I can make the leaves and branches of her memory disappear but the roots remain.'

Chandra tossed her head and started to walk away. 'Death is stalking you,' she cried angrily. 'The house will tumble about your ears one day, and you'll be buried under the rubble.'

The roots will push deeper and deeper into the soil, I said to myself, *and the walls of my mind will crack and fall on the earth in a million shards. The day that happens I shall sit astride my old horse and gallop away to the east with my belongings in a bundle tied to the end of a stick. The villagers will stare at the bundle. It will grow smaller and smaller, turn fainter and fainter, and finally disappear beyond the field of golden paddy. They'll know I'll come back again some day, back to the village—a king.*

A few days later . . . I waited for Chandra and my midday meal but she didn't come. I gazed out at the field of flowering aniseed till my eyes ached. But still she did not come. Not that day. Not the next. I waited for her for a while, then took out my rusty old axe and began sharpening it. I spent the whole afternoon rubbing the axe's lip against a flat, grained stone till it sprang into life, dazzling bright, with joy! The muscles of my body had swelled with the hard exercise. The hot blood leapt and danced in my veins. I felt wonderfully alive! I felt drugged with happiness.

I thought I would be able to cut down the ashwatha saplings by the evening, but long before that Chandra arrived with a platter full of rice in her hand.

'Why didn't you come all these days?' I asked roughly.

She raised her eyes to mine and held them. 'A tiger waylays me on the path every day,' she said solemnly.

"Where are you going?" he asks. Then he orders me to place the platter on the ground. "Stroke my tail as I eat," he says, raking my body with his fierce tawny eyes, "or else I'll send you to the devil." The tiger eats your share every day.'

I grunted in disbelief. 'I've heard that story a million times. My mother used to tell it to me when I was little.'

'So what?' Chandra snapped. 'That doesn't make it a lie!'

'"I'll kill that tiger when I grow up," I used to tell my mother. One should kill off one's enemies. Hunger and thirst are enemies. They should be destroyed.'

Chandra rocked on her heels, laughing. 'I doubt if you'll kill the tiger. You'll talk sweetly to it and stroke its tail. Won't you?'

'I don't know.'

'Ma was testing you,' Chandra said after a while. 'She wanted to see how long you could hold out against hunger. "He'll come along when he's really starving," she said. But the days passed and you didn't come. "He's not human," Ma said, sadly, one day. "He's just like his parents. The father uprooted himself from his native habitat and set his eyes on the other end of the world. The mother abandoned her young and went off in search of happiness. Both forgot the way home. He'll go away, too, some day . . . " Ma brushed the tears away from her cheeks as she ladled the rice into your platter.'

Chandra watched me as I ate my rice and murmured, 'But I know you won't go. I feel it, here, in my heart.' She touched her hand to her breast. Picking up the empty platter she walked away. I gazed upon her departing form as she wove her way swiftly between tufts of aniseed flowers. When I couldn't see her any more I picked up the axe and started lopping off the ashwatha branches.

One by one the strong, sturdy stumps, thick with leaves and dripping with sap, dropped to the ground. The blood sprang up in my veins as I swung the axe this way and that.

I felt the heat rise in my limbs and saw it stand on my skin in glittering, rolling drops. I smelt it, strong and musky. It was like the scent, warm and moist, of flesh and bones and sweat and blood, that rises from the horse on cold winter nights. It crept into my nostrils. The fumes intoxicated me and I felt as though I was drunk with wine. They lifted me high on a wave of exhilaration. I was filled with love for my body. I wanted to stroke it, hug it, caress it. I lay down on the ground and rolled my limbs in the soft dirt. My sweat mixed with the dust of the earth.

When winter ended, a flute player came to my house. Spring was in the air. I felt it in the swift, warm tug of the wind. I saw it in the soft drifting of the leaves, light and brittle, from the trees. In the fields the pea greens ripened into gold. The season of collecting faggots was over.

One such day, late in the afternoon, the flute player came from who knows what distant land. He wore a patchwork robe of motley colours and on his head sat a turban so large it hid his brow. His thin bare legs were coated to the knees with red dust. I had never seen him in the village before.

'I don't sell flutes,' he said to me, 'I'm a seller of melodies.' Putting his flute to his lips he played the strangest tune I had ever heard.

'What is this tune you play?' I asked him, puzzled. 'I understand some of it but not all.'

The flute player looked up. Under his heavy brows his eyes were like deep, dark pools. 'This is my own melody, son,' he said. 'I have no guru. I wander over hills and meadows, through towns and cities, by streams and rivers, and play as I go along. Sometimes I hear the soft

Sirshendu Mukhopadhyay

lapping of mountain brooks in my strains, sometimes the swish and quiver of falling leaves.' He put the flute back to his lips and breathed into it. And now the swift, dry winds of spring caught the strains and sent them flying, like arrows, towards the sky. Away they flew, over banks of aniseed flowers, beyond fields of golden paddy, across the blue mountain. Away, away, on the wings of the wind, over towns and villages, lakes and rivers, deltas and estuaries, and city ports on the shores of alien seas to a destination unknown.

And now the wind returned the strains, wafting on its wings the faintest fragrance of that faraway land. Like the soft lilt, sad and sweet, of a cuckoo's song. And on that path, treading on beams of light, and skimming over clouds of shadow, someone was coming. I heard his footfalls—soft, wary. I knew who it was. My father.

What a long path it was! What a weary path! I closed my eyes. *That's my father*, I said to myself. *So many days have gone by. So many nights. The horse is old now. But my father is still on the way home.*

The flute player was playing a different tune now—a strange, new tune that turned the light of the day into the dark of night. As he played, tears welled into my eyes and rolled down my cheeks. 'What does it mean?' I asked him, weeping bitterly. 'Tell me.'

But the flute player didn't care to answer. He played on and on. And as he played, the strangest sounds filled my ears. I heard the great cobweb of cracks on the parched dry land shuddering, vibrating with joy as it soaked in the rain. Rain pelting down from the clouds massed high on the blue hills, rain that reaches deep into the nerves and sinews of the earth. Rain that swells and softens the hearts of the waiting paddy, sending their curling, unfurling emerald shoots pushing vigorously through the fissures. Like tiny flames, the saplings rose, swift as green lightning, shattering the breast of the earth, reaching up to touch the sky.

'What it means is this.' Now the flute player stopped to explain. 'Just as the bud unfurls its petals one by one and blossoms into a flower, just as the tree sheds its old leaves and wears new ones—in silence, in secret—so in man's life, too, one season goes and another appears. Endure the season of sorrow so that the season of joy may follow. Remember that when a field catches fire, the falling ash enriches the soil for the next harvest.'

'Where did you find this tune?' I asked wildly, weeping all the while. 'Teach it to me. I'll wear a robe like yours and wander all over the world. I'll play it as I go along.'

'You surprise me, son,' the flute player said. 'This robe has been fashioned from a thousand remnants picked up in my wanderings. Why should you wear one as motley as this? A bright, happy spirit like you? I flaunt these thousand hues without because I have no colour within. In my soul all is grey and dark.' The flute player rose to his feet. He smiled and walked out into the warm winter sunshine, the red dust glistening on his thin bare legs. No one called out after him. No one begged him to stay. He faded away into the distance and his melody with him.

I spent the rest of the day in a state of drunken delirium. Drunk. Not on wine but on music. I was no longer myself. I had become a mad flute player in a motley robe, a creator of melodies. These melodies had lain dormant within me for aeons. But the time of birth was at hand. They came tearing out of my veins, shimmering and dancing in my blood, driving me mad. I wept as I sang. 'Why! Oh why,' I cried out piteously, 'why did the flute player leave me his tunes? They tie me in a million knots. They won't let me rest. I try to blow them away with the wind and the storm but they remain rooted, steadfast. I try to burn them to ashes but no fire can scorch them. Like tame pigeons they hum in my blood and flit this way and that. I wish they would spread their wings and, rushing out of my soul, soar away into the purple sky.'

The flute player walked on. The path was rough and scattered with stones. It wended this way and that, over the hills and down the dales. Hot, dry winds blew over him, tugging at his skin, cracking it. His feet were torn to pieces by thorns and flints. Yet journey's end was not in sight. He walked from the east to the west. From where the sun rises to where it sets. He went the way my father went; the path my mother followed—leaving her son sitting by a fire of leaves. Don't waste your tears on the old horse. When a field catches fire, the falling ash enriches it for the next harvest. Rain will fall on it from clouds massed high on the hills. Driving, persistent rain will seek out the secret spaces of the earth. Dead seed, buried deep within the hollows, will tremble into life. Paddy shoots, creeping up like green worms, will turn their faces to the sun. But the flute player will not return. No—never. I flung myself on the earth and wept the days away.

One morning, while giving the horse his grass and water, I realized he had aged some more. Silently, secretly, in front of my eyes but beyond them. I leaned against him and tried to think of my mother. But I couldn't recall her face. Like the dew which vanishes from the grass in the rays of the morning sun, my mother's face had vanished from my memory. The edge of her tattered sari, her eyes, dark and still as the quiet shadows on the lake, seemed to me a vision from another life.

The village elder crinkled his eyes at me and said, 'Why! You're a man now, tall and big and strong! When did you grow from boy to man?' I hung my head, smiling shyly. 'Your body is like your father's,' he went on, 'but you have your mother's eyes.' He looked at me appraisingly. 'Well!' he said after some time. 'Now that you're no longer a boy you must start earning your living. There's no sense in whiling the days away. Look after the house. Give the horse his grass and water.' I wondered if I should tell him about the flute player. I hesitated. But he must have seen the thought in my eyes for he smiled and said, 'I know. I know. The flute player came to you. He comes once—only once.' His large head went up and down, up and down, like a marionette's on a string. 'That's why I say, don't sit and mope all day. Don't let the days go by. Look after the house. Give the horse his grass and water.'

Chandra came to me a few days later. 'I hear you paid money to a flute player and bought his melody?'

'Hunh,' I assented gruffly.

She held me with her eyes. Her form swayed, moved towards me. 'You bought a melody but not a flute?' she asked, her eyes burning into mine. 'What's the use of buying a bird if you don't have a cage? With what will you hold it? If you buy at all it must be something tangible, something you can touch, see, smell and hear. Something that will bring you joy. And which you can sell if it brings you sorrow.'

The minutes passed. My eyes were on the ground. 'How much longer,' Chandra said, laughing softly, 'can I go on lugging your platter of rice? You're big and strong now, big enough to feed a woman. Why don't you work for a living instead of sitting at home all day staring at the mountain?'

'I don't know,' I muttered sadly.

'The village elder says that a strong sturdy youth like you needs a woman in the house.' Chandra stuffed the edge of her sari into her mouth to stifle her laughter and ran away from me, fleet-footed as a doe. The soft, warm, woman-smell of her came wafting on the air as she went across the aniseed field, past Phaganlal's earthen hut, skirting the pool of green, scum-laden water, hair flying, the striped end of her yellow sari streaming in the wind. A flimsy veil of cloud, sprinkled with silver sequins, misted the sun. Shadows flickered, rested awhile on her face. Breezes blew gaily about her and honeybees followed her, humming in gentle voices.

The old men of our village were annoyed because I had bought the flute player's melodies. 'You'll have nothing left,' they said, shaking their heads at me sorrowfully. 'Your father went away. Your mother followed.' But the young men spurred me on. 'You were quite right,' they cried, slapping me on the back encouragingly. 'You're young. You're a man. You must earn and squander what you earn. Buy what you will—bird's eggs or melodies— it doesn't matter. Don't listen to the old. They've let their lives slip through their fingers. When they die, next winter, we're the ones who will remain.'

On hearing this I went to the old horse. He laid his great weary head on my shoulder. I didn't know when I had changed from boy to man. When my limbs had lengthened, my skin had become taut and my face roughened with manhood. But the old horse knew. He rubbed his head against my shoulder as if acknowledging my new identity. His great trunk of a face quivered with emotion. I pressed the rough stubble on my cheek against his silky mane and said, 'Don't worry, old one! You're my father. I'll look after you.' Hearing this, he sighed, a great gusty sigh that blew out of his ribs like a column of steam. *Don't grieve because the horse is old. Don't spend your days in fear of the winter. Remember that you can't stem the flow of running water with your hand. It will*

*slip through your fingers. If the old horse dies next winter
you will still be here.* 'You're my father, old one,' I said.
'Don't worry. I'll take care of you.' The horse pressed his
cold tired body against mine and drew warmth from it. I
flung my arms around his neck. I felt safe, secure, as
though I stood under the protection of a great banyan tree.

'What do you mutter to yourself all the time?' Chandra
asked me one day. I turned my eyes, gentle, silent eyes,
on her. Her limbs were moist and shining with the heat of
youth. Lights twinkled in her eyes. What kind of light
was this? I had never seen anything like it before. The
smell of her—bitter sweet, like spiced wine—came drifting
into my nostrils. But it couldn't be wine. It must be some
flower—wild, exotic. But what flower? What did it look
like? What colour was it? She pulled me by the arm and
said, 'Come with me. I have something to show you.'

'What?' I asked.

'It's a king's palace.' She sighed for some reason. A
deep, deep sigh. 'A very strange king's,' she added.

'Where is it?'

'It's close,' she laughed, 'very close. You should be able
to see it. But you don't.' Chandra gave the sari she wore
a tug. It slipped away, first from her breasts, then from
the rest of her, and fell to the ground. She pressed her
hands over her eyes and said, 'The king doesn't take what
is his. But he doesn't give up his ownership rights either.
Why should I spend all my days guarding it for him? Don't
I have other work to do?'

I looked at her body. It was soft and slippery as though
moulded out of ochre clay. Tears dripped from between
the fingers that covered her eyes. I felt a sudden rush of
fear sweep over me.

'I can't work,' she moaned. 'I can't rest. My days go by—
sad and empty. Hasn't your flute player told you that?'

Sirshendu Mukhopadhyay

The scent of that alien, unseen flower trembled in the air. My chest felt tight and hot. Sharp tears pricked at my eyelids. I had thought that I would grow up and kill the tiger that waylays her every day. But how many tigers could I kill? The village elder had told me to attend to my house. The other old men had warned me not to buy the flute player's melodies.

Chandra put out her hands and drew my head to her breast. 'I understand some things about you,' she said. 'But there's a lot I don't understand.' The tips of her breasts, taut and strong like stems of plucked flowers, passed over my brow and eyelids, then softened and melted away. 'You'll go to the mountain to pick faggots one day,' she said, 'and I'll stay and guard your house. And I'll light a fire of leaves at dusk and sit by it so that you can see me on your way home.' Her words brought back to me what the flute player had played in his first tune. I hadn't understood it then. I did so now. 'You had nothing,' the flute had throbbed in anguish. 'No home. No loved ones. You lit a fire of leaves and stared all evening at the mountain. But it was all in vain. The ones you waited for weren't really yours. They forgot the way home.' Suddenly I burst out weeping. I pressed my head on Chandra's breast and wept loud and long. She was weeping too. I could feel her tears fall, thick and fast, on my hair. 'If you don't leave me I won't either,' she said. 'We'll make a home together.' She took me gently in her arms and kissed my lips. Then, naked as the day we were born, we lay down together.

Spring was drawing to a close. The old horse was older. All he would do now was nibble at his grass and doze in the sun. Hot winds blew above his head, ruffling his mane, sending tremors over the dappled skin, puckering it. 'The season of famine is at hand,' the old men said gravely. 'Ponds and pools will be sucked dry. The earth will crack into a million shards. We can only watch and wait for the rains.'

In the field the grass was turning yellow. I led the horse to it, every day at dawn, and left him there. He would graze all day, snuffling out the tenderest shoots, and come back to me at sunset. One day he didn't return. I waited for him till the shadows of dusk gathered about me and the mountain turned dark and hazy. Still he didn't return. Presently, a moon—a round, brilliant moon, flooding the earth with light—rose over the horizon. I sat for a long time straining my eyes for a glimpse of him—bent and crooked with age, hobbling on painful feet, his shadow trailing wearily behind him. I thought and thought and then came to a decision. Knotting one end of a rope into a noose I left the house.

'My loved ones left me when I was a child,' I muttered to myself as I stepped on the path. 'I couldn't help them find the way home. But I'm grown-up now. I won't lose you, old one. I'll look for you and bring you back—wherever you may be.' I walked through the rice fields, waving and rippling in a sea of moonlight, past the shrine of Mahabir under the ancient banyan tree, and crunched my way painfully across stretches of crackling, yellowing pea stalks.

But my horse was not to be found. I walked myself into a frenzy. I whirled like a hurricane from field to field, calling out in a hoarse, cracked voice, 'Come home, old one. Come home.' But all I heard were the echoes of my own voice ringing in my ears. 'I'll look for you till the end, old one,' I muttered, clenching my teeth. 'I won't go home without you.'

Leaving the fields behind, I entered the forest. Trees grew tall and thick around me. Light and shadow flickered in changing patterns about my feet and in my ears was the hiss and crackle of leaves. A strange fear came upon me as I walked. Someone is here, I thought, close behind me. A tremor ran through my limbs, chilling my spine. I felt an unseen presence take my hand and lead me on. Where was it taking me? Was this where I wanted to go? I trembled and cried out in an agonized voice. I don't know what I cried. And then I found I was standing in a tract of marshy land. The forest was behind me and before me was a sheet of gleaming water. I had never come here before.

I had never seen such a vast, shimmering sea of moonlight. Standing across the water was my horse. He stood very still, his eyes unblinking as though straining to see something. His ears quivered a little as though waiting for a call. 'Old one!' I cried softly. 'Old one!' I called again. He didn't respond. He stood just as he was. Absolutely still. I went slowly up to him and placed a hand on his back. 'I've found you, old one,' I said. 'I'll never lose you again.' He turned his head and looked at me. Then, with a nervous whinny, he shied away. I realized then that he didn't know me. I was a stranger. I walked towards him, calling over and over again, 'Old one! Old one!' Suddenly he took terrible fright and, turning his face in the other direction, galloped away as fast as his ageing legs could take him.

I ran after him. I called out to him. But he didn't see me. No—not even in the terrible, pitiless light that flooded the earth as fiercely as though it came from the midday sun. My hands gripped the noose of my rope. Then I called out to him for the last time. No response. Only a sharp whinny of fear. I threw the rope. He stood still. I realized that the noose had fallen around his neck. The end of the rope which I held in my hands trembled as though it were alive. 'I won't let you go, old one,' I moaned softly. 'No, never.' I moved stealthily towards him.

Suddenly a strange sound entered my ears. The horse was neighing in an old man's voice, quavering, fearful. I felt a tug at the rope. I realized that he was trying to dash into the forest—away from me. I ran after him, crying, 'I won't let you go.' And now the pull became stronger, the voice passionate, angry. It rained curses on me. But I held steadfast to the rope. 'I'll fight you to the end, old one,' I said to him, 'but I won't let you go.' The horse bit and strained at the rope for a while, then, beaten, came to a shuddering halt. I went up to him and laid a hand on his back. The dappled skin was hot and damp and smelled of fatigue and terror. I examined the noose. It had fastened itself tightly around his neck, cutting deep into the flesh. I tried to loosen the knot but, soaked as it was with sweat and blood, it felt as if it was welded by fire. I kept pulling till my fingers were torn to bits and sweat broke out, cold and clammy, all over my body. But the knot wouldn't loosen. The old horse trembled with fear and pain. I put my teeth to the knot and tried to bite it through. The veins on my temples swelled with the effort. My mouth was full of blood. And now the horse turned his eyes on me. Huge, unblinking eyes filled with sorrow. Not for himself but for me. I pressed my cheek against his mane and sobbed, 'I'll set you free, old one. I'll set you free.' I looked into his eyes. Great sad eyes that sought to wipe away from my soul the pain and shame of patricide. 'I wanted to hold you back, old one,' I cried out in my misery. 'I wanted to hold you with this noose.' Then, to my horror, I saw his eyes change. They started curdling, turning opaque. Dying. Yes—in that dazzling silver of the moon I saw his eyes die. I flung the rope away and fled. Across the sheet of bright water, past the trees, through the corn fields, crying as I went, 'I don't know who used my hands to kill you, old one . . . I don't know.'

Sirshendu Mukhopadhyay

My father went to a distant land to seek his fortune. My mother went to the mountain to pick dry leaves and faggots. My old horse went out to the swamp to graze on soft grass. None of them returned.

The village elder called us all one day and said, 'Let me tell you a story. A holy man used to sit by a burning crucible under the shade of a giant banyan tree. All those who saw him, travellers and householders alike, thought him a great saint and folded their hands before him in reverence. One day a man came up to him saying, "Sadhu Baba, I wish to offer you some food," and handed him a stack of *rutis*. But immediately afterwards, as though ashamed of his humble offering, he said, "These are dry rutis, Baba. With what will you eat them? Give me your *lota* and I'll bring you some milk." The sadhu was pleased and handed him his lota. But the man went away and didn't return. The sadhu rolled in the dust in a paroxysm of grief and called out to each passer-by and told him the story. "See how I've been cheated!" he cried. "The rascal fed me a few rutis and ran off with my silver lota."'

'And then?' we asked eagerly.

'The man who loses his lota is a fool,' the village elder smiled. 'But he who weeps over his loss is a greater fool.'

The village elder died just before the onset of winter. The other old men sat together in a knot. 'Death follows birth,' they said to one another. 'Then a man is reborn. Just as wave follows wave in the sea, so also in the ocean of life. Man walks, falls, picks himself up and walks again. There's no end to this game.'

The old men of the village were fearful for their own lives. 'Winter is coming,' one of them remarked. 'It is time to leave our homes.'

'What homes?' another asked fretfully. 'Leaf huts— lashed by the rains during the monsoons, burned to dust by the summer sun!'

Winter came slowly. On painfully crippled feet. Like the worn hooves of the old horse. Laying its head on the old men's shoulders, it breathed in the little warmth still left in their bodies. They swept up leaves in their feeble arms and, lighting a fire, sat in a circle around it.

'We were set adrift on the tide as soon as we were born,' one said to the others. 'That is why we never had a roof above our heads nor walls around us!'

'We were walking on the road to an unknown village along with many,' another said. 'Then darkness fell on the land and we couldn't see each other. No one knew who walked beside him. We cursed the dark but our souls were filled with wonder at its beauty.'

'Who knows where I am headed?' one murmured wistfully. 'I only know that I must return. Like the fine pollen of flowers I shall be blown by the wind and fall to the earth. And then, one day, clouds will gather on the mountain tops and the air will grow heavy with moisture. Rain will fall in torrents and drench the earth to its foundations. Then I shall bloom in the sheets of flowers that will cover the land. I shall flow with the gurgling stream. I shall play with the breezes and float on the clouds.'

At these words the young men of the village laughed in mockery. And that was the reason I set up home with Chandra.

'Light a fire after dusk,' my mother had said to me. 'I'll see it from the mountains and know you're safe.'

'Come and stay with me,' the midwife had urged. 'Live in my house as a son.'

'The paddy seed hiding in the bowels of the earth will swell with the rains,' the flute player had said. 'Shoots will burst out of their shells and, shattering the breast of the earth, rear their heads to the sky. Don't grieve for the old horse. One season follows another.'

Sirshendu Mukhopadhyay

'Look after the house,' the village elder had advised me. 'Feed and water the horse. Don't let the days go by in idleness. Remember that the flute player comes only once.'

'Don't buy the flute player's melodies,' the old men of the village had warned. 'You'll have nothing left if you do.'

'You're my father, old one,' I had said to the old horse. 'I'll look after you.'

I had looked after the house. I had lit a fire at dusk. Yet my father went away to an alien land. My mother went to the mountain to gather leaves. My horse went to the swamp to graze on tender grass.

In the Opinion of This House

Uttar Paksha

Bani Basu

This story is about Najma Chowdhury, the lady who has just come rushing into the railway platform of a mofussil town and is glancing at her watch with anxious eyes. She is wearing a navy-blue jamdani from Bangladesh, covered all over with motifs in white thread. A white shawl and poncho starred with silver sequins rests lightly on her shoulders. Two small but flawless stones are winking and blinking from her ears. There's another on her ring finger—a large diamond, blazing like white fire. The air is languid with the scent rising from her person. An expensive French perfume.

In the ensuing debate it is Najma Chowdhury who stands for the motion.

It is seven-thirty in the evening of a cold, depressing, wintry day. To top it all, it is drizzling—lightly but steadily and monotonously. The platform is deserted. No passengers. Not a coolie or railway official in sight. Even the hawkers seemed to have called it a day. Drip! Drip! Drip! The sound of falling rain on the sheets of corrugated tin above her head is hardly music in her ears. Not the music of the jaltarang. Definitely not. If anything at all, it sounds like the spine-chilling overture of a horror movie or radio play. It is dark inside the station—the density dispelled somewhat, it is true, by the faint light from a fluorescent bulb, but lurking close by like a shameless cat, ready to spring any moment. 'Tell the coolie,' they had said to her, 'to take you to the Ladies compartment.' But there was no coolie. Besides, it was probably not safe to travel in the Ladies compartment alone at this hour. By they, of course, she meant one person. Lily's cousin—that excessively enthusiastic young man who had abandoned the wedding house and its numerous festivities in order to drive her to the station three miles away.

Najma knew that it was only her ability to instil a certain diffidence in her male admirers that had prevented the gentleman from following her into the station. It had started from the moment she had seen him, one hand on the steering wheel, wavering between the two doors, wondering which one to open for her. She had pre-empted him smartly by pulling the one at the back and settling herself against the cushions. It wasn't a very polite thing to do but she couldn't bear over-solicitous men. There's a word called 'chivalry' in the English language which, Najma was convinced, men exploited shamelessly in order to con women. There's a subtle difference between taking care of a lady in a sensible, responsible way and being overtly familiar. Young, inexperienced girls couldn't see it. But Najma was a mature woman, a social worker. She had taken part in workshops, meetings and processions from the age of seventeen. She had met many men in her career and could see through their masks. She knew which cloud was merely hot air and which would bring rain. She kept a smile on her lips at all times—a smile with about as much life in it as a bunch of paper flowers in a vase. No one could call her rude. But the smile registered a temperature that varied. In the case of Lily's cousin it was almost frosty.

Fortunately for her she had a return ticket. She had bought it on stepping off the train on her way to the wedding venue. The Bengali race was really very irresponsible, she thought. You could call it warmth or hospitality or whatever you wished but, in effect, what Lily's family had done was nothing short of oppressive. And who was suffering the consequences? Not they but her.

She had come early in the hope of being able to leave early, reaching Lily's house at four-thirty in the afternoon—after a two-hour journey from Kolkata. It had been quite an effort and had involved considerable self-sacrifice. She had been working on the annual accounts of the Centre and had had to abandon them halfway even though the work was urgent. The audit was to take place next month. She had planned to catch the five-thirty passenger local on the way back. That would drop her off at Howrah around seven-thirty. After that it was another half an hour by bus to Park Circus. Hopefully, the office rush would be over by then.

But her plans had misfired. She had reached Lily's house to find her deep in her prenuptial beauty sleep. Her mother and aunts, worn out with the morning's chores, were catching quick naps in various parts of the house. The men were busy supervising the catering and decorations. The rites were to be solemnized at a very late hour—well after midnight.

Najma's announcement that she would be leaving in half an hour was met with a storm of protest. 'Najma di!' Lily exclaimed, 'how can you even dream of such a thing? Heaven forbid—a girl gets married only once in her whole life! And you say you'll go away without seeing the one

and only bridegroom I'll ever get to have. Go away
without even a meal? Impossible!'

'Arré! Arré! I have to get back home, don't I? Do you
have any idea of how long it takes? Nearly two hours by
train, then half an hour by bus. And your house is quite a
distance from the station. Three miles at the very least.'

'You can spend the night here. Please stay on and see
the wedding, Najma di. You've never seen a Hindu
wedding at close quarters before.'

No, Najma thought grimly. *And I have no desire to.
You've been sold off cheap at the cattle market and will
be branded tonight with much pomp and ceremony. Then
slaughtered. Three-fourths of your throat will be hanging
on one side like a sacrificial camel's on Eid. You may
scream as loud as you wish with the one-fourth that's
left, for the rest of your life. No one will hear you.* Aloud
she said, 'You've forgotten there's a family-planning
programme in Baruipur tomorrow morning. You've been
let off because of the wedding. I don't have the same excuse.'

'All right, all right! You win. But why are you in such
a hurry? You can catch the six fifty-five local, surely!
Sukanto da will take you to the station. Won't you,
Sukanto da?' Najma stole a glance at Lily's Sukanto da,
the young man who had bustled into the room at least six
times while she was there with a hearty, '*Ki ré*, Lily? I
hear you wanted me!' He was grinning from ear to ear.
'Of course I will,' he answered. 'I can even drive her
straight to her home in Park Circus. Only—I won't be
here, then, to hold the bridal plank.'

Najma lowered the temperature of her smile in a single
jerk. She knew what these Sukanto *das*, Proshanto *das*,
Rafiq *das* and Jalil *das* were like. They were spiritual
descendants of those royal princes who, in Mughal times,
flung kerchiefs from the ramparts of forts at the women

they desired for the night. The only difference was that these modern equivalents lacked the guts of their ancestors. And their power. These kept their handkerchiefs in their pockets and lurked in dark corners waiting for opportunities. Najma had absolutely no doubt about it.

The time had now come to get the bride ready for the wedding. And, as is quite natural, Lily got totally lost in the intricate mazes of make-up. Eye shadow, blush-on, glimmer, lipstick, lip gloss, in all their finest nuances, took hold of her. Even elderly ladies are known to go berserk on such occasions. As had Lily's mother. Lily was her only daughter and she had eyes for no one—not even her VIP guest. Najma tried to slip away a couple of times but she was caught by someone or the other and forced to return. It was six-thirty by the time a meal was served to her in the bride's room. Lily's aunt filled a thala with whatever had been cooked and hovered around Najma, apologizing so humbly for the delay that it seemed as though she was serving royalty. 'Don't be afraid,' she said over and over again, 'Sukanto will take you all the way home if you miss the train.'

'Afraid!' Lily exclaimed. 'Najma di doesn't know the meaning of fear. If she did she couldn't have become the secretary of the Shakti Centre. She's not a faint-hearted mouse like you.'

'It isn't a question of fear,' Najma smiled, endorsing Lily's statement. 'But there is such a thing as inconvenience.'

'That's true. If you feel travelling to Kolkata would be inconvenient at this hour, why don't you stay the night? We are humble people and cannot offer you the comforts you are used to but if it isn't too difficult—'

Najma had absolutely no intention of spending the night here. These people were all strangers to her. Barring Lily she hadn't seen even one of them before. The house seemed to be bursting at the seams with friends and relatives. Where would she sleep? Of course no one intended to sleep. She was quite sure of that. They would stay awake all night, teasing the newly-weds with crude comments and vapid jokes. She didn't want any part in it.

'I haven't told my father,' she said crisply. But who would accept such a lame excuse?

'You!' Lily exclaimed, laughing. 'Even you are afraid of your father, Najma di?'

Najma sighed. No matter how much you educated them, these women would never learn the difference between true independence and whimsical, irrational behaviour. She made it a point, always, to inform Ali Saheb about where she was and when she meant to return because she knew he would worry.

Now, looking beyond the faint light of the platform, at the rain which the wind was blowing hither and thither like the torn slats of a lattice curtain, she thought that spending the night at Lily's house would perhaps have been a more sensible option. She had stayed in so many unknown places before. In a sweepers' colony in Bihar whose lanes and alleys were littered with vegetable peels, crushed egg shells and swine shit. In a filthy Muslim slum in Pilkhana which stank of garlic, urine and human faeces. But she hadn't minded. She was a social worker and social workers were not supposed to think of their comforts. The situation was different here. She had visited Lily's house as a guest. And it was that which had raised a wall. Work and socializing had to be kept separate, she told herself.

Trains on this line became more and more infrequent as the evening advanced. The one she was waiting for now was the seven forty-five local. After the six fifty-five—the seven forty-five. A gap of fifty minutes. What a nuisance! Lily's Sukanto da had offered to wait with her and see her into the train. But, hitting the icy wall of her disdain, he had had to go back. The train was coming in now . . . she could see the lights from where she stood. Najma braced herself to board. The Ladies compartment shot past her absolutely empty. There was no time now to regret her decision. She stepped forward quickly and entered the compartment nearest to where she stood.

It was fairly crowded. Looking around she could spot only one vacant space. And that was between two gentlemen. Well, you could hardly call them gentlemen. A gentleman would have had the courtesy to move up and give a lady the corner seat. She had seen men at close quarters all her life and knew all there was to know about them. She was convinced that they were all, without exception, dirty dogs. It was only the fear of the law and social condemnation that forced them to keep their unruly paws well hidden. They were all waiting for opportunities.

Tearing through the charcoal expanse of a winter dusk the train rushed on like one demented. Like Najma. She too had been rushing like that, from the age of seven to thirty-two, through a pitch-black night. There had been hundreds of signals on the way. Red-eyed warnings. But Najma hadn't taken heed of them. Nor was she now. Time was precious. She had no intention of wasting it by stopping midway. She had a goal to reach. Freedom. Total and complete freedom. The first step of which was independence of thought and action. There could be no question of gifting it away to a stranger. She had almost mastered the ability to take care of herself, to be responsible for herself; and she wanted other women to be like her. She wanted to mould them in her own image. But the women around her were so dull! So insensitive! It was such an effort!

Najma had studied in a madrasa till she was eight-and-a-half years old. Then, with her maternal grandmother's help, she had run away from home and joined a missionary school. Mother Marianne had been her first inspiration. It was from her that Najma had learnt the meaning of freedom and how important it was for a woman.

Getting her mother out of her grandfather's mansion in a peasant village of Murshidabad had been a harrowing experience. Though she was only ten-and-a-half years old at the time, she had done it. Ignoring the blood-flecked eyes of the proud and indomitable Nawab Nausher, she had ripped the iron curtain of the zenana apart and brought her mother to the town in which her father lived and worked. When her grandfather had tried to stop her she had bitten his hand. 'Go then!' the nawab had laughed at his tiny granddaughter—so like himself. 'Let's see how far you can get. If you can stall the nikah—so be it.'

Najma had done just that. She had prevented her father from taking another wife. She had achieved what her mother didn't even know was possible to attempt. Her mother's helplessness had stung Najma into a realization of what her life's mission would be. She had to educate the women around her. They had to be taught to stand up for themselves. To demand their rights.

There were others like her of course. Friends of the weak. But what had they achieved? Bride burnings and Khomeini. Even today at the turn of the twentieth century! The cover of the book bore a different picture but the text was nearly the same. There's a veil within that is harder to shed than the external one.

If at all, the slave woman was wearing an extra shackle now. She was being sent out to work. She was earning money. But that didn't enhance her image in male eyes in the least or lessen her responsibilities in the house. *So what if you're working?* the eyes said to her. *Do you expect your husband to look into the nitty-gritty of your household? You're highly educated. Very good. Teach your children. Training her child to be a good, responsible citizen is a mother's primary duty and divine privilege. In fact that's what a woman is born for. Housework? Well, of course. It's woman's work after all. Surely you don't expect Mian Saheb to . . . ? Think how embarrassing it would be for him. And since you're going out anyway why don't you do the shopping? Don't overspend though. Try to get the cheapest rates. The electric bill? But that's on the way to your office. Why don't you just drop it off?* The post office, the bank, the doctor, the kerosene queue— no one quite knows how and in what order all these have fallen on the slave woman's back. The same back on which her lord and master, weary with his day's work, has spread his bedding and is taking a peaceful nap. Women's liberation! Pooh! A mockery.

There is, undoubtedly, another lot. They've burned their bras, chopped off their hair, donned shirts and pantaloons and been indoctrinated in the ism of 'living together'. Najma wears jeans too. It's convenient for work. But those who flaunt them, as a flag of their emancipated status, everywhere—from official meetings to family celebrations and even at the graveyard—are the ones who pose a greater danger.

Under the auspices of the Shakti Centre, Najma organizes workshops and seminars at which these issues are raised and discussed. Academically and analytically. What is the definition of freedom? What are the exact parameters of the term 'equal rights'? Apart from the biological one, is there any value or significance to a woman's existence? Does she really represent the second gender? Is she truly a second-class citizen of our planet Earth?

At this point in her cogitations, Najma's thoughts took off on another track. Siraj made it a point to come to all the seminars and symposia she organized. Hunh! As if his anxiety for women's liberation was giving him sleepless nights! He had managed an executive committee membership with a large donation and attended all its meetings—a crooked smile dangling from his lips like a cigar. He even had the audacity to offer his opinion. 'Women need protection, Najma,' he told her every now and then. 'They need a man's love.' Najma, of course, was buying none of that. 'What do you mean by a man's protection?' she snapped at him in private. 'Every girl in this Centre is being taught judo, karate and sword fencing. Do you know that? And what is this "love" you're talking about? On which women are supposed to thrive? What percentage of it is sex? And what percentage is shameless, unadulterated opportunism? It's a blasted, one-sided social contract.' Siraj, however, was unfazed. 'It's a little difficult to explain,' he said, smiling at her agitation. 'I'm a mere male, that too with little or no education. But I can demonstrate. And I'll do so willingly if you allow me to . . . '

Najma glanced at her watch. It was only half past eight. There was still a long way to go. Wrapped in her thoughts she hadn't noticed that a good many stations had come and gone and that the crowd in the compartment had thinned considerably. The two men who had been sitting on either side of her, solid and immovable as banana trunks, had left. She moved to the window seat and raised the glass. A fine drizzle of rain blew in, spattering her elbow. She moved away a little but didn't lower the glass. The compartment reeked of foul-breathed, sweat-stained humanity. She wanted some fresh air to blow the odours away. Gusts of wind tugged at her hair, blowing the strands around her face, caressing her cheeks, chin and forehead. She loved the sensation. Glancing out of the window she saw that the train was cutting across a paddy field—a huge expanse stretching to the horizon. The trees and bushes on either side had bunches of glow-worms sticking to them. Date palms, bent and shrivelled like old women, stared at the disappearing train with vacant, lacklustre eyes. Najma felt a curious empathy. It was always so. She had bonded with Nature ever since she was a child. Was Nature only a birth giver? she asked herself now. This vast, deep, wondrous, awesome Universe with its mysterious inner workings! What was it in essence? What was the true essence of a woman? Why was she deemed different? Were the distinctions society made between male and female legitimate? Did they arise out of an inherent need? Najma shook her head. She couldn't accept the fact that men and women were intrinsically different. If at all, the difference lay in the fact that the female was naturally endowed with a greater share of good judgement, balance, and sensitivity to beauty than her male counterpart. Except of course . . .

One of the ladies who visited the Centre had a very large behind. As secretary, Najma had thought it her duty to give her some practical advice. 'Mrs Biswas,' she had said to her once, 'you should wear saris. I think it would be wiser.'

'Why?'

'You'll look better in a sari. It will suit your figure.'

'Oh! But men with figures like mine wear trousers—don't they?'

'Of course, but they don't have a choice. You do.'

'Why should I accept the other option? Just to look a little more attractive? So that the men around me have a little more to feast their eyes upon? Even if I'm much more comfortable in trousers?'

Bani Basu

Irrefutable logic! Najma hadn't been able to deny it. 'Mrs Biswas,' she could have said but didn't, 'being gracefully dressed is not a crime. Why are you thinking only of the men? You can think of our eyes too.'

The matter was really quite complicated. Mistakes like this were being made all the time. The watchwords of the present age were 'egalitarianism' and 'utilitarianism'. Between the two they were slaughtering beauty and grace.

Najma glanced around her, shivering a little. She felt strangely at odds with herself. As though the vast outside world she had been contemplating on and this railway compartment were situated on two different planets. This one, in which she was trapped, was filled with noxious, dangerous fumes. She wondered why she felt like that. Tilting her head back, like a hound on the scent, she sniffed the air, inhaling deeply. And, at that very moment, she identified the source of her uneasiness. He sat a few benches away from her. A crude, coarse-looking man in a cheap, checked shirt and soiled tericot pants with a dun-coloured shawl flung across his shoulders. He had a very wide jaw covered with stubble and starred with large fleshy warts. He was looking at her out of the corner of his eye. They were sharp eyes, full of cunning. Najma felt vulnerable. As though an open knife was being flicked to and fro over her. Following the direction of his glance she saw that it rested on her ring. An eight-and-a-half carat diamond brilliantly cut and set in white gold. She had no idea what price it would fetch today were she to sell it.

The ring was a family heirloom which had found its way from her maternal grandmother Noor-a-tun Begum's finger to hers on the former's deathbed. That was ten years ago. Najma had been very close to her nani. Though very young at the time, she had understood the old lady as no one else had. She had known where her sorrow lay and had empathized with her entirely. Nani had been born in a Syed family and been married into one. But her marriage hadn't been happy. Her husband had two other wives and between them and their children they had made life hell for her.

This ring, the family believed, had originally belonged to Arjumand Banu Begum. It was a love token given to her, in secret, by the young prince Khurram in the Meena Bazar of Agra. Later, as beloved wife of the emperor, Arjumand had borne the brunt of his passion and given birth, year after year, till she had died of anaemia. Mumtaz Mahal! Light of the Palace! Empress of Hindustan! had died of anaemia, enabling her husband to build, over her remains, a magnificent tomb which came to be ranked among the seven wonders of the world.

Nani had made her promise never to take the ring off her finger. Life, in those days, was safer for women. No one had heard of chains being snatched in broad daylight from windows of buses or of women being forced to part with their jewellery, at knife-point, in full view of the public. But despite this, and despite the fact that Najma's work took her to a great many strange, out-of-the-way places, Najma had kept her promise. The ring meant a great deal to her. It carried the imprint of her nani's love. It was also, in Najma's eyes, a symbol of struggle. Mumtaz's struggle. Her mother's and her grandmother's.

Someone had said to her this very evening, 'You'll be travelling by train, Najma. That too at night. Take the ring off and keep it in your purse.' But Najma had turned a deaf ear. Now, seeing the man's greedy, glittering, animal eyes fixed on the diamond, she felt a small stab of fear. Twisting her little finger around the ring she twirled it slowly, in the opposite direction, till the diamond rested on the inside of her hand. Then, balling her fingers into a

Bani Basu

fist, she slid it into her poncho. Casually. As though it felt the winter chill and needed to be warmed. She wrapped the poncho more securely around her and moved a little in her seat, trying out another position. A position of greater vigilance. She took care not to glance in the man's direction though every nerve and sinew of her body sensed his agitation. His legs were shaking violently, the knees knocking against one another. He didn't seem to know what to do with his hands. They kept fluttering from his knees to his pockets and then back to his knees. He threw the shawl off once and draped it again, pulling it more tightly around his chest. He passed his hands over his face. He was smoking bidi after bidi with quick impatient puffs. But his eyes, like an accomplished hunter's, were fixed on his quarry. Unblinking. Unwavering.

Najma took a strong hold on herself. The man couldn't be a gangster or dacoit, she reasoned. Though big and muscular with an air of brutish strength, he looked more like a factory hand. Najma tried to draw strength from the thought.

There were five passengers in the compartment now. The man, herself and three others. An old woman, clutching a bundle of rice to her lap, was sleeping soundly by her side. Two men, whose looks proclaimed them to be simple village yokels, were sitting at the far end, smoking bidis and talking to one another. Should she ask them for help? But who knew what they were really like! For all she knew she might fall from the frying pan into the fire.

There were stones in her ears too. But they were American diamonds. Synthetic. Not valuable. People wore such stuff these days. No one went around wearing real gems. She could pretend that the stone on her finger was also an American diamond. She could bluff her way out of the train that way. Was the man still looking at her?

Was he trying to form a plan in his head? He couldn't be a hardened criminal. If he was he would have leaped on her by now and taken the ring away at gunpoint. No one would have tried to stop him. People were afraid of goons and would keep well out of the way. He was only an ordinary, uncouth rustic whose greed had been aroused at the sight of the diamond. Najma glanced in his direction out of the corner of her eye and got the shock of her life. His eyes were on her and he was practically slavering at the mouth. A runnel of ice-cold water crept down Najma's spine. Her heart all but stopped beating. Was he only after the diamond? Or her as well?

It was nine o'clock. A whistle blew and the train snaked into a station. The old woman rose and, resting the bundle on one hip, moved towards the exit. One of the men from the far end rose too. Putting out his bidi hastily he followed suit. Now, there was only one passenger left between Najma and her assassin.

Suddenly, in a lightning flash, an idea struck her. Gathering her things together she rushed to the door. As though she had almost forgotten that this was where she had to get off. She ran, swift as an arrow, along the platform, and leaving four compartments behind her, climbed into the fifth. This one had a fair number of people in it. Najma heaved a sigh of relief. 'Thank Heaven I never lose my head in an emergency,' she congratulated herself. 'Keep your wits about you always,' she exhorted the students of the Health and Self-Protection classes over and over again. 'Presence of mind is the only thing that can save you in the face of grave danger. Lose it and you may have to pay for it with your life.' Moving to the window, she raised the glass and let some fresh air blow over her.

And then . . . her body froze, slowly, till it became a column of ice. The man had followed her. He was sitting at the extreme end by the window. There was a bidi in his mouth and he was striking a match. The compartment was dimly lit but there could be no mistake. The warts on both sides of his face were clearly visible in the light of the flame. They stood out—ugly and terrifying—like demon's teeth. Najma couldn't fool herself any more. She knew what he wanted.

Stations came and went. Simlagarh . . . Pandua . . . Mogra. Two or three people got off each time but no one got in. There was only one other passenger left in the compartment now. Presence of mind. That was the important thing. Najma babbled the phrase soundlessly. What should she do now? Get off? But the man would get off too and what would have been impossible in the brightly lit, crowded platform of Howrah could easily be accomplished in a dark, dingy, deserted suburban station.

And now the man rose. He was coming towards her. But no. He didn't come all the way. He seated himself, five or six benches away, his elbow resting on the window sill, his eyes fixed upon her face. Najma tried to swallow but couldn't. Her tongue and palate were as dry as dust. What could she do now? The thought hammered in her brain. It felt like pulp . . .

Flickering lights. A station approaching. Srirampur. The last passenger rose and disappeared into the dark vault of the night. They were the only ones left now. Najma and the man who was waiting to rape her. Her heart thumped wildly against her ribs. She tried to pull herself together. 'There's no point in getting off here,' she reasoned, as calmly as she could, above the hammering in her head and heart. 'Howrah is only a few stops away. If I can keep my courage till then . . . the crisis will pass. I mustn't let him know I'm scared.'

The train started moving. The man rose. Came towards her. Now he was sitting on the opposite bench, facing her. The compartment was hazy with bidi smoke. Most of the bulbs had cracked and fused and the few that remained shed an opaque, unhealthy light. They were like eyes filmed with rheum and catarrh. Like the eyes of the very old. Unfeeling. Indifferent.

And now the man did something very strange. He started moving from bench to bench. From left to right. From back to front. He wasn't moving so much as leaping about. Najma stared at him in horror. *Just like an amoeba*, she thought suddenly, *caught in a magic web*. Words hit her head, splintered and shattered like the strange form before her eyes. *Splitting atoms . . . binary fission . . . from one to two . . . two to four . . . eight . . . sixteen . . . thirty-two.*

The man was all over the compartment. His checked shirt, sweaty pants, filthy shawl and smouldering bidi were everywhere—in fragments and together . . . knocking against the walls, hitting the roof, rolling on the floor. Leaping, dancing, squatting, flying from this end of the train to that. Now she saw nothing but eyes. Bulging, glittering eyes like a prehistoric toad's. Now he was flying towards her—an enormous, slippery, poisonous moth— loathsome, deadly. But no—he wasn't a moth. He was an ape. Huge and black with a slavering mouth. He was swaying towards her, stretching out paws covered with dark, prickly fur. Najma screamed and flailed her arms in the air. But they felt weightless, like arms in a dream. All the martial skills she had learnt for her self-protection, what she had taught others melted away, became blurred and insubstantial like a fleeting dream. Suddenly, one of the remaining lights went out with a flicker. Sweat streamed over Najma's cold, cold body. Why was the train slowing down? Were they approaching a station? The train was stopping. Why? Oh God! Why?

Najma's nerves couldn't bear the strain any more. She fainted away. But not before seeing, in a lightning flash, a shadowy figure leap into the compartment. Najma lost all sense of time and place. Somewhere, from the dark, smoky recess her mind had reached, she was still fighting, tearing at the dim, dank cobwebs entangling it. 'Siraj! Siraj,' she was crying. Soundless babble. 'Is it you? Have you been following me like a shadow? Protecting me? Is it only today? Or has this gone on for a long time? Aeons? How many aeons? Women need protection . . . your pet theory . . . and they need—'

On coming to, with Siraj's strong muscular arms around her trembling form, Najma continued from where she had left off. 'While so-called civilized society is a jungle—men will be animals. There's no such thing as freedom. A woman can protect neither her jewels nor her honour by herself. I admit it today. Siraj, I don't want the lakh of rupees you've put aside for the bridal dower. No contract. No stipulations. All I want is a promise from you to leave me free. To live by my own choices. With dignity. I have worked all my life for women. To win for them the right to follow their own goals. Can I give up this right in my own life? Save me the humiliation of admitting before the world that I was wrong.'

Najma was babbling away but only her lips were moving. Not a sound could be heard. At this point, Siraj cried out in a strange, alien voice. 'Arré! Didi, don't be so scared. I've beaten the rogue to a pulp and thrown him out of the train. Open your eyes and see for yourself. Always remember that men who try to rob and frighten women are cowards at heart. Hit back and they'll run like rats. I saw him leaning over you from the platform and . . . '

Najma opened her eyes. A young man stood before her. Slim and handsome, with a neat, black beard. He looked a bit like Siraj but was much younger. A college student—perhaps. And one who obviously believed in body building.

Shikha's Address

Shikhar Thikana

Suchitra Bhattacharya

'What's your name, darling?'

   'Mou. Moutushi.'

   'Un hunh. Not your pet name. The real one.'

   'Kanchan Kuntala Sen.'

   'And your father's name?'

   'Aninda Kanti Sen.'

   'Excellent! Where do you live? What's your address?'

   'Seven by three, Ballygunge Station Road.'

The answers came, pat, in little Mou's indistinct babble. They sounded as practised as a well-trained parrot's. Afraid that she might get lost some day, Aninda had been conducting these question–answer sessions from the time Mou had begun stuttering her first syllables. For Mou it was a game—more enjoyable in the repetition. She always answered 'Mou, Moutushi' to the first question, knowing full well what the next one would be. Moutushi! Was that a pet name or a love name? What was the right word?

The thought shot through Shikha's head and faded away just as quickly, as she stood before the dressing table, adjusting the pleats of her sari. She could see them in the mirror—Mou sitting on the bed, her toys spread out in front of her, and Aninda lying sideways, his elbow resting on a bolster. Their eyes met. Though talking to his daughter, Aninda was looking at her. Why? Shikha wondered. Was he trying to gauge her appearance? Or her thoughts? Men were like that perhaps. Aninda, Debashish, they were all the same. They needed to assess the value of their possessions from time to time. Their methods might be different but . . . Shikha turned her eyes away. She knew that though plagued with a thousand questions, Aninda would never articulate them. But he couldn't hide his uneasiness either. It rose into the air and clouded it like a fine sweat on a summer afternoon. Yesterday evening for instance. He had fallen into such a deep silence after . . .

'You telephoned? *You?*'

'Yes—'

'What did he say?'

'He avoided giving a direct answer at first. Then, after I requested him several times, he . . . '

'What did you say?'

'It's the boy's birthday tomorrow. I haven't seen him in a long time. I asked if he would let me . . . I . . . I'm missing him dreadfully.'

'Didn't you feel awkward? Humiliated?'

'Why should I feel humiliated? He's my son after all. For his sake—'

'You'll go to that house again! Even after the way they insulted you?'

It wasn't as if that thought hadn't passed through Shikha's head. It had. But there is a thirst so strong that all shame and humiliation dissolves before it; an emotional need so intense that it defeats logic and reason. Aninda knew it as well as Shikha did. Yet . . .

'You should have told him to bring the boy to some other place.'

Aninda made it a point never to utter their names. Debashish's and Mantu's. Shikha wondered why. Was there an element of envy behind this shying away? Or something else? Whatever it was it disturbed her. Aninda knew all there was to know about her past. And yet, he always . . .

Her silence provoked him.

'It seems as though it is you who is yearning to go to that house.'

'No, it doesn't. I requested Debashish to bring Mantu to some other place. Any place. But he refused.'

There was no reply. Aninda got busy with Mou. A little too busy.

Shikha moved away from the dressing table and went to the almirah. Standing on tiptoe she plucked a shopping bag from the topmost shelf. She had bought everything yesterday evening on her way back from the office. Two sets of clothes, a cricket bat and four balls, a sweatshirt with a sticker, a box of chocolates. She wondered if the clothes would fit. A growing boy like Mantu . . . She hadn't seen him in seven months. How much could he have grown in that time? Seven months! It seemed like eternity. Or more. She telephoned him from the office, sometimes, in the afternoon. Not very often. And she didn't speak for more than two or three minutes. That, too, if he picked up the phone. She was afraid of being caught. She went to his school now and then and stood peering through the gates as the children came running towards it, chattering and giggling. Sometimes she caught a brief glimpse of him making his way to the cycle rickshaw in which his grandmother sat waiting to take him home. Sometimes she didn't. But even when she did she never saw his face. Not clearly. She didn't dare go near them. Who knew what the lady would say? Tearing her unwilling eyes away from the scene she moved silently away. Aninda knew all this. He knew and understood how she felt. Why, then, did he behave as he did? This morning for example. The first thing he did on waking up was yell at the top of his voice, 'Shikha! Come here this minute.'

Shikha was in the kitchen, boiling milk for her daughter. Her maid hadn't come in as yet.

'Shikha!' Aninda's voice, loud and importunate, tore through the air. 'Can't you hear me?'

Turning off the gas, Shikha ran into the bedroom. 'What's the matter?' she cried, staring at her husband. 'Why are you shouting?'

'Mou has fever. Touch her and see.'

Shikha went to the child, sleeping peacefully on her cot. She looked like a flower, her limbs spread out like unfurling petals. A shaft of sunlight, coming in from the window, hovered delicately over her. Shikha placed a trembling palm on her forehead. It was cool—most innocently so.

'Of course not,' Shikha exclaimed, relieved.

'Are you sure?'

Shikha touched her cheek to her daughter's, then pressed it against her neck and breast. 'Jah!' she laughed at her husband's fears. 'She's perfectly cool.'

'Nonsense! Fetch the thermometer.'

'Don't be silly. There's nothing wrong with her.'

'Nothing wrong? Or are you deliberately denying the truth?'

'Why should I deny it?'

'It might be inconvenient . . . today in particular.'

'What do you mean?'

'What do I mean? It is obvious that you care more for them than for us.'

'Us? Who do you mean by us?'

Suchitra Bhattacharya

'My daughter and I.'

'Only the two of you? Am I not part of you?'

'Are you?'

Mou's face clouded in the mist that rose to Shikha's eyes. Aninda's too. What was Aninda trying to say to her? Was it possible that he had never accepted that other part of Shikha's life? That he had only pretended to. That he had acted a part these three or four years. The part of a perfect gentleman—refined, sensitive and humane . . .

Shikha packed the presents she had bought for Mantu carefully in the shopping bag. The pain that lay in a hard, heavy knot on her chest rose to her throat. She turned around slowly and looked at Aninda.

'I want to ask you a question,' she said. 'Will you give me a straightforward answer?'

'What is it?' Aninda's voice was sharp. His back stiffened as though in self-defence. As though he had to get ready to ward off an attack.

'Do you really want me to go?'

'Why do you ask me that? Of course you must go. Have I ever stopped you from doing anything you wanted?' Aninda smiled—a tight, strained smile that stretched his mouth but did not touch his eyes. 'You're thinking of what I said this morning and brooding over it. Can't you take anything lightly and easily?'

Can you? Shikha thought. *Can anyone?* But though the words were on her lips she didn't utter them. She smiled, a forced painful smile—much like Aninda's. 'I wasn't thinking of this morning,' she said.

'Then—?'

'I won't go if you two don't like it.'

'We two?' Aninda was smiling now. A real smile.

Shikha moved to the bed and pulled the child towards her. Pressed her head to her bosom. Then she looked at

Aninda with quiet eyes. 'You and your daughter,' she said. *With whom I live*, she thought. *Where I live. My address.*

2

Shikha's steps faltered as she came within view of the house. She stopped for a moment. Her legs were trembling badly and she could feel her heart pounding. Dhub! Dhub! Dhub! Weird sounds! Her throat and tongue were parched dry. *How strange*! she thought. She had been so happy! She had looked forward to this meeting for so many days. And now everything—her joy and expectation, her eager longing—had vanished. Should she go back? No. That would be silly—to come all this way and then funk it . . .

Shikha took out a handkerchief from her vanity case and mopped her streaming face. She moved the shopping bag from her right hand to her left. It was a late afternoon in mid-April and very, very hot. The sun seemed to be raging and fuming out of a sky as white and clear as glass. Huddling in the faint streak of shade on the footpath she walked a few more steps. The street was deserted and the houses on either side shuttered and silent. The inhabitants, she knew, would be sleeping, warm and languid, in the summer heat. Shikha breathed a little sigh of relief. She had chosen the right time. There was no one around who would recognize her and ask her questions. But even as the thought came to her mind, her eyes fell on an open window on her right. Someone was looking out. Wasn't that Piklu's mother? Shikha drew the end of her sari hastily over her head, shielding her face. She quickened her pace and almost shot past the house. But the very next moment she was overcome with self-loathing. Why did she have to steal away so guiltily? Even if the lady had seen her, even if she had asked her a few questions— she would have, of course—how could it affect her? She hadn't committed a crime. The matter was simple. She hadn't got on with her husband. They couldn't stand one another. They had fought and sparred, flung accusations at each other all the time. The bonds between them had loosened over the years. Then . . . then she had found someone else. Someone she could love and trust and make a home with. What was wrong with that? If anyone had suffered from the break it was she. Debashish had kept everything—his home, money, parents and son. It was she who had lost all she had, or thought she had. Where were all these people at the time?

The thought strengthened her somewhat but the trembling in her legs would not cease. She walked doggedly on till she reached her destination. Looking on the house, its rose-red façade shimmering in a blaze of sunlight, the last flicker of courage she had clung to deserted her. She stood at the front door through which she had walked in and out innumerable times in the past. How alien it looked to her now! How strange and forbidding! The closed door wasn't a door. It was Debashish, his father, mother, brother and sister-in-law, flanked against her, barring her entry. Beyond this human wall stood Mantu, biting his thumbnail and looking at her with troubled eyes.

With this last thought her courage returned. She shook herself free of all her doubts and fears. Putting out her hand she pressed the bell. She could hear it ring, a long, loud insistent sound.

Debashish opened the door. 'Come in,' he said.

Shikha tried to smile. The same smile she had smiled at Aninda. 'I'm a bit early,' she said.

Debashish didn't hear her or pretended not to hear. 'Sit down,' he pointed to the sofa. 'Mantu is sleeping. I'll wake him up.'

Shikha looked at his back as he walked away from her. He had lost weight in the last few years. He had aged and shrivelled. Her chest contracted. A ripple of pain passed through it. If Debashish had only . . . if he had understood her just a little . . . but he had never been able to see beyond his own little world. She wasn't angry any more. Anger dissolves with time. Turns to pity, even empathy.

Shikha sank into the sofa nearest to her and looked around. Everything was just the same. The old grandfather clock with its swinging pendulum over the door. The tall enamelled vase on the bookcase. The wooden cabinet full of cups and medals—each in its allotted space. Rabindranath and Netaji on the walls. Only the sofa covers had faded a little. And the colour of the walls looked dimmer. Was everything kept exactly as it had been, as Shikha had arranged it, because . . . because? Had Shikha really left this room? These walls? That door? Her head was swimming and her thoughts were getting fuddled. She leaned her head against the faded upholstery. She ran her fingers on its surface. Something to hold. Something to connect with. Suddenly her head shot up. Her back stiffened. There were footsteps in the passage. Who was it? Her father-in-law? Her mother-in-law? Her hand went up, involuntarily, to her head and she drew the end of her sari lower over her brow. But no. The footsteps went past her. To the next room. The dining room. Was the dining table still there? With its blue sunmica top and six chairs?

Shikha heaved a sigh of relief. Or was it disappointment? She couldn't tell. 'Strange,' she murmured to herself. Why was she still thinking of them as her in-laws? All her bonds with them had been severed by law. They were nothing to her now. Why should Aninda Sen's wife cover her head before Debashish Bagchi's father as though he were her father-in-law? She yanked the sari off her head and stared at the swaying curtain with hard, bright eyes.

And it was at this moment that Mantu pushed the curtain aside. Mantu. Debashish's son. Her son.

'Why do you stand outside?' She smiled at him. 'Come in.' Shikha rose to her feet. She was breathing hard. Short, heavy gasps. Mantu stood at the door like a statue. Immovable. 'Come, son,' she called out to him. 'Come to me.' And now her voice shook with something like fear. 'Won't you?'

The statue moved. Walked slowly, step by step, and entered the room. There was a smile on Mantu's face, a pale wan smile that twisted his childish features like a spasm of pain. Shikha couldn't bear that look. Running towards him she sank to her knees on the floor and, taking him in her arms, covered his face with kisses. 'This one is for your birthday,' she explained between kisses. 'This one is for seeing you after such a long time. And this one . . . ' She felt the boy stiffen. A tremor ran down Shikha's spine. Why was he not responding? Why were her love and caresses leaving him cold? Had anyone in the house briefed him in any way? When they talked over the phone he sounded different. Normal and cheerful.

'Why darling?' Her voice sounded strange and hoarse even to her own ears. There was an edge to it. 'Won't you talk to me? Why? Why?' Tears stung her eyes. She pressed her lips tightly together to keep them from brimming over. And now eight-year-old Mantu spoke to his mother for the first time. In a twenty-eight-year-old voice.

'Why did you lie to me?'

'What . . . What lie?'

'That you miss me. That you cry for me.'

'Of course I do. I cry . . . '

'That's a lie. You're married to another man. You have a daughter.'

'Who told you that?'

'Nobody told me. I've heard it.' Mantu stood before her, arms akimbo, like an aggressive adult. 'Thamma was talking to Baba yesterday. "Why did you tell her to come?" she said. "You drove her out yourself. You told her never to come near the house again. Never to contact the boy!"'

Yes. Debashish had said all that. And more. A flood of memories washed over Shikha. Could she share them with the child? He was so little. Later, perhaps, when he was older. She shook her head. No. She could never, ever, tell him the things his father had said. Shikha's arms dropped to the ground. She rose slowly to her feet. 'What you have heard is true,' she said quietly. 'Everything you've heard is true.'

'Then why are you here?'

Shikha stood before her son, biting her lip. There were no simple answers to questions like this one. Even if she tried to explain, would he understand? The word 'love' had so many connotations. It could be interpreted in so many different ways. But the boy was waiting for an answer. She had to give him one.

'I don't know,' she said.

Mantu turned and darted out of the door swift as an arrow. She could hear the sound of running footsteps in the passage. And now on the stairs. Shikha looked around the room with blank, bewildered eyes. The shopping bag with the presents in it lay on the floor, untouched. She picked it up and placed it on the sofa. Carefully. As though it contained something brittle. The front door was open. Should she leave? Or wait for someone to come and shut it after her? Wait? Even after what had happened?

She didn't have to. Debashish hurried into the room. 'Why did Mantu run off like that?' he asked her. Shikha looked away. She couldn't meet his eyes. 'He's getting terribly spoiled and wayward,' Debashish said ruefully. 'He doesn't listen to anyone any more.' Silence. 'He says whatever he feels like,' Debashish murmured. His voice was gentle and full of concern. 'Was he rude to you?'

Shikha shook her head. Debashish stood looking at her for a while. She took a few steps towards the door but her feet wouldn't move beyond the big sofa. 'Take this with you,' Debashish said. Shikha turned her head. She had managed to push back the tears by now and could look at him with unclouded eyes. There was a long brown envelope in his hand. 'It's a letter from an insurance company,' he said, holding it out to her. 'You opened a policy ten years ago but haven't kept up with the premiums. It has probably matured by now.' Shikha stretched out her hand and took the envelope. Their eyes met for a few moments. After years and years.

'I have a request.' Debashish's voice was soft but firm.

'What is it?'

'Your letters should not come to this house any more. Please make the necessary arrangements. You have another address now.'

'Hmm . . . '

Hmm! It was just one sound. Faint. Almost inaudible. Who knew it would wrench her lungs this way?

'I must go.' Shikha moved towards the door.

'You're leaving something behind.' Debashish went to the sofa and picked up the shopping bag.

'No,' Shikha's voice was metallic. Like a wire pulled so taut—it would snap any moment. 'It's for Mantu. There are a few things in it. Birthday presents.'

'Why are they lying here then? Your loving son refused to take them, I suppose.'

Now Shikha turned to him and spoke. 'Not my son,' she said. Each word was enunciated carefully, precisely. It fell on the air—clear and distinct. 'Your son. Scion of your line.'

3

Neelima opened the door and stared at her daughter. 'You!' she cried out in surprise as Shikha rushed into the room. 'Alone? Where's Mou? Hasn't Aninda come with you?' Question after question, hurled at her, battering her. Shikha shuffled her feet loose from her slippers and, tilting her head back, took a few deep breaths. As though she needed to fill her lungs. As though they had been empty for a long, long time.

'Why don't you answer me?'

'I've come alone.' Shikha walked into her mother's bedroom. Her mother's? Or her own? Hadn't this room been hers when she was a girl living in her parents' house? Wasn't that bedstead the one on which she had slept for years and years? She went straight to it and stretched herself out on the embroidered bedspread.

'Aren't Dada and Boudi at home?' Shikha lay on her back and looked at her mother.

'No. They've gone to see a film.' Neelima approached the bed, slowly, step by step. Her eyes were clouded with questions. Doubts and fears. A cow whose shed has caught fire once shies away from the faintest whiff of smoke. 'Why do you look at me like that?' she asked her daughter. 'What's wrong with you?'

'What could be wrong? Nothing at all.' Shikha pressed her palms against her temples and massaged them slowly.

Suchitra Bhattacharya

Grasping her hair with both hands she pulled the strands, tightly, from the roots. 'I'm very tired, Ma,' she said. 'I've come here to rest. I'll lie down for an hour.'

A look of alarm sprang into Neelima's eyes. Fixing them on her daughter's face she asked in a voice that shook slightly. 'Tell me the truth, Buri. Have you and Aninda quarrelled?'

'No, Ma. Don't worry. We're fine.'

'Then—' Neelima's eyes were still full of misgivings. 'On a Sunday . . . that too in the evening . . . you've come all the way from Jadavpur to Beleghata . . . to lie down?'

'Ma!' Shikha rolled on the bed, laughing. Peal after peal of noisy laughter. 'You sound just like an astute lawyer cross-examining the accused. Don't you believe me? Can't I come to you whenever I wish? Alone—if I feel like it? Do I have to bring Mou and Aninda? Do I have to check if it's a weekday or a holiday?'

Neelima dropped down on the bed and clutched Shikha's shoulder—so tight the girl winced. 'Don't lie to me,' she said in a hard voice. 'You are hiding something. Out with it.'

Shikha stopped laughing and rolling. She lay on the bed motionless, one arm flung across her eyes . . .

'Tell me the truth, Buri.' Neelima placed a hand on her daughter's head. 'You say you are fine. Yet . . . ' Suddenly a flicker of fear sprang into Neelima's eyes. Memories of her daughter's past streaked through her head like flashes of lightning. Could it be that . . . ? Shikha raised her head from the pillow and, burying it in her mother's lap, burst into tears. Silent tears that shook her form with their intensity. For a long, long time.

'What's wrong with Mantu?' Neelima asked, at last, suppressing a sigh.

Having cried her heart out, the heavy, icy lump in Shikha's chest melted slowly, bit by bit. She felt lighter, freer. Had she come here to weep then? Had she known she was carrying so many tears frozen within her? That she had no other place in which to shed them? She raised her head and, still hiccuping painfully, wiped her eyes and nose with the end of her sari. She took a few deep breaths. 'Today was Mantu's birthday,' she said. 'I went to see him.'

Neelima's brows came together. 'They didn't let you see him?'

'It isn't that,' Shikha spoke slowly, carefully. 'It was Mantu who wouldn't come to me. He ran away. He called me a liar. He knows that I have remarried. That I have a daughter.'

'Is that why you are crying?' Neelima stroked her daughter's head, comforting her. 'Don't worry so much. When he grows up he'll understand. He'll know what his father was like. How he treated his mother. Why she couldn't stay . . . ' Even as she spoke these words, a thought struck her. 'Did you tell Aninda you were going to see Mantu?' she asked anxiously.

Shikha was silent.

'Did you?' the mother probed. 'Did you take his permission?'

'Why should I?'

'What do you mean by that? Your husband should know what you are doing and approve . . . '

'It's my problem, Ma. My own, personal problem. It doesn't concern Aninda. Why should I seek his approval?'

'What are you saying, Shikha?' A tremor of apprehension ran through Neelima's frame. Was history repeating itself? 'No part of a woman's life is hers alone,' she explained.

'And even if there is, she should share it with her husband. This is exactly why . . . the first time . . . you had to—'

Her mother's words plunged into Shikha's ears like a hissing torrent. Drop by burning drop, the molten lead spread to her brain and filled the veins and arteries around her heart. The sensation was familiar. She had felt like this before. Aeons ago—it seemed to her now. Between the time she had left Debashish and married Aninda. She had spent those months in her mother's house. And every moment she had felt . . .

'Women have to put up with a great deal,' her sister-in-law had advised her. 'They must accept the fact and learn to endure.'

'You're too stubborn, Buri,' her brother had said. 'Husbands and wives quarrel all the time. But no wife leaves her husband and family. That's foolish.'

Shikha had never reacted to anything that was said to her. 'But this is my home too,' she could have told her brother. 'Just as it is yours. You grew up in it. So did I.' But she didn't. She couldn't. No girl can. She knows that once she crosses the threshold of her father's house, it rises, tall and forbidding, against her, barring her re-entry.

Was her mother trying to instruct her in the ways of the world as her brother and sister-in-law had done, with unflagging zeal, all the days she had spent here? Was she trying to tell her those very things that had driven her, with unseemly haste, into marriage with Aninda? She rose from the bed and stood before the mirror. She passed a hand over her hair and straightened her sari. Her face was flaming. She went to the bathroom and splashed water all over it.

'I'm going, Ma.' Shikha pushed her feet into her slippers.

'Going? So soon? Have a cup of tea first.'

'No.' Shikha smiled at her mother. 'Aninda doesn't know that I'm here.'

Neelima wouldn't ask her to stay after hearing these words. Shikha knew that. She stepped over the threshold, then turned around to face her mother. 'I came to this house for myself, Ma,' she cried out passionately. 'To weep once, just once, till I had exhausted my tears. I have no other place where I can weep only for myself.' But though her lips moved, not a sound emerged from her throat.

A cool, sweet wind blew over Shikha as she stepped off the bus. It was the middle of April—the season of squalls. Dust started rising in spirals from the ground, enveloping her. Shielding her face with the end of her sari, she walked rapidly across the street. But, before she could reach the pavement, the lights went out. Load shedding. Darkness—deep and dense. But only for a few moments. Then the faint outlines of houses and people appeared. Eyes are wonderful things. They see; get used to seeing—even in the dark.

Shikha stood for a moment, battling the dust. Then she started to walk, groping, hesitant. Stepping quickly aside as autos and cycle rickshaws rushed past her. Cars came racing up the street, their headlights flashing, banishing the dark—if only momentarily. Lightning streaked above her head, tearing at the seams of the sky. She was surrounded on all sides by shadows. Shikha started to walk faster. She had to get home before the storm broke. It would be any moment now. She was nearly home. Turning left she entered the lane on her right. A few more steps to the bend and then . . .

But she couldn't make it. The storm rushed towards her like a herd of dancing buffaloes. Ha! Ha! Ha! Throttling the sky with an iron grip it laughed. A weird, maniacal

Suchitra Bhattacharya

laugh. Lightning slipped and slithered across the sky, cackling with mirth. Dust lashed at her, stinging her eyes and lips, rushing into her nostrils, threatening to throw her to the ground.

Shikha flattened herself against a wall. There was no point in trying to go on. She would fall and hurt herself. A few yards from her, the tin roof of a shop got blown away with a grinding metallic sound. But people were still rushing past her, trying to go where they had to go. Bracing themselves against the gale, two boys were walking backwards. Others saw what they were doing and followed suit.

Was it possible to reach home that way? Walking backwards—eyes shut against the dust? Shikha's heart beat in a strange kind of way. How would one recognize one's home? Identify one's address? Terror swamped her. Her head swam and her brain felt light and fuzzy. This was it, she thought. This storm. It would never lift. Never exhaust itself. The gale would only get stronger, more tumultuous, the darkness more impenetrable. Shikha covered her face with both hands.

'What's your name, darling?'

'Buri, B-u-r-i.'

'Un hunh. Not your pet name. The real one.'

'Shikha. Shikha Bhaduri. No—Bagchi. No—not Bagchi. Sen.'

'What's your address?'

Shikha put out a hand and touched the dark. Clasping the lashing wind to her breast she let it flow all over her body. Does one have an address? Somewhere? Anywhere? Who knows? Perhaps one only walks backwards, on and on. Till one reaches some place. One's real address. The only address that never changes. The moment of birth.

Even as the thought struck her, Shikha moved forward. Reeling and staggering like a demented woman, she started walking towards the bend in the lane.

Suchitra Bhattacharya

Notes on the Authors

Rajshekhar Basu (1880–1967): More popularly known as Parashuram, Rajshekhar Basu was an eminent scholar and humorist. Educated at Patna and Kolkata, he stood first in MA in Chemistry from Calcutta University and joined Bengal Chemical Ltd, Calcutta, in 1904. Though a scientist by profession, his wide interests included lexicography, Sanskrit classics, linguistics and music. His portrayal of urban educated Bengali youth of the 1920s and 1930s and the peculiarities of Calcutta's social ambience is unique for its sense of humour, acute observation and sympathy for human foibles. His books of short stories include *Gaddalika* (1924), *Kajjali* (1927) and *Anandibai* (1957) which fetched him the Sahitya Akademi Award in 1958. He also wrote a number of essays which reveal his scientific temper, logical thinking and precise diction. He received the Rabindra Puraskar in 1955.

Bibhuti Bhushan Bandopadhyay (1894–1950): One of the stalwarts of contemporary Bengali fiction, Bibhuti Bhushan Bandopadhyay is widely known as the author of *Pather Panchali*, his magnum opus and a bona-fide classic. He is justly celebrated for his acute power of observation, his love of nature, and his profound sympathy for and understanding of simple men and women. His early life was spent in abject poverty. His father roamed from village to village earning a precarious living as an occasional priest. It was left to his mother to provide the barest necessities for the household. The interrelationships among the members of the household had a lasting impact on the young Bibhuti who later faithfully reconstructed the same in his first novel, *Pather Panchali* (1929). He was a schoolteacher throughout his active life. In almost two decades of literary activity he produced more than fifty works including seventeen novels, twenty short-story collections, travelogues, children's literature, a Bengali grammar, autobiographical compositions and a translation of *Ivanhoe*. His major compositions apart from *Pather Panchali* include its sequel *Aparajita*, *Aranyak* and *Ichhamati*, for which he was posthumously awarded the Rabindra Puraskar.

Tarashankar Bandopadhyay (1898–1971): Eminent Bengali novelist and short-story writer, Tarashankar was born in Lavpur, a village in the Birbhum district of Bengal. He came of a once prosperous zamindar family and this helped him understand the tragedy of Bengali zamindars—the subject matter of many of his novels and stories. Though a good student, he could not complete his graduation from the St Xavier's College, Calcutta, because of his participation in the freedom struggle. He joined the civil disobedience movement in 1930 and was imprisoned for six months. The death of his favourite daughter, because of lack of treatment owing to his dire financial condition, affected him deeply and in many ways contributed to making him the writer he became. His novels reflect a precise understanding of the socio-economic patterns of Bengal villages at the threshold of change and their underlying uncertainties, most memorably depicted in his greatest novel, *Ganadevata* (1942), which won him the Jnanpith Award in 1966. Tarashankar's claim to literary greatness rests largely on *Ganadevata* and its sequel *Panchagram* (1943). Other important works which clearly reveal his development as an artist and his willingness

Notes on the Authors

to address diverse themes include *Dhatridevata* (1939), *Kalindi* (1950), *Nagini Kanyar Kahini* (1951), *Arogya Niketan* (1952), *Saptapadi* (1958) and *Uttarayan* (1958).

Premendra Mitra (1905–1988): Eminent poet, short-story writer and novelist, Premendra Mitra started off as a journalist, shifted to film-making and finally settled down as a writer. He is regarded as one of the foremost of young writers associated with *Kallol*, a journal of the 1920s which critiqued and broke free of the Tagorean school of literary writing. Although he authored a number of well-known novels, his fame rests primarily on his books of poems and short stories. His first book of poems, *Prathama*, came out in 1932 and was followed by such acclaimed collections as *Samrat* (1940), *Pherari Fouj* (1948) and *Sagar Theke Phera* (1956) which won the Sahitya Akademi Award in 1957 and the Rabindra Puraskar in 1958. His notable collections of short stories include *Panchashar* (1929), *Benami Bandar* (1930), *Putul O Pratima* (1932) and *Aphuranta* (1935). He is also the author of the well-known 'Ghanada' series of stories.

Gajendrakumar Mitra (1908–?): Novelist and short-story writer, Gajendrakumar Mitra received his education in Varanasi and Calcutta, before joining the book trade as a canvasser. For a long time he was co-editor of the literary magazine *Katha Sahitya*. He has authored more than 500 short stories and forty novels, receiving the Sahitya Akademi Award in 1959 for his novel *Kolkatar Kachei* and the Rabindra Puraskar in 1965 for *Paush Phaguner Pala*.

Ashapurna Devi (1909–1995): Novelist and short-story writer, Ashapurna Devi started writing from a tender age and, in a literary career spanning over five decades, produced more than 150 novels and short-story collections. A large number of these are children's books. Her stories mainly depict the domestic world of middle-class people with their little joys and sorrows. She won the Jnanpith Award in 1978 for *Pratham Pratishruti* (1964), her most successful novel.

Jyotirindranath Nandi (1912–1982): Born and educated in what is now Bangladesh, Jyotirindranath Nandi came to Calcutta in 1936. His story 'Nadi O Nari', published in *Parichay* in the same year, was an immediate success. In 1946, his first collection of short stories, *Khelna*, came out, and by the late 1940s he became known as an outstanding writer. His novel *Suryamukhi* was serialized in *Desh* in 1948, and thereafter he published more than fifty works which reveal a mastery in portraying emotional crises.

Narendranath Mitra (1916–1975): Acclaimed as a great short-story writer, Narendranath Mitra gave a new dimension to the Bengali short story. He graduated from Calcutta University and took to journalism as sub-editor of *Ananda Bazar Patrika*. Middle-class Bengali life and the concerns arising out of famine, war, and the problem of refugees in the wake of Partition form the core issues he addresses with his trademark simple style and sympathetic insights. His memorable short-story collections include *Charai Utrai* (1951), *Narendranath Mitrer Shreshtha Galpa* (1952), *Sabha Parba* (1960) and *Sandhya Raga* (1968).

Samaresh Basu (1924–1988): Novelist and short-story writer, Samaresh Basu had little formal education. Coming to Calcutta at the age of thirteen, he worked as an ordinary hawker, a clerk in a jute mill and as a tracer at the Ichhapur Ordnance Factory during the Second World War. His varied experiences and unmitigated struggles were evident in his first novel *B.T. Roader Dharey* (1952) and later in *Jaggadal* (1966). In the 1960s he produced a string of extremely controversial novels like *Bibar* (1966), *Patak* (1969) and

Prajapati (1969). A sizeable number of readers protested against the excessive use of sex and obscene language in these books, with *Prajapati* even being sued for obscenity. Samaresh Basu was also a brilliant writer of travelogues and, under the pseudonym 'Kalkut', penned the unforgettable *Amrita Kumbher Sandhaney*, a travel diary of the Kumbh Mela. He won the Sahitya Akademi Award in 1980 for his novel *Shamba*.

Prafulla Roy (b. 1934): Novelist and short-story writer, Prafulla Roy has written over a hundred novels, 150 short stories and ten collections of children's stories and essays. Many of his works have been made into award-winning films and telefilms and television serials. He received the Sahitya Akademi Award for his novel *Krantikal*, which has subsequently been made into an award-winning Bengali film.

Sunil Gangopadhyay (b. 1934): Born in Faridpur (now in Bangladesh), Sunil Gangopadhyay came to Calcutta as a refugee in 1947. Despite extreme poverty which forced him to work even in his teens, he managed to continue his education, completing his master's degree from Calcutta University. He began his literary career as a poet, starting the epoch-making magazine *Krittibas* in 1953. He stormed the field of the novel with the trendsetting *Atma Prakash* (1966) and went on to become one of the leading novelists in Bengali with such cult classics as *Sei Samai* (1982), which won him the Sahitya Akademi Award, *Purba Paschim* (1989) and *Pratham Alo*.

Sirshendu Mukhopadhyay (b. 1935): Born in the town of Mymensingh (in present-day Bangladesh), Sirshendu Mukhopadhyay earned a master's degree from Calcutta University and worked as a schoolteacher for some time. Subsequently, he joined *Ananda Bazar Patrika* as a journalist. His first novel, *Ghoonpoka*, came out in 1967 and has been translated into fourteen languages. He has published more than forty novels and over seventeen collections of short stories. In 1991, he received the Sahitya Akademi Award for his novel *Manab Jamin*.

Bani Basu (b. 1939): A prolific writer and novelist, Bani Basu studied at Lady Brabourne College and Scottish Church College, Calcutta, before obtaining a master's degree in English Literature from Calcutta University. She was the head of the department of English at the Bijoy Krishna Girls' College, Howrah, from where she retired recently. Since 1980, her writings have appeared regularly in *Desh* and *Ananda Bazar Patrika*. She translates extensively into Bangla and writes essays, short stories and poetry. Bani Basu is the author of such acclaimed works as *Shwet Patharer Thala, Ekushe Paa, Gandharvi, Pancham Purush* and *Ashtam Garbha*. She has been the recipient of the Tarashankar Award for *Antarghaat* (1991) and the Ananda Puraskar for *Maitreya Jataka* (1996).

Suchitra Bhattacharya (b. 1950): Novelist and short-story writer Suchitra Bhattacharya was born in Bhagalpur, Bihar, and graduated from Calcutta University with honours in Bengali literature. Her writing focuses on contemporary social issues, especially those concerning the urban middle class. Over the past two decades she has published around twenty-five novels beginning with *Aami Raikishori* (1988), and a number of short stories. Her major novels include *Dahan, Hemanter Pakhi, Chhera Taar, Parabas, Kaancher Manush, Alochaya* and *Jalchabi*. Her novels and short stories have been translated into many Indian languages such as Hindi, Oriya, Tamil, Malayalam and English. Among the various awards that she has received are the Katha Award and the Tarashankar Award.

Copyright Acknowledgements

The publishers gratefully acknowledge the following for permission to translate and publish the stories in this anthology:

Sahitya Akademi, New Delhi, and Dipankar Basu, great-grandson of Rajshekhar Basu and sole copyright holder of the original Bengali story 'Anandibai' by Rajshekhar Basu.

Mitra and Ghosh Publishers Pvt. Ltd, Kolkata, for Bibhuti Bhushan Bandopadhyay's 'Mouri Phool' (Aniseed Flower), published in the collection *Bibhuti Rachanabali* Vol. 2, and Gajendrakumar Mitra's 'Ekti Galpa' (The Family Retainer), published in the collection *Galpa Panchashat*.

Shishu Sahitya Samsad Private Limited, Kolkata, for Tarashankar Bandopadhyay's 'Agradaani' (The Brahmin).

Mrinmoy Mitra, son of Premendra Mitra, for Premendra Mitra's 'Janaika Kapurusher Kahini' (The Story of a Coward).

Susanta Kumar Gupta, for Ashapurna Devi's 'Cactus', first published in the magazine *Saptahik Sharadiya Basumati* and later part of the short-story collection *Bachhai Galpo*, published by Mandol Book House, Kolkata, 1979.

Ananda Publishers, Kolkata, for Narendranath Mitra's 'Ras' (Sap), published in the collection *Galpa Mala* Vol. 2.

Prafulla Roy for his story 'Raja Jaye Raja Aashe' (The King Is Dead, Long Live the King), first published in *Desh* in 1967 and later included in the short-story collection *Prafulla Roy-er Shreshtha Galpo* (1978), published by Dey's Publishing, Kolkata.

Sunil Gangopadhyay for his story 'Palatak O Anusharankari', first published in *Shreshtha Galpo* (1982), Dey's Publishing, Kolkata.

Sirshendu Mukhopadhyay for his story 'Gharer Path' (The Way Home).

Bani Basu for her story 'Uttar Paksha' (In the Opinion of This House), published by Ananda Publishers, Kolkata, in the collection *Mohana*.

Suchitra Bhattacharya for her story 'Shikhar Thikana' (Shikha's Address), published by Ananda Publishers, Kolkata, in the collection *Moyna Tadanto*.